THE EDGE OF ETERNITY

OTHER BOOKS BY ELAINE EGBERT:

Moccasins Through the Rye
Hardly an Angel in Sight
Once in Old Frisco

To order additional copies of *The Edge of Eternity,* by Elaine Egbert, call 1-800-765-6955.

Visit us at *www.rhpa.org* for more information on Review and Herald products.

The Edge of Eternity

Elaine Egbert

REVIEW AND HERALD® PUBLISHING ASSOCIATION
HAGERSTOWN, MD 21740

The author assumes full responsibility for the accuracy of all facts and quotations as cited in this book.

This book was
Edited by Penny Estes Wheeler
Cover design by Edgerton • Bond Image Design/Mark Bond
Cover photo illustration by Edgerton • Bond Image Design/Mark Bond
Cover photos: PhotoDisc
Typeset: 11/12 Bembo

PRINTED IN U.S.A.

03 02 01 00 99 10 9 8 7 6 5 4 3 2 1

R&H Cataloging Service
Egbert, Anita Elaine, 1938-
The edge of eternity.

I. Title
813.54

ISBN 0-8280-1425-6

This book is a work of fiction, and any resemblance to persons living or dead is purely coincidental.

Dedication

Dedicated to those with loved ones who have chosen not to answer Christ's gentle call, but who, in faith, continue to pray for them.

Preface

It is indeed a sobering task to write a fictionalized story about something as important as the second coming of Christ and those things that will happen just before He appears. We are told that we cannot even imagine how difficult those days will be. Nor can we accurately envision the joy we will feel when at last we look upon Jesus' dear face.

As I worked on this manuscript I often felt overwhelmed from the enormity of what those living through those last days will have to experience. The temptations they must face, and in many cases the persecution they will undergo, can be frightening indeed. Our adversary is determined that none make it to the kingdom, that none, in their hearts, crown Jesus as their Redeemer and live totally for Him, that none believe that God truly loves us and cares what happens to us. The devil spares no effort to sidetrack us, to keep us from focusing on our Father and His will for us.

It is vital, therefore, that each of us studies the Bible for ourself, that we make a concerted effort to spend significant amounts of time communicating with Him so that when our time comes to stand alone we, through the power of the God we have learned to love and trust, will be able to stand for the right though the heavens fall.

This is my prayer for you, and for myself.

—Elaine Egbert

I can do all things through Christ which strengtheneth me.
—Philippians 4:13

Chapter 1

June

Aaron Chandler succumbed to the makeup man's last-moment flurry, put on his audience face, and stared at the teleprompter. In seconds the on-the-air light would flick on, and he would make his usual evening report to millions of people across North America.

It had taken years to become America's number one news telecaster, fighting—and winning—over savage competition. Surviving. Years of running around, disregarding the deceptively simple needs of food and sleep; nosing out information, intruding in people's lives, closing his eyes to the lovely to seek out the horrible. And lately there was certainly enough of the horrible.

Watching the unlit on-the-air light, he forced himself to ignore the burning beneath his breastbone. He needed to take a few days off to look into that, but how could he and stay number one in the news world? Through practice he'd taught his body not to wince at the sharp pains. Remarkable, wasn't it, how a man could explode on the inside, yet outwardly seem calm and in control?

The light began to blink, 11, 12 times, and then it glowed a steady green. The timing was perfect. The teleprompter began to roll.

"Good evening. I'm Aaron Chandler with *The Chandler Report* for June 28. Talks have reopened between China and Japan in an effort to come to a compromise over land disputes. World leaders agree that . . ." A sour bubble climbed his throat. "A military envoy was dispatched to Iraq this morning on a peacekeeping mission. . . ."

The words on the teleprompter ended, and the on-the-air light switched off. While commercials rolled, the makeup man came in again, blotted his forehead and dotted his nose with powder, sprayed down the stubborn cowlick on his left temple, and vanished.

"Ten seconds!" The men behind studio cameras vied for position. Then the blink, the steady light. Now Chandler reeled off the usual stuff—reports about a bombing attempt in New York and the mass murder in a remote little town in Montana. He reported an unusually savage weather disturbance that was shredding the islands in the Pacific, and the latest information on the tangle of tornadoes that had cut great swaths through Mexico City. Sweat prickled his spine. If only his listeners knew of the secret dangers that lurked above the smudgy overcast they now called the sky, dangers greater than any natural disaster recorded in history. If they only knew, they'd not be out there half-listening to him while they swallowed their convenience suppers.

"On a more pleasant vein, plans for the Bring God Back to America kickoff this July 4 have been well-received throughout the nation. The concept of America's restoring God to His rightful place in this land was born in the mind of Phyllis Rondell, the First Lady.

"Religious leaders eagerly endorsed Mrs. Rondell's plan and have organized the first of many nondenominational religious thrusts that are designed to enhance Americans' moral, ethical, and spiritual lives.

"At the root of the movement is the belief that God will no longer bless a nation that does not honor Him and that does unto others as they themselves would not like to have people do to them. By making citizens aware of God's sovereignty, it is hoped that a new unity will result, enhancing the development of neighborly goals and morals.

"We switch now to Merle Faygo in Eureka, California, for a report about that city's upcoming celebration planned in conjunction with this movement."

The steady green light on the camera a few feet from his face went off. He had 20 seconds. *Thank you, Merle.* Aaron fished a couple antacid tablets from his pocket and slipped one into his mouth; chewed—swallowed.

"Now, on the environmental front. Record temperatures are scorching the New England states, causing power outages and death. . . . Torrential rains in Nevada have virtually closed Las Vegas for a second week. Some residents there claim that the bizarre weather is actually God's judgment against the gambling industry and its promotion of lack of responsibility to home and country. . . . Heavy winds destroyed millions of acres of corn in Kansas and Iowa, and . . ."

Somehow Aaron finished his report. Minutes later he stuffed his laptop into his briefcase, stopped at Travel to pick up his tickets to Bismarck, then headed for his apartment.

He used to relish on-the-scene assignments. The excitement of outguessing other newsmen regarding where the action would be was like a full-scale chess game and had always given him an extra shot of adrenaline. All modesty aside, he had an uncanny knack for being at the right place, asking totally obnoxious questions without offending, and somehow staying in the good graces of those he interviewed. Coupled with the sharp-styled deadline writing he had to do and the race against the clock to report his findings at the exact required time, it made for an exciting life.

Now he tried to rustle up the old excitement, but the pain searing his stomach kept intruding. Perhaps he'd pack his overnighter, then lie down for a half hour. He needed to focus on tomorrow's assignment—an on-the-scene introduction of the asteroid alert system whose headquarters—secret until now—had been set up in North Dakota by a coalition of governments. Leaders from around the world would be there. Reporters would swarm the place, digging for that hidden something to spring on an unsuspecting audience—the tiny detail exposed—that might launch them into the number one news-reporting spot.

He popped another Tums.

CHAPTER 2

Nick Wheatley clutched the steering wheel of the cantankerous old car, willing it to run smoothly, yet it coughed and shook, bouncing him around on the slippery leather seat. Determined to fix the thing, he jammed on the emergency brake and tried to get out. But the door wouldn't budge. As the shaking intensified, the car began to roll backward. Puzzled, Nick snatched out the key, but the motor refused to die. The car kept rolling—faster and faster. He yanked at the wheel, trying to steer.

Nick didn't know for sure when his dream ended and reality took over, but suddenly he jerked awake. Instead of a steering wheel he clung to his brass bedstead, and the bed trembled beneath him.

It was happening again.

"Earthquake!" He jabbed Marj and then was across the room and down the hallway. He shot into Elissa's room, yanked her from her bed, and hurried back into the hall. Gillie already stood there, his face a pale oval in the dimness. He grabbed the boy and pushed him toward the front door. They must get out, just in case . . .

It was all over by the time they stood barefooted on the rain-wet grass. Marj, always slow to awaken, sagged against him.

Relieved, Nick hugged his family close. "Not as bad as last night's, was it? But you can never tell at first."

As if in answer, the sky opened and unleashed a pounding rain that sent them for cover. Back inside, Nick pondered the situation while Marj dried off the kids. What if the tremor they'd just experienced was merely the warning of a larger quake about to happen? Perhaps they should all bed down in the living room where they could get outside quickly.

He sized up the situation, then reassured his family. "It's going to be OK. You all stay here. I'm going to get the sleeping bags and check on Dusty."

The tremor had stopped before Nick could get back inside for his oldest son, and he still hadn't joined them. Being a light sleeper, Dusty was usually the first to feel the quakes, so it seemed strange.

Nick headed through the kitchen to the big bedroom he'd added behind the garage. Here Dusty could hole up and play his music without disturbing the others. It was his fortress against a world he suddenly mistrusted.

As usual, the door was closed. Nick opened it and peered into the quiet darkness, then with a sigh flicked on the light. The only sign that Dusty had been there was the mug of root beer he'd taken with him when he'd stormed out of the living room earlier that night. It sat on his bedside table—warm, untouched.

The fist in Nick's chest tightened. He'd been sure he'd just seen Dusty's car in the driveway where it belonged.

Marj came in. "Any damage?"

"No. You seen Dusty?"

"Why?" Irritated, Marj picked up the mug and wiped at the ring of moisture it left on the nightstand.

They stood silent, apart. Dusty was a sore point between them.

Nick shrugged. "Maybe he went out back when the earthquake started. I'll check around."

The rain still poured down, but it felt good against his skin. At least rain was something predictable. It fell. You got wet. You dried off. You went on from there. He wished the rest of life were as predictable.

Dusty's car was in its place, but the boy was nowhere around. Nick's stomach soured as he went back inside, stepped over the children in their sleeping bags, and headed for the bedroom. Marj perched on the edge of the bed drying her hair, the question loud on her face.

"I'm going into town to see if—uh—Dusty might be—"

"But it's past midnight. Everything'll be closed."

Nick dressed quickly. "I've gotta check the garage anyway. See if there's any damage."

"I suppose he's with those hoodlums again," Marj said, concern lining her face. "I'm telling you, Nick, you've got to be more firm with him."

Nick shrugged. He didn't know *what* to think anymore.

It was hard to see with so much rain sheeting off the windshield. The wipers thwacked insistently, but didn't help much. Nick inched down their graveled drive, across the little log bridge, and out onto the country road.

Maybe Marj was right. Maybe he'd been too soft on the boy who was a youthful replica of himself. It hadn't been easy for the kid to be left without his mother and then to get a quick replacement. Nick had tried to put himself in Dusty's shoes, to understand how a 4-year-old would feel when the dearest person in his life walked away. Many children grew to love their stepparents, but it hadn't happened that way in the Wheatley family, so Marj had become a thorn between Nick and Dusty. Dusty blamed Nick for that, and for the fact that Shannon had left them both.

Smears of light appeared in the distance. Town. The rain eased off a little, and he pressed the accelerator. *Lord, please help me find Dusty. Keep him from . . .*

The streets were nearly empty, except for one car that sat idling outside the pool hall. Three heads turned as Nick inched by, straining to see through its rain-streaked windows.

A rough-looking bunch of teens huddled around one table in the otherwise empty pool hall. With a quick glance around, Nick turned to leave. Then the restroom door burst open.

"Dusty!"

His son spun around. "What're *you* doin' here?"

"That's my question too."

Dusty's face closed, his brown eyes hard steel. Nick reached out. "Let's go home, son."

The boy shrugged his stocky shoulders and pushed through the front door. Smeary faces pressed against the parked car's windows, and Dusty waved them away.

Inside Nick's car the atmosphere grew heavy, and not just

from the stench of cigarette smoke that clung to his clothes. As usual, Nick struggled to find the right words, but it was even harder when tense feelings lay on the surface.

"After the earthquake I checked to see if you were OK."

Dusty glared at him, his full lips pressed tight. A mile later Dusty still hadn't spoken. Nick wanted to reach out, to assure Dusty that he cared, but the set of his shoulders warned him that touch at this point could set off an explosion. Nick's thoughts reached for God, seeking help.

"Why'd you leave home without telling us?"

Dusty forced a laugh. "And I s'pose you'da let me go?"

"No. Seventeen-year-olds shouldn't be out so late."

Dusty's hands balled into fists. "Right. I'm not old enough to be out, but I *am* old enough to mow your lawn, run your errands, keep an eye on those two bratty kids, and take anything off Marj she feels like throwing at me. Man, I'm sick of her always picking at me. And you? You just sit there and let it happen. If you were a man—"

For a split second Nick wanted to smack the boy, but he'd never done that and never would. Besides, letting his own feelings get in the way would be counterproductive. He *had* to get to the bottom of this.

"I know you're angry, son, but Mom and I—"

"Marj is *not* my mother, and I'm not going to pretend she is any longer just to keep *you* happy. My mom, my *real* mom—" He choked.

They rode in stiff silence the rest of the way. The car hadn't stopped before Dusty jumped out and headed for the back door, kicking at Committee as the yellow dog wagged out to greet him.

Later, too tense to sleep, Nick lay on the bed, listening to the children breathe. He thought about the quakes that had been shaking them out of their sleep oftener than ever. Well, they had earthquakes in their personal lives, too, and somehow those seemed even more threatening.

What could he do for Dusty? The boy's face, so like his own, swam before his eyes, gradually becoming Shannon's. Dusty's mother had been the light of Nick's life, the fairy-tale princess who had kissed him—the toad—and turned life into a fairy-tale dream. For awhile, that is. Even before they'd married he'd known that Shannon deserved to be more than a grease monkey's wife. But she'd rebelled when her parents had told her that, and they'd had their golden time in the sun. How hard he'd tried to make their marriage work, to give her everything she could want. When Dusty had come along he was sure things were fine. And they had been, for a couple years. But then?

The old insecurities threatened, gnawing at his self-confidence. He tried to stop his train of thought. *Lord, it's no help going over this again. I need to concentrate now—on Dusty. Please help—*

The alarm jolted him awake. A wave of nausea—like car sickness—washed over him. He rolled off the couch, dreading the day. He had so much unfinished business. Why had he promised to meet the mayor at the garage that morning? His whole body felt like it needed a good dose of Scope.

~ ~ ~

Two hours later Nick ran his hand over the Model T fender and smiled at his sandy-haired reflection. *I'd sure like to own a baby like this.* He pulled the rag from his back pocket and wiped his hands.

"That's about it, Mayor," he said, easing the hood shut. "Magneto was bad, but everything else checks out. Should run right pretty now."

Mayor Jordon opened the door and wedged his ample body behind the steering wheel. "I envy you, Wheatley, spending your time working on cars. Least they don't talk back to you." He shook his head, setting his chins in motion. "Folks think a public servant has 28 hours a day and doesn't need sleep. This Bring God Back to America campaign, for instance. Parade next Saturday is everybody else's idea, but I'm left with making most of the arrangements and following up. Plus being Grand Marshall and driving this little darling." He patted the dashboard, not trying to hide his pride in himself. "I suppose it's all right if I can help make our city—our country—a better place to live. After all, that's what you folks elected me for."

Nick bent to crank the car. "Well, sir, we appreciate your business. Any trouble with the T, just give me a call."

The old girl coughed once, then chugged away smoothly.

Nick pushed the button to lower his garage door, hoping no one had seen it open. He found it hard to say no if someone needed help at an inconvenient time. It had happened too often, spoiling other Sundays he should spend with his family.

Casting a satisfied glance around the shop, Nick put his tools away. He could hardly believe that 10 years had passed since he'd taken the plunge to buy the business. There were years of struggle to pay for it, and more struggles to buy the new equipment he needed to keep up with computerized systems. But he'd given honest service, always done more than expected. He'd kept his prices fair and got in a little witnessing on the side. It all added up to customers coming back—and bringing others. Yes, with God's help Wheatley's Auto Repair had earned a sterling reputation and was doing fine now. He smiled to himself. *Fine enough to keep the kids in church school, a roof over their heads, and a nest egg in the bank. And that's not bad for an ugly-mugged guy with only a high school diploma.*

He locked up and climbed into his old green "Beater" for the 15-minute drive home. Already the K-Mart parking lot swarmed with shoppers waiting for the doors to open. Another group of people lined the curb in front of the city hall waving "If you love God, why aren't you in church?" placards, while others knelt on the curb to pray.

He waved at them before turning toward the county road. At least they weren't hiding their beliefs under a bushel.

This parade Mayor Jordon had mentioned—Karmerville's response to the Bring God Back to America campaign—tweaked Nick's curiosity. In his New Year's address, President Rondell had challenged each community in America to redouble its efforts to put God back at the helm. The president had said that God couldn't bless people, cities, or nations that blatantly ignored Him and continued their money-oriented self-seeking. People had become greedy, thinking only of financial gain and amusement. Fewer citizens cared for one another or gave God a place in their lives. Perhaps the increasing number of disasters that had plagued the nation through the nineties were sent by God, like an emphatic tap on the shoulder, to remind America who really should be in charge. Change had to happen, the president emphasized. And it started with individuals. And communities. Even small towns.

Television preachers and church groups had latched onto the idea, sponsoring rallies and special services all over the country, but the official kickoff was on July 4th, the United States' Independence Day. It was great to have so many people focusing on spiritual things again and to hear folks openly praising God, but something about it made Nick uneasy.

All the churches in town were to be represented in the Fourth of July parade—even the Seventh-day Adventist church, though their elders had debated heatedly about being part of a secular function that occurred on the Sabbath. Yet as they considered the shortness of time, their desire to witness to a world obviously winding down had won out. The Pathfinders—a club for kids similar to the Scouts—had prepared a float on Nick's flatbed trailer. It held a plaster representation of the Ten Commandments, highlighting the fourth one, and a froth of spun-glass clouds surrounding Jesus and three angels. Excited about doing something as controversial as attending a parade on Sabbath, club members begged to walk next to the float and hand out brochures announcing a satellite evangelistic series the church was beginning shortly—Revelation and the End Times. Who could tell? Maybe it was part of God's plan and might lead a lot of honest people to the Lord.

Nick smiled as his thoughts sifted back over the years. Ever since he was a kid he'd heard his parents and the old folks saying that Jesus was coming soon. He could still see them, huddled in white-haired groups, nodding as they agreed that nearly all the Bible prophecies had been fulfilled; all but the gospel going to the entire world. People were turning from God, they'd said, dirtying His name by using it profanely. And the false Sabbath—it had nearly obliterated the true day of rest. With childlike trust, Nick had believed Jesus' coming was immediate; probably before he was old enough to get baptized. Surely before he finished his teens. Absolutely before he married and had children. But the years had gone by, and here they were.

If Christ came today would he be ready? Though time with God was a priority in his life, the answer sent a shudder up his spine. Other things—making a living, caring for his family—had a way of creeping in.

~ ~ ~

During the past couple years Aaron Chandler had given increasingly bleak commentaries about the deterioration of society and the physical world. Skirmishes between countries were more frequent; natural disasters and terrorist activity occurred with numbing regularity. Maybe hunger was at the base of it all, Chandler suggested. Hunger not only for food, but for meaning to life. And life, well, it seemed cheap to a lot of people. Illegal immigrants flooded the country in spite of quota numbers, nearly bankrupting the welfare system, and even the new Social Identification and Protection System (SIPS), which had replaced the Social Security system, hadn't stemmed it. Fear rested on the land like a heavy hand, boosting the crime rate and making safety a joke, even in Kramerville.

Things on the environmental scene weren't any better. Since that asteroid in '98 had narrowly missed Earth, many more had threatened. All sorts of plans for safety had been devised, and scams drained thousands of dollars from people who longed for a little security from what might fall from the heavens. Maybe the asteroids had something to do with the weather going crazy. Or maybe pollution had changed weather patterns. Who could tell?

Lately folks read spiritual causes into everything. President Rondell's advisers, who were well-known seers, said that if citizens returned to the piety of their forefathers, God would gather up the ill winds and save the world. In an effort to orchestrate reform, frantic government leaders had devised programs, three-month plans, and miracle cures to curb the country's deterioration and the resulting threat of destruction from above. There had to be a fix to all the problems, they insisted. People were more intelligent than ever. Surely this newest plan would hold that answer.

With a sigh, Nick downshifted. The Bible foretold all sorts of troubles. And then the end was supposed to come. But first there was to be a great reawakening of spiritual fervor. Could this Bring God Back to America movement be the starting gun?

He braked and turned onto a gravel lane that squeezed through the trees, crowded the brook, and ended at his home.

As usual, Committee ran out to greet him, flailing his crooked tail as his joy spilled over. Bending to pat the dog's rumpled sides, Nick resolved to forget his worries for the rest of the day and just enjoy his family. Who could tell? With God's help maybe they'd even have a chance to discuss some of Dusty's new lifestyle ideas in a casual way. Nick simply had to deal with that before school started again and ate up another year of their lives.

The fist in his chest tightened as he climbed the front steps. *Lord, please don't let this day end up in another skirmish with Dusty.*

CHAPTER 3

With a smile of anticipation, Brenna Kenrick slipped a bottle of sparkling grape juice into her shopping cart, then headed for the checkout counter. She was small and delicate boned, and her husband called her his hazel-eyed beauty. As she waited in line, memories from seven precious years with Wally sifted through her mind. She recalled the first time she'd seen him, seemingly so self-assured as he stood before his college class on the first day of his career as a biology professor. During his opening statement, he'd dropped his pen, then the chalk, then scattered his notes all over the floor.

Somehow she'd known that he'd become more than just a teacher to her as she slipped from her front-row seat to help him gather up his things so class could resume. The biology labs, strung like diamonds on a glistening strand of Tuesdays throughout the school year, had produced many precious moments.

Then there was his proposal, their wedding, the trip to Greece—and she the princess. The funny little apartment that was much too small held so many memories! And the look on Wally's face when he'd first glimpsed Jared, their firstborn, still made her smile. And then Keely had made their family complete.

Brenna's heart brimmed with joy as she loaded the groceries onto the checkout belt. She didn't deserve to be so happy. The years ahead looked bright, and tonight they would launch those years with their best anniversary yet. Somehow she must manage to express to Wally how much he meant to her. She would do all in her power to help him relax a bit—to enjoy their quiet evening together.

Perhaps they could reminisce. He used to like to do that, yet he'd been so tense lately that maybe he wouldn't want to. Lots on his mind, he'd said when she'd asked. Classes. Heavy student load. But now that his summer class was ending, maybe he'd let down a little—take some time to do the things he wanted to do. Maybe the mischievous sparkle in his eye would resurface, and he'd become his teasing self again.

The kids had already been taken to her friend, Felicia's, to sleep over. There'd be no moist-sweet kisses tonight, no cuddles while she tucked them into bed. Her heart tightened. But this celebration was for them, too, a making-better of an already good relationship. An investment in their future. Yes, tonight would be special. She had her plans.

Wordlessly the checker rang up her things. Brenna watched the monitor. When the total flashed onto the screen, she keyed in a number and then placed her hand on the SIPS scanner to confirm identification. In a moment the green light blinked, verifying that her bank had accepted the charge.

Once home and with things put away, she switched into gear. Turn on the oven, slip in the casserole—Wally's favorite—start the potatoes, toss the salad, decorate the table with their wedding candle and fresh flowers. With a glance at the clock she dropped a flow-through bag of potpourri into the teapot and turned it on to simmer. Then she brought out her gift to Wally and placed it on the coffee table. She smiled to herself. Fifteen minutes to spare. As usual, her planning had worked out. Everything was ready in time.

In the bedroom she flicked on the TV, only half-listening to the usual reports of weather upheavals and Middle East skirmishes. She'd just taken Wally's favorite dress from the closet when *The Chandler Report* began.

"Can we really put God back into America?" Aaron Chandler intoned. She turned the volume up.

"Nationwide polls declare that Americans desire a more religious country. Seventy-seven percent of those polled believe that if Americans would put God first, as they did when our nation was founded, the catastrophic upheavals that Planet

Earth has experienced in the past few years would cease. Eleven percent feel that God has nothing to do with what is happening in our world today—that we have environmentally punished the earth so completely that it will continue its downward spiral and eventually snuff itself out.

"Which opinion is correct remains to be seen. In five days most communities around our country will endeavor to invite God to stand at America's helm once more. This year Independence Day will take on a new tone. Not only will historical independence be celebrated, but our dependence upon a higher power will be officially recognized. It remains to be seen if we, as a nation, can bow to this Power once more. . . ."

With a fleeting thought of their promise to take the kids to fireworks on Saturday night, Brenna switched off the TV and hurried to the living room. She started the CD player, dimmed the lights, and lit the candle on the dining room table. In only moments Wally would arrive.

~ ~ ~

Two hours later Brenna paced in front of the living room window. Car lights, like twin fireflies, zipped past the house or turned the corner and vanished. As each disappeared the tightness in her chest grew. Why was Wally so late? True, he'd driven to Spokane for a morning business appointment, but said he'd be back to his office by midafternoon at the latest. An hour after he should have been home, she'd called his office, thinking he might have become involved in working with a student. She'd even phoned his buddy to see if he'd dropped by there.

A wreck? Her heart lurched. Telling herself she was being silly, she nevertheless had tuned in the area news and let it run ever since she'd turned off the oven and snuffed the candle. She knew Wally remembered their anniversary. She'd seen him slip a greeting card bag into his desk drawer just the night before.

The tight feeling began to cut off her breath as she curled up on the couch and stared out the window. He always called if he was going to be significantly late. That was one thing about Wally—his thoughtfulness.

Oh, Lord, please protect him, wherever he is. Don't let him be hurt.

As she waited, her thoughts drifted back over the years. How natural it was to call upon God now. Somehow He had become the focal point of her life. At first she had resisted the Adventist propaganda, thinking it stuffy and extreme. Besides, she'd thought she could never be forgiven for all the things she'd done in the past. But when she realized how much her understanding Wally's beliefs meant to him, she'd agreed to study. Gradually, through his explanations and the studies with the pastor, it had all made sense. Then came the joy of knowing she had a wonderful future to look forward to, no matter what happened in her day-to-day life. She'd never forget the tears that Wally fought back the Sabbath she was baptized—the day before their wedding.

They had thrown themselves into being involved with the church. The women had been motherly to her, patient with all her questions, and very kind on the day that she had brought a real chicken casserole to a church potluck.

Their marriage had gone smoothly until the last few months when Wally began pulling into himself. He would sit for hours, not angry, but silent. He spent a lot of time reading books she wouldn't even pretend to understand, books explaining New Age concepts, and how channelers were the key to the world's crises. She knew he was worried about his students, and how easily they accepted such enticing error. Naturally he was trying to help them.

It was late now. Her heart jumped as she saw familiar lights turn the corner and creep down their street. So, he was coming at last. A curious mixture of joy and anger warmed her. He could have called! She would not let him know that she had missed him so much.

Brenna hurried to their room and stuffed her new nightgown into a drawer. She stripped off her clothes, all the while listening for the garage door to open. Jamming her arms into the sleeves of her old robe, she mussed her golden hair, which Wally loved so much, grabbed a book, and settled in the bedroom chair. But the garage door didn't open. Finally she went out to see what was keeping him. Then, ashamed of her fleeting anger and "I'll-make-you-pay-for-this" reaction, she watched her trembling fingers dial the police.

~ ~ ~

Three a.m. Brenna sat in the big wing chair in their living room, numb with fear. She couldn't remember the house ever being so empty, so quiet. There was no childish stirring in the kids' rooms, no even breathing coming from Wally's side of the bed. Since calling the police she'd not stopped praying for him—the *every-thought-I'm-thinking-is-a-prayer-for-you* sort of praying. She tried to hang onto her faith in God, that He would not let some dreadful thing happen to Wally—not at this stage of their lives when she and the children needed him so much.

She swallowed the lump in her throat. The Spokane and Moscow police officers had asked her a lot of questions. Had they quarreled? Were his clothes still in the closet? Did she suspect an affair? Had he seemed despondent lately, or had he been ill? Had he made any large withdrawals from their bank account? And by the way, did he carry a substantial life-insurance policy?

With God's help she had remained polite, even though some of the questions were ridiculously personal, and others had been tinged with suspicion about her role in the whole thing.

"We'll get right on it, Mrs. Kenrick. We'll call if we hear anything."

We'll call you. How many times had she wanted to call since then, but stopped herself? Were they really investigating?

Her imagination flared again. What if there'd been a wreck and his wallet had been thrown free so no one knew who he was? No. Impossible. Not with SIPS identification. Not unless—

She envisioned a fiery crash—flames licking at his small car—hungry for him. *No! That's not using my faith.* Then a new scenario nibbled at the back of her mind. What if, coming home, one of the growing number of gangs had waylaid him at a stop sign? If that was so, she would be getting a phone call. *Hostage. Money.*

Stifling her panic, she picked up her Bible to search for the promises she'd underlined during the past seven years. "Thou wilt keep him in perfect peace, whose mind is stayed on thee: because he trusteth in thee."*

The verse pointed an accusing finger at her. Where was this trust she claimed to have—this perfect peace? She'd been worried before, and surely would be again. But it was her duty—no, her *privilege*—to trust God to work out things in her life. She gave herself a mental shake. She wouldn't be any good to anyone fretting like this. Rest. That was what she needed. And she would prove her trust in God by going to bed and getting it.

She'd already crawled into bed when she remembered that she hadn't brushed her teeth. Dutifully she arose and went to the bathroom. Her reflection, usually rosy-cheeked but now pale, peered at her from the mirror. It was when she opened the medicine cabinet that she found a large Hallmark envelope, recycled white and practical, just like Wally. Relief nearly overwhelmed her. Wally knew how compulsive she was about brushing her teeth. She'd just been too busy, and then too preoccupied, to follow through. What had she done? Ruined some intricate plan of his by not opening the cabinet soon enough to find mystery directions?

Fingers trembling, she tore the envelope open. "Happy Anniversary to My Wife," it read. A folded paper fell out. There were only a few lines.

Brenna, I have been thinking about relationships a lot lately, more especially my relationship with you in light of my changing belief in the Adventist religion and the things I always thought true. I must be alone for awhile to think these things over. I need to be away from you and the kids so nothing colors my thoughts, for I have some important decisions to make. I'll be gone for a few days until I can sort things out. Will explain when I return. I'll phone you in the next couple days. Please try not to worry, and give the kids a hug for me. Wally

The card, with its sweet message, was unsigned.

She stumbled back to bed and lay there, dry-eyed and numb. This couldn't be happening to them! After what seemed a long while something inside her broke—she could almost hear it—and she couldn't stop the sobs that threatened to wrench her very insides out.

When the first storm was past, she reached for the phone, and matter-of-factly reported her findings to the faceless voice at the police station. Then she dialed another number. She needed help, and there was only one person she'd trust with news like hers. After a couple rings a sleepy voice came over the line.

"Pastor Stafford here."

---

* Isaiah 26:3.

Chapter 4

July

Glad that it was almost sundown, Nick sank into his recliner, raised the footrest, then gazed through the living room window across the scorched countryside. He felt thankful that the past week's record high temperatures and the brownouts had finally ended, and looked forward to recharging his spiritual batteries. He'd be able to spend some extra time with the Lord over the Sabbath. Sometimes during the noise and bustle of the hectic week, he missed God as he'd miss a dear friend. "Well," he muttered aloud with a sad chuckle, "He hasn't gone anyplace."

His thoughts reached toward heaven. *Thank You, Father, for taking things into Your hands and stopping the heat wave. Satan's pulling out all the stops to keep us from distributing those telecast pamphlets. Bless the Pathfinders as they hand them out tomorrow.*

"Finished," Marj said as she came in from the kitchen. Tossing a smile Nick's way, she put on a CD, the children's signal that it was time for sundown worship. A moment later Gillie bounded into the room and leaped onto the sofa. Elissa, doing her best to look grown up, settled beside him, yet sat there chewing her fingernails. Only Dusty was missing.

Wishing he didn't have to, Nick called out to him. Their family outing the past Sunday had been a disaster. Dusty, still angry about being brought home after the earthquake, had remained sullen, and his attitude hadn't improved. Nick's stomach soured as he reached for his Bible. "Let's read a few verses from Matthew 24."

Marj tensed. "Dusty's not here yet."

Nick turned the pages, avoiding her eyes. "He'll be here."

"But Nick, we've always waited for everyone before starting worship, and I don't think we should change now just because Dusty's out of sorts."

Nick put the Bible down, and stared out the window. It was peaceful outside. Why couldn't it be that way inside, too?

Dusty had just slouched into the room when the doorbell rang. Gillie sprang to answer it. "It's Mayor Jordon."

Nick stepped onto the porch and pulled the door closed behind him. "I didn't hear you drive in," he said, shaking the man's hand. "Dog's letting up, not announcing you."

The mayor chuckled; his big belly jiggled. "Sorry to drop by so late, Wheatley, but I've got problems with the T. She's coughing and wheezing again. Not as bad as last Sunday, mind you, but enough that I'm concerned about getting her through the parade tomorrow."

A sheepish grin settled on the older man's face. "Me and the Mrs. went for a little drive this morning—to cool off, as it were. Took Whistler's Road, and you know what that's like. Maybe something shook loose. I'd have come sooner, but I had a meeting with town council this afternoon and we just got out. If I wasn't all thumbs—"

Nick glanced at the T, then toward the horizon. Only half the sun was left.

"Mayor, I'm sorry—"

"I know what you're going to say—it's your Sabbath." The mayor smiled understandingly. "But this is an emergency, Wheatley, and God's reasonable. He's not going to hold you accountable for doing what you can to help that parade go off like it should, seeing it's all to honor Him in the first place."

Nick searched for the right words. How could he best witness? By complying with the mayor's request, or sticking to the letter of God's law—the fourth commandment? What example would he be setting for his children if he left family worship to go to the garage?

The words "Remember the sabbath day, to keep it holy"* popped into his mind. He gathered up his courage and looked Mayor Jordon in the eye.

"I'm sorry, sir, but I can't work on your car until after the Sabbath ends. It's what God—"

Mayor Jordon tensed. "Look, I'm not asking you to do a major repair job. You understand that. Just to look at the old girl and adjust that little thing so she'll run right again. Won't take you five minutes." A red flush spread over his jowls. "You know, Wheatley, until now you've been a pretty decent chap—down to earth, not a Bible-thumper like most Advents are."

"I—"

The mayor held up his hand. "Used to be one good deed deserved another, friends helped each other. I can't even count the times I've donated to your church when they came pounding on doors and asking for money. Nobody worried about breaking into *my* holy day when they came begging. Furthermore," his eyes narrowed, "I've put myself out for you a time or two. Remember that business loan you had trouble getting a few years back? The one for your expansion?"

Nick did—he'd been pleasantly surprised when it had unexpectedly cleared.

"Couple of words from me and your fate changed. Didn't know that, did you?"

His laugh was mirthless. "I brought my cars to you—even the antiques. Word about your work wouldn't have spread as fast without my help. Seems you could be reasonable on this point, if not for my sake, then at least for the town and our parade. After all, tomorrow's a pretty special day—for us, our country, *and* for God."

"I'm sorry, Mayor, I just—"

"Now don't go telling me you never work on your so-called Sabbath. Last year when Gotlieb's mother died on Friday night you fixed up his car so he could drive on up to be with his old man. There was even an article in the paper about that—something about you pulling Gotlieb's ox out of the ditch, to put it in the religious vernacular. Well, the T's my ox!"

Nick had wondered when that newspaper article would cause trouble. How could people understand the difference when he couldn't even explain it himself?

"I'm sorry, Mayor. Any other day—"

The deep red flush had spread all the way to his high forehead.

"Have it your way. Two can play this kind of game, you know."

Nick listened as the old car sputtered down the drive. *Just a small adjustment . . .* He hated the trembly feeling he got during confrontations—the uncertainty about if he'd done the best thing. Maybe he'd ruined his chance to witness further to Mayor Jordon. Only God could tell.

Lord, go with him. Help him understand—please? And if You could, help his car to run OK.

~ ~ ~

Sabbath dawned cool and bright—the perfect kind of morning that made Nick feel good all over, like he did when an engine purred in response to his skillful touch. From their bedroom window he watched the creek trickle along through the gap between the trees at the lower end of their property. It looked so calm and unaffected by everything around it that he couldn't help comparing its beauty to what God had accomplished in his life over the past few years. Silently he prayed for God's blessing for the day, for his family, and for God's leading and control over all his words and actions. And he prayed for Dusty, who had too much of his father in him, and did not purr in response to anything.

It had been a terrible night. He'd spent it tossing and turning, rehashing everything Mayor Jordon had said on the front porch. He didn't relish the idea of seeing the man at the parade that afternoon. Already he'd had to fight his old foe, smoldering anger, over the way the mayor had acted the night before. But he had given that to the Lord, and now it was his job to trust the Father to help him keep things in perspective. God would bless their golden opportunity to bring the gospel truth to those who had never paid attention before.

With a prayer in his heart, he checked his tie, picked up his Bible, and headed downstairs.

There were only five cars in the lot when they arrived at church—minus Dusty. Inside, Nick stowed his Bible on their regular pew and headed for the foyer to welcome the worshipers. Uncharacteristically grim, Paul Norawalt met him.

"We've got trouble."

Nick sobered. "What's up?"

"You go by your shop this morning?"
"Nope."
"The float's been trashed."

~ ~ ~

The 15 Pathfinders ate a hurried meal in the church activity room before the parade began. Wide-eyed and unusually quiet after learning of the crime that had been committed against their float, they accepted the pamphlets Paul Norawalt gave them, and for the first time Nick could remember, listened attentively to their instructions.

Though their float was ruined, they had decided they would still walk along the parade route to distribute the pamphlets. After a prayer that they'd all behave in a way that would be pleasing to the Lord, they walked the three blocks to the parade's lineup area.

Ten minutes from starting time Mayor Jordon's aide hurried over, a tense look on his face. "Who's in charge here?" he asked.

Paul lifted his hand.

"The mayor is terribly upset about your float and wants you to know the police will be investigating."

Paul started to reply, but the aide continued. "I'm afraid I have more, uh, bad news for you." The aide glanced away and began to speak, as though reciting. "Uh, I've just been informed that because of an old city bylaw prohibiting solicitation or disbursement of religious literature of a specific nature during secular public gatherings on holidays, you folks won't be allowed to give out your papers."

Nick sucked in his breath. "I've sat on Town Council, and I've never heard of that bylaw before."

The aide avoided Nick's eyes. "I don't know much about it either," he mumbled. "Mayor Jordon just told me to give you the message. But your kids march, don't they?" Nervous, he grinned. "I've seen 'em in your church parking lot. Mayor says they can march right behind the Salvation Army band. Music and everything, you know." He took a step backward. "Don't want to disappoint the young ones, now do we?"

"I think I know what this is all about," Nick told Paul. "Give me a minute and I'll be right back."

He shoved his way though the group of officials that crowded the mayor and his Model T. "Mayor Jordon, could I have a word with you?"

The mayor brushed him aside. "Not now, Wheatley. I've got a parade to run."

"But—"

"Look, I'm sorry about your float and that bylaw, but if we're going to bring God back to America, we'll have to start by obeying *all* our laws, whether or not we like them."

"Mayor—"

"Wheatley, I'm busy right now. It's almost time to start. Just let the kids march, and we can talk later."

Righteous indignation surged through Nick. He remembered Jordon's parting words the evening before. *He's doing this to get even with me for not fixing the T last night. And there's not a thing I can do about it!* Nick fought his anger. *Help me, Lord.*

"Thanks, Mayor," he managed to say in a kindly voice, "I do understand."

After a short conference with Paul, they gathered the children and headed back for the church. There was no logical reason to remain. Back in the sanctuary they tried to explain the unfairness to the kids and made plans to pass out the brochures the next day. After prayer, asking the Lord to help them not to become bitter, they locked up and headed for the parking lot.

Gillie got there first, and so was the first to discover that several of their vehicles had been vandalized with spray paint. The Wheatley van was the worst, sporting the words "Sundown Sissies" and "Nuke SDAs." As Nick watched the fear creep across the children's faces he swallowed back his own anger. The Pathfinders, as well as others, would be watching to see how he took this latest blow.

"It's going to be OK," he said, opening the van door. " 'All things work together for good to them that love God.'† Just don't you worry."

---

*Exodus 20:8.

†Romans 8:28.

CHAPTER 5

Brenna broke the spaghetti before dropping it into boiling water. It was another Sunday—a day of endless hours, of holding herself tightly so she wouldn't think, and wouldn't lose her mind. The kids' giggles reached her from the living room where they built and destroyed wobbly Lego towers. The lump in her throat moved up again. Build and destroy—that's what life seemed to be about.

It had been three weeks since Wally had shattered her life, but it might as well have been a lifetime. She'd spent those weeks wondering why, vainly trying to trust in God instead of worrying, forcing herself to keep things as normal as possible for the kids' sake. It had been an exhausting struggle.

She got out the lettuce and began tearing it into pieces. It was like her life—being ripped into ragged bits and nothing she could do about it. She'd heard from Wally only once since he'd left, on July 5 when he'd called after the children's bedtime. He'd been polite but distant, and hadn't talked long. He didn't tell her where he was, but said that in case of an emergency she could pass a message through a friend she didn't know. No, he wasn't angry with her—just needed space to think awhile. Meanwhile, would she read the book he'd left on his nightstand? They'd discuss it when he got back home.

Memories of the first few days after he'd left were blurry now. She didn't know how she'd gotten through them, only that the ache had filled every inch of her and it had taken untold willpower just to keep going. If only she could have called Mama to ask her advice, the way she used to. But Mama was gone now. Still, Pastor Stafford had been wonderful, coming to visit when he could, and calling her each day to pray with her over the phone. But he couldn't take Wally's place—couldn't bandage the hurt that had left her raw and wounded.

She'd read part of Wally's book, but soon laid it aside. It described typical Christianity as a religion that binds believers with chains of guilt, that sucks all joy from their lives. It discussed cults whose beliefs grasp people's minds like tree roots clutch the soil, so securely that it can't wash away with the rains. But it also detailed what the writer insisted was a better order of things, information God had personally given him about what modern Christianity should be. Among other things, this modern Christianity embraced a better way of communicating with God through channelers or one's own inner mind.

Brenna's stomach cramped from nervousness at the thought. How could Wally even *read* that book, knowing everything the Bible taught about spiritualism and its deadly tentacles? Tears filled her eyes, but she fought them back. *Lunch is almost ready. I can't let go now.*

She'd just offered the blessing when she heard the front door carefully open and close, and Wally came into the kitchen. The children swarmed him, hilarious in their joy, asking why he'd been gone so long. They poked through his pockets to find the candies he always brought after a lecturing trip. He glanced at her only once, then shuffled to the living room—each of his legs encased in a clinging child—to dig larger gifts from his suitcase.

Brenna took the solitary moments to compose herself. Shaken, she determined not to muddle their time together with crying. But she had so many questions, and by the masked look on Wally's face she feared they'd go unanswered.

Later, after the children had eaten and were playing with their new toys, Brenna began clearing the table.

"Can that wait?"

Suddenly shy, she faced her husband. She pushed a strand of wiry hair from her forehead. "Sure."

"Well, sit down then."

An awkward moment passed before he spoke. "The grass is pretty long."

"Yes."

"You should have hired someone."

Tears clawed at the backs of her eyes as she struggled to swallow her pain. "I suppose. But why don't we get to the real issue?"

He eyed her. "Issue?"

"What's this all about? Why did you leave?"

He gave her a long look, then sighed. "Well, there's no easy way to put it, so I'll just say it straight. For quite awhile I've needed to do some heavy thinking. That's not always possible considering that I'm either busy with classes or the children or duties at home. Because my decisions will affect all of our lives, I felt it very important to have the solitude necessary to really think them through." His eyes fastened on hers, begging understanding. "The bottom line is that I've drawn some pretty detailed conclusions about what our church teaches."

"Our *church?"*

"There's no easy way to say this, but our church has led us down a very narrow, dark pathway. The entire truth about God has not been taught. By keeping us tied so rigidly to so many rules, the church forces us to subdue our natural freedoms. By use of fear, it thrusts us into a mold, as it were."

Words tried to jump from Brenna's mouth, but she held them back, waiting.

Wally began to pace. "If we question that mold or let our minds expand beyond their confined limits, then we are shamed, shunned, or written off. Don't you see? That's the way they keep us enslaved to what they call our consciences. And that keeps us from the real freedom of God's love, and the growth that love produces." A tight smile trembled on his lips. "It also keeps 'fright money' coming into the church coffers."

Brenna's stomach turned. She couldn't believe this was Wally—*her* Wally—who had supported the church so faithfully since before she'd known him. Not that the church was God. No, of course not. But after prayerful, careful study, she believed that, more than any other, the Adventist Church taught biblical truth. And Wally—through the Holy Spirit—had enabled her to see it. It was a joyful thing. Liberating!

She wanted to cover her ears and flee from the room. She

felt as though she were on a roller coaster as it crested the first big rise. There was nothing she could do to stop it.

His face softened. "I know, I know. Don't think I've forgotten how hard I tried to get you into the church I used to love—to teach you everything that I knew, and bring you along with me. It seemed so right, so important then. I'd grown up being taught all those things, believing. But you hadn't. Still, you accepted it because of me."

Brenna stiffened. "I accepted it because I *believed* it. And I still do."

He opened his mouth to speak again, but she forged ahead. "And I can't believe you've let yourself change so much. You know that Satan will try to delude us. You know that there'll be a shaking of God's people before He comes."

His eyes lit up. "My point exactly. I know what I've been taught, what I taught you. But so many of those things are wrong—enslavers."

"The Sabbath? Christ's second coming? Surely you can't think—"

"Brenna!" His voice was cold. "Did you read the book?"

"Part of it."

He flopped back into his chair. "Part? I asked you to read it all so that we could discuss it, so we'd both have the same background information. I've read many volumes about the subject, but this one graphically explains the truth, and simply enough that even a *child* could understand it. It seems you could have done that much for me, if you're really interested in learning where I'm coming from."

One tear escaped. "Wally, the things that book says—it talks about accepting guidance from unseen thought leaders and—"

"And?"

"I can't ever do that. Don't you see, the Bible is really the only book we can base our beliefs on? And the Bible warns us about these delusions!"

He measured out his words. "Perhaps the Bible is part of the conspiracy."

Her voice was a whisper. "You don't believe the Bible anymore?"

"Don't get me wrong. It was useful in its time, but it's

outmoded now because God has given us new light." Wally scraped back his chair and stood up. "I know one thing. I don't want our children to have to cope with the load of guilt that was strapped to me while I grew up! 'Don't do this! Jesus won't like it. Don't even think such and such if you want to go to heaven!'" He scowled. "Can't play this on Sabbath; afraid to see and do and feel. Everything's bad. No, that's not what I want for Jared or for Keely."

Brenna couldn't move. A darkness that had nothing to do with lack of sunlight rested its cold hands on her shoulders, pressing her into her chair. A thin whistling, like wind whipping through icy branches, filled her ears.

"What are you saying?"

He softened, reached for her hands. "Sweetheart, you know I love you more than life itself. I always have, ever since you first scrambled across the floor to pick up my chalk. But in spite of that, I can't live with such a rigid religion—especially when I know it's wrong. You've accepted it so completely that you've become rigid, too." He kissed her palms.

"You used to be carefree and young. Now you're bound and tied by duty. And, like my parents did—bless their hearts, for they meant well—you'll pass those crippling teachings along to the children. Fear and guilt will become the major part of their lives. It feels so good to be free from those feelings that choked me all of my life. I just can't watch history repeat itself in our kids."

He glanced toward the living room. "Sweetheart, please read the book. Don't go into it with your mind already made up—give it a chance. We'll talk about it every night until you understand the background and what it says. We've been hoodwinked, and it's up to us to keep the children's lives free from the kind of error we've begun to teach them."

He smiled the grab-my-heart smile that was so precious to her. "It should take only a couple weeks to really cover the subject. You're intelligent. I'm sure it'll make sense to you."

"And if I don't read it?"

He sobered. "Look, I'll make you a deal. As we study, if I learn that I've been wrong, I'll return to the church. I promise."

"But if neither of us changes?"

He stood up, turned, and walked into the kitchen. He opened the refrigerator before replying. "I don't want the children to have to undergo the problems of a broken home."

She was being forced into a corner. "Are you saying that if I don't change my ideas you'll leave us?" Somehow she knew he'd already thought this through.

He faced her, straight on. "No, I could never leave you three. Truth is—and it tears me up to say this—we three would have to leave you."

The words piled up around her. She didn't want to recognize them. She forced herself to pick them up, one at a time, to set them in order in a frightening attempt to make sense of them. "You mean you'd take—?"

He nodded. "I don't want to hurt you. You know that. But if we can't come to an agreement there's no other choice."

Brenna stared at her slender hands. They'd picked up broken chalk from a classroom floor. They'd been able to soothe the children, to help earn a living, to work together to make meals and clean floors and fashion wee dresses. They had spanked occasionally, and caressed and fixed and loved. But there was no way they could help her now. The dark weight pressed harder.

"Please, sweetheart?"

She felt the last shred of joy flee from her heart. "I'll finish the book," she whispered.

CHAPTER 6

August

Lucita Fernandez reached for the stack of updates and focused on the monitor again. Double-checking her last input, she hit the "enter" key, and the big eye blinked away the information and a blank form popped up on the screen. Taking the top paper from the stack, she keyed in a SIPS number. It took only a moment for a record to appear, complete with all pertinent information about Slone Jonathan Carrister, 2944-739-91686. She scanned down the long police record, then added the newest felony information—a drive-by shooting at the market near her home. With a sigh she reached for another update.

It boggled Lucita's mind to realize that with a few keystrokes she could bring up a detailed record for any person legally living in the United States—and so could prospective employers if Slone Carrister ever got out of jail.

Her thoughts wandered as her fingers flew across the keys.

Though not what she wanted for her career, she enjoyed her job at the Social Identification and Protection System office, where she'd been since its beginning two years earlier. How angry the rights to privacy groups had been when SIPS replaced the Social Security system. They'd picketed the government buildings, and every other place they could think of. But as SIPS became more common, the advantages were clear. With its birth the government had put an end to stolen identification, credit card fraud, welfare scams by social sponges, illegal immigrants taking scarce jobs, and a host of other social problems. And now, riding on the brittle crest of success, SIPS officials enthusiastically claimed that the new system would bring a golden tomorrow.

She'd never forget going to the high school gym to have the grain-of-rice-sized chip inserted in the fleshy place near the base of her left thumb. To begin with, it was painful and had taken a few days to heal. Nor would she forget being fingerprinted. This information had been coupled with the old Social Security information, creating a new record to which vital information would be added as time passed, one that no other person's would duplicate. It created an almost foolproof system of identification, and few questioned it anymore.

Thousands of records were being added each day as new Americans were born or naturalized. In hospitals and birth clinics tiny chips were imbedded and fingerprints recorded as soon as an infant was born. Vital information keyed into the terminal connected the infant and its mother, instantly creating a new SIPS record. The revolutionary process had nearly eradicated abductions, for schools and medical offices required SIPS identification before providing services, information which could be read through use of a small scanner and a monitor.

Working at SIPS was preferable to working at La Cucharita, Papa's restaurant, where her sisters had worked while growing up. Papa had strongly opposed Lucita's request to work at the federal agency, believing that her safety and virtue might be sullied in the outside world. A young woman was much safer in a world growing more and more *loco,* he insisted, if constantly surrounded by family members. But she felt a close warmth connected with Papa's protection. The pride in his eyes proved that he cherished her. The fact that she was pretty, he said, meant no safety for her. Too often young *hombres* cast admiring glances her way. Who could blame them if they were overcome by her beauty and tried to take undeserved liberties? Only Papa's watchful protection would safeguard her.

In truth, she didn't know if she was pretty. She had a round face and a figure that would never be pencil slim. Olive skin, wavy hair, and a nose too wide for her liking. But Mama said that her smile was so bright and genuine that even the homeless felt loved at the sight of it, and that was the important thing.

La Cucharita was small, and two of her sisters still worked

there. Times were hard, and jobs in the neighborhood scarce, so in the end, and against his better judgment, Papa had relented and allowed Lucita to venture into the world with all its social hazards. Still, Papa kept a tight rein on her, as he had all his girls, but he meant well, and she never doubted that she was loved.

At last the workday ended. Glad it was Friday, Lucita boarded the bus and eyed her fellow passengers. Though they had different names, colors, and social standings, they had one thing in common. *Numeros.* Old or young, rich or poor, they each had a 12-digit number that would follow them throughout their lives.

When she left the bus, Lucita glanced down the narrow Seattle street toward St. Luke's Cathedral. Papa didn't like for her to walk this neighborhood alone, even in the daylight hours. But the few minutes she customarily spent in the cathedral's quiet grandeur before catching the next bus made her more able to cope with the pressures that surrounded her, including the lack of privacy at home.

She stood on the corner for a moment, checking the shabby doorways between herself and St. Luke's. Some of the businesses were closed for good, but not the pawnshop or tavern she must pass. Only a few people moved along the street, and they seemed harmless enough. Still, last week, just a block away, a woman had been raped and killed at curbside. She, too, had been on her way to the cathedral. Lucita's heart skipped a beat, and for a moment she hesitated.

Then, gathering her courage, she hurried the two blocks. Inside, she dipped her fingers into a basin of holy water, then made her way to the altar where the Blessed Virgin floated in clouds at the feet of the Christ. She caught her breath at the beauty of the statues and the stained glass windows. The fragrance of wax candles combined with the perfume of the yellow roses someone had laid at the altar. Dropping to her knees, Lucita found her crucifix and let the stillness wrap around her.

The hassle of the day faded as her prayers drifted heavenward. Christ was truly up there; she knew that for sure, for hadn't she felt His loving presence when she knelt here before Him?

After awhile she moved into a tiny alcove that housed Saint

Anthony. To the side was a velvet-draped altar and a rack of candles. Lucita dropped a dollar into a little metal box and lit one of the candles. Feeling small and vulnerable, she watched the thin ribbon of smoke meander toward the ceiling as she whispered to her patron saint, carefully reminding him of her golden dream, begging him to somehow intervene with Papa and make it possible. Papa had told her to put the notion out of her mind—not to mention it again. And in part she had obeyed.

The minutes passed. Someone else came into the alcove, lit a candle, knelt, left. She stayed longer, pleading until her knees throbbed from the cold stone floor. Then, pushing aside a vaguely restless feeling, she returned to the bus stop.

As she waited for number 91, several others joined her. From across the street a surly group of teenagers eyed them, gesturing, laughing. Still thinking of her prayer in the cathedral, Lucita turned her back to them. If Papa would let her keep the money she earned, in another year she would have enough to quit work and attend university. And then perhaps her dream of becoming an interpreter would come true, and she would travel all over the world.

At last Lucita spied the familiar green-and-white bus. She was slipping into line when someone touched her sleeve.

"Señorita?"

The tiny white-haired woman wore a big smile and the brightest blue eyes Lucita had ever seen. "Dearie, I saw you come out of St. Luke's, and I thought you might enjoy something good to read." She thrust a small booklet into Lucita's hand. "This has been such a blessing to me."

The Secret to Answered Prayer, the title read. Well, she needed answers. Lucita returned the woman's smile. "Thanks so much."

And then the bus was there. After boarding, Lucita turned to wave to her new friend. She couldn't help noticing that the old woman now stood alone, and the gang had started across the street toward her. Resisting the impulse to call out to the driver, she lost sight of the woman as the bus turned the corner.

As she clung to the overhead strap and struggled to stay upright, Lucita scanned the back cover. "If you need answers to prayer this book is for you," she read. Religious and political people often handed out propaganda, and though Lucita usually accepted, she always threw it away without reading it. Yet there was something different about the old woman and their 10-second contact, something that drew her to take a closer look.

Like Papa said, every religion had an angle, and it usually involved money. She sighed as she remembered how angry he'd been the time her sister had brought home a Mormon tract. Life hadn't been the same for several weeks. Well, she didn't have time for extra reading anyway, for she needed every spare moment to study the German she was teaching herself. Her decision was made, and that was that. She'd discard the book when she got off the bus.

Just then the bus lurched, throwing her against the man standing beside her. And when she regained her balance, she slipped the booklet into her pocket and held on with both hands.

That evening after helping with supper cleanup, Lucita sank onto the couch beside Mama to watch the local news before Papa returned from the restaurant. Half listening, Lucita leaned back and closed her eyes, happy to relax for a moment before getting out her German. Suddenly she sat up and stared at the screen.

". . . unidentified elderly woman that was apparently robbed and then murdered at a bus stop near St. Luke's Cathedral. Anyone with information about this crime is asked to call the Seattle Police Department."

Lucita's heart stopped. She recognized the bus stop with St. Luke's towering in the background. Would she also recognize the old woman?

Overwhelmed, she turned to tell Mama, then changed her mind. If Papa learned that she'd been in that neighborhood he'd never let her ride the bus again. Excusing herself, she headed for the room she shared with Teresa, her older sister. When she picked up her coat to hang it, something fell out of the pocket.

Dazed, Lucita stared at the booklet at her feet. *Why was that old woman so foolish?* Everyone knew it wasn't safe to be alone on the city streets. She sank to the floor and read a passage. It seemed harmless enough—almost comforting.

She flipped through the pages until she came to the last

one. There, at the bottom, carefully written in shaky cursive were the words "For more information, or for additional literature, please contact the Seventh-day Adventist Church or your friend, Myrtle Flemming." Her phone number followed.

Ears buzzing, Lucita eyed the book for a long time. Then she got up and headed for the phone.

CHAPTER 7

Nick stared at the filthy words scrawled on his bay door and shook his head. "I've got no idea who might have done it."

Sergeant Clay clicked his ballpoint pen in rhythm with the rap that blared from the car parked at the curb. "You cross anyone recently?"

Nick shook his head. The truth of the matter was that he'd had few customers lately, few enough that he was beginning to worry about his business.

The policeman scribbled something, then continued. "Employee problems?"

"Uh-uh. Except I laid off Frank White, but he'd never do anything like this."

"Anyone quit lately?"

There was Chuck, who had been with Wheatley's Auto Repair since its birth. They'd worked together like brothers, carefully plotting the shop's growth and monitoring its health. That's why Nick had been caught off guard when, at the beginning of this business slump, Chuck had stepped into the office, looking miserable.

"I've had an offer from Beckett's Automotive."

Nick's stomach had tightened. His competitor. Lower priced, but also inferior service. Together he and Chuck had fixed quite a few cars that Beckett's had botched. Together they had laughed when Beckett had approached Chuck before. Surely Chuck's work ethic would never allow him to cut repair corners like Beckett's did.

"What're they offering you this time?"

Eyes averted, Chuck had fiddled with his wrench. "More than I can afford to ignore—unless you can match it, of course." And then, dead serious, Chuck had named a figure.

For a long moment Nick had groped with the reality of his finances, trying to rearrange the figures that lined up in his mind. After all, Chuck was his best mechanic, and he generated a lot of business.

Nick finally shook his head. "You're worth much more, my friend, but you know how business has been lately."

Chuck sighed. "Well, with Millie's illness and all—sorry, Nick. I'm going to have to give notice."

Nick turned back to Sergeant Clay. "Chuck quit two weeks ago."

Sergeant Clay's eyebrows lifted. "He went to Beckett's."

"Yes. Now only Shorty's with me."

"Well, then." The man pocketed his pen. "If you think of anything else, let us know. We'll be in touch."

Nick went inside and raised the bay door. Hot or not, he'd keep the door up until evening so customers wouldn't see the graffiti. Then he and Dusty could paint it out.

Nick turned to look at the black lettering above the service window. *"God is my partner."* Every year since he'd opened he'd touched up the words, remembering Who it was that had helped his one-bay business flourish into the four-bay operation he now owned. It hadn't been easy, but then, with the Lord all things were possible. Surely God would help the business through this slump. Meanwhile, Nick reasoned, it was his duty to continue to give good service.

He stepped into his office, closed the door, and bowed his head as he always did before starting work. "Lord, I give You today. Help me be a good witness and guard my words and actions. Keep me cheerful in spite of my troubles. Thank You for Your care and guidance and for paying the price for my sins. May I always be true to You. Amen."

The morning went slowly with only two minor repairs. Shorty had made quick work of them, and then, seeing that the appointment book held only a tune-up for the afternoon, Nick had suggested that Shorty take the time off. "I'll call you if we get busy, but I can manage around here."

Fighting against his tendency to worry, Nick turned up the radio and began some long overdue cleaning in the parts room. Opening a tall metal cabinet, he sorted through its contents, some of which had been there since the day he opened. Unwillingly he recalled the times that Shannon had chided him for saving everything he'd ever owned whether it was any good or not. *If she could just see me now—no customers and all.* Thoughts of her predictions that he'd never make anything of himself or his grubby little garage were certainly not what he needed to remember just now. He worked faster, pulling stuff from the shelves and forcing himself to toss much of it onto his "discard" pile.

The music ended and *The Chandler Report* began. Nick half-listened as he sorted goods and memories.

". . . believe the disturbance is caused by the asteroid shower that leading geologists predict. Meanwhile, California sizzles under temperatures that have already reached 118 degrees. Power in coastal California has been intermittent, leading to lengthy blackouts and cooling problems. Meanwhile, an early ice storm has blanketed central Canada and the Dakotas. A hurricane rages off the panhandle of Florida and is due to cross the Keys later today. Texas has reported multiple tornadoes, and the wheat belt remains parched. The weather fronts are building up for something more catastrophic than our country has faced before, predicts Onna Schleier, the visionary who predicted last year's double hurricane in Florida.

"Meanwhile, on a happier note, a news release from Rome states that Pope Philip will conduct a prayer tour through the United States in November. President Rondell, who attended a Vatican dinner for world leaders, made the following statement: 'I am greatly encouraged that Pope Philip has agreed to aid us in our refocus on spiritual matters. Putting God back at the helm of our nation is of major importance to us at this troubled time. His words and blessings as he visits will do much to aid us in that endeavor.'"

Nick stopped to listen.

"In a news brief the Vatican stated that it is Pope Philip's purpose to encourage each person to be faithful in church attendance every Sunday, and to promote the idea of bringing all mankind back to God, regardless of past differences or trespasses. He states that our world cannot expect God's mercy if we are not willing to put Him first in everything. What that means to the common man remains to be revealed to us in November. And now, a message from our sponsors."

Nick dropped to his knees and pulled an old distributor off the shelf. This business about the pope and the world leaders was unsettling. The alliance among Rome and America had continued to strengthen since the early nineties due to Pope John Paul II's worldwide concentration on social issues. Now Pope Philip carried his predecessor's work forward, and though Nick admired the man's stand on abortion, the importance of family, and other concerns, he could see how the church leader's charismatic reputation had developed to the point of near-worship from most countries around the globe. Pope Philip had gone from place to place, settling disagreements folks had never thought would be settled. Nick would watch with great interest what became of this visit.

He pulled a small cloth bag from the cupboard and, puzzled, dumped its contents—two plastic bags of white powder—onto the floor.

What on earth was it? Crack? Some other drug? Certainly nothing used in the garage. Puzzled, he flipped through possibilities of who could have put it there, not liking any of them. He should call the police, but there'd be an investigation. That was all he needed now with his flagging business. He stood there, undecided . . . wondering.

"Hallo-o-o?"

Nick tossed the white stuff back into the cupboard and hurried to the bay.

An elderly man stood there. "I wondered if anybody wuz around. Didn't see no one." He took off his ball cap and scratched his head. "Name's Will. I'm passin' through and don't have no appointment, but I wonder iffin you'd have time t' look at my brakes? Car sorta pulls to the left when I step on 'em, and I don't want no trouble poppin' up whilst I'm on the road."

Nick smiled. "Be glad to. Just drive her onto that lift there and I'll take a look."

The old man shuffled to his car, then inched it onto the lift. As Nick approached the car he noticed a Bible on the back seat.

Nick pointed to it. "Any good?"

Will's eyes locked on Nick's. "Best readin' they is."

Nick nodded. "Where you from?"

Will chuckled, a warm, bumpy sound. "Well, young feller, that's hard to say. I've been travelin' fer a good spell now."

It took little time to adjust the brakes, so while the car was up Nick did a quick spot-check of the car's general condition. Everything else looked fine. He let the car down, wrote up the bill, and handed it to the old man.

"Mighty reasonable service you give here, lad," the old man said, examining the invoice. His eyes wandered around the bay, then rested on the words on Nick's wall. His smile widened. "Say, He's my Partner, too, an' I wanna tell you somethin'." He rested his trembly hand on Nick's shoulder and grew serious. "Things are fixin' to get pretty tough in the next little while. But don't get discouraged. Just keep yer mind on yer Partner and a prayer on yer lips. He'll get you through it. An' don't fergit—He's promised to give us the words when we need 'em."

With that, the old man paid his bill, backed out of the garage, and drove off. Nick watched until the car had rounded the corner. Strange old man—comforting words. And Will was right. Keeping his mind on his Partner was what he needed to do.

~ ~ ~

The late afternoon sun beat down mercilessly, reflecting off the bay door and intensifying the heat. Nick taped out the last window, then climbed back down the ladder.

"Please put these things back inside," he said, handing the tape and newspaper to Dusty.

Sullen, Dusty took the items and slunk into the office. How long did it take kids to get through this ugly stage of life, anyway? He and Marj had been walking on eggshells for a long time now, weighing every word and action so as not to set the boy off again.

A moment later Dusty returned, hands thrust deep into his pockets.

Nick eyed his son. "You want to spray the top part?"

Dusty shrugged.

"Then hand me the nozzle and I'll start."

Nick began spraying the paint, careful not to overlap the edges too much. The throb of the compressor drummed into his head, eclipsing everything else. When he finished as much as he could do from his position he called for Dusty to turn the compressor off, but Dusty was nowhere in sight.

Nick climbed down and went to find the boy. As he entered the garage, Dusty emerged from the parts room. Startled, he fastened his gaze on his father. "You done already?"

Nick swallowed his annoyance.

"No. And I need your help out here or I never will be done. Would you remove the tape, please?"

Dusty's lip curled in a silent snarl. He jerked off the masking tape, then headed for his car.

"I'm going to McDonalds. Be home later."

Nick watched Dusty's car head down the street, then turn a corner. *Strange. He's going in the opposite direction from McDonalds.*

Inside, Nick flopped onto the waiting room couch. He needed a few minutes to think, to decide what to do about that white stuff he'd found in the parts room.

Lord, who could've put it there? Frank? Shorty? He shook his head. *I don't want to get anyone in trouble—but I know it's a felony to hide the stuff—I could be in serious trouble here. Turning it in could cause trouble too, put* me *under suspicion. What'll I do?*

He sat for a long while, mulling the whole thing over. The law was the law. As he could see it, he had no choice. He must turn the stuff in, regardless of the outcome. After all, there was a principle at stake here.

He went to the cabinet and reached inside. He paused, felt around, then turned stone-cold, for the white stuff was gone.

Chapter 8

September

August had crawled by, tedious and exasperating. Usually Brenna loved the long summer evenings with their lingering twilight, for she spent them playing outside with the children, consciously creating lovely memories for them to cling to when they grew up. But this year . . .

She turned another page of the book that was tearing her life apart, whose subject was almost the only thing Wally would discuss anymore. Her fingers tingled against its evilness. But she had promised Wally she'd read it through and try to understand what he saw in the strange mixture of spiritism and Christianity. With each page she begged God for His forgiveness and for words to win her husband back to the truth with understanding, loving-kindness, and reason.

Something caught in her throat as she recalled how Wally had spiritually nurtured her when they first married, how on their wedding night the first thing he had done was to draw her into a close circle of prayer to their heavenly Father and dedicate their marriage to Him. Those worship times had become daily occurrences, strengthening times she had looked forward to, knowing that he cared for more than her physical well-being. What had happened to change all that? Where had they gone wrong?

It was almost suppertime. Brenna gladly set the book aside and headed for the kitchen. Yet, an uneasy restlessness filled her. She wanted Wally to come home. She wanted him to stay away! She needed to feel his arms around her, to hear him telling her everything would be all right, but she dreaded discussing this latest chapter. Sometimes she wished she could turn her back on her world and everything in it. Just run to some safe place where life was happy once again, where her heart didn't feel torn at every turn.

Pausing by the sliding glass door, she glanced into the backyard, where 5-year-old Jared and 3-year-old little Keely constructed their endless sand roads and towns. For several moments she watched, half-praying for the dear little souls that God had entrusted to her. Once she thought Jared noticed her, but then he looked away, his face unsmiling, thinner, somehow remote. Could he feel their tension too?

She watched his poor little claw as he dragged it through the sand, then looked beyond to the woven fence he had climbed and fallen from when he was 2. Could it have been Jared's painful accident that had shaken Wally's faith in the truth? Again she felt the horror of the moment he had struck the ground, injuring the growth plate near the wrist. That fall had crippled their son's once-perfect left hand and shattered their hope that it would ever be normal.

Shaking off useless self-blame, she glanced at her watch. Wally would be home from the university soon. Maybe if she worked things right, was light and happy and smiling, she could sidetrack him from their usual discussions and they could enjoy a pleasant family evening. She would try.

~ ~ ~

Later, with dinner finished, they lingered on the terrace. Wally took Brenna's hand and stroked her fingertips the way he had so long ago. "There's a Knights of Truth meeting tomorrow night, and I'd like you to come with me. A scientist from Seattle will be there. He's the secondary Priest of the Knights and claims to have solid evidence about immortality. I know you have a hard time with that concept."

Warnings from Pastor Stafford's recent sermon resurfaced. *"Never put yourself on enchanted ground. Stay away from those who try to prove things to you that you know are contrary to what the Bible teaches. So-called proof can be very misleading, most convincing."*

"I can't go, Wally. I wouldn't want to take the children, and you know how hard it is to get a sitter on such short notice."

He squeezed her hand. "Already taken care of, my love." He bent to kiss her forehead. "I contacted Janey before I left work. She'll be here by 6:00. I thought we'd go for a bite to eat before we join Whalen."

~ ~ ~

Whalen's home sprawled across a rise overlooking the little university town and the fertile Palouse country in which golden wheat fields crowned the gentle hills stretching westward. Already Whalen's driveway was filled with finer cars than she and Wally would ever own. Uneasy, she glanced down at her simple navy dress and wished she'd worn something else.

Wally led her through the portico that opened into a courtyard bursting with orchids, airy ferns, espaliered shrubs, and flowers. An ornate cross stood near a waterfall that dribbled into a natural-looking pond. Her tenseness washed away. Why should she worry about the evening? These were just people, people who apparently treasured the same gifts of nature she enjoyed. She would not waste her time worrying. She would just listen, take good notes, and then be ready to help Wally understand the truth about immortality, as he himself had once taught her.

Luke Whalen was a gracious host, immediately setting Brenna at ease with his easygoing, lighthearted manner. "I'm so happy to meet you at last," he said as he handed her a glass of lemonade. "We've become good friends with Wally. It would be nice if you'd decide to join us on a more permanent basis, too."

After introductions, everyone settled in Whalen's spacious living room. Dr. Max Orcott, president of Orcott Scientific Research Bureau based in Seattle, finally stood to speak. He was a birdlike man with disturbing eyes that seemed able to see through her.

"I have exciting news this evening, because help for our battered world stands in the wings. Before I begin, let me say that I'm not one for convention. *Please* don't call me Dr. Orcott, as titles tend to separate, and I just want to be one with you." His smile twitched on, then off, never reaching his eyes. "Max will do just fine."

He cleared his throat and looked at the ceiling as though his notes were there. "From the beginning of history the question regarding what happens once a person dies has been a subject of profound interest. Religion poses several theoretical answers—none of which can be concretely proven. Some religious groups believe that the departed goes directly to heaven; others, directly to purgatory. Some believe that the departed is reincarnated into a new being. A few sects believe that the person merely sleeps until such a time that God will come in blazing clouds and awaken him to a new, perfect state of life. Then there are those who believe that once a person dies, that's all there is. *Kaput. Finis."* He sighed. "Believe it or not, I was once among this latter class.

"Tonight, however, I wish to document some experiences my colleagues and I have had in the course of our research. You will see pictures of a few incidents that completely changed my mind about what lies beyond the grave and how much the living dead have to do with what happens to us every day."

"Living dead?" Brenna shuddered.

"These things have altered the way I look at life, and consequently, the way I worship."

Max eyed the guests as he spoke. "Today the world is looking for answers to social problems, spiritual problems, mental problems. But the answers seem elusive. Well, I've got good news for you! There's a new world order just around the corner. It will put an end to the senseless squabbling all around us, if we are open to celestial guidance from those who have moved beyond the door humans call 'death.' When we focus on things that are important, and learn to offer worship to the highest being of the universe—when we put things in perspective—we can see things in a different and more positive light. And that is what I'm here to share with you tonight. What I will show you has become part of a documentary on life after death which is soon to be released by Geographic Science Filmworks. But you are getting in on the ground floor." He flashed a tight smile. "The great Privileged Beforehand, as it were."

Max rubbed his hands together, then switched on the video. Brenna watched Max walk across the screen to the edge of a graveyard, then sit on a stone. Soon a misty form lifted from the ground at his feet, then became as solid as herself. She listened to the taped discussion between the apparition, named Viktorr, and Max. She saw Viktorr rest his hand on Max's shoulder and tell him to spread the word to others, for there were wonderful things in the future, and they must prepare for them.

Enchanted ground! Prickly heat inched up Brenna's backbone and her heart seemed to stop.

Max switched off the video. His smooth words, which seemed to mesmerize the others, began to tug at her too. When his eyes finally settled on her they narrowed momentarily, and an uncomfortable warmth flashed from them. Was he reading her thoughts? Heart doing double time, she glanced at the door, then nudged Wally. "Honey, let's go home."

He gave her a "don't-bother-me-now" look and turned his attention back to the speaker.

Brenna closed her eyes. This was the type of situation that Pastor Stafford had warned about, but how could she leave without making a scene that would embarrass Wally? She'd just have to sit it out, but she didn't have to pay attention.

The video started again. Words, smoother and sweeter than honey, filled the room with a heavy denseness she'd never known possible. The hair on her arms rose as a sensation of extreme cold, and at the same time moist heat, enveloped her. *Enchanted ground!* Riveted to her seat, Brenna tried to close it all out, to concentrate on praying to God, but it was hard to form the words.

At last the video ended. "Let's move on out to the courtyard," Max murmured. "We'll have a session there."

Eager, the others moved outside. Brenna touched Wally's arm. "We need to go home to the children," she said, hoping he'd understand.

"No."

Something clammy slid over her. "I *must* go."

His glazed eyes found hers and he looked at her for a long moment before handing her the car keys. "I'll get a ride home with someone," he mumbled, before he turned and walked away.

~ ~ ~

Long after Wally had drifted off to sleep Brenna lay awake. Though she tried to shut them out, Wally's last words before he fell asleep resounded in her memory. *"What Max said tonight makes so much sense. Somehow I knew there was something more out there. So often I've felt Dad's presence—like someone trying to direct me, but of course I thought that was impossible. We're fools not to accept guidance that God sends us, through whatever means He chooses."*

Brenna stared into the corner of their darkened room, shuddered, then pulled the sheet over her head. She felt spied upon and somehow violated. Once again she tried to pray.

~ ~ ~

The next evening Wally stood across the bedroom, watching her, so near and yet so far away. With his eyes narrowed and his arms clasped across his chest, his body language screamed that he was shutting her out. Looking at him now, there was little to remind her of the considerate man she'd married.

"So you're going to break your promise."

Brenna brushed her hair aside. "What promise?"

He came closer. "You told me you'd finish reading the book. That was our deal when I agreed to stay. That you'd finish it so we could discuss it."

Brenna had honestly tried to keep her word, tried to force herself through each contaminating page. But after the meeting at Luke Whalen's house, after what Wally had said . . . She searched for the right words.

"Honey, you know I don't want to lose you, but I can't finish that book. When I read it, I—I feel like I'm turning my back on God! It's so opposite of everything the Bible says. I just . . ."

Wally's eyes flashed. "Forget about the Bible as it now reads. It's been tampered with—a tool of the devil to mislead you! It was revised by men who thrived on producing guilt. It's designed to control through fear and guilt. The sooner you put it behind you and look for God's real kingdom, the better off you'll be."

He crossed the room and took her in his arms. How she wanted to rest there, to feel the safety she had in the past. She forced herself to relax against him as he kissed her hair, her forehead, massaged the back of her neck. "C'mon, honey. Don't fight this. You promised to see it through, to give it an honest look."

He who loves his mother or father more than me . . .

Reality's chilling hand settled over Brenna. "Wally, you know I love you and I don't like us to be so far apart in our beliefs, but I can't turn my back on God and everything that I know is true." Her voice quivered. "No matter what happens."

Without a word Wally flopped onto their bed and pulled off his shoes, letting them thud onto the floor. She waited for his words to drop, as well.

Just then Jared burst into their room. "Mom, Keely squashed my tunnel!"

Keely was right behind him. "It was an ax'dent!"

Jared spun around and shoved Keely to the floor. "Liar! You did it on purpose!"

"Jared!" Brenna separated the two children.

Jared's eyes narrowed, a reaction so like Wally's it scared her. "She's bad! I don't want to play with her anymore."

Keely faced Jared, tears running down her cheeks. "Jesus doesn't want you to push me," she sobbed. Then she pulled away from Brenna and ran to Wally.

Brenna tried to gather her wits. "Children, please. You know it makes Jesus sad to see you squabble."

"Enough!" Wally shouted, slamming his fist against the table and turning on her. "I won't let you smother these kids with religious guilt trips." His glare darkened. "Bible-thumpers love to twist young, defenseless minds. Now, back off and let me handle this." He swooped both children into his arms, and then his voice went soft.

"C'mon. Daddy brought you something."

Stunned, Brenna watched them go into the living room.

Lord in heaven, what shall I do? She believed in honoring her husband, of holding him up before her children. But lately, if she mentioned Jesus in Wally's presence, he stopped her, cut her short. It was frustrating, and it hadn't taken the children long to begin to challenge her right to direct them. Dared she intervene now?

She could hear them in the living room, laughing at something Wally had said. She slipped to the door and looked in. The three of them sat on the couch, their backs to her.

". . . so at my meeting last night I got one for each of you. If you ever get scared or don't know what to do about something, just hold it tightly in your hand and repeat the words I told you. God's power is in this little charm, and He will always help you know what is right and wrong. Can you remember that?"

"Ooooh, it's so smooth," Jared whispered as he turned it over and over in his hand. Keely dutifully chanted the words.

Wally hugged her. "Good girl. Now don't forget, and keep it under your pillow at night."

Later, when she put Keely to bed, Brenna asked to see what Wally had given her. Keely's eyes sparkled. "It's my charm, Mommy," she said, feeling beneath her pillow for it. "Isn't it cute?"

Brenna took the tiny replica of a snake wrapped around a cross. Her fingers recoiled. Metal was usually cool to the touch, wasn't it? But there was an eerie warmth to the snake.

~ ~ ~

It was hard to go to work the next morning. After Wally left for the university, Brenna distracted the kids long enough to discard their charms. Then during breakfast another squabble broke out. "Jared tore my toast!"

"I did not!"

Brenna broke in. "Kids, who can remember what our memory verse for this week says?"

Keely's hand shot up. "Be ye kindly 'ffectioned one toward another."

"Do you know what that means?"

Keely frowned. "No."

Brenna put a new piece of toast on her plate. "It means that we should be kind to each other, to treat others like Jesus treats us. Then we'll be happy, don't you think?"

Suspicion hovered in Jared's eyes. "Daddy says we mustn't

listen when you tell us things like that." He scooted off his chair and headed for his bedroom. "I'm getting my baby snake."

A moment later, unable to find his charm, her sweet little boy threw a tantrum in the middle of the kitchen floor.

~ ~ ~

At the hospital the hours lagged like years. She ministered to one patient after another, trying to smile and make them feel better. But as she went about her duties a terrible foreboding closed in on her. Finally she slipped to the phone and called the day care center.

"Sally, how are the kids doing?"

"Fine. Why?"

"They were just a little upset when we left home this morning. Call me if you need to, OK?"

Sally laughed. "Don't worry, they'll be just fine."

"And Sally, don't let them leave with anyone but me." Her words echoed in her ears.

Sally was quiet for a moment too long. "Oh, sure."

Feeling exposed, Brenna returned to her duties. Maybe she was just letting her imagination get away from her, making mountains out of molehills. But she had a definite feeling that all was not well, that Wally was up to no good, and she'd better be watchful.

Wally didn't come home for supper that night and it was after 11:00 before she heard the garage door close. She set her Bible on the nightstand, thankful for the quiet hour she'd spent with her Lord, reading and asking Him for guidance for what lay ahead.

When Wally walked into their room, he tossed her a weary smile. "Long meeting tonight. I'm tired."

He readied himself for bed, then slid in beside her. "I've got to lecture in Seattle for three days next week. Dr. Briley just told me. I'll be late tomorrow night getting things together, so don't wait up."

He switched off the lamp and turned his back to her. "My, it feels good to lie down," he sighed. And he was asleep.

CHAPTER 9

October

"You've defiled our home!" Papa shouted, waving Myrtle Flemming's booklet in Lucita's face. *"Madre mía!* My sin was letting you work away from me. Now I must confess to Father Matthew that I have not kept evil from entering our home, or faithfully governed my daughter."

Lucita cringed as Papa slammed his fist on the kitchen table. She'd never seen him so angry, even when the deliveryman had tried to compromise Cinta at the restaurant.

Papa stepped closer, his breath hot on Lucita's face. "Where did you get this?" he demanded, flinging the booklet across the room.

Mama's raspy breath scratched at her ears. "Tell him, *niña.*"

Lucita clung to the back of the kitchen chair and fought back frightened tears. How could she explain that she had not meant to be wicked or to disgrace the family?

Groping for the right words, Lucita remembered the evening of Myrtle Flemming's murder. That weekend she hadn't been able to sleep for the awfulness of it, and at SIPS on Monday had finally called the phone number written in the back of the booklet, hoping that she'd been wrong about the sweet-faced woman's death. But there had been no answer.

How close she had come to being caught as she pulled up the old woman's SIPS file without authorization, something that could have cost her job.

Lucita quickly scanned her monitor. Seventy-nine years old. No children. Long ago, a secretary, and church affiliation: Seventh-day Adventist. There was that name again. At the top of the record flashed the word "Deceased." Below it, yesterday's date.

Lucita had gagged. There was no choice. She must phone the police and tell them about the boys she'd seen crossing the road. She had begged them not to contact her at home. Papa would be furious if he knew that she had gotten off the bus in that area of town. The police had complied, interviewing her at the SIPS office at lunchtime.

When she'd arrived home that night she had determined to destroy the book, but tucked it in her bottom drawer until she could do it privately. Still, the memory of her brief encounter with the old woman with the gentle smile didn't fade. Several days later, in spite of what Papa would say if he knew, she had shoved her German textbook aside and read through the entire booklet in one evening.

Passages had burned into her mind. *"Prayers uttered to beings other than the God of heaven are useless. It is popular error to believe that one must route his petitions through a long-dead saint or the mother of Christ. These have no ears to hear, no voice to speak, no thoughts to think, for they are not alive, but as all who have gone before us, wait in their earthy graves for Christ's second coming. God's love for us is unfathomable. He desires to be approached personally through prayer directly by each of His children; there is no need of an intermediary to carry our words to Him."*

At first she had thought those words blasphemy and had thrust the book away lest its words contaminate her. Yet, as she pondered their meaning, she had become intrigued. *Speak directly to God?* She thought of the virgin Mary, and of St. Anthony, before whom she lit candles and bowed nearly every working day. Surely she had not misunderstood what the church taught. Surely these holy beings in heaven could hear her prayers and then plead her cause before God.

Time and again she had determined to destroy the book, then stopped short, seeking answers and comfort for her increasingly troubled thoughts. She had learned the truths of her church at Mama's knee, and from Aunt Rosa too, rest her soul. It was all too confusing. She must go see the priest.

"Lucita!" Papa's anger yanked her back to the present. "Where'd you get the book?"

Lucita's stomach soured. "Remember when that old woman was murdered by the Ravens?"

"Sí."

"She, uh, gave me the book just before that happened."

Papa glowered. "You were near St. Luke's?"

"Yes. She was so kind. She touched my arm; put the book into my hand. I couldn't be rude and refuse it. You've taught me to be polite."

Remembering, Lucita fought for control. "Papa, I saw those boys cross the street toward her after I got on the bus. When we turned the corner I couldn't see anything more, but I should have said something—helped, somehow."

"Why have you hidden this matter from me?"

Lucita swallowed hard. "I knew you would be angry, Papa. I have told the police."

"So. My daughter sneaks. She's involved with police matters. She's—*madre mía!* Why did you bring the book home?"

Lucita could fight the tears no longer. "I've thrown it away many times."

Papa spun around and faced Mama. "So you are in on this too!"

"No, Papa. She knew nothing about the book. I took it out of the trash myself."

Papa threw up his hands. *"Mi corozón!* What did I tell you? Those *Adventistas* have cast a spell over you. Now what shall I do?"

Calmness settled over Lucita as she put her hands on Papa's sagging shoulders. "There's no spell. The book just talks about Christ's love and His death for us, and how much He loves us. I don't see how that can hurt anyone."

Papa shrugged away. "But what can *you* know? You're only a woman." He shoved the booklet into Lucita's hand. "You will destroy this and have nothing more to do with Advents."

Defeated, Lucita sank into the chair, took a last look at the familiar handwriting inside the back cover, and then ripped the booklet into shreds. Papa scooped the pieces into a pan and held a match to them. As Lucita watched the pages curl and blacken, fingers of smoke drifted upward, much like the smoke from the candles in the cathedral. Her chest tightened. *Will God notice this smoke, too?*

At last Papa faced her again. "Sunday you will go to Confession and beg Father Matthew to forgive you. You must never read anything like that again. I will not have a heretic in our family. Understand?"

Two weeks passed and those blue eyes kept reaching into Lucita's heart. There had been something else about Myrtle Flemming, too. Was that look she'd seen so briefly the look of someone who really loved the Lord best of all, the way Aunt Rosa had loved Him? Aunt Rosa whose heart was so akin to her own?

Lucita sighed. Passages of the book interrupted her thoughts at the most inopportune times. She didn't know why, but she couldn't free herself from them. And with them came a curiosity about the woman she had seen so briefly. *Seventh-day Adventist.* That's what she had been. Were all the members of her church as kind?

Curious, she looked in the phone book and found the nearest Adventist church. She would call from work tomorrow to find out when services were held. Then, on Saturday, she'd go shopping, but on her way, just happen by the church. Just to see what it was all about, that's all.

~ ~ ~

So she did. The church was so small and plain inside, cold and bare without statuary or candles or stained glass. There wasn't even a cross. Papa's words came back to her. *They are heretics . . . they hold nothing sacred.* Lucita eyed the audience who sat reading, whispering. A row of teenagers passed a magazine back and forth and one laughed right out loud.

For a moment Lucita considered slipping out as quietly as she had entered. But then she changed her mind. She must satisfy her curiosity, once and for all. Only then could she put Myrtle Flemming's memory to rest.

After group singing and the collection basket going around, and after a black-robed man dunked three children in a tank of water, an elderly gentleman stepped to the plain wooden pulpit. "Welcome, brothers and sisters. It's good to be here this Sabbath morning."

Sabbath?

He smiled, his face dark under a frizz of white hair. "Please get out your Bibles and turn to Revelation 3, verse 8."

Pages turned. Where had the people found the books?

" 'I know thy works: behold, I have set before thee an open door, and no man can shut it: for thou hast little strength, and hast kept my word, and hast not denied my name.' "

The man set his book aside. "Brothers and sisters, have you noticed an open door before you? Have you wondered what would happen should you walk through it? Do you have the courage to take God's outstretched hand, grasp it, and step out in faith, holding back nothing?

"I do not need to tell you that we now stand on the brink of eternity. There cannot be too many more months or years that we will gather together here, for all the signs point to the soon-coming of our Lord."

A chorus of amens filled the room.

The preacher nodded. "There is no more time to hold back, my friends. Everything is wrapping up."

Wrapping up?

"We have all been aware of recent drastic swings in weather. We have watched news reports about famine, and strange illnesses and the havoc they are wreaking, and the seemingly unexplainable accidents in the world of transportation. We have heard dimly disguised whisperings about asteroids that may crash into the earth and destroy it, and the equally disturbing comments casting blame for the earth's problems upon groups of people who do not keep Sunday, who do not worship the beast on his day."

Beast?

"Brothers and sisters, it will take courage to walk through the door that is now swinging open. Actions that destroy our complacency, that invade our comfort zone, always take courage. But I'm here to tell you we need not make the journey alone!"

Amens rang out again.

"We have a Saviour! Jesus Christ is His name, and He has agreed to take on our infirmities, to encourage us when we become fainthearted, to *show* us the way as He walks with us! And

He will be our joy, our strength, our *salvation* if only we let Him."

"We all know what is coming in November, and we have been full of conjecture about what the pope's visit to our country means. As you know, he will come to our own great city, and some people may actually worship him. But we are told that we are to give worship only to the God of heaven.

"I believe the time is ripe for the harvest. We must be watchful, keep our lamps trimmed and burning."

Lucita glanced around. *Lamps?*

"The time will soon come for us to leave the city, to step out in faith, to trust the One whom we have worshiped for so long. Our Lord will send angels to protect us, and He Himself will be with us in Spirit. The Holy Ghost will help us through all our hard times. All God asks is that we give Him our hearts, that we hold no other gods before Him, and that we take Him at His word.

"We each need to use the short time of freedom we have left to us to cement Christ's words into our minds, to know where we stand for Him, to let Him speak His words of love to us through His printed Word, the Holy Bible. We must give up false pride and allow Him to lead us in paths of righteousness, for He is our Good Shepherd.

"Will you rededicate yourselves to Him today? Will you grasp Christ's hand through faith, and walk through that door that has opened before you? Will you raise your hand just now, saying, 'Regardless of what lies before me—the problems, the trials, the heartbreak—I want to be Your child. I want You to lead me, and I ask for the faith You have promised to give to me'?"

As hands raised, a young man stepped to the pulpit and waited quietly while some recorded music began to play. Eyes closed, he began to sing:

"Take my life, and let it be
Consecrated, Lord, to Thee . . .
Take my love; my Lord, I pour
At Thy feet its treasure store;
Take myself, and I will be,
Ever, only, all for Thee,
Ever, only, all for Thee."

The harmony of the unseen orchestra swelled, carrying the promise to the God above. It did not arise in wisps of incense or candle smoke, but it arose, just the same. Lucita could feel it, could sense something in that group of people she hadn't sensed before.

The woman ahead dabbed her eyes, and again the amens arose. But the music was not finished. It changed pitch, swelling around them, growing urgent.

"Teach me, Father, what to say;
Teach me, Father, how to pray . . ."

The melody enfolded her, the soloist's velvety voice putting words to the feelings so long unidentified in her heart. And, after a time, he held out his hands to the audience. "Join me now in singing to our heavenly Father."

One by one those around her joined in. The words were beautiful—finding a place deep within her that she had not known existed.

"I would be like Jesus, I would be . . ."

Love for Christ filled Lucita. He was there to love her, to bless her. Not to chastise her, and somehow she knew He had led her to this place.

When she'd left home earlier that day a storm had been brewing, angry-looking clouds piling up in the west. Now, as the audience stood to sing the closing hymn, the storm crashed upon them, its great thunderings adding emphasis to the deep notes that swelled from the organ.

A few minutes later she stood watching it from the foyer. Rain slammed to the ground, creating a curtain so heavy that she couldn't see the street. And then someone touched her elbow. She turned to see the kind-faced man who had given the sermon.

"Bless my soul," he said, motioning to the rain. "You'd better not go out there. You'll float away!"

Lucita liked his easy way.

"I was wondering if you wouldn't join us at our potluck dinner today. Most everyone's staying."

"No, thank you so much. I have errands to run," she began, suddenly needing to get away to think.

He laughed. "You'd need the ark itself to get anywhere

right now. They said this'll last a couple hours." The preacher beckoned to an elderly woman. "Sadie, this is—I'm afraid I didn't get your name, Miss."

"I'm Lucita Fernandez."

He smiled and shook her hand. "I'm Washington Bannister, pastor here, and this is my wife, Sadie. I must go take care of a few details. She'll look after you real careful like."

It had been instant friendship. Though they looked nothing alike, Sadie reminded Lucita of Aunt Rosa. And in the end she had stayed for the potluck meal of the strangest foods she'd ever eaten, lingering on to listen to a discussion several young people had about what they called "the last days." Their ideas were frightening, but they seemed upbeat about things growing worse, as they predicted.

Before Lucita left, Pastor Bannister gave her a packet of magazines and two booklets he said would help her understand a little more about their church and what was happening in the world just then. Then he, along with her other new friends, invited her to come back as often as she could.

The rain had eased off as she headed toward the bus stop. If she hurried she could catch the uptown bus in time to get into the SIPS building before the Saturday afternoon shift ended. She'd stow her new reading materials safely in her locker where she could get to them during lunch hours.

When she had finished her shopping she headed home, suddenly queasy about the questioning she'd certainly undergo. Papa was sure to ask why she'd been gone so long. She looked out the window as the bus made its start-and-stop journey homeward. Once again the clouds gathered, blacker this time than she'd ever seen them before.

Chapter 10

November

Aaron leaned against the press box railing and faced the camera. "We're looking toward the corner where His Holiness, Pope Corrado, will soon appear. Soon the voices of a 300-member choir will fill this square, and the hope of the Catholic Church—and possibly of the world—will stand before us.

"As you can see, thousands of people are pressed into this relatively small area behind me as they vie for a glimpse of the Man of the Century. Security is tight here in Seattle, and for good reasons, for there has been another threat on the Holy Father's life."

Buzz panned to the great platform that had been erected for the occasion, scanned the line of religious and political dignitaries seated there, then zoomed in on the glistening throne beneath the scarlet canopy.

"Pope Corrado, who will soon sit upon this magnificent throne, comes from a humble beginning . . . and even now he is a man of simple tastes, great passion, and a tender heart for those who suffer. It is his goal to lead us into a time of spiritual renewal that will bring all people together as brothers to follow the true God of heaven."

Now Buzz panned to the street, closing up the space between them and the corner three blocks away. "We switch to Sam Birch, who is interviewing worshipers along the road where Pope Corrado will soon pass. Sam?"

Aaron adjusted his earpiece, as Sam's mellow voice took over. "Sir, you are the owner of a Seattle restaurant named La Cucharita?"

The man's chin lifted. "Yes."

"You and your family have been waiting here since 2:00 this morning. Why did you come so early?"

The man smiled. "In my house hangs a picture of the Holy Father. Now I can see him with my own eyes, and bow before him. It is the answer to my prayers for years."

"And this is your family?"

The focus drew in the women who pressed close to the restaurant owner. The youngest face—lovely—caught Aaron's eye. Instantly he picked up on her feelings. Hadn't he become an expert in reading expressions? He watched for a moment longer, knowing she didn't want to be there.

Aaron pulled the earpiece off and wiped the sweat from his brow. "I can't believe how hot it is here—never seen it like this in November!" The 87° F temperature would also make headline news. He kept his eye on the monitor. Sam was going strong and would continue his interviews with the faithful until given the signal to quit.

He pressed his fist into his stomach, trying to breathe around the pain. The newsman beside him jockeyed for position, almost knocking him over. He swore. Up here he was just one of them; got no special privileges. Only his ratings set him apart.

He glanced down the street again, awaiting the moment. The pope . . . everyone's hope. It was a cop-out, though. They expected this *man* to make changes that couldn't be made, do things no state leader could do. It was sickening, the way religious leaders parroted his words, accepting at face value his lofty talk about religious and ethnic tolerance and the nations' ability to work together to rescue their suffering planet. Now even political leaders had begun to look to the Papacy and its worldwide influence as the only power able to bring order out of a world gone crazy. Aaron didn't buy it. The pope was just a man—one who had been propped up on a golden pedestal when nothing else had worked out. He had no more connection with God than anyone else did. The only one he'd ever known that truly had had a connection with God, if there *was* a God, was Grandie, and of course she was gone.

He sighed. Grandie had often held him on her lap to read the books she'd bought to use when he visited her. How he'd enjoyed those stories! *Joseph. Jesus and the loaves and little fishies. Funny little Zacchaeus scrambling up the tree.* The people and stories had come alive when she had read them to him. Still, they were only stories contrived to control people through religious fear. He'd learned that later. It was puzzling, if he let himself ponder it. For Grandie had seemed to have peace. He knew she'd prayed for him until the day she died—she'd said so in the letters that had followed him around the world—those letters with the shaky handwriting and the lavender scent. Funny how she'd always gone to church on Saturday, and had never made much sense about the things he'd told her. He doubted if she'd have paid any attention to this visit by the head of the Catholic Church.

Well, the pope had better hurry if he planned to work a deal with God. When this asteroid thing broke, when security was finally lifted so they could mention its threat, the world would really go crazy. Then they'd need anything they could find to glue them together.

A few moments later the cries of a great throng arose from the distance, then grew steadily nearer. Aaron took back the audio, ready to catch the action. Suddenly a police escort followed by a white limousine rounded the corner. Security agents trotted beside it, eyeing the crowd. As watchers cheered, many prostrated themselves on the street.

"His Holiness, Pope Corrado, has driven into view."

The limo stopped at the crimson runner. "He steps from his car, stands with bowed head." Finally Pope Corrado climbed the carpeted stairs, then turned and stretched his hands toward the worshipers.

"Bless you, my children," he began.

The applause was deafening.

"It is with great solemnity I stand here today."

A sickly hue settled over the throng. Aaron looked up, then nudged Buzz. "Look at that!"

Clouds swirled overhead, their yellow-green tint easily recognizable.

His heart lurched. Not here—not now!

Buzz's wide eyes met Aaron's. "Shall I shoot it?"

"Not yet. Stay with the pope!"

Seemingly oblivious to the threat overhead, crimson-vested priests surrounded Pope Corrado, waving their censers of incense. Little rivulets of smoke arose in the still air.

"Our world has made great strides in turning back to God. Most of us have put hatred for other peoples behind us. Most of us have agreed that we need to honor God by worshiping Him on His holy day. Still, we are tormented by disasters of nature that wipe out thousands of lives at the swipe of her mighty hand. Human storms also persist. Crime has grown to intolerable proportions. Some refuse to recognize God's sovereignty, refuse to honor Him as commanded in the Holy Scriptures and by the Mother Church. Until all people heed God's command—"

An explosion of thunder eclipsed his words. The throng screamed and pointed upward at the long finger of cloud that jabbed toward them. Litter swirled upward; people bolted.

Pope Corrado looked up, then giving a mighty shout, lifted his arms and uttered words Aaron couldn't understand, but the look on the pontiff's face was one of supreme authority. Immediately the great finger retreated, letting the debris sift back to earth. Then the clouds parted ever so slightly to allow a golden beam of sunlight to slip through and bathe the pontiff in the most glorious light Aaron had ever witnessed.

Buzz swore. "He commands even tornadoes?"

A hush settled over the crowd as Pope Corrado fell to his knees, arms reaching high, and tipped his face to the light. For several minutes he remained there, as though he were listening to something. Then he bowed his head.

At last he stood. "My children, in His great love and mercy God has just given me a message for you. You must listen carefully, for your lives depend upon it."

Urgency strengthened his voice. "Until all people heed God's commands, there will be no peace or safety in this world. You have just seen His mighty finger, pointing down at us. You can see the results of His anger, for many have laughed in His face, made His name common, ignored His holy day, and trampled upon His laws given on Sinai. We must turn back to Him—as an entire nation, entire world—and give Him His rightful place. He has shown me that His patience will not endure much longer. There is no time to waste."

The hair on Aaron's arms raised. "Very shortly world and church leaders will meet to discuss earth's tenuous condition. They will define a plan which cooperates with God in putting an end to the suffering that goes on around us. I ask you to spend the coming days in prayer. Seek a closer relationship with God. Prepare your hearts to do anything He asks. Pray that your leaders' minds may be open to Him so He may bring this planet back under His protection."

The pontiff lifted his hands in blessing. "Now go in peace and obedience."

As the choirs sang their song of adoration, thousands of worshipers prostrated themselves before Pope Corrado, as did the church leaders on the platform. Except for one man, that is.

For an instant Aaron was back on Grandie's lap. They held the book together. There was the towering golden image, there were the throngs of people bowing before it. And there were three Hebrew boys who would not bow.

He yanked himself from memory's persuasive grip. "Buzz, we'll describe the procession, then switch back to Sam's live interviews."

Aaron swallowed the pain that gnawed at him, and with a terribly unsettled feeling faced the camera once more.

CHAPTER 11

That's it!" Dusty shouted, glaring at Nick. "You don't have enough work to keep yourself busy, but you make me come in after school to help. I'm not doin' it anymore."

Nick sucked in his breath. "Son, we made a deal."

Dusty flung his broom aside. "Yeah? Then just go tell the cops. You can't prove anything anyhow."

Nick took a deep breath. How could he forget the evening he'd confronted Dusty with the marijuana he'd found at the garage? The boy had finally confessed to putting it there, yet insisted he'd never used the stuff.

"I was just holding it for a guy 'cuz he was in a jam. His friend didn't show up to get it and he was scared of the cops."

They had holed up in Dusty's room for a long time that night, and for the first time in months had had a civil conversation. In the end Dusty confided that he wanted to become a doctor but didn't see how he'd get the money. He said he'd let his relationship with Christ slip in the last little while, but he planned to do something about that. If only he hadn't been so stupid! Nick and Marj were right about his buddies, he'd admitted. They weren't good for him, and he'd break off their relationship right away.

Though uneasy, Nick had accepted Dusty's explanation at face value and had agreed not to turn him in, for if the boy saw his wrong, why pin a record on him? After all, God was merciful; why shouldn't he be merciful, too? But there were stipulations. Dusty couldn't hang out in town late at night, and he'd be expected to help at the shop after school each day.

Reluctantly, Dusty had agreed. Nick had made him shake on it. "I'm taking your word, son, and Wheatley men have always kept their word."

Dusty had avoided eye contact at first, but finally relented. "OK, Dad. Whatever you say."

It had been a deal, but Nick didn't know who it was hardest on, Dusty or himself. If he could just tolerate the boy's moods.

Now, as they eyed each other, Dusty stood tall, fists clenched. "I'm outta here."

"Dusty—"

"Forget it," he growled, spinning on his heel. The shop door slammed behind him, leaving Nick to wonder what he should do next.

~ ~ ~

That evening Nick sat in the living room, pretending to watch TV while he tried to make sense of his situation. Supper was long past, and Dusty hadn't come home. It didn't show trust in God when he worried, he knew that. Yet Dusty's problems, added to the concern of his flagging business and the frequent flashbacks to his ex-wife Shannon's dour predictions regarding his future, made a pretty ugly picture. He'd asked God for help, for *wisdom*. He'd been faithful about tithing and studying the Bible, but nothing seemed to make a difference.

Lately Marj had been unhappy because he'd kept the garage open on Sundays. She'd even asked if he was tired of being with the family and used work to stay away. He supposed he should have told her how slim their business bank account had become, but he hadn't wanted to worry her. It seemed important to him to protect the family as long as he could.

Nick leaned back and closed his eyes. *Lord, I don't know what to do about all this stuff. Ever since my go-around with the mayor, things have gone downhill. I know Your coming is near, and that things will close down for people who are trying to be true to You. I'm so eager to see You—to live where I can talk to You face-to-face. If only I could be sure that these things aren't happening because of something I shouldn't have done. Have I been such an awful dad? Did I mistreat the mayor or anyone else? If there's something I should remember, please bring it to my mind! Religious writers say the time will come when there'll be nothing but trouble and we should leave our homes. Am I supposed to give up my work? Where would we go? And what about Dusty?*

Marj came from the kitchen. "Want a hot drink, honey?"

Nick raked his hand through his hair. "Naw. Thanks, though."

She sat down beside him. "Nick, you've seemed so stressed lately. Want to talk about anything?"

How could he talk to her about Dusty? She'd say what she always said, that he should be stricter with him. But her relationship with the boy was even worse than his. Still, there *were* other things he should share with her. She was a good wife, and he trusted her intuition about everything except Dusty.

"I'm concerned about the business," he began, taking her hand. "You might as well know that things are really bad there. I didn't want you to worry. I thought maybe things would pick up after summer, but they haven't. There's not enough work even for me, so I had to let Shorty go."

Marj frowned. "But what's happened? You used to be the busiest in town."

"I shouldn't make wild accusations, but everything started to deteriorate after that Friday night thing with Mayor Jordon. You know, the float trashed, our car defaced, then my shop door. Later my tow truck, and then that fire out back of the shop. Lucky I happened to go by that evening, or that could've been total disaster."

Marj began to rub his neck, to soothe him.

"Then losing Chuck to Beckett's. That was the worst."

"He took a lot of business with him?"

"Yes, then Best Car Rentals dropped its contract with us, as well as City Hall. It doesn't look good, Marj."

"What if you could prove that Mayor Jordon had something to do with it all?"

His laugh sounded harsh in his ears. "I wouldn't even try. He's so influential, it'd be a losing battle, don't you see?"

There was nothing else to say, so they sat quietly, she waiting for the 10:00 news, he for the sound of Dusty's car. *I should go out and look for him. No, I shouldn't. Lord, no matter what I do it won't be the right thing. It's a lose-lose situation.*

Aaron Chandler's familiar face finally filled the screen.

"In response to Pope Corrado's request to world powers, a 24-hour cease-fire has been called in Israel to honor the American tradition of Thanksgiving. After his urging that the entire world celebrate a time of thanksgiving for God's blessings upon humankind, the Israelis agreed. It is Pope Corrado's hope that this temporary laying down of arms will be extended so the aborted peace talks can be resumed.

"Marloid's disease, a newly identified virus, has broken out in Hong Kong. Strict measures are being taken to keep it from spreading to other areas of the globe. On the national front, nature continues to go berserk. Within three hours 17 tornadoes raked Tennessee, Alabama, and Georgia, and conditions there remain unstable, defying humanitarian efforts to aid victims."

The report continued. Trouble everywhere. Innuendos that God was bringing it all upon the victims as punishment for turning from Him . . . Suddenly feeling the need for a few minutes alone with his Lord, Nick headed for the bedroom to find his Bible. *And* listen for Dusty.

He settled in his chair and opened the black book, but the news followed him into the bedroom.

"Locally, City Council is studying a plan for mandatory business closure on Sundays, honoring Pope Corrado's plea that each principality provide time to worship God on that day. If voted, Sunday closure would affect all but humanitarian services and gasoline sales."

Nick glanced across the room at the orderly row of religious books. This sort of thing had been predicted. Without Sunday business he probably wouldn't make it. How would he keep the family afloat?

Shannon's face threatened, but he forced it away.

One thing he knew for sure; he needed to spend time with his Bible and on his knees seeking God's guidance. With a sigh he opened the Bible. Then, hearing a sound outside, he switched the lights off and peeked through the blinds.

A car was coming up the lane. It was Dusty's. His lights were off, too.

CHAPTER 12

December

Quieting the children once more, Brenna struggled to hear Pastor Stafford's sermon.

"Are there times when you feel that you cannot go further? Is it as though Satan has put his thumb on you and is pushing down without letup?"

Yes!

"Does it seem he's handpicked you for agonies the depth of which you never knew were possible?"

Brenna's nails bit into her palms.

"Then let me share with you the secret for receiving strength for your journey and knowing God's will for you."

Desperate for spiritual food, Brenna tuned everything else out.

"There are three crucial items to remember when we face difficulties, things our Lord has told us. The first—"

A tap on Brenna's shoulder broke her concentration, and she turned to find Mrs. Morett's frowning face closing in on her.

"My *dear,* the children are so restless, we can't hear. Why not take them to the mother's room?"

Forcing back tears of shame, Brenna gathered their things and herded the children down the aisle and into the foyer. The front door stood open, a way of escape from frustrations over those who didn't understand how badly she needed both this sermon and Christian companionship that could support her right now.

Go home. Listen to music. Read Bible stories to the kids.

"No." She hissed the word aloud, yanking herself up

short. I *will not feel sorry for myself.* Determined to gain what she could from the rest of the sermon, she headed for the mother's room only to find the mothers in there visiting with each other.

Brenna handed coloring books to Jared and Keely, then strained to hear Pastor Stafford above the conversation and loud speaker's static.

". . . which brings us to the second statement."

Brenna grabbed a pencil.

"Hey, Brenna, how old was Keely when she was completely potty trained?"

Brenna sagged. "A little over 2."

The mothers resumed their conversation as the lump in Brenna's throat grew.

Oh, Lord, give me patience . . . help me cope . . . I feel so frustrated and alone.

Brenna led the children toward the side door, needing to escape before the tears came. Disappointment over missing the sermon nearly crushed her. If things were just different at home . . .

"Ah, there you are, my dear," cooed Mrs. Morret as she clamped her fleshy hand on Brenna's arm. Acrid, the woman's breath preceded her words. "I know it's hard to raise children nowadays because everyone's so permissive, but experience has shown that quietness in church must be taught by first training the child to quiet periods at home. And expecting prompt obedience at all times, of course," she added, a smug look on her face. "Now, my dear, from my observations I'd suggest—"

Brenna edged away. "Excuse me, I must go."

Mrs. Morret tightened her grip. "Just a minute. If you'd just—"

Brenna pulled away. "Come *on,* kids." She hurried out, not caring what Mrs. Morret might think. There was no time to lose. She *had* to get away!

Fighting back tears, she started the car and eased out of the parking space. As she pulled into the street a pickup careened around the corner and slammed into her right front fender. Stunned, she glanced at the children to make sure they weren't hurt, and then toward the church. Everyone was watching, and at the front of the crowd stood Mrs. Morret, who shook her head knowingly.

Brenna rested her head on the steering wheel, quit fighting the lump, and let the hot tears come.

~ ~ ~

Pastor Stafford and a couple other men had pulled the fender away from her tire enough that she could drive home. When Wally arrived later that afternoon he spent several minutes examining the damage before coming into the house.

He skipped the *hello's.* "Well, that's at least $1,200 worth of damage, and our deductible is $500. What happened?"

Brenna sagged. "I didn't see the guy coming when I pulled out of the church lot."

"You get cited?"

She nodded. *The children. Aren't you going to ask if they're OK?*

"Figures," he said, fiddling with his pendant. "You seem in such a muddle anymore."

Tears stung her eyes. "Sorry, I just—"

"I don't want to hear it, Brenna," he said levelly. "I've had enough of your blubbering and your preaching about what's right and wrong, of your unwillingness to try to understand the new light that I've found. You wear your self-righteousness like a cloak, all the while smothering the kids with guilt. Using Jesus as a weapon to force them to do what *you* want them to do. Well, I'm a patient man, but you're tearing our home apart and are unwilling to listen to reason. I'm simply not going to stand by and watch it happen. I'm not going to allow the kids to be manipulated like that."

He headed for the bedroom, opened the closet, and took out some shirts, his eyes taking on the look she'd found so chilling in Dr. Orcott. "I've taken a room in the community. I'll be in touch later. Too bad the kids are napping. Tell 'em I love them." And he was gone.

She stood at the front window for a long time, watching the spot where his car had disappeared. Only dimly aware of her surroundings, she tried to make sense of what had just happened. Wasn't God supposed to help in such cases? Numb, unfeeling for the moment, she sifted through her thoughts.

It was her fault. It had to be. If she'd been more open to listening to Wally and helped him to see the little errors creeping into his thinking. If she'd prayed harder and sought God's direction more faithfully, surely she could have avoided this. And now Wally was gone. She couldn't blame him for not liking to be around her anymore. It was purely true that the darkness of his new beliefs, and her feelings of somehow being responsible for not being able to talk him out of them, surrounded her with such intensity that it cast a pall over all their time together. If only there were someone she could talk to.

Only gradually did Brenna become aware of Keely tugging on her jeans. "Mommy, I'm hungry!"

Forcing her inner turmoil aside, Brenna tousled the child's hair. "How about an ark supper?"

As she spread peanut butter and mashed bananas on toast she'd trimmed with animal cookie cutters, her thoughts returned to the one thing she had managed to hear in church that morning, and a sliver of hope entered her heart.

"I will instruct thee and teach thee in the way which thou shalt go: I will guide thee with mine eye."* She glanced out the kitchen window, a prayer in her heart. *Lord, help me always to be able to recognize Your eyes.*

~ ~ ~

Sunday, a week after her accident, was Jared's birthday, and she still hadn't heard from Wally. It had been a tough week, for she constantly battled the lump in her throat. It required constant concentration to not break down at work or at home when the children were awake. Bless the children! They were used to Wally being away for short trips, so they hadn't asked many questions—yet. She wished she could do the same, for he was always on her mind. Often his face swam before her, gentle and caring, but more often she saw him as he'd looked when he walked out the door Sabbath afternoon. His face was closed. Hard. Decisive. And hiding thoughts she couldn't begin to contemplate.

The only thing that kept her going now were the dreams she'd begun having. At first those dreams, spun during the restlessness of solitary nights in her big bed, were of her as a child cuddled in Mama's lap. The gentle rocking, and Mama's soft voice as she sang, had comforted her. But last night her dream had been different, had given her a sense of direction, at least for the moment.

Mama had come to the house for lunch—was sitting at the kitchen table doing something with Keely. Happiness filled Brenna as she watched them laugh and talk together. Presently Mama got up and crossed the room to where Brenna was stirring soup. She wrapped her arms around Brenna and gave her that familiar squeeze.

"Everything's going to work out, my lamb, please believe me. These hard times come in marriages, but Wally's an intelligent man, and you're an intelligent girl. You must do your part in making him feel welcome here. Don't make him feel guilty for following what he believes is true. Perhaps you should listen to what he has to say more openly. In time you will both find the way and be better for it. I'm sure of it."

Mama had shown her such love as she voiced her welcome encouragement that Brenna had awakened this morning filled with a down-deep joy and sense of well-being. Only as the morning wore on did reality begin to engulf her again. After all, it was only a dream. Mama had been gone for four long years. Still, a tiny corner of warmth remained.

Later, as Brenna put the finishing touches on Jared's alligator cake, she glanced outside. Gusty winds shook the trees, and dark clouds pressed down from overhead. She pushed from her mind the three major storms that had caused extensive damage to her little town during the last two years—the submerged houses, mudslides, and that place that opened up to reveal a major fault reaching from the mountains to the sea. In a few hours seven little boys would arrive to help celebrate Jared's sixth birthday, and she had planned some outdoor activities. She needed to stay focused on that.

She added another dollop of green frosting to the cake, then began etching the creature's scales. Mentally searching her store of children's games, she tried to think of some alternate things the children could play indoors without demolishing the house. Wondering how long the storm would last, she switched on her little kitchen TV.

Aaron Chandler's face flickered, then became steady. ". . . reported Dr. Max Orcott."

Brenna paused to watch.

"Several sightings have been made, the latest one this morning somewhere on the Nevada desert. Orcott claims that the messenger left him a detailed communiqué that is now being deciphered by a scientific team not connected with the Knights of Truth. We will bring you more information as it becomes available. And now to the weather . . ."

A cold fist clenched Brenna's heart. Seeing Max again—his probing eyes, his voice—brought back the memory of the last time she had gone anywhere with Wally, to the meeting at Luke Whalen's.

With a sigh, Brenna stood back to inspect the alligator. No work of art, but it should do for a rowdy handful of kids. She forced thoughts of Wally from her mind, picked up the rolls of green and white crepe paper, and headed for the living room.

Later, sitting on the couch with the aftermath of the party surrounding her, she smiled down at Jared, who sat on the floor gloating over his gifts. As usual, Keely was at his side, trying to "share" his things.

It looked as though another squabble was in the offing, so Brenna forced herself to get up. "Keely, honey, Mama needs your help. Can you come to the kitchen with me?"

Keely jumped up. "Can I wash the dishes, Mama?"

For a while they busied themselves with the cleanup, Brenna cleaning along after Keely. Soon Keely lost interest, and finally wandered off to play birthday party with her family of dolls. Jared had taken his treasures to his room and closed the door. As dusk came on, a quietness settled over the house.

Brenna reached for the mop just as the doorbell rang. She hurried to the door to find Wally, his arms loaded with gifts and a pizza.

"I thought I'd come by to say hello to the kids and help celebrate Jared's birthday. Looks like you had a party."

She fought to still her trembling hands.

"Yes."

Wally walked in as though he'd never left her life, put the packages on the couch, then headed for the kitchen. "Thought you guys might be hungry. Actually I came by earlier but saw all the cars. Didn't want to interrupt the festivities." He slid the pizza into the oven and turned it on to warm. His eyes made short work of looking her over. "How've you been?"

Brenna gaped. *"How* have I been? Just the same as any woman whose husband has walked out, I suppose. But I'm—*we're*—managing."

He smiled as though he'd been gone only since breakfast. "Well, you're *looking* good, anyway."

She could think of nothing else to say, though she had wished many times since he'd left that they could sit down and really talk things out. Oh, why didn't he just go find Jared and then leave? She wasn't up to any more wrenchings right now, he should know that.

But he just stood there, his eyes caressing her. She glanced at his neck. Was the charm still there? She couldn't tell. Suspicious, she tried to make sense of what was happening.

"Honey, I've been thinking. Maybe I should come back home. It's no good for us to live apart like this, and I know it's been hard for you." His words came quick—as though rehearsed. "Two people who love each other should be able to work things out. We can pick up where we were, make a real home for the kids. We'll study together again. We don't have to go so fast, and I won't push you so hard." He crossed the room but as he reached for her, she moved aside, unwilling to let herself be sidetracked from what he was saying by his touch.

Something flickered in his eyes, then disappeared. "It's so important that you understand the things I've learned about God and what He really wants us to do. I know it scares you; you think that there's something strange about my new beliefs. And face it, they *are* very different from the way I used to believe. But honey, I want us to be saved—together—and going the direction we are, that will never happen. Why, right now Max Orcott's down in—"

"I saw the news," Brenna interrupted. Her mind cleared, and she suddenly felt calm. "Wally, there's nothing I'd like more than to have our family back together again, but it can't be under the same circumstances as when you left us. I won't study into your new beliefs, for I think they are a work of the devil. The children must be raised with the knowledge of how much God loves them. I want them to know He is to be obeyed, honored, worshiped. I want them to know the truth about life after death—and the truth about Jesus' dying on the cross being our only security."

"But—"

She forged ahead. "When you were here you told the children they didn't have to obey me anymore. That was wrong, Wally, and they were getting quite unmanageable. Well, they're not perfect now, but things are more peaceful. You're welcome to come back—" Her voice broke. "I'd love to have you, but you would need to understand that it couldn't be like it was right there at the last. It would have to involve your return to our church, and being willing to lead your family in that direction."

This time she didn't resist as he reached for her. "But sweetheart, asking a man to turn his back on new truth."

"Daddy! Daddy's home!" shrieked Keely, bursting in upon them.

Keely tackled Wally's legs, and of course Wally turned from Brenna to swoop the child up. And then Jared was there, wide-eyed with happiness, jabbering on about all the things he'd gotten for his birthday.

When the children had quieted enough to carry on a reasonable conversation, Wally tousled Jared's hair. "I haven't forgotten your birthday, Tiger," he said, pulling something from his pocket.

Jared opened the tiny package. "A red knife!"

"It's Swiss. See all the blades?" Wally opened it. "Be careful. They're sharp."

The knife wasn't very large, yet Brenna stiffened. Jared wasn't particularly careful. He'd probably cut himself or Keely.

"Wally, I don't think Jared is old enough to—"

Wally's look silenced her.

"Come see what else I brought."

The children raced after Wally. The front door opened, then shut, and for a moment it was quiet. Then they were all back inside.

"Oh, isn't he cute?"

"Look at his funny little nose! I'm gonna name him Rascal!"

Brenna hurried to the living room to find Jared holding a

tiny brown-and-white puppy. With a lick of its pink tongue, it wiggled out of his arms and onto the floor. Cavorting around the children's feet, it squatted and made a puddle.

Wally, looking sheepish, went to the kitchen and came back with paper towels. "I've got to go now, Brenna, but if it's OK I'll drop by after work tomorrow and we can finish our conversation. Think of what I said, and I'll think of what you said. Somehow, we'll work things out."

She watched as he competed with the puppy for one last hug, then turned and walked through the door.

~ ~ ~

That next night Brenna switched off her bedside lamp and sank back onto her pillow. It had been a hard day at work, and she'd made several mistakes. Dr. Faswell had been kind about her preoccupation, but she could tell he was nearly fed up.

She'd do better tomorrow. It was just so hard to put everything out of her mind now—Wally pushing to come home, Jared's new phase of disobedience and aggressiveness against Keely, and the constant TV news about Dr. Orcott and the direction he was receiving from a "guiding spirit from the heavenly realm." In fact, that very evening Dr. Orcott had been the main feature on *The Chandler Report.* It was only because of Wally's affiliation with the man that she had watched the clip, resisting those eyes that reached out and tried to suck her in. It was when Aaron Chandler said they'd actually filmed Orcott's interview with one of the messengers that she'd switched the TV off. *Be wary. Don't put yourself on the devil's ground.*

She'd gone, instead, and spent an extra half hour with her Bible, soothing herself with the familiar old words about the dead being in their graves, knowing and seeing nothing until Christ would awaken them at the resurrection. Then she'd again read Paul's instructions in James 1:5, the guide she'd taken for her life whenever she was in difficulty. *If any of you lacks wisdom, he should ask God, who gives generously to all without finding fault, and it will be given to him.* How often she had read and followed those words. She whispered another prayer to God for His protection that night, then turned over to go to sleep.

She had already dozed off when she was suddenly wide

awake. Opening her eyes, she listened carefully. What had roused her? Had Keely called? Or was it the phone? She waited, endless moments between each second, but heard nothing.

Still uneasy, she settled back, determined to get some sleep. If only she could quit remembering Dr. Orcott's eyes. She breathed deeply and gradually relaxed. Then, from the world halfway between sleep and reality, she sensed that she was not alone. Though she had heard nothing, she instinctively knew someone was watching her! Something prickled against her spine.

There'd been so many break-ins lately, no one was safe anymore. She sucked in her breath and slowly turned her head. She looked toward the hall, glad she'd replaced the night-light bulb. But what was that? There was someone in the doorway.

She swallowed her scream. *Lie quietly. If it's a robber, let him take what he wants and leave. Offer no resistance. Lord, don't let the kids wake up now!*

And then she heard her name. The sound surrounded her, gentle, soft, somehow familiar. A voice she hadn't heard for a long while.

The form moved from the doorway toward her, slowly, almost gliding. "Brenna, it's me. Mom."

Brenna blinked her eyes, then sighed in relief. It was only another dream. The comfort these night memories of Mom brought her was so welcome. No need to worry. She'd just lie back, relax, and go along with the illusion.

The form came closer. She could smell the gardenia fragrance Mom had always worn, hear her gentle breathing. Such a realistic dream . . .

"You worked pretty hard today," Mom soothed. "You need to slow down a little. You seem so jumpy and tired."

Mom stopped halfway between the doorway and her bed. "I've been watching what's been happening in your life. You're such a good girl, such a good mother, and I'm so proud of you. I'm glad you stand firm for what you believe."

Mom settled on the foot of her bed.

"But honey, about Wally. I know he's been saying things

that seem strange to you. Still you should listen to him."

An eerie awareness crawled from up Brenna's toes to her spine. Her thoughts tumbled over one another in an effort to set things chronologically straight. Being dead, Mom could not know anything about the strange things Wally had been saying to her. How could Brenna's memory conjure up this scene?

Mom reached out and patted Brenna's foot through the covers, as she had so often done during night talks when Brenna still lived with her parents. "Your church is right in many things, and I'm glad that you're a faithful believer. But they are wrong about a couple of things. One is what happens after we die."

Mom got up and moved around the room, her slippers flapping against her heels with each step she took. Then she moved toward the head of Brenna's bed, between Brenna and the hall door. Her hair stuck out on one side of her head, as though she'd just gotten up from bed, and Brenna could see the nubbins of her old chenille bathrobe outlined from the hallway light.

The woman sighed and shook her head. "You see, dear, God has sent me to talk to you tonight because He loves you so much. He wants you to listen to Wally—to listen to Max Orcott—for there is truth in their message. The world is in more trouble than you realize," Mom said. "Unless people start to pull together, there's no hope."

Gradually Brenna realized that she wasn't asleep. *This was no dream!* This was really Mother. Brenna stared at her. She didn't know whether to scream or to get up and embrace her. She was so *real!* Had she been wrong all these years? But the Bible said— Suddenly Brenna didn't know *what* she believed.

Sweat beaded on her lip as Mom fiddled with her robe collar as she always had.

"Honey, study the book Wally gave you. I know it's hard, but see it through! I've learned so much since I left you. I want you safe and . . ."

Fear, like a burning coal, pierced Brenna. The hot-at-the-same-time-as-being-cold feeling she'd noticed at Whalen's home closed in on her. This wasn't Mother, *it was—*

God, help me!

Trembling, Brenna slid her hand across the sheet—*closer to the thing*—toward the nightstand. Not taking her eyes from the apparition, she groped until she felt it—her Bible. Barely able to hold on to it, she clutched it to her breast. Then, finally finding her voice, she opened her mouth.

"G-get thee behind me, Satan!" Her voice came out in a rasp, shaky, breathless. She tried again, this time stronger.

The form began to back away. "But Brenna! Wait, honey, you don't understand!"

"In the name of Jesus Christ, get thee behind me!" she screamed, tears streaming down her face. She lunged for the lamp and snapped it on.

The form backed into the hallway. *Would it go to the children?*

Fear pushing her, Brenna sprang from bed and darted into the hallway. Where had it gone? She hurried to Jared's room, then Keely's. It had vanished. Her heart drummed against her ribs so hard her chest ached. She felt lightheaded, but dared not give in to it.

Satan! He'd been here—really *been* here. He'd tried to fool her, and it had almost worked! Skin crawling, she crept around the house, her eyes nearly bulging from their sockets. She turned on every light she could find, chasing away shadows where the hateful being could hide. Silly, she knew. Light wouldn't keep the archenemy away, but at least she wouldn't wonder if he was in the corners.

Trembling, she carried each of the children to her room. Tomorrow she would move their beds into her room, but for tonight, they'd sleep together in her king-sized bed.

Then, as the children slept, she read all the verses she knew about the dead. She must never be fooled! Mama had looked so real. She'd sounded and smelled so genuine.

Now, more than ever, she understood that God had to be first, last, and always in her life. She needed to guard against letting anything come between them that would allow her to be fooled, that would mar their relationship. She needed to be willing to give up anything—be single-minded toward God, her only safety.

It was only when the sky began to lighten that Brenna slipped back into her bed, weary, yet refreshed by God's promise to guide her with His eye.

---

* Psalm 32:8.

Chapter 13

Nick shuddered as he stared at the Saturday headlines Elder Munsey held up. *"Town Council Votes Sunday Closure, Opens Churches."*

"It starts tomorrow, folks, just like that. We knew it would come someday, and now it's here. Things are tightening all over the place."

Paul Norawalt stood. "But shouldn't we appeal this bylaw? Several families in our congregation depend on Sunday income."

Elder Munsey shook his head. "Our counsel is to cooperate with the government in order to hold back further troubles. We need the freedom to spread the gospel for as long as possible, for issues like this no-work-on-Sunday can escalate very quickly. Lack of cooperation could bring on other problems sooner than necessary."

Elder Munsey leaned on the podium. "Folks, the church leaders feel that it's time to start moving in new directions. Our church leaders have set up a Web page for quick info regarding situations that affect its members. We know that the time will come when we can't worship as a church family any longer, so we need to develop small home groups where we can seek the Lord's guidance, and encourage each other. We must also plan where to go when circumstances worsen."

He grinned. "Don't look so sober, folks. We're planning for the future. The one we've been waiting for all these years. True, our immediate circumstances may become difficult, but we've had our orders and known what's coming for a long time. After all, our *eternal* future should be our focus."

A deep joy sprang up in Nick's heart. *It's all about seeing Jesus' face!* He sighed and slipped his arm around Marj.

~ ~ ~

Two Sundays later, Marj flashed a smile across the breakfast table.

"Nick, I'm glad that bylaw keeps you home on Sundays. Let's go for a ride later and enjoy the snow."

It was a pleasant afternoon. They'd laughed and talked about the future, and then stopped at the park for a snowball fight with Gillie and Elissa. But on the way home, the van's engine began to miss. Twice when Nick stopped, it had sputtered, choked, and died.

Marj touched Nick's arm. "I hope it doesn't do that during Gillie's field trip tomorrow. I don't want to get stranded with a carload of kids on those back roads."

When they reached home Nick stayed in the van. "I'm going to the garage to run a diagnostic. I don't want you to get stuck, either."

"But Dad!" Gillie yelped. "It's Sunday. You'll get in trouble."

Nick tousled Gillie's hair. "I don't think so, son. We just can't work on *customer's* cars. There won't be any trouble."

"But—"

Nick chuckled as he drove away. Many times he'd wondered if Gillie thought at all. But underneath that yellow hair, gears were actually turning!

Nick had just hooked up the instruments when Arnie Tate, the grocery store manager, poked his head inside.

"Saw yer lights 'n wondered if you was here."

He rolled a wheel through the door. "I'm sorta inna spot. April and me gotta leave for her folks' place inna hour. Takin' her old auntie along, and that should be a thrill." He rolled his eyes. "Innyhow, that back tar keeps goin' flat. Since yer awreddy here, d'you think you could fix it quick afore we head out?"

Nick shut the door. "That's risky business with this new law. Tell you what, why not take my loaner? She's no beauty but she runs good, and there'll be no charge."

Arnie grinned. "That's mighty nice of you, Wheatley! I'll—"

At that moment the customers' entry door burst open and

Sergeant Clay stepped in. "What's goin' on here?" he interrupted, his quick glance taking in everything.

Nick shrugged. "Just visiting with Arnie here."

Sergeant Clay eyed the van. "Well, why's that connected up, then?" His eyes narrowed. "Sunday work ain't allowed, y'know."

"But that's my *own* car!"

Sergeant Clay smirked. "Right. What's *he* doin' here then?"

"Just talking, like I told you."

Sergeant Clay opened his ticket book. "Oh, I see. And that's why he brought his tire in. Makes perfect sense to me."

~ ~ ~

The next Thursday Nick glanced toward the front of the county courtroom to see which judge was hearing that day's cases. Gratified that it was Judge Rochetti, he waited for the proceedings to begin, concentrating on quieting his jumpy stomach. How he hated speaking in front of a group of people! In public, words that were usually at his beck and call became elusive. Trying to find them left him speechless—or stammering. Not a good way to be when prompt and intelligible answers were required.

However, not many observers had come that day, and besides, Judge Rochetti was practically a friend. Nick had fixed his car a number of times. Perhaps it wouldn't be so bad, after all.

A few minutes later the judge peered over his glasses. "Mr. Wheatley, who is representing you?"

"Nobody, Your Honor."

"You wish to speak for yourself, then?"

"Yes, sir, it's a fairly simple matter."

Judge Rochetti's eyebrows shifted as he read the paper in his hand. "I see. Were you in your place of business last Sunday?"

"Yes, my wife needed the van for a field trip. I'd just put it on the diagnostic to see—"

"You *were* doing some work, then?"

"Yes, sir, on my own car."

Judge Rochetti glanced back at the paper. "This report states that Mr. Abernathy's car was also there, awaiting repair."

"W-well, yes, but—"

"Then I do not see that this is a simple matter, Mr. Wheatley. In a moment I'm going to ask Sergeant Clay to step forward and give me a full report. Are you certain you don't want legal advice?"

"Sir, if you would j-just let me explain."

Judge Rochetti leaned forward. "Do you or do you *not* wish counsel, Mr. Wheatley?"

Money. There simply wasn't any. And he couldn't tell them he couldn't afford it! "No, sir."

Judge Rochetti leaned back in his chair. "Very well. Sergeant Clay?"

Nick could hardly believe his ears! It sounded as though the officer and the judge had rehearsed beforehand. It was a simple matter, Sergeant Clay said. Nick was working on his own car but was getting ready to fix Abernathy's tire, as well.

Finally Nick was allowed to speak, but as usual, under the pressure of the moment, he couldn't quite put the words together. Finally the judge declared a 10-minute recess and went to his chambers.

Numb, Nick awaited the decision. Shannon's mocking smile pressed in. If she heard about this trouble with the *law* . . . Her gloomy predictions for his future pummeled him. Thoughts of Dusty interrupted his unwelcome reverie. Wouldn't *he* make something of it all!

Judge Rochetti returned in five minutes. "You may approach the bench, Mr. Wheatley." The courtroom went silent.

"Mr. Wheatley, according to Sergeant Clay's report and your testimony, it is true that you were not officially open for business this past Sunday."

Nick relaxed.

"However, according to the *meaning* of the law, you *were* open for business. You were there fixing your own vehicle. The purpose of the law, Mr. Wheatley, is to enhance Sunday worship by keeping that day separate from secular activities such as repairing cars. You had your car in a place of business. No one can deny that. Whether you would or would not have taken it upon yourself to work on Mr. Abernathy's tire is merely a matter of conjecture. The fact is that you were *work-*

ing in your place of business. That, in my opinion, openly defies the bylaw."

"But, sir—"

"I haven't finished, Mr. Wheatley. Because I believe your *intentions* were good, I am prepared to revise normal consequences somewhat. I shall reduce your fine to $200 with three days of community service, to take place on the next three Saturdays. You will report to the Police Department at 9:00 on each of those days and work eight hours doing whatever project is assigned. Sergeant Clay will supervise."

Nick sucked in his breath. "But Your Honor, I can't do that."

Judge Rochetti didn't look the least bit surprised. "And why not?"

"You know that Sab—Saturday is my sacr—*holy* day," Nick began. "I'll gladly do community service on any other days you say."

Judge Rochetti's eyebrows drew together. "Then perhaps I need to adjust the consequences to fit your liking." He thought for a moment, then smiled. "How about the regular $500 fine and next week in jail? Do you think you could fit that into your schedule?"

Nick met the judge's unwavering gaze. There was no choice, that was plain.

An hour later Nick slumped at the kitchen table, staring at the court order.

"You're right, Marj, I should have hired a lawyer, but there's nothing I can do about it now. I've gotta turn myself in within the hour. An attorney won't help now. I'm just being made an example for others, that's all."

Annoyed at him, Marj threw up her hands and flounced out of the room.

Father in heaven, I can't seem to get things right. I shouldn't have taken the van in, but I didn't realize . . . I don't have enough money to pay my monthly bills now. Where will I get that fine money?

A touch on his shoulder interrupted his prayer. Elissa, unaware of what was happening, and wide-eyed with excitement, settled onto his knee and wrapped her arms around his neck. "Daddy, Kathy just called. Her mom's taking her to the mall to buy stuff for her hair, and she invited me. Could I have $5?"

Nick tried to gather his thoughts. "Uh, things aren't going so well right now, sweetheart."

Elissa sobered. "OK, Dad."

She was not a child to sulk, nor did she often ask for things. Shannon's face swam before him. It was a pretty sorry father that couldn't spare five bucks for his only daughter!

He reached into his wallet and pulled out his only bill, a ten. "Oh, things aren't *that* bad, Elissa. Just don't spend it all in one place," he said, forcing a smile as he wrapped her slender fingers around the money.

Chapter 14

Grateful, Lucita stepped into the church foyer. Because of Papa's watchfulness, it was getting harder to slip away from home on Saturdays, but as often as she could she joined her new friends for the sermon and fellowship dinner, and coddling by the sweet-faced Sadie Bannister.

Sadie had just wrapped her comforting arm around Lucita. "Child, you've gotta eat more. You gonna blow away with the next wind if you don't."

Lucita laughed. "How are you today?"

The older woman gave a squeeze. "Oh, 'bout the same, child. When you commence to get old all sorts of miseries get you. If I'm not forgettin' where I put my glasses or leavin' on the stove burner, well, I'm lockin' myself outta the house, and that's the truth. Other day when I came back from the doctor's I had to wait two hours for Washington to come home an' let me in. I was plumb tuckered by then, so all I did was go in an' put my feet up."

Lucita had heard rumors about Pastor Bannister's wife having heart trouble, but the twinkle in her eye and the strength of her hug made her wonder if it could be true.

It had been a good church service. Pastor Bannister talked about obedience to God's commands—stressing that the commandments God had given to Moses were rules for the people's own good and happiness rather than a way of holding something over their heads. "If you love me, keep my commandments," Christ said. Lucita had never thought much about the commandments, but she was sure she didn't break any. After all, she didn't worship any other god, she didn't steal, didn't flirt with the men at the office, even when she had the chance to, and she was careful to honor her parents—*or was she?*

There might be a problem with the Sabbath commandment, however, if it truly meant what Pastor Bannister said it did. When she got home she'd have to look in Papa's Scriptures to see if the commandment really said Saturday was the proper day to worship. It didn't seem likely.

Sadie headed toward the fellowship hall, Lucita in tow. "Want you to taste my casserole, child," she said. "Bet you'll never guess it's not really chicken."

They sat around the tables, eating and talking. And then Sadie leaned close. "You have a Bible?"

Lucita shrugged. Referring to the holy book as "the Bible" always bothered her. It was a Protestant title—almost sacrilegious, knowing that the word only meant book. *The Holy Scriptures,* they were called in *her* church, who held the writings in highest regard.

Sadie's eyes took on a far-away look. "You know, I don't have children." She eyed Lucita thoughtfully. "I've got Mama's Bible that I've kept all these years. When she died she told me to pass it on to my daughter someday. Well . . . I just thought you might like to have it, seein's that I have no kin of my own to leave it to."

Lucita sucked in her breath. "I couldn't take your—your, uh—*Bible.*"

The older woman smiled. "Oh, yes you can, child. I been watchin' you and am impressed that you've got an honest soul. I know you'll make good use of it." She patted Lucita's hand "Besides, I was thinkin' that if I'd had a daughter I'd have wanted her to be just like you. Seein' Mama's Bible in your hands would make me happier than you could imagine."

Lucita's heart filled with a new kind of warmth. These people might be wrong, but they sure had a way of making you feel loved.

"Well, in that case—"

Sadie reached into her satchel, kissed her old Bible, then pressed it into Lucita's hands.

The cover was cracked and worn, the pages well-used. Lucita thumbed through the book, heart pounding, for never before had she looked into the Scriptures for herself. Wasn't it for the priests to explain what the strange words meant?

As she paged through it she noticed underlinings here and there, and the margins held personal comments written in tiny, neat script.

"Mama taught me out of this Bible, y'see," Sadie said, tears filling her eyes. "I could teach you things I would want my daughter to know, too, if you like."

Lucita hedged. "Thanks. This is a *lovely* book."

"You must remember to read it first thing each mornin', and before you sleep at night."

Lucita's heart skipped a beat. "But—"

"Child, if you let it, it will plant a burnin' joy inside you that will stay with you till the day you die."

"But the trouble is Papa. You see, he doesn't like me to read things from other churches." She told Sadie about Myrtle Flemming's booklet and how she had had to hide her religious materials at work.

"Why, praise the Lord," Sadie crooned.

"Praise the Lord?"

Sadie's chuckle filled the room. "A' course! The good Lord says 'blessed are ye when ye are persecuted'! Well, you haven't really been persecuted, but there's been resistance against your learnin' more about God, an' it shore hasn't stopped you. Can't you see, child? The Lord's a-tappin' your shoulder even now. I believe you can pick up your blessing at noonday just as well. Lord knows you'll be a-tryin'."

Sadie shook her head and leaned back in her chair. "Now, ain't that somethin' about that Myrtle Flemming. Shy as a bird and reedy as willow grass, but she shore did work for the Lord!"

Later, as Lucita was leaving SIPS after stowing Sadie's Bible, Melanie, her supervisor, noticed her. "Lucita! You here again?"

Lucita laughed. "Can't seem to stay away."

Melanie smiled. "Well, I'm glad to see you. We've just received notice that a large amount of extra input is required over the next few weeks. We must add Saturday shifts now until we finish. Do you think you could work Saturday afternoons for awhile? It would mean four hours a week overtime pay."

Lucita thought about the extra money. She'd been saving all she could for her hoped-for university classes, but because of handing most of her check over to Papa each week, she hadn't put much aside. Besides the money, work would give her a good excuse to be away from home so she could attend church on Saturdays without worrying Papa.

"What time would you need me?"

Melanie shrugged. "Oh, 1:00 to 5:00 would be best."

Relieved that the extra work wouldn't involve Saturday mornings, Lucita began planning how to ask Papa.

The bus ride home was pleasant that evening. Christmas decorations on the light poles and the festive store windows somehow distracted from the reality of how dangerous the city was. It seemed that since Pope Philip had visited Seattle two things were happening. Good people were getting better, but the bad were getting worse. Robberies and drive-by shootings had nearly doubled since last Christmas. Muggings, murders, and—she shuddered—*rapes* were at an all-time high. Papa had even had security bars installed on their home windows, as awful as they looked.

After helping Mama fix supper, Lucita put the plates on the table. She'd just placed the last knife and fork when Papa arrived.

Mama greeted him with her usual smile and patted his back. *"Hola, mi esposo.* Your dinner is nearly ready." She hurried to the table, pulled out his chair so he could sit, then bent to kiss his cheek. "You are tired?"

"Sí, but I shouldn't have come home. We need more help."

"Ah, but you must rest also. What good is a restaurant owner who is too tired to run his business?" Mama slid a plate of fried chicken in front of Papa.

"During holiday time we're always extra busy." He glanced at Lucita. "Perhaps Lucita could work Saturdays until January."

Lucita smiled at Papa, suddenly glad she'd run into Melanie that afternoon. It wasn't that she didn't want to help Papa; she simply wanted to go to church. But she could hardly tell Papa that. Now because of SIPS, she had a great excuse.

"I'd be glad to help, Papa, but I've been asked to work

Saturday afternoons at SIPS. There's lots of extra work right now, and everybody has to."

"So now they want you six days, do they?" Papa eyed her. "They'll give you more money, no?"

She nodded, suddenly realizing that the overtime money she'd anticipated would have to be turned over to Papa, too.

"Well, it's important that you do your share at your job, my little pigeon, but remember that the restaurant is what gives us our home and allows Mama to cook delicious food such as she has this night." He chewed thoughtfully, then brightened. "But it will be OK, don't you see? You can help out at La Cucharita on Saturday mornings *before* you go to SIPS. That way we will have even more food ready by the time our first customers come."

~ ~ ~

On Monday morning the manager called a general meeting for all SIPS employees. "As you may have heard in the news," he began, "the new Complete Records Act has just been voted. This regulation requires that religious preference be included in each security record, which in turn means that we're facing quite a task, as religious input has been optional in the past.

"We're responsible for updating all Washington State residents' records. Your assignments are on the duty sheet. From the file room, pull hard copy of the records for each person in your alphabet range and double-check to see that religious info is correctly entered. In the case of infants where preference is not stated, list both parents' denominations, mother-slash-father. If no preference is shown the field should remain empty.

"When you finish, Clerical will print labels and mail deadline-dated retrieval cards to those with incomplete records that will require more input on our part as they are returned."

The manager smiled. "All in all, this is a major task, but what it really means, folks, is quite a few extra dollars in your pockets."

Back at her desk, Lucita ran her finger down the page until she found her assignment. *Fernandez: Sa-Sm.* She typed a query and a moment later realized that it was a very long list.

~ ~ ~

A couple evenings after Christmas Lucita answered the phone.

"Lucita? This is Jennifer Merryweather, from church, you know?"

Lucita's mind did a quick search. "Yes. How are you?"

"Uh, Pastor Bannister asked me to give you a call. I don't quite know how to say this, but he thought you'd want to know Sadie had a heart attack this morning."

Lucita went cold. "She's OK now?"

"I'm sorry, dear. I know you were fond of her. We just thought you might want to know that her funeral will be day after tomorrow at 3:00 in the afternoon. At the church."

A tear splattered onto Lucita's hand. "Thank you. I'll be there."

She set the receiver in its cradle, then buried her face into her hands. First Myrtle Flemming. Now Sadie Bannister. Why was this happening? Numb, she pondered quietly until Mama came into the room.

Mama stiffened. "What wrong?"

Lucita fought for words. "A friend died today, *Mamacita.*"

"Ay, I am sorry. Do I know this girl?"

"No, Mama, she's from—work." Lucita became suddenly conscious of her fib. "I'll be late Thursday because I'm going to her funeral."

Mama wrapped her arms around Lucita, warm, protecting her for the moment. But her mother's words frightened her. "And I shall go with you, *niña,* for look at your sadness. This is not a time for you to be alone."

~ ~ ~

Though Lucita tried to dissuade her, Mama arrived at SIPS in a taxi to pick Lucita up for the funeral. When they finally pulled up in front of the Adventist church, Mama blanched.

"Your friend was from this church?" Mama's eyes widened in horror. "A heretic?"

"She wasn't a work friend, Mama. She was an elderly lady that went to church here."

Mama clutched Lucita's wrist. "You came here again? Are you *loco?* Papa will be so angry. You'll bring a curse on our family." Mama's eyes widened in fear. "Remember Father Matthew's sermon at Mass? The Scriptures say you must obey your mother and father! Don't you care about us anymore?"

Lucita's knees went weak. Was going to Sadie's funeral worth this trouble? Still, what difference did that make now? Mama would tell Papa about the church, and she would be in trouble anyway.

Lucita picked up her bouquet of red carnations and eased away from Mama. "I'm sorry to disappoint you, but I must go in."

Mama set her chin. "You go, then. But Papa will hear of this."

The plain white casket that perched atop the skirted table below the pulpit seemed naked, decorated with only a spray of carnations. Where were the wreaths, the abundant bouquets of flowers that marked a mourning people's sadness at seeing one of their own fall? Bewildered, Lucita made her way up the aisle and put her small bouquet on the floor in front of the table. Then she found a seat and opened the program that had been handed to her as she entered the church.

Wasn't Sadie Bannister respected? How would she feel, looking down and seeing that no one cared enough to make things nice for her? And how sad Pastor Bannister must be. Did no one care about his feelings, either? She glanced around the overflowing room.

Puzzled, she turned back to the program and noticed italicized print at the bottom of the page. "In lieu of flowers, Pastor Bannister requests donations to the literature fund that Sadie eagerly supported."

Strange. Strange people.

There was music, both happy and sad, the eulogy, a life sketch that brought tears to Lucita's eyes, and then a sermon almost irreverent with the happiness that it portrayed. It depicted Sadie waking up in the resurrection and looking up to see her Lord coming in the clouds of heaven. Why, the preacher actually said Sadie was now asleep, and that her soul knew *nothing!* That she would lie covered with dust, rotting away until Jesus saw fit to awaken her with His trumpet.

Blasphemy!

Suddenly Lucita understood why Papa didn't want her to

have anything to do with the Advents. They really *were* heretics! Her skin began to crawl, and she felt as though something evil was about to overtake her. She should get up. She should leave now while she could. But it was too late. The prayers had begun. How could she be that rude?

Compromising, Lucita remained seated while the others knelt. She would not worship their way or accept any more of their delusions. She would throw out the books and pamphlets crowding her locker. She had been a fool to bring such shame on her family.

When it was over she noticed the rear doors were closed and there was nothing to do but go with the others past the casket up front. Well, she might have to pass, but she would not look—would not join the heretics in their evil ways. She crept along with the line of mourners, poor deluded people that thought Sadie could not see what was happening. And what was wrong with Pastor Bannister? His gentle face was sad, but not agonized with grief as she'd imagined he would be.

But try as she would, as she passed by the casket she could not keep her eyes away from the soulless body that filled it. Sadie's spirit had flown back to God, but look at those sweet dark cheeks. The same gentle chin and sensitive mouth. Lucita eyed her hands, gnarled with arthritis but no longer in pain. Those hands that had done for everyone, that had so gently touched Lucita, that had ministered to others. Those hands that had wanted to caress a tiny daughter, but had never had the privilege.

Tears sprang to her eyes as she crossed herself. This woman she'd known so short a time had become like a mother—a *spiritual* mother to her. Too bad she had been so deluded. Surely she had not known that she had turned her back on God by joining this church and accepting what they believed. Lucita choked back a sob and tried to slip around those who were offering their condolences to Pastor Bannister, but he reached out and caught her arm.

"Lucita, thank you for coming. Sadie had special feelings for you."

Lucita choked back a sob. "I know."

"Don't feel so sad, my dear. Sadie's resting now, knows no

pain, thinks no thoughts. The next thing she will see is Jesus' face." His chin wobbled, then steadied. "She was not a strong woman, you know. I'm sure God realized she couldn't withstand the troubles about to befall us, so He let her go to sleep instead. It's a blessing."

Lucita gasped, then wavered between her need to comfort him and to confront him. Confrontation won.

"How can you act like her death doesn't matter? The truth is that your Sadie is watching you right now. Where are your prayers for her soul? She was a good woman, but she will be in Purgatory until prayers send her on to heaven."

Pastor Bannister's eyes teared. "No, Lucita, that's not true. Do just one thing for Sadie, would you? Read the Bible she gave you. Read in it the truth about death. Look inside the back cover where she's listed some texts."

The others were crowding close now, so Lucita turned away without giving the promise that Pastor Bannister wanted.

Thunderstorm clouds had gathered again and the wind flailed around her as she left the church. The decorations on the street now seemed a mockery. She hailed a cab and headed for St. Luke's, for it was obvious that if anyone was going to light a candle and pray Sadie Bannister into heaven, it would have to be her.

It was dark when she left the church. For once the street was nearly deserted. Wishing she had enough money for another taxi, she headed for the bus stop, the corner where poor Myrtle Flemming had first caught her in this web of foolishness.

She hurried down the street, eyes sweeping the doorways ahead. She had nearly covered the distance when she heard a snicker from behind. Three young roughs had fallen in step with her.

"That chick's on the street alone," one chuckled.

"And you know what that means."

"Yeah. And being the gentlemen that we are, we should give her what she wants."

Lucita's heart nearly jumped from her chest as she began to run. In her fright she dropped her purse and lost a shoe. The cry that lodged somewhere inside tore at her throat. Her legs would run no faster.

"Help me, God!" she screamed, as one of them grabbed her coat sleeve and hurled her to the hard cement.

CHAPTER 15

January

Brenna rolled up the soiled sheets and tossed them into the laundry cart. Forcing herself onward, she sprayed the bed with disinfectant, then wiped it down. When she had finished she looked at the room, now ready for the next patient. *The bed's hardly cold. It's like he was never here. Gone. Erased—even though his parents' crying is so fresh in my ears.*

His lover had not brought him to the hospital until he had to, until the bitter end. Before she'd even had a chance to share Jesus with him, to give him hope of a happy ending to his short life, he had breathed his last. She fought back tears. That's what hospital work was all about. People coming. People going. Worst of all, people going forever.

She could still feel his warm hand in hers as she'd passed the SIPS scanner over his palm. The computer-clock would register the exact time of death. *And positive identification. No way to fake the dead's identity now.* Later on, the doctor would key in the deceased's cause of death.

His lover, gaunt and pallid, had followed the body, weeping, bereft. His parents had followed, too, mixing their tears with heated accusations about the other man.

During the final minutes of the patient's life, as Brenna sensed the intense pain his parents were suffering, she had offered to pray with them. Their jaws went slack in amazement. "How dare you?" the father had bristled. "You want to pray to a God who allows this kind of thing? I think not!"

What comfort was there for them, then? How would they

cope—face their tomorrows—their *nights?* Without Jesus, how would they manage?

~ ~ ~

At lunchtime Brenna slipped into a chair in the corner of the hospital cafeteria, glad for a few minutes on her own. She needed a time during which there was no need for pretense that her life was happy and everything was fine. She looked forward to this time each day—a few moments for her own thoughts uninterrupted by the children or colleagues. A time to sort herself out, regroup, plan. With a sigh, she bowed her head.

Lord, thank You for this sandwich. Right now I'm so tired I don't even want to eat it, but I will. I'm so worried. How can I cope with everything facing me now? How can I keep a happy face around everybody when I feel like I'm coming apart? I ought to trust You more to work things out for me—for us. Please, help me to get through this day somehow. I'm really scared about seeing Wally tonight. I'm afraid of what he's going to do about the children. I feel so alone. Please increase my faith. Take charge of things. I know You will, but Lord, I'm so confused . . .

Three doctors, still in green scrubs, settled down at a nearby table and began an animated conversation. Tuning them out, Brenna bit into her sandwich, forced herself to chew and swallow. Her thoughts churned back over the past few weeks, again and again trying to make sense of things. They'd had a miserable Christmas—miserable because Wally was not there and she was down in the dumps and the children had whined almost constantly. And then on December 28 he'd finally called. They'd talked for quite awhile about the children and the bills and safe things, always skirting the real issue. Eventually he'd suggested that he come by after the first of the year so he could share some news with her.

She shuddered, her imagination conjuring up all sorts of scenes: the children clinging to Wally; his accusing eyes on her because she wouldn't study The Book; his distracting her with some inane request while he whisked the children into the car and vanished with them.

Enough! She would not allow her mind to carry on so. She forced her attention elsewhere. She watched a young couple struggle with their trays while holding small children in their arms; noticed crotchety Mrs. Flarrety as she ladled soup for a nervous customer. Then one of the doctors swore.

"It could be Marloid's in its early stages," he said.

Dr. Haber's eyes narrowed. "Mark my words, it will be an epidemic."

Dr. Grants set his fork aside and leaned forward. Brenna stopped chewing and tried to hear. "She has all the signs. But how could it crop up here? This morning's national Internet report said that there are 11 confirmed cases in New York and 21 in Los Angeles. No cases elsewhere."

Dr. Haber shook his head. "But we don't know how the virus passes. Just a week ago there were no known cases anywhere in the States. They think some tourists brought it in, but they don't really know yet. Supposedly those infected are in quarantine, but you know how well that works."

Brenna shuddered. Marloid's disease had been big news of late. In fact, Aaron Chandler had done a special on it. Apparently it had first been noticed in Hong Kong and until this week was supposedly contained there. The first sign of the virus was what seemed to be a perfectly innocuous cold sore on the mouth. But it didn't stop there. Accompanied by an increasingly fierce headache and progressive trembling of the limbs, the ulcer grew rapidly, oozing and running, and everything that its thick ooze touched also erupted with pus and gore. With it came a burning itch that people described as being stabbed with hot knives. Within 48 hours the flesh began to turn purple and slough away, gradually eating into the tissues until it attacked the blood vessels. The victims they had tracked so far had finally bled to death. All in all, Marloid's added up to several horror-filled days and then death for those unlucky enough to contract it.

Dr. Blake glanced around to make sure no one had heard, then spoke softly. "I say we don't mention this unless we're sure. You know how panic goes. If we're not careful we'll have the whole town in an uproar, afraid every little pimple is Marloid's." He shook his head. "Too bad they can't identify a carrier type. You guys hear anything more?"

"They're still trying to isolate the virus. Nobody's too anxious to get near it, though—it progresses so rapidly."

Dr. Grants shook his head. "Let's just hope it's really contained, or we'll have a real mess on our hands."

Brenna shoved the last half of her sandwich back into the bag. What with her own problems, the early morning death, and the specter of Marloid's, her appetite had vanished.

Head throbbing, she headed back to work.

~ ~ ~

That evening after supper Wally taught Jared the safe way to whittle with his new knife and then played Legos with the children. Finally he sent them scampering to their rooms with the promise of a wonderful surprise if they'd "let Mommy and Daddy talk" for a few minutes.

Brenna sank into an armchair across from Wally. A silence thick enough to slice followed.

"You had something you wanted to tell me?"

He tossed her a half smile. "You're getting too thin," he announced.

"And that's what you came to tell me?"

He crossed the room, knelt, and took her hand. "Of course not, silly. I really wanted to see you, to see if you'd changed your mind."

Brenna's heart flopped against her ribs. Why did he keep doing this to her? To have him so near and yet so far away was torture. Why must she keep making the same decision over and over?

"I'm afraid I haven't. Wally—"

"I was hoping you'd come to Nevada with me."

"Nevada?"

"I'm taking a leave of absence this next semester. Going to Nevada."

Brenna withdrew her hand and got up. She walked to the big window, looked out at the thin sprinkle of snow that covered the lawn. "Whatever for?"

Wally was beside her then. "I have a chance to help Max with some research. You remember Max Orcott, don't you?"

Brenna's knees went weak. "Sure, but why do you want to help him with *his* kind of research?"

Wally held up his hands. "Now don't start in on me. You

have only yourself to blame for not understanding what's going on. You refused to read the book—to discuss any of these issues with me, remember?"

Weary, Brenna sank back into the chair. "I'm sorry I jumped on you like that. What'll you be doing?"

"Max has had a number of face-to-face meetings with Taelon, The Messenger. You know, the one he met in Nevada a couple months ago. He knew of my interest, and—well, he asked if I'd like to come on down and help him document what's going on. I was hoping you and the kids would come along. Max has a place there."

Brenna grasped for straws. "But what about your *job?"*

Wally turned his back, gazed out the window, then spun around again. "I—uh, have some vacation time coming, some research time. See here!" His eyes flashed. "At a time like this, when I have this opportunity you're worried about my *job?"*

"No, no," she objected, but he cut her short.

"Oh, you're worried about *money,* that's it. 'Money is the root of all evil,' that's for sure. Well worry no more. You'll get your money."

He stormed to the door, leaving her speechless. She thought he'd slam it behind him, but instead he turned back. "God doesn't always continue to strive with us, you know," he said evenly. "You've failed your test, my dear. You didn't know it, but this was your last chance."

He closed the door behind him, totally forgetting the surprises he had promised the kids.

Chapter 16

Aaron elbowed his way to the front of the tangle of news reporters who crowded around Surgeon General Grady Wilmore. Ever watchful, Secret Service men and Armed Forces personnel held the more eager ones at bay. In an increasingly common declaration, the reporters were told that under the new Citizen Security Law they could neither report nor record the impromptu press meeting, a fact that was sure to rankle even veteran news personnel.

An Independent Press field reporter spoke up. "But it's the right of the American people to know the latest on Marloid's disease. Is it true that new cases have been verified in the Northwest?"

Grady Wilmore leveled his gaze at the questioner. "At this time there is no statement to make. When there is you will be notified."

Aaron raised his hand but did not wait to be recognized. "Can you assure us that to the best of your knowledge there has been no verifiable case of Marloid's outside New York City or Los Angeles?"

Wilmore ignored Aaron's question, instead pointing to a rookie reporter at the rear of the room.

"Sir, is it not the right of Americans to know what threatens them?"

Mr. Wilmore's benign smile flicked across the group. "Is it best for the American public to continually be bombarded with rumor rather than fact? To be sent into paroxysms of hysteria that impede clear thinking?"

"Mr. Wilmore—"

The surgeon general adjusted his tie and with a cursory nod announced, "That will be all, gentlemen, ladies. This briefing session is closed and by presidential declaration is not to be reported. When there is news to share, you will be informed. Thank you and good day."

A bad taste climbed Aaron's throat. Three days, and they were still getting the runaround. Unofficial word had come to him from his sources both in Idaho and in Nevada that several Marloid's cases had been hospitalized within the past week. It was true that breaking the news in an unwise way could cause untold panic among the general public. That was why it was important for Aaron to be the first to zero in on the story, to give the truth in an intelligent and useful way, so that people could know what was happening. So they could use common sense in their activities, and possibly prevent contamination. He jammed his notepad into his pocket and headed for the door.

The wraps on this story made him nervous. As far as the public knew, Marloid's was merely one of those inconvenient fly-by-night diseases that washed through and then was over. Word was that it had been successfully contained in the two bigger cities, and then snuffed out, but long experience had taught him that the quieter the authorities were about a story, the more danger potential it had. Like the asteroid thing that was still being suppressed.

Toying with the idea of flying right out to the small university town in Idaho where rumor placed the disease, he climbed into his rental car and headed for the airport. Once there, he could ferret out whatever news there was—whether or not it was available for public knowledge.

He had that old gut feeling that had served him so well in the past. *This is big. Somehow I have to be the one to break this story.*

He swore as he pushed his way through the traffic. Women drivers, old people, teenagers weaving in and out. They made him crazy. A Pepsi truck pulled out in front of him. Aaron swerved, then laid on the horn. He hated to think of flying back to Atlanta, making his evening news report, and then doing an all-nighter to Idaho. *Perhaps there's another way.*

Without setting his turn signal, he eased into the left-turn lane, and though a sign prohibited U-turns, whipped around and headed back in the direction he'd just come.

The secretary behind the cherrywood desk was unmovable. After putting down the surgeon general's appointment book, she met Aaron's gaze. "I'm sorry, but Mr. Wilmore is booked for the afternoon. He does have a 15-minute opening on Thursday. Would you like for me to book you?"

Aaron despised businesswomen—all polish and efficiency with talons barely hidden beneath the surface. It was his opinion that though they'd infiltrated a man's world, they clung to a woman's penchant that urged them to become subtle as mother tigers, guarding those for whom they worked.

Aaron forced a friendly smile. "I appreciate the offer, but I'll be out of the country then. You *do* know that I have a newscast to attend to each evening?"

She remained stony, protective. "I know who you are, Mr. Chandler."

"Then you understand that I must move quickly, no matter what I do or where I go. That being true, and knowing that I must make flight connections in less than two hours, you would understand that I could not take much of Mr. Wilmore's time. Five minutes would be quite adequate, I can assure you."

She wavered. "Perhaps I could slip him a message."

"I could finish with him in a shorter time."

She stared at him.

Annoyed at her stubbornness, Aaron pulled the big one out of his persuasive hat. "Let's just say that I have something extremely confidential, possibly *lethal,* to tell him. If it gets into the wrong hands—"

He could tell by her face that he was making ground.

"It's urgent that Mr. Wilmore learns about this promptly, before someone else does."

Her eyebrows twitched as she eyed the appointment book again. "I might just squeeze you in for a moment when Senator Craven leaves. You said five minutes?"

Aaron didn't allow himself to grin. "That will do just fine, ma'am. I appreciate your consideration."

~ ~ ~

Impeccable in his pin-striped suit, Grady Wilmore arose and extended his hand as Aaron stepped into the plush office. "It's been awhile, Chandler. I see you often, though, on the tube."

"Yes."

"I understand you're in somewhat of a rush, but do sit down and tell me how I can help you."

Aaron came right to the point. "I want to know the truth about this Marloid's."

Wilmore's smile vanished. "I'm sorry—"

There was no time to waste. The feline in the front office had said five minutes, and Aaron took her at her word. "I'd hate to let a little story about a man and his gun just happen to slip," he said softly.

Their eyes locked. Quickly and unobtrusively, Wilmore reached beneath his center drawer, then withdrew his hand.

Aaron gave a knowing smile. "I thought you might want to turn your recorder off. Now, may I speak plainly?"

Wilmore blanched. "Chandler, there really is no firm news now, though there could be at any moment. They're afraid of the reactions. This thing is big—I can't say anything else now."

Wilmore pressed his fingertips together, watched them closely. "Tell you what. Since we're 'friends,' I'll cut you a deal—on the QT, of course. You *can't* leak that I've made any, uh, special concessions to you. When something's ready to break I'll give you as much advance warning as I possibly can, though it won't be much."

He took a card from his pocket and wrote on it. "I'll call your office and leave an urgent message using the name Philburn. Here's my unlisted number and a code name you can give when my aide answers. That will get you right through to me."

Aaron took the card. "Thanks."

Though Wilmore glared at him, his words sounded smooth and friendly. "It's important that we keep this between just the two of us—uh, everything, that is."

"Agreed," Aaron muttered, turning on his heel and letting himself out of the office.

~ ~ ~

The call had come at 2:00 the next morning when he'd

barely fallen asleep. Annoyed at the interruption of his much-needed rest, he'd snapped at the network operator. But the name "Philburn" put him in an entirely different mood.

"Thanks, doll. Sorry I'm such a bear when I'm awakened. It's a box of chocolates for you."

He switched on the lamp and hurried to the chair where he'd dropped his jacket when he came in from the broadcast. Taking Wilmore's card from his breast pocket, he grabbed his legal pad and reached for the phone.

Thirty minutes later he was on his way to the airport. Destination—Moscow, Idaho.

~ ~ ~

The small university town was just coming to life when the network Lear jet touched down on the airstrip. From the window he spied Merle Faygo and his cameraman, who had come down from Spokane.

After the 10-minute drive to the hospital, Aaron climbed out of the car. "I think it's best if I go in alone. Less obtrusive than a group of us. You guys hang around out here, and if things look like they're getting out of hand dial my pager." He touched it to make sure the "on" button was in position. "And keep the camera under wraps."

Orienting himself in new places came easily after so many years of having to look like he knew where he was going. He tucked his clipboard under his arm and slung a stethoscope around his neck. Then gripping the medical bag Merle had provided, he pushed through the swinging glass door. As he'd expected, a directory was posted just inside.

When the elevator door opened on the third floor, he stepped out, glanced both ways, and then headed for the communicable disease section.

A thick-lashed, dark-haired nurse named Kenrick was at the desk talking to an older nurse. At the end of the hall a lanky police officer chatted with a photogenic student nurse. Aaron nodded at the peach-faced cop, then stepped quickly to the door labeled "Quarantine—No Admittance."

Inside, the curtains had been drawn. Aaron waited for his eyes to adjust, then glanced around. The whir of a dozen air purifiers created an accompaniment to the patient's rapid breathing. He stepped closer. What appeared to be a young woman lay in the bed with a sheet covering the central portion of her body. His stomach turned at the sickly-sweet odor that rose to greet him as he bent to see her face. A yellowish crust covered most of it, spreading down her neck and arms. The ooze looked thick and creamy—and made his skin crawl. He swallowed hard.

Though her eyes were closed she did not lie there placidly, for her limbs kept up a rhythmic trembling, as though she were dancing to unheard music. Occasionally she tossed her head and muttered something.

As he watched he noticed something he'd not seen at first glance—large purplish holes on her arms.

The deadliness of what was contained in that room seemed to close in, eager to claim him, too. He must leave, must try not to breathe the tainted air. She coughed, and a fleck of her spittle landed on the back of his hand.

Stifling a retch and his urge to flee, he took her chart from the holder at the foot of the bed, and scanned it. *Quarantine. Lissy Hammond, University Apartments, age 22, admitted two days ago, married. Diagnosis: Confidential—see Dr. Blake.*

Right on! He had what he needed. Aaron took a quick snapshot, gave a last glance to the frightful creature on the bed, then peeked out the door. The policeman was so taken up in the young beauty's attention he didn't even notice Aaron leave.

He stopped in the restroom, scrubbed his hands, then scrubbed them again. Outside he gulped cleansing breaths of fresh air. But his skin still crawled and nausea filled his throat.

A little later he and Merle sat together in a motel room. "Let's see what we can scratch up," Aaron said, consulting the notebook he'd scribbled on in the hospital room.

He picked up the phone and dialed. "Mr. Hammond? I'm with the university student insurance department. I need your help on a couple of things."

The man on the other end hesitated. "I was told this situation was not to be discussed, sir."

Aaron used his most understanding tone. "That's crucial. Not with anyone except your doctors. And of course myself, as I need to supply proper information to the insurance company so we can get your wife's hospital insurance cleared."

"But—"

Aaron thought fast. "Understandably, Dr. Blake is very busy right now. He asked me to give you a call. Do you have a moment?"

Aaron winked at his companions, then began rattling off his questions.

~ ~ ~

That noon, just after grim-faced news correspondents from around the nation left the hastily called medical news conference led by Grady Wilmore, in Washington, D.C., Aaron Chandler stared into the TV camera once again.

"We interrupt your regular programming to bring you a breaking story. A confirmed case of Marloid's disease has been identified in the small university town of Moscow, Idaho. The victim, whose name is being withheld at this time, was treated in a Los Angeles emergency room for a dog bite she sustained two weeks ago. New cases of Marloid's have been reported in Los Angeles, New York, and Las Vegas. Emergency measures are being taken to stop the spread of the mystery disease, and to isolate the carrier. Pending further information, persons in affected areas are requested not to travel and are advised to boil all water that will be ingested or used to clean fresh foods, and to avoid large groups of people.

"We go now to Merle Faygo in Moscow, Idaho."

Aaron waited until the on-line light went out, then got up. That should boost the ratings. There might be questions from the other networks regarding how he could break the story so much earlier than the rest, but he trusted himself—with the help of Grady Wilmore—to put them off the track.

Aaron winced. *Good thing I stumbled onto Grady's little fiasco when we were in college. You never know what tidbit of information will serve you later on.*

He dug in his pocket for a Tums and popped it into his mouth. Wincing, he felt a tender spot at the corner of his mouth. A sudden cold sweat squeezed from his pores as he hurried to find a mirror.

Chapter 17

March

Lucita sighed in relief as she left Rudolfo at the SIPS entrance. How tired she was of his shadowing her whenever she was away from home or work. The problem was bigger than Papa fearing it wasn't safe for her to walk the streets alone anymore. It was that he didn't trust her to stay away from that awful Advent church. And so he'd hired the dart-eyed young tough to shadow her. The trouble was, it had put an end to her stopping off at the cathedral to pray for Sadie Bannister before she went home each day, for how could she pray with those surly eyes boring into her?

She shuddered as she remembered the young thugs who'd knocked her down on the evening of Sadie's funeral. Praise God, in spite of her going against Papa and fraternizing with heretics, God had had mercy and sent a police car along just in time. What had ended up as a few scratches and losing her purse could have been much worse. In the scramble she could have lost her virginity, or even her life!

Ever since, Papa had been on the rampage, threatening to make her quit her job, to go into the convent, anything to make sure the heretics didn't put their spell on her. Well, he could rest his mind. She wouldn't go back to any but the mother church if her life depended upon it. She wasn't proud. She could admit when she'd been wrong. Besides, she owed her allegiance to Papa, but even more to God. Yes, that was it. She owed her first allegiance to *God,* and she wanted nothing that might keep her from rightness with Him. Lately, it seemed that her heart reached out to Him almost constantly.

Lucita glanced over her shoulder to make sure Rudolfo had stayed outside, then hurried up the steps. She hadn't returned to her locker since the funeral, instead keeping her things with her at her workstation. Perhaps it was foolish, but she was almost afraid to look at the reading materials the locker contained, especially the Bible. Papa was right. The Adventists were heretics, and she didn't want to have their spell on her.

~ ~ ~

She typed in her password and reached for the stack of records to be processed. The Statement of Religious Preference forms had flooded in, overloading workers with hours of extra input. After keying in the last record she was no longer able to quell her curiosity. She checked to make sure Melanie was busy, and then broke a company rule. Heart pounding, she quickly pulled up a record not in her assignment range: Washington Bannister.

The minister was 70 years old, had been an Adventist pastor for 40 years, and he had not moved since Sadie's death. There were no close relatives, nor had he been in trouble with the law. Though he had an alarmingly small bank balance he did own one thing of value—a small cabin on four and a half acres in Pinebrow Heights, northern Washington.

Lucita smiled, remembering Sadie's animated story of a deer coming right up to their cabin front porch. The thought of Sadie didn't remain pleasant, though. Again she remembered promising Sadie to read the old Bible. Guilt threatened her, but she pushed it away. Promises to her father were more binding, weren't they? Still, how could it matter? Weren't all Scriptures the same? Why not read a few lines in the old woman's book and therefore fulfill her hasty promise?

Disquieted, Lucita turned back to work.

~ ~ ~

Later, in the lunchroom, Lucita's rice and beans sat forgotten as she thumbed through something called The Book of Psalms. As she read passages underlined by a hand now still, warm comfort wrapped its gentle arms around her, comfort she had so long desired. Why, God was her friend, and this book His message to her. Why hadn't she read the Scriptures—the *Bible*—before? Her food forgotten, she continued to read until the five-minute chime sounded.

Carefully she wrapped the book in its tissue, then hurried to her desk. She wanted to read more. She had to. But there wasn't time enough on her short work breaks. And she certainly couldn't take the Bible home, for Papa would be terribly angry.

She crossed herself. *Blessed Mary, help me find a way.*

~ ~ ~

When the living room clock chimed twice Lucita left her bed and tiptoed to the bathroom. On an upper shelf of the linen closet was a small box of fancy towels they seldom used. She removed a few, then took out her precious Bible. Sinking down on the bath mat beside the tub, she opened it to the back cover. As Pastor Bannister had said at the funeral, Sadie had listed several texts about death on that page.

Adrenaline-filled because of doing something against Papa's will, Lucita found the first text. "The living know that they shall die: but the dead know not any thing. . . . Also their love, and their hatred, and their envy, is now perished."[1]

Strange. A spirit would still have its love, its hatred, its envy, wouldn't it? Unless what the funeral preacher had said was really true.

"The dead praise not the Lord, neither any that go down into silence."[2] "His breath goeth forth, he returneth to his earth; in that very day his thoughts perish."[3]

Lucita continued reading for a half hour, then set the Bible aside and got onto her knees. Though she had not brought her rosary she sensed that God would accept her prayer, this once, without it. Overwhelmed with great love for Him, she made the sign of the cross.

"Our Jesus, honorable Son of God, it's me, Lucita," she whispered. "Please, may I tell You something? In this book Sadie Bannister gave me You told Your disciples how to talk to Your Father, God. I noticed that You didn't say for them to talk to a saint in heaven, but straight to Him. Then You died and rose and went back to heaven. For some reason people quit talking to You, but maybe they were a little scared, like I feel right now.

"Please forgive me if I am being too impulsive in speaking directly to You. I don't want to do wrong." She paused for a moment, waiting to see if she would feel differently, but nothing happened.

"I've tried to be good and do what Papa tells me, most of the time, anyway." A tear dropped onto her nightgown. "Oh, Jesus, so many things confuse me. Papa tells me I must not look at things outside my church. My church tells me that there are certain things I must do to guarantee my salvation. They also tell me that my Aunt Rosa's and Sadie's spirits left them when they died, and that they are trying to come to You. I've been taught that it is my duty to pray for my loved ones, and to burn candles in their names so they can get to You sooner. Is Aunt Rosa there yet, Lord? Does she see me and know the turmoil I'm in? Or is this book telling me the truth? It seems to say that when a person dies *nothing* happens except he just *quits*. And that he'll stay right where we bury him until You come back someday. How can this be? It's all so confusing!

"Papa doesn't want me to read the Scriptures because I'm female, and he feels that I can't understand it. Maybe he's right, but I'm sneaking with it in his own house. Is this a mortal sin? Please help me know what's right and I'll do it."

Lucita knelt there for a long while, savoring the satisfaction of talking directly to Jesus for the first time in her life. At last she glanced at her watch. She'd been reading and praying for over an hour. Reluctant to leave Jesus' presence, she crossed herself, then got up and looked in the mirror.

How did God really see her? As an individual? Or as one of many? Her black hair, mussed now, fell in loose waves onto her shoulders. Her dark eyes peered from her round face, and she could see the joy in them. She couldn't help but smile! Where did she go from here? She had so many questions and no one to ask.

She had just stooped to pick up her Bible when the doorknob rattled. Then someone tapped on the door.

"Lucita! What takes you so long in there?"

Fear shot through her as she hid her Bible, then flushed the toilet. "Sorry, Papa," she whispered, as she slipped past him and back to the bed she shared with her older sister.

~ ~ ~

She must find a way to get away from Rudolfo. How Papa could trust the smirking youth was more than Lucita could understand. And Rudolfo had certainly not let him down. He waited for her in front of her house every morning, and in front of SIPS every evening.

She had continued her morning Bible study in the bathroom as long as she dared each morning, and she was getting desperate to have the questions her study had produced answered. Though she toyed with the idea of going to see Father Matthew, she remembered he was Papa's friend and worked for the church that had taught her to pray to a saint instead of to God. Somehow she must speak with the Adventist pastor, even though that would be going against Papa's wishes and breaking the commandment. She would never become an Advent, certainly not. But someone had to help her understand the things she'd read in Sadie Bannister's Bible.

Finally she could put it off no longer, so during lunch hour she went to the lounge pay phone. "It's me, Lucita Fernandez," she said when Washington Bannister's deep voice answered. "I have some questions." She hesitated, gathering her courage. "Could I come to see you?"

He cordially suggested they visit on Sabbath right after the fellowship dinner. After she explained why that was impossible, he paused. "Well, Lucita, would you like to come to the church tomorrow at about 2:00? Mrs. Simeon will be cleaning, but we could talk in my study."

She would have to leave work. Lucita's thoughts scurried before her, already deciding to feign sickness in order to leave work the next afternoon. "Yes, I'll be there."

~ ~ ~

The time with Pastor Bannister passed all too quickly. How easily he had answered her questions about death. It had always seemed strange to her that souls already in heaven must return to their decayed bodies so Jesus could raise them, transform them into new and clean beings, and then take them back to heaven. The way Pastor Bannister explained it seemed much more reasonable.

Yet, thinking of Aunt Rosa and Sadie Bannister moldering in the ground was pretty gruesome. Knowing Aunt Rosa was watching her had so often given her a warm, close feeling. There had even been times, kneeling there before the likeness of her patron saint, when she'd actually felt Aunt Rosa's presence, or at least had thought she had. It was all so confusing.

She glanced at her watch, then out the bus window at the early rush-hour traffic. She had talked too long with Pastor Bannister and missed the bus she'd needed to catch. How would she ever get inside SIPS without Rudolfo seeing her? And what if her supervisor saw her and realized she truly was not sick?

~ ~ ~

Only an emergency would draw Papa away from the restaurant at 7:00 in the evening. Enraged, he had burst through the front door. Earlier, Lucita had taken refuge in her bedroom, excusing herself from Mama's presence by saying she had a headache. And by the time Papa came, it was the truth.

Trembling, she lay on her bed, a cool cloth over her eyes, awaiting the inevitable.

Papa didn't even knock. "What is this Rudolfo's told me?" he demanded. "You left work without him?" He pulled her to her feet. "What have you to say about this, girl?"

Lucita's mouth went dry. She could lie and maybe get out of it. Or she could tell the truth and have sudden destruction come upon her. She looked at Papa, his smoldering eyes underlaced with worry. His right cheek twitched as it always did when he was upset. His grasp, though firm, was not rough. *He's afraid for me!*

"I—I didn't feel so good this afternoon—uh, sometimes the computer monitor gives me a headache." She rubbed her temples. "I thought, well, I decided to go for a *ride* to get some fresh air. I knew you wouldn't want me *walking* alone."

Papa stared into her eyes, his look so long and penetrating that she nearly buckled. Finally she closed her eyes.

He gave her a little shake. "Look at me when we're speaking. Where did you go?"

She sank onto her bed. "I told you, Papa."

"Are you seeing a man?"

"Papa!" She added a hint of disgust to his name.

He watched her for a long while, then walked to her window. "Are you sure your headache is from your computer? Or is it maybe from getting too little rest?"

"What do you mean, Papa?"

His eyes bored into her. "Maybe my daughter's sick, maybe she needs a doctor, who knows? She spends so much time in the bathroom each morning. She's there when she should be sleeping."

A chill raced up her spine. "The bathroom?"

"Don't think I haven't heard you, my daughter. A good father sleeps with one eye and both ears open, is that not so?"

"Yes, Papa, and I appreciate that you take care of us."

"But my ears sometimes hear things that puzzle me." He headed for her, a strange look in his eyes. "You don't mind, do you?" he said, opening one drawer after another to search them. Puzzled, he finally eyed her again.

"I hear pages turning, turning. And you stay in there so long. I wonder what it all means."

He turned on his heel and left the room.

She heard him go into the bathroom and open the drawers, then the linen closet. *Blessed Father, help him not to find the Bible, please!* She held her breath. Had she hidden it carefully enough when she'd put it away this morning? She could imagine him lifting the towels and the sheets and finding nothing, starting his search on the shelf above.

He finally returned with nothing in his hands.

Thank You, Father!

Lucita sat quietly on her bed, willing her heart to settle down.

"I will call the doctor," Papa said.

"But—"

"He will see if you have an illness. After all, I am responsible for keeping my family well." He stepped to her bedroom door. "My daughter, you are not to spend so much time in the bathroom each morning. You need your sleep, and so do I."

He turned back to face her. "Another thing. Do not leave

your building without Rudolfo. If you get sick, call me at La Cucharita. Tomorrow I will buy a pager for Rudolfo so I can send him for you if necessary." Anger tinged the edges of his words. "You must promise me."

Despair claimed her, for she knew she must visit with Pastor Bannister again.

"Lucita?"

She stared at her feet. "I promise."

~ ~ ~

She had prayed long and hard, lying on her bed that night after Papa had confronted her about leaving work. It was no longer safe to keep her Bible at home, and even if she did she would not be able to read it there. Two mornings ago Papa had tapped on the bathroom door when she'd been there only five minutes. She would have to find another way.

Now she smiled at the elderly Black man who sat in the restaurant with her. How kind he had been to offer to come and have lunch with her two days each week. How convenient that the restaurant occupied the ground floor of the SIPS building and had an inside entry.

As they waited for their soup and sandwiches she opened her Bible. "Pastor Bannister, how did the commandment day of worship get changed to Sunday? I didn't find anything about that in Sadie's Bible."

---

[1] Ecclesiastes 9:5, 6.

[2] Psalm 115:17.

[3] Psalm 146:4.

CHAPTER 18

May

Aaron slapped a $20 bill into the driver's hand and jumped out of the taxi, briefcase in tow, Buzz on his heels. Having had their plane locked into a holding pattern for over an hour and then fighting Washington's usual traffic, there'd be no chance of getting a good place for the president's emergency news conference. If they didn't hurry they'd miss the entire thing.

Jogging the last three blocks between snarled traffic, Aaron swallowed the sour-tasting stuff in his mouth and tried to ignore his burning stomach. He hated going to a conference unprepared. He despised not knowing what he was up against, but there'd been no advance warning of President Rondell's intentions to speak, no press information that would make it easier for them to know what might fly. Too bad he hadn't kept pressure on Grady Wilmore—gotten a tip from him.

Soaked from their dash, Aaron wiped the rain from his eyes and headed for the White House guard station. It really *was* something big, then. He'd never seen security tighter. Dozens of plainclothes agents and military personnel kept watchful eyes on the crowd, carefully checking credentials before admitting them to the nation's number one residence.

As he had expected, the briefing room was already crammed with reporters. The door had barely closed behind them when President Rondell arrived. The man's usually rosy face was gray and drawn. There was no smile, and no spring to his step. Aaron tensed, his mind racing, ready to put his special verbal twist on whatever might come.

"Ladies and gentlemen of the press, I have called this special conference to share some grave information." The president paused, then seemed to reach inside himself to find strength. "There is no way that what I have to tell you can be made to seem pleasant. No doubt it will cause you a certain amount of fear, and I must ask that you listen to my entire message before drawing any conclusions."

The room hushed as the reporters drew a collective breath. Faces looked up, eyes questioning.

"The Department of the Air Force has spotted a small asteroid that is on a collision course with Earth. If we collide with it extensive damages will occur. However, emergency measures are being taken to attempt to divert its course so that it will not make a direct hit. You will be hearing more about this situation and protective forces within the next day or two. For now, the public needs only to know that it is there and that a solution is already underway."

Annoyed, Aaron shrugged as he fished for his notepad and pen. After all the hours he'd spent on the story of the asteroid and the alert system in North Dakota, it had been held back by National Security and they'd never been allowed to air it. And now news of the threat rolled off the president's glib tongue as though it was brand-new.

Aaron turned his attention back to President Rondell.

"There is more. As you know, Marloid's disease is increasingly active on our continent and could escalate into a very contagious situation unless protective measures are taken. . . ."

Aaron's stomach turned, recalling the sticky-sweet stench in the hospital room in Moscow. Now hundreds of cases were erupting at odd, seemingly unrelated places around the world, and scientists still had no idea how it was passed. *It's going to make AIDS look like kindergarten play,* Aaron thought.

"Conjecture regarding the source of Marloid's points to the possibility of transfer via fruits coming in from Mexico and South America. Though it's not conclusively proven, as a safety measure I have ordered a ban on fruit imports from those countries until further study can be completed. This will certainly inconvenience consumers, but it is important that we take swift measures to protect our national health. Studies of the disease continue on a round-the-clock basis, with hopes of learning how to counteract it.

"It has been a hard year, weatherwise." That was such an understatement it was almost a joke, but no one laughed. The president droned on. "Disaster-aid coffers are depleted because of the hurricanes, tornadoes, and earthquakes that plague our nation. The homelessness these disasters have produced has caused our crime rate to triple. Our nation—our *world*—is clearly in serious trouble. America has always been in the forefront in dealing with problems that assail the world's safety. Unless we find a way to do something about the grave matters that face us now, we may have a very short future."

President Rondell sagged against the podium, and for a moment Aaron thought he might collapse.

"Yesterday I received a phone call from Dr. Max Orcott. On numerous occasions Dr. Orcott and his crew have been approached by the extraterrestrial, Taelon, who reportedly brings messages from God. After speaking with Dr. Orcott via telephone, I contacted a good number of church leaders, including the leader of the World Church. Together, by televideo, we examined Earth's situation, Taelon's message, and its ramifications. After careful study, these esteemed church leaders have mutually concluded that Dr. Orcott's claims are genuine, and that heed should be given to the special messages delivered by Taelon."

As the president took a sip of water a hiss of voices rose from the room. Aaron could hardly believe what he was hearing. An "extraterrestrial" given respect? Credibility? It was impossible! And they were supposed to listen and report without laughing? But then, it was no laughing matter. The president cleared his throat, and the murmur silenced.

"As Taelon explains it, God has withdrawn His protection over our nation and, in fact, the world because humans continue to dishonor Him. He says that a common error has been made by many Christian leaders. Many have taught that the Ten Commandments, as given to the biblical Moses, are no longer in effect—that they became obsolete upon the crucifixion of our Lord. In some cases this attitude has been adopted to make life less restrictive, to allow people to do what they wished without regard to others.

"Taelon states that God is displeased with this course of action. Each of God's commandments was given to provide a better quality of life for those who people His earth. He cannot bless a nation or a world whose citizens take advantage of others, who do not respect others' property, who bear false witness, and do not honor Him on the Lord's Day. The message is that unless people everywhere are willing to change their ways, and *promptly,* our future looks very bleak indeed.

"Through Taelon, God is giving one last warning to our nation, for we stand foremost in the Western world. His day—Sunday, in honor of Christ's resurrection—is to be hallowed as a special time to honor Him. All businesses must be closed, and secular activities put aside, according to the commandment of God. To quote Taelon: 'Men and women have long accepted the blessings of God as their rightful due. Instead, these blessings are a privilege God has given because of His great mercy and love. These blessings are now being withdrawn because of the ungodly willfulness of those who people the earth. Without God's protection natural disasters increasingly plague Earth, and the results are terrible indeed. But there are greater disasters to come if we do not heed the warnings. At all costs, God must again be put in first place.'"

President Rondell put down his notes. "Keepers of the press, I am therefore proclaiming Sunday the official day of worship in America. Beginning next month, each American or foreigner harbored in this country will be required to attend a church on Sunday to worship God, regardless of other days he or she chooses to worship. We must repent as a people. All of us must do our part to avert the tragedy that is about to befall our country, and the world.

"These measures may seem extreme. Some would say that this is a violation of the separation between church and state. However, extreme circumstances demand extreme measures. Some will argue that these requirements are contrary to our laws granting freedom of religion. Yet, only by devoting ourselves to the God of heaven, as *He* asks, can we be saved from utter destruction brought on by His wrath toward a thankless people.

"It is with regret that I recognize the hardship this could

cause our Islamic and Jewish citizens, worshiping as they do on other days. It will inconvenience others, too. Yet in times of war drastic measures are sometimes needed. I am here to tell you that we now are in a time of war—*spiritual* war. I seek the cooperation of each man, woman, and child as we press toward a better tomorrow. I ask that families gather together this evening in their homes to discuss how they can rearrange their affairs so they can make God a priority, thereby helping our country to be a better place, a *safer* place to live. There is no time to waste."

President Rondell removed his glasses. "Gentlemen and ladies of the press, a hard task lies before you. It is yours to set the stage for spiritual renewal, yet to do so without promoting hysteria. Be careful, but be complete. And—God bless as you go about your difficult work."

~ ~ ~

Aaron glanced across the aisle at Buzz, whose head had flopped against the backrest, and envied his ability to sleep soundly no matter where he was. Willing himself to concentrate on what he must say to his audience that evening, Aaron reached for his laptop. Of course, they would go *Special,* but could he cover such a large, multifaceted story in the short time allotted him? He leaned back in his seat. *How shall I begin?* Going to church on Sunday?

Something uneasy from long ago pushed at the edges of his memory. What was it? Something about Grandie. *Ah, yes.* Grandie's books and her lap. That was it. Nestled in her lap he'd studied a picture of wonderful, billowy clouds so vast they'd spread across two pages of the book. Winged angels with dainty feet poking out beneath their robes hovered around the edges of the clouds and looked at the Man sitting at the center of the picture—the one wearing the crown.

Grandie had hugged him close. "Someday Jesus is going to come back to get us and take us on a big cloud like this to the most *wonderful* place." Her voice had always grown soft, yet excited, when she spoke of it. "Hard things are going to happen before then. We need to study the Bible and learn to trust Jesus so we'll be ready to go through that time."

When he'd asked Grandie what hard things she was talking about, she'd sighed and kissed his cheek. "Oh, things like being told that we must worship on the wrong day, and getting in trouble if we don't." Then she'd changed the subject, insisting only that they both needed to learn to love Jesus more, and that He would take care of the rest.

Restless, Aaron set his laptop aside and got up to stretch. His stomach felt like it was eating itself, and he was out of antacids. More uneasy than he'd felt for a long while, he focused on the problem of presenting mandatory Sunday worship as a rational and good thing.

Then for an instant he let himself slump against the wall. *This, then, is what Grandie was talking about. The dear old woman had been right!*

CHAPTER 19

It was like a nightmare that spun on forever, this dreadful aftermath of Dusty's being nabbed with a stash of drugs. Nick stared into the boy's deep-set eyes, so like his own but now hostile. "Son, you *must* cooperate with the police and Mr. Jones. Possession of that stuff was bad enough, but protecting pushers doesn't make good sense."

Dusty glared, fists flexing. His lips twisted into a cynical smile as his glance bounced between Pemberton Jones, the cop, and Marj. Rigid, he turned away from Nick.

"What would *you* know about good sense, Dad? You've never had much of that."

Nick held his tongue. When he spoke, his voice was even. "I've made my share of mistakes, but we're not talking about me now."

"Well, maybe we should!" Dusty spat, spinning around. "You don't know so all-fired much, y'know. Still you're always trying to tell me what I should do. What about you? You screwed things up with my *real* mom and then buried yourself in that grease pit you're so proud of, and then you brought *her* in—" He jerked his head toward Marj. "Now you're going broke 'cause you're a fanatic about Sab—*Saturday!* You wimped out and spent a week in jail for something you'da fought if you were man enough. But no! You have your nose in the Bible all the time and you keep praying to a God that doesn't even care what happens to you." He slammed his fist into his hand. "And then you sit there and try to tell me to turn in guys that are guilty of nothing? You want me to snivel and get all religious? To talk to this—this *cardboard lawyer* you hired for me? No thanks."

Marj's icy hand slid down Nick's arm. *"Please,* Dusty. We just want to help."

Dusty leapt from his chair and sent it flying backward. Livid, he glared at Marj for a long moment before flicking an obscene gesture toward the three of them, then turning his back.

"I'm done here," he growled as he stormed toward the door.

Devastated, Nick sagged in his chair. The boy was right. He had made a mess of his life. He probably *should* have done something more about Shannon, and he *should* have hired a lawyer to fight his bout with the law. That week in the city jail last December had been both horrible, yet good. The horrible part had been knowing Marj and the kids were out there worrying about him, wondering what was going to happen next. The good part was that he'd met Tong Wu, his pint-sized cellmate, who was in on a shoplifting charge. In their three days together the man had learned about and accepted Jesus because he was so curious about why Nick read "that black book" so much. Now, if he hadn't been in the jail to *tell* him . . .

After Tong had been released, Nick had had enough solitary hours to sort out his feelings about Shannon and the way he had let her memory intrude on his life. Though they seldom had contact, he'd allowed memories of her to infiltrate his thoughts and, if the whole truth were to be told, to influence his actions. That had hardly been fair to Marj. And it had made him less effective with Dusty, of that he was uncomfortably sure. No wonder the boy saw him as ineffectual. All this time Shannon's last words as she had stepped out of his life had clung to him, uncomfortable as burrs at the end of a long, dry, summer. Now he asked the Lord to help him see things as they really were, to stop letting whatever Shannon might think interfere with his feelings about himself. She would always matter to him in a painful, sad, way—that happened when you gave your whole heart to someone, and then the relationship crumbled. But what she had thought so long ago should have no bearing on his life now. It was what God thought of him that should matter. And he was doing everything he humanly could to stay near to Him.

At long last, after praying and dedicating himself anew to the Lord and His purposes, Nick had felt at peace about his ex-wife. He prayed that in times of indecision or insecurity he would no longer let her cutting words and visions of her mocking face control his life. He needed all his strength—yes, and *all* his fatherly influence—to help Dusty and the other children follow in the pathway the Lord would lead them. He sensed that the months just ahead could be rough, and he needed to stay close to God if he was going to lead his family safely through.

A hand on his shoulder pulled Nick from his reverie. "I can't do much with Dusty if he won't cooperate," Attorney Jones said. He adjusted his tie with a nervous tug. "Perhaps it would be better if I come back and try to talk to him alone, unless you've decided not to proceed."

Nick thought about finances. He'd already tried to get a loan from the bank, using his business as security, but he'd been turned down. If he could just afford a different lawyer, one Dusty might respect, might like. As it was, he was going to have to put the house up for sale just to take care of daily expenses, let alone find enough for legal fees.

Lord, help me here. I know this guy isn't the best, but he seems to be a good man and I can't just let Dusty flounder. Surely after all these years of learning about You Dusty'll come around.

Nick stood and held out his hand. "Please help us. Dusty's young and hot-headed sometimes, but I think he'll cooperate when he's had time to cool off."

Mr. Jones picked up his briefcase. "Right. And, uh, about the fee?"

Shannon's face threatened again, but Nick shoved it away. "I'll be getting it to you right away. We have an appointment with a realtor today, and I'm sure I can raise some immediate revenue from equipment in my garage. I'll be back in touch within the week."

Jones's lips stretched into a tenuous smile. "Right-o. I'll carry on until I see you next."

~ ~ ~

Nick stood on his front lawn and eyed the family possessions lined up in neat rows. He wasn't a sentimental guy, but he dreaded having strangers paw through their things, even if they were offering them at their yard sale. He thought of the garage machinery he'd just sold to Beckett's Automotive at such a loss. He'd worked so hard to get each piece, and everything else now strewn about his yard. And now it would all slip away, as though it had never been.

Forcing a smile, he turned to Paul Norawalt. "Thanks, buddy, for your help and for everything you've done for us here in the last while. Don't know what we'd have done without you."

Paul grinned, but his blue eyes, still boyish, remained somber. "It's a shame," he said, "the way things are going. But—well, Memorial Day's a great day for a sale! Wish I could hang around to help out, but I promised that I'd run the roofing crew today. Rain's got us way behind, and those folks are pushing to move in. Oh, before I forget—" He hurried to his truck and returned with a stack of plastic drop cloths. "I brought these just in case. I'll call you this evening to see if you need help loading the piano or something."

Paul, a contractor who built houses and apartment buildings, had gone beyond the call of brotherly love, and in typical kindness had graciously offered Nick the chance to manage one set of his apartments and live there, rent-free. Three small bedrooms and a bathroom were no palace, but it would be a roof over their heads until business picked up, or until the Lord came.

A car drove up the lane as Paul left. Nick sighed. Soon the place would swarm with browsers. *Lord, I hate to have everything end like this—my family stripped of their home and comforts. Help us to take it all in stride, and thanks for a friend like Paul. If we didn't have his apartment to go to . . .*

The car stopped. A woman dressed in shorts and a halter climbed out and without a glance toward Nick began sorting through the kitchen things. She spotted the cookie jar—something that had belonged to Nick's mother and held many boyhood memories for him.

"Oh, ain't this cute?" she called to her husband who sat in the car reading his newspaper. She turned it over and the lid fell off. "They want $15 for it, can you imagine?" She set it aside without replacing the lid. As she turned to the table of clothing and began to paw through the neat stacks, Nick swallowed sudden anger. With a shrug, he headed for the house.

In the bedroom he picked up his Bible, then fell to his knees. *Lord, let me take this in stride. Help me to be willing to let go of everything except You. I know You will help us—that good will be the final result, for You have said as much in Your holy Word. Help me to keep a right attitude and be thankful that we can raise some money. Help me to be a good example and a source of strength to my family. Don't let me be eaten with anger and muddy the waters with it. Help me to trust You. And Lord? Be with Dusty, please.*

He stayed on his knees for a long while, waiting for the peace that the Lord had promised would become a part of him. Then, arising, he set his Bible in its place on his nightstand and went out to face his new reality.

CHAPTER 20

June Again

The distinctive sticky-sweet odor hung heavy in the halls, drifting from patients' rooms toward the nurses' station. Brenna pulled on her latex gloves and adjusted her face mask, then picked up the disposable meds tray and headed for the Marloid's ward.

Sick apprehension climbed her throat. *Keely and Jared—what if I take Marloid's home to them?* Trust is what she needed, more trust that God would oversee what happened in their already shattered lives.

With one elbow she pushed open the swinging door and entered the grim room. Narij's dark eyes peered over her mask. "Let's start with Mr. Gundersson. He's had a bad morning."

Brenna set the tray on the table at the center of the room. Reluctantly, she glanced over the seven beds filled with patients in all stages of the disease that spread so quickly it was packing hospitals all over the country. Its telltale oozing ulcer began on the lip but did not react to cold-sore medicine. *"The one that keeps going,"* people were calling the disease.

She stepped to Mr. Gundersson's side. His eyes fastened on her, begging relief through the powerful medication she carried. No longer able to swallow pills, he'd been receiving the medicine crushed in a bit of water. Pain leaped from his eyes as he struggled to swallow it.

"Wh-where daw-tur?" he grunted, his lips oozing with sores, his eyes wild with pain.

His putrid breath pushed from his crusty-cavern mouth.

The ulcers were already traveling down his throat, making it nearly impossible for him to speak. Brenna's unwilling eyes traveled along his body. *His purple-tinged torso, deeply pocked limbs.* There was no use trying to put anything on the oozing flesh that sloughed off much as overcooked meat dropped away from a bone. No medication could be given by needle. Nothing scientists had found would help. Only the passing of a few days until . . .

Brenna pulled herself away from the gruesome thoughts. "The doctor will be here soon. Try to rest until then."

The wealthy banker sobbed, now reduced to a miserable husk of humanity. Automatically, she reached out to pat his shoulder, ready to give her bedside dose of comfort, then yanked her hand away. *Avoid touching patient.* It was an iron-clad rule. *Contact spreads the disease.*

"Mr. Gundersson, I'm sorry you're in so much pain. Our God can help you bear it. May I pray with you?"

The man's rheumy eyes widened and pinned her down. He lifted his closest hand, a seeping claw, and flailed it at her. "No! Wan' no part u' God!"

Saddened, Brenna stepped back and watched Narij try to medicate a new patient.

"There's got to be something more that we can do," her colleague said. "She spilled her medicine. Can you bring more?"

~ ~ ~

Back at home, Brenna took her third shower of the day. She scrubbed so hard she chafed her skin, then lathered again in an attempt to cleanse herself from her day with Marloid's. She wished she could wash her lungs where the odor hung, unbidden.

A dreadful thought lurked at the back of her mind. Youngsters across the nation had been orphaned by the disease, but social agencies were unable to find foster homes for them. What would happen if *she* contracted Marloid's as she cared for her patients? Who would take care of Jared and Keely? *If they went to Wally . . .*

Nearly six months it had been since she'd seen the first case. That was the day that Aaron Chandler had walked down the hallway to the end room to see the Hammond woman, then broadcast a heartstopping description all over the nation. The young police officer had gotten in trouble for letting the newscaster pass—had been dismissed from the force, if rumor was correct. Even she'd received a mild reprimand for not challenging the famous newscaster when he passed the nurses' station, though she didn't place who he was until he had already gone.

Brenna turned off the shower and toweled dry. Wally's latest letter lay open on the bathroom counter. She'd read it a dozen times, longing to find something between the lines that would tell her he was coming to his senses. Instead he wrote of his excitement over being allowed an audience with Taelon, how enlightened he had become, how convinced he was that the messenger actually *was* from God.

"I can't explain what it is like to speak with Taelon. His voice is audible, and yet you feel it inside of you before you really hear anything. Soon he's going to heal the illnesses of the faithful—God's given him the power. Remember the stories in the New Testament where Jesus healed those who had even a shred of faith in Him?"

Brenna shuddered, her mind's eye conjuring up the being that no one had been able to photograph. Yet his likeness, drawn from Max Orcott's descriptions, was displayed on opportunists' T-shirts throughout the country, proclaiming "Taelon for World Peace!"

She refused to remember Wally's next sentences—would not let them ruin another day for her. But once read, they'd wormed their way into her memory.

"I keep thinking of Jared and how much fun it would be for the little guy to be able to play ball when he gets bigger, not to have to worry about that useless hand of his—people making fun of him. I was thinking—"

Brenna recalled the times people's ill-disguised stares at that hand had left her seething. What Jared referred to as his "flipper" didn't really bother him yet. But it would. Soon he would go to school, and then the kids . . . It would be wonderful for his hand to be normal. They'd planned on reconstructive surgery when he was older. But suppose he really *could* be healed and she was resisting it because she wasn't open enough to realize truth when she saw it? Brenna pulled herself up short, crumpled the letter into a tight wad, and hurled it into the wastebasket.

"No, he *won't* take my baby to Taelon! He's nothing but the devil, and I don't understand why Wally can't see that."

Something inside her broke. There was no reason to stop her tears now. No one was home to witness her weakness, her frustration, her sorrow. Sobs tore at her chest, tears soaked her cheeks, and dripped onto the bathroom counter.

"Don't you see, Wally? Jared's hand *will* be fixed! God will take care of that when He comes."

When her tears were spent and she'd calmed herself she dressed and headed for the day-care center and her world of responsibility. She'd planned an evening picnic in the backyard with the children, but it was so very hot, unusually hot for June.

"You wouldn't think it possible, but he brings a cool freshness to the area when he appears. On the hottest day you can sit in complete comfort and listen to him speak. Honey, if only you could see, you'd believe . . ."

Wally had been gone nearly half a year, and since he'd left it seemed that everything else had gone crazy too. Besides the ongoing Marloid's rampage, seven catastrophic airplane accidents had occurred on one day, throwing Chicago's O'Hare Airport into a devastated frenzy. Then there'd been simultaneous building bombings in San Francisco and Phoenix and Washington; the freak ice storm in May that had created a two-week deep freeze of the South and Southwest, laying waste the citrus and other crops the country depended so heavily upon; the two-month truckers' strike that had crippled food deliveries throughout the nation; the fires, the floods, and another spate of tornadoes. There was the asteroid so many people were afraid was going to demolish Earth's growing power. There were the gang wars between illegal immigrants and legal immigrants, who both made social demands, and the Middle East skirmishes that threatened to escalate and bring the world into another conflagration. And now the stock market was in another spell of wild fluctuation, closing businesses, bankrupting families and throwing them onto the streets. Murder during robberies dominated the local news. No one was safe. Nowhere.

Then President Rondell's messages, follow-ups of his Sunday observance proclamation last month, had insisted that residents' lack of moral fiber and spiritual dedication was greatly to blame. Additional SIPS security would be put into place—tying economy more closely to the identification system. Even now it was getting hard to make purchases of any sort without first being scanned. Illegal immigrants and fugitives from the law were being uncovered in that way. And the people were lining up behind it, grasping for any straw of safety.

Church folk had not escaped. Worried members lingered in the foyer, endlessly discussing whether they should attend church on Sundays as well as Sabbaths, just to keep the peace. Or was it time to sell what they couldn't carry and move away from even the small towns? The doomsayers expected catastrophe with every new day, but others, wearing thin, skeptical smiles, nodded, murmuring "They've been crying wolf for years, and we're still here."

Why, just last week Pastor Stafford had said he felt things would get a lot worse before they got better, that they should just go about their business for awhile, trying not to stir things up, go along with the law as far as they could without breaking the Sabbath. Cyberspace contact with church headquarters would let them know when it was time to leave their homes.

So Brenna took her children to church and tolerated the stares that came her direction, the ill-disguised whispers of those few who were not quite comfortable having the family of one of Taelon's closest followers in their midst. It was heartbreaking to go to church longing for the strength and encouragement a church family could bring, and then go home more lonely than she had felt to begin with. But the children needed their Sabbath school. They enjoyed it and were blessed, and she wouldn't take that from them. If it weren't for hours spent with her Bible before the children awoke each day she . . .

"I could come and get him. The healing takes only a few moments . . . is painless. Think what it would mean to our son, Brenna. Can you deny him this chance?"

She clutched the steering wheel as she pulled to the curb at Sally's. *God, please help me not to let this thing rattle around in my head. I need to spend time with the kids tonight, to encourage them, to laugh with them. Help me to set aside my concerns for awhile and feel rest in You.*

She glanced up at Sally's window. Keely stood there, nose flattened against the glass. Her little face broke into its usual sunny smile when she spied Brenna, and she disappeared from the window. A moment later the front door opened and Keely, followed by Jared, hurried out.

"Mama, we made clocks," Keely squealed as Brenna scooped her up.

Jared slipped his bad hand into Brenna's. "Mommy, is Jack Belamont really the best first baseman in the world? Chuckie said so."

Baseball. Suddenly aware of Jared's misshapen little paw in her hand, she drew in her breath.

"Think about it, Brenna. It would mean so much to him."

~ ~ ~

Together they'd made tacos for supper, Keely tearing the lettuce into chunks much too large, and Jared managing to cut tomatoes into ragged little pieces.

After a game of tag in the backyard, and taking the garbage can out to the street, Brenna called the children inside.

"Baths, and then storytime."

At last they settled down in the living room, cuddled together on the loveseat. It had been a great evening, the best they'd had for a long time. Brenna inhaled the fragrance of Keely's still-damp hair and hugged her close.

"Do you guys know that I love you?"

Jared grinned. "Uh-course."

Keely twisted around and took Brenna's face between her soft little hands. "Why doesn't Daddy love us?"

Brenna's mouth went dry. "Oh, honey, h-he does."

Keely shook her head, her eyes grave. "No, Mama. He's always gone. I can't hardly remember what he looks like."

"It's true," Jared stated in his businesslike way. "Tommy said Daddy's a bad man and he's gonna get the church people kilt. How come he worships Satan?"

Brenna sucked in her breath. "Who said he does?"

His voice was a whisper. "Mrs. Morret told Tommy's mama at church. Why *does* he, Mama?"

The evening's joy vanished as she groped for words. "Daddy's just a little mixed up right now, that's all. Every morning and every night when I have my special time with God I pray for him. I know that God will help him to understand what is right and what is wrong."

"I want to pray for him too, Mama." Jared slipped off the loveseat. "We need to pray really hard because I want my daddy home again."

The children's prayers tore at her heart. *Do You hear them, God? They're so full of faith, and they know You can do anything. I forget that sometimes, but help me to remember. . . . What if Wally doesn't choose to listen to You again? Will these babies get discouraged and think You don't answer prayer? Lord, what shall I do?*

For an instant she forgot everything else in the room as her thoughts focused on her God.

Prepare them.

"Prepare them?"

Prepare them for what's ahead. The thought filled her mind.

"But they're too little to understand."

Explain.

After their amens, Brenna sat down again. "I have some things I want to tell you before you go to bed." Expectant faces turned toward her. "We're all worried about Daddy. We will always pray for him, but we must make sure of one thing."

"What, Mommy?"

"We must remember that Daddy can choose to let Jesus help him do what's right, or he can choose to have his own way, just like Adam did back in the Garden of Eden. Children"—her voice broke—"we must not stop trusting Jesus even if Daddy doesn't choose to do what God asks."

"But Mama, if Jesus says, you *hafta!*"

"No, Jared. People *choose* whether or not to obey Jesus. And some really hard times are going to come to the people who love Jesus. The Bible tells about it, and I will try to explain it to you in the next few days. Lots of people who want their own way are going to do what Satan wants them to do instead of following Jesus' way."

Jared's eyebrows squeezed together. "What do you mean, Mommy?"

They had to hear it sometime. "You see, some people made a new law. You've heard people talking about the Sunday law, haven't you?"

The children nodded.

"That law says that everybody has to be in church on Sunday. From now on."

Keely made a face. "That's silly, Mommy. Everybody knows Jesus said to go to Sabbath school on *Sabbath,* not Sunday."

"But honey, not everybody believes the way we do. Jesus woke up from the dead on a Sunday morning, and because of that lots of people decided to worship on Sunday instead of Sabbath."

Jared squirmed around to face her. "So why'd they make a rule we hafta go to Sunday church?"

"Well, some folks think that all the bad weather and plane accidents and bad diseases like Mommy's working with at the hospital are happening because Jesus is so angry with the people who won't keep Sunday. So they think He's sending trouble to everybody to punish the people who still worship on Sabbath. The Sunday people don't quite understand that God still wants us to worship Him on Sabbath and to keep all ten of His commandments. They want to make everybody go to church on Sundays because they think that then God won't be mad at us anymore and so the bad things in the world will quit happening."

Jared's eyes popped open in shock. "Is God *mad* at us?"

"Oh, no, sweetheart. That's only what some people think. They're just trying to understand why so many bad things have happened recently."

Keely squirmed. "Will they stop happening, Mommy?"

Brenna took a deep breath. *Lord, help me not to scare my babies!* "No, sweetheart," she said. "The Bible tells us that things are going to be very hard for everybody just before Jesus comes to get us. Even for the people that really do what He asks."

"For *us,* Mommy?"

"Yes. Some people will have to go find other homes. Some might have to hide in the woods. Some might even be put into jail because they do what Jesus asks them to."

Jared squared his shoulders. "I won't let them put *you* in jail, Mommy."

Brenna smiled. "I know you'll take care of me, honey. And Jesus will too. He put His promise right in the Bible—the promise that wherever we go, in the mountains or in jail or anywhere else, He will be with us. Remember how He took care of the children of Israel when they wandered on the desert?"

"Yup."

"Well, He will take care of us, too, and will help us be strong and brave if we just keep asking Him and try to do what He asks us to do."

Jared slid onto the floor. "Let's ask Him right now."

They prayed again. She would tell them more tomorrow, get them ready for what might happen. But this had been enough for tonight.

Brenna had just tucked the children into bed when the phone rang.

"I'm coming home for the weekend," Wally announced. "I'm bringing Jared back down here—just for a while, mind you."

Stunned, Brenna gripped the door frame. *No . . . No . . . No.*

"Honey?"

Brenna forced words out. "I'm here."

"I can't talk longer. A whole line of people are waiting to use the phone. The healing's next week, and they want to get folks here for that. But I'll see you in just a couple days."

He hung up, the click loud in her ear. She stood there for a long time, trying to think, not succeeding. When she looked up she saw her mother standing mere feet away, her gentle face filled with compassion.

"I know you're confused, sweetheart, but let Jared go with Wally."

Brenna sucked in her breath, choked on her own saliva. "I—"

Mama edged closer and put out her hand. "It's God's will."

A heavy wind swirled around Brenna, pounding in her ears. Then everything went black.

CHAPTER 21

Aaron mopped his forehead as he squinted across the steaming camp that had mushroomed in the desert hills south of Winnemucca, Nevada. At its eastern edge three large tents formed a triangle that faced the morning sun and the special platform said to be Taelon's touchpoint. The smallest of the three tents, the one assigned to the National Press Association, was crowded with broadcasters eager to follow up on the claim that Taelon would conduct a healing that very day.

The camp had been laid out in a triangular pattern, following Taelon's instructions, in honor of the Holy Trinity for whom he claimed to speak. Now the place was awash with hopeful infirm who camped in their pup tents, camp trailers, or motor homes. Religious nuts, they were, in Aaron's opinion, for in spite of all the talk, no one had been able to produce a picture of the mystical "being." Typically skeptical about all the hype, he smiled to himself. They were probably dealing with amateurs—excited folk who forgot to wind the film, or didn't load their cameras in the first place. People who didn't keep a cool head when the unusual happened. He'd show them, if there *was* anything to show.

Aaron eyeballed the homely board platform. "Buzz, let's lead from here, then do an eyewitness tour of the camp, and interview a few of The Chosen. That way, if we get a shoot on Taelon we can quickly wrap and be out of this oven."

Buzz positioned the tripod, then peered through the camera's eyepiece. "I'm ready."

Aaron wiped his forehead before beginning in his polished, practiced tone. "The platform is empty now. Heat presses down on the desert encampment of The Chosen who await the appearance of Taelon, the extraterrestrial being who reportedly makes contact with scientist Max Orcott of the Orcott Scientific Research Bureau based in Seattle, Washington. As primary priest of the Knights of Truth, Dr. Orcott has quickly moved to the top of the organization because of his uncanny ability to dialog with a being as yet to be captured on film."

Buzz panned to the largest of the tents. "They wait here, huddled under the white canvas that has become the focus of our nation during the past few days. Inside, beyond the raised flaps, you can see Dr. Orcott, his scientific aides, and invited members of the clergy. Tense, they watch. They discuss. They make notes on their laptops."

Aaron took a long swig of an electrolyte-enriched drink. The heat was beginning to clamp his head in a vice. He'd have to get out of it soon, or he wouldn't be worth anything when—*if* Taelon appeared. He motioned to a young man waiting off-camera. "Dr. Wallace Kenrick, professor of biology at the University of Idaho, is probably Orcott's closest colleague. Dr. Kenrick, why do you believe Taelon will appear here today?"

The young man brushed his hair aside and smiled. "One of Dr. Orcott's specialties is interpreting dreams as they relate to phenomena. Perhaps you have read his latest article on the subject in *Scientific Exposé*. About a year ago he began experiencing a repeated dream that eventually led him to this place. To date he has had 42 meetings with Taelon, mostly private, but some with others in attendance. According to what Taelon said the last time he visited, he was to come on the day of the next new moon."

"Today?"

"Yes."

"Have you personally seen Taelon?"

Kenrick's face lit up. "On a number of occasions."

"Could you describe him for us?"

Kenrick pulled at his lower lip. "He's very tall, 14, 16 feet tall. Looks human. He's well-built, and of a somber nature. As to his age—"

Just then a windless breeze ruffled Aaron's hair. Cool; refreshing. A glistening haze settled over the platform. Instantly Orcott's tent emptied as scientists and clergy rushed toward the platform. As Kenrick hurried to join them, Aaron pinned his eyes on the raised wooden deck. Then as he watched, a radiant being materialized, his hands held high for silence.

Earlier, Aaron had walked the entire encampment, looking for hidden special effects equipment, for he didn't want to play into a hoax. But now he knew the truth. It was no wonder that Kenrick had trouble describing Taelon. Though he appeared to be human, he was enormous, regal, and there was something different about him that Aaron couldn't quite place. Was it his attitude of complete control? His effervescence? Did he really *glow?* Aaron blinked. Looked again. The creature was as solid as he or Buzz. It wasn't trickery, then.

Then a vibration, unlike anything Aaron had experienced, began in his chest and quickly spread through his limbs, filling him with delicious anticipation. Before he could figure it out, a great voice boomed from the platform.

"I bring you a message from the true God," Taelon said, making the ground beneath their feet tremble.

Aaron glanced at Buzz, who stood bug-eyed, letting his camera roll as it pointed toward the ground. Aaron hissed his name, bringing him back to reality.

The voice surrounded them. "God is not pleased with how Earthfolk have turned away from Him. He wants all people to worship together, to unite to show Him honor. But Earthfolk have not listened, and have brought much evil upon themselves by their laxness. People have had only a glimpse of God's disapproval in the hurricanes, diseases, and floods that have increasingly plagued Earth in recent months."

The great being passed his hand, palm outward, before his face, then stretched it toward his audience, palm up. "The Chosen, however, are attuned to God and His wishes. In response, the Father wished to show His appreciation. His heart is saddened by the disease and sorrows Earthfolk suffer, and today has granted me the honor of bringing healing to those who have come pursuing it."

Shouts of praise filled the camp as dozens moved toward

the platform. Crippled people, young parents carrying babies, a woman with a red-tipped cane, three children bald from the effects of chemotherapy, AIDS couples, clinging to each other, and Marloid's victims—all hoped for the miracle of new health.

"You must give your hearts to the Lord of this earth; you must follow all of the commandments, you must give your God the honor that He deserves. Then, and only then, can He remove the evil forces who at this very moment pummel your world. Until all obey, there will be safety for none. It is God's will that you take heed."

Those surrounding the platform prostrated themselves on the ground. Others followed suit until only the news media stood, trying to catch the action, to report, to ply their trade.

And then Taelon grew taller, brighter. He turned his eyes toward heaven and lifted his arms. "Oh Holy One, bestow Your mercy upon Your followers, these Your Chosen, who have come to bow before You. Grant me the gift of healing, that I may be Your instrument and prove Your mighty power."

A chill surrounded Aaron, but accompanying it was a heat he'd never before experienced. Too warm and too cold, all at once—enough to make one's hair stand on end.

And then Taelon's hands began to glow. He beckoned to the three bald children, caressed them, touched them with exquisite care. The brightness grew, and Aaron blinked. When he opened his eyes again, the children's heads were no longer bald. They themselves looked larger. Stronger. Healthy.

"Praise Jesus Christ, the One God of heaven!" someone shouted.

Taelon stopped abruptly. After an uncomfortable silence, he uttered one sentence. "Praise the Lord *of Earth!*"

The hair on Aaron's arms arose, and the fluttering beneath his ribs caught his breath away. Too shaken to stand, he sank to his knees.

Except for the Marloid's cases, whose fate Taelon seemed unable to change, the healings continued every time Taelon's hands glowed. And then, finally, Kenrick, the professor, made his way onto the platform and prostrated himself for a long while. The camp went silent, waiting to hear.

"Please have mercy on my little son. An accident crippled his hand . . . but I couldn't get him here. In Bible times Jesus healed from afar if one's faith was great enough. My faith knows no limits. Please, oh *please,* heal my child."

Taelon towered over Kenrick. "I could do that if I wished. But you must be willing to obey God's requests, as well. It is His desire that the boy live here with you and that your wife be brought into belief. Only then will I heal Jared."

Taelon turned away from Kenrick to address the crowd. "Unbelievers block God's blessings from us. They do not worship Him on His holy day. It is God's will that you do whatever necessary to convince these dissenters that God's commandments must be kept." His words wrapped around Aaron.

"Give the God of this earth His reverence and honor. Put away your selfish ways. Submit, obey, and I shall come to heal again."

Aaron blinked, and Taelon was gone.

~ ~ ~

In the helicopter on their way back to the airport, Aaron asked to see the videotape Buzz had shot. Through the eyepiece he scanned it, making mental notes regarding editing they needed. There was the empty platform, the tents, his lead. And then came the voice.

"Buzz! Look at this!"

Buzz squinted into the eyepiece. "Bingo!"

The close-ups were crystal clear. Taelon had been captured on film. Now, if only they could release before other networks did!

The thud of the rotors pummeled Aaron's eardrums as he fished in his pocket for a Tums.

Suddenly agitated, he nudged the pilot. "Can't you move this thing any faster? We've got work to do."

Chapter 22

Brenna heard someone crying, a whimpering, faraway sound. She struggled to arise, gather her thoughts together. *Has Keely had another bad dream?*

The sound grew louder and somehow closer. Though her eyelids seemed glued shut, she fought through the darkness of her heavy sleep, struggling to open them, willing them to obey. But she was so *tired!*

Why was her bed so cold, so hard? Where was her blanket? The crying grew shrill in her ears, and as she listened she felt her mouth move to its rhythm. And then she realized it was she who was crying. Mustering her willpower, she forced her eyes open. She was lying on the kitchen floor.

Confused, she sat up, then sagged against the stove. And suddenly she remembered. Wally's call. And the shock of seeing her "mother" again!

Pushing aside her weakness, she scrambled to her feet and glanced around the kitchen, then hurried through the rest of the house to make sure "Mama" was not still there. Only 15 minutes earlier Wally had told her he'd be home in three days—and to have Jared ready. What should she do—could she do?

Panic's evil taste filled her mouth as she fought to keep a cool head. It was important to think clearly, especially now. It went without saying that she couldn't let Wally take Jared to the desert, but how could she stop him? He was, after all, Jared's father. Vainly she tried to pull her thoughts together, thoughts now sluggish as chilled honey. She must make some sort of plan. It was all happening so fast.

She remembered how much Wally loved surprises. He'd sounded so eager, so sure of himself, and he *could* be here by this time tomorrow.

Father, what shall I do? If we just take off, where will we go? I can't just leave my job—we need money to live on. She hurried to the bedroom for her Bible, then forced herself to sit down quietly. A moment later she began thumbing through the precious book, looking for something, anything, that would help her focus again.

Lord, I don't want to do something irrational. But I can't let Wally take Jared, can I? Please, please guide my thoughts.

She turned a few more pages, then noticed an underlined text that had given her comfort in the past. *"And thine ears shall hear a word behind thee, saying, This is the way, walk ye in it, when ye turn to the right hand, and when ye turn to the left."** She read it again and again until it burned its way into her mind. She would take the text as her promise in her time of trouble. Her part was to keep her ears attuned to God's whispers. He would be a faithful guide. She needn't know the entire way—she must only follow His leading, one day, one step, at a time.

Thank You, Lord, and please help me to stay open to Your promptings. Thank You for Jesus and His wonderful sacrifice on the cross. Help me not to disappoint Him, or You. Clear my mind. . . . Bless my children.

It was obvious they must leave soon. What was the first step?

Your job.

It was unthinkable to leave without making arrangements. She must call now, tell them something had come up and that she needed a few days off. But where could she go?

Flee to the hills.

The hills? The only person she knew who lived in the foothills was her childhood friend, Yolanda Maravstoski, who was already making quite an impression on the art world. They'd been such good friends, the kind that could communicate without talking. Maybe Landie would let her come visit for a few days. That would give her time away from danger, time to plan more adequately.

A few minutes later Brenna hung up the phone. Landie had been overjoyed. "I've been working too hard," she'd said, "and I need a few days' break too. Nothing would be more enjoyable than a visit from you. Will Wally come, too?"

Landie was still unmarried, always too busy with her "passion," as she called her work, to take time for any man.

"No. It'll just be the kids and me."

"Oh." Landie with her quick imagination had probably guessed there was trouble of some sort.

Things had not gone as well with her hospital call, and the supervisor put pressure on Brenna to give two weeks' notice. Brenna felt awful, but uncharacteristically refused to back down, for it was her children's safety, their eternal welfare, she was thinking of, and right then her feelings and the situation at the hospital must take second place. "I'm sorry for the inconvenience, but I have a family emergency and I must go. I'll be in touch."

The voice on the other end had grown cold. "As you choose, Brenna, but you must understand that I cannot guarantee your job when you return."

She'd have to cross that bridge when she came to it.

She'd been saving for church school tuition for the kids', tucking a few dollars away whenever she could. In the morning she'd go to the bank and draw down the account. She could also take a few dollars from their joint checking account. Wally still fed it to take care of the mortgage and car payments. Her thoughts became more rational, easier to sort. She sat down and made a careful list of what she should pack and the last-minute details she must care for. After spending an hour on the note she'd leave Wally so he wouldn't worry that they'd been kidnapped, she finally sank into bed, eager for a couple hours' sleep before the children awoke.

The next morning she sold her fur coat and Grandma's stamp collection at a terrible loss, then packed up, and with the kids and Rascal, Jared's dog, in the car, headed for the hospital to retrieve her check.

Excited about the "vacation," the children peered, bright-eyed, from the scant area she'd left them on the back seat. Rascal, food, clothes, sleeping bags, anything she thought she might need, had been stuffed into the car until it rode low on the road.

As Brenna neared the main intersection in town she noticed a familiar red car. Heart plummeting, she looked again. Wally *was* home early, but just happened to be looking the other direction. Automatically she swerved onto a side street, praying that he hadn't seen her.

No time to go to the hospital! Forget the check, the bank, and fueling up. Just leave.

Another block. Her hands shook. Checking the rearview mirror to make sure Wally hadn't followed, she pulled a quick left onto 95 North.

Landie had been understanding, welcoming her guests with open arms, asking no more questions after Brenna had sidestepped the first ones. Perhaps she should share more—perhaps she would. But she would wait for God's whisper.

Brenna soon relaxed in the quiet surroundings of Landie's mountain A-frame. A true artist who preferred good conversation, her friend disdained the tinsel world of television and usually turned it on only for the news or a concert. After one of their long evening's reminiscing, Brenna tried to explain her treasured faith to her friend.

Landie had smiled. "But Bren, I've heard lots about Adventists. They're good people, I know, but aren't they just . . . how can I say it nicely? Just a little off the wall?"

They had talked for hours, Brenna praying all the while. Finally Landie had stood and stretched. "I've never lied to you, my friend, and I never will. I really don't make any sense out of what you've told me. Besides, I'm too set in my ways to get involved with any religion. Be good to other people, make a contribution to society, enjoy what I can, pay my taxes. That's about all I can do, I expect. Anyhow, my bones are tired. Whadda you say we get some sleep? We can talk more tomorrow. But kiddo, I think you've got everything wrong."

~ ~ ~

Eleven days later, with breakfast over, Brenna stood looking out Landie's living room window, admiring the wooded hillside. A stream, barely visible through the pines, beckoned. Since her arrival she'd gradually relaxed, worrying less that Wally would find them. She knew he was back on the desert, for she'd seen the news report from Nevada—the heartbreaking one where Aaron Chandler had interviewed him before he cried out to Taelon about healing Jared.

However, Brenna knew she couldn't stay at Landie's forever, though her friend had been welcoming and cordial. Perhaps it was safe to go back home. She sucked in a deep breath. This afternoon while the children played at the water's edge she would decide what must be done.

The phone rang, and Landie hurried to the kitchen to answer it. "Yes? Oh . . . Sure." She glanced at Brenna. "Uh, that information is in my studio. Hang on a minute."

Landie shot Brenna a cheery smile as she hurried away. "I'll be just a sec, Bren. Then let's do something fun."

Brenna smiled, then ambled into the kitchen. She'd clean up the breakfast things while Landie was on the phone. After a quick glance into the backyard to make sure the kids weren't getting into anything, she let her thoughts drift back over the past couple of weeks.

~ ~ ~

The sound of her name yanked Brenna back to the present. She paused, dishcloth in hand, wondering why Landie had mentioned her name on the phone, for her presence was supposed to be a secret.

". . . over a week now. No, I don't know how long."

Brenna held her breath and listened.

". . . outside playing. . . . No, she didn't say anything. . . . *Court order?* No, I won't tell."

Brenna froze. *Lord, help me!* She still hadn't told Landie why she'd left home so quickly.

She simply wouldn't have understood why his dad shouldn't take Jared to the desert. It would be his right, after all.

Lord, what shall I do?

Brenna froze in the doorway as Landie hurried out of the studio. One look at Brenna's face and Landie gasped, "You heard?"

"Yes."

Several emotions crossed Landie's face in an instant, then the old look of conspiracy filled her friend's eyes. "Hey, Bren, I don't know exactly what's going on, and I promised not to tell, but, oh, you're my friend."

Brenna braced herself. "It was Wally. How'd he find me?"

"SIPS. You bought gas in Potlatch. You also phoned before you came. Phone company traced the call."

"Well, what did he say?"

"He wants the kids. He's going to take them to Taelon's meetingplace with him. He's got a court order giving him temporary custody."

Fire shot through Brenna. "But he can't have them! He'll—"

"Bren, he's *going* to get them. He was calling from town. He's on his way right now."

Brenna wanted to cry, to scream, to force her foolish world to stop hurtling down such a godless pathway.

Lord, help me!

A warm calmness sifted over her. "How long do I have?"

"Ten, 15 minutes, if you leave right away. You'll have to take the dirt road out or you'll meet him."

Brenna dashed inside and grabbed her purse. There were still a few clothes in the car, and the sleeping bags. She'd just have to trust the Lord for the rest.

She couldn't see the kids outside. Panic threatened. Had Wally already arrived? "Keely! Jared!"

"They're in the car," Landie called. "*Hurry,* Bren!"

Brenna hugged her friend, then jumped in. "Will you get in trouble?"

Though Landie grinned she looked scared. "I'll handle it. Just *go.*" She pointed. "Follow that road about five miles, then turn left onto the blacktop. That'll get you over to U.S. 200. Luck of the Irish go with you!"

Brenna eased the car down the lane, not wanting to stir up dust that Wally could follow. She glanced into her rearview mirror. In it she saw Landie, with Rascal tucked under her arm, trying to erase the tire tracks by brushing the dirt with a pine branch.

God, bless her. Help her understand. And help us too!

~ ~ ~

She'd found the blacktop and followed it to Highway 200. Quickly she turned east, toward the Montana border. Half an hour later, Keely had fallen asleep, but Jared hung over the back seat, breathing in her ear. "Mommy, why did we leave Aunt Landie's so fast? Why did we leave Rascal?"

How can I tell him I didn't want his dad to see him?

His dirt-stained face filled the rearview mirror. "It was time to go, honey."

He was quiet for a long moment. "Mommy, the speed thing says eight-oh. Does Jesus want you to drive so fast?"

Brenna gave herself a mental shake. A quick way to be found would be to get stopped for speeding.

"Thanks, Jared. I'm slowing down."

She topped a rise, then passed an oncoming police car. A couple minutes later she noticed that it now followed her. The sound of wind grew loud in her ears.

~ ~ ~

Wally glared at his wife. "What do you mean, Jared can't come? I've got a court order."

Brenna glanced at the policemen who surrounded them, then hugged the children closer. "Wally, you know what you're doing is wrong. You can't take him to the desert and let the—that *creature* touch him! Think of what you are doing."

Wally didn't waver. "I've given you every chance. You know that. And what you're saying about Taelon is way off base, but then you wouldn't know that because you were too closed-minded to find out."

He softened, but for only an instant. "Look, I'll give you your choice. You let the children come with me and I won't press kidnap charges. You can go on home. Or you can come with us and I'll drop all charges. Those are your options."

Brenna glanced from one policeman to another, seeking understanding and help, but their stolid expressions confirmed that there was none forthcoming. *What shall I do, Lord?* She couldn't let the children go to Taelon's encampment without her, but wise counsel and good sense told her to stay away from places like that; never purposely put yourself where you could be deceived. Still, if she went she could try to keep their minds on Jesus, distract them from the delusion.

"Wally, let me go home. I'll take Jared to the doctor again.

We'll get his hand fixed."

Wally's eyes narrowed. "Only *two* choices."

The world was closing in on her. Wally reached for Jared's good hand. "Come on, buddy."

The sound of a thousand winds filled Brenna's head as she stooped to pick up Keely. *Somehow God will provide a way for us to get away. He's promised!* On wooden legs she followed Wally to his car, then watched herself put her girl-child into the back seat. She grasped the door handle on the passenger's side of his car and without another word climbed into the front seat.

---

*Isaiah 30:21.

Chapter 23

August Again

Unsettled, Lucita listened to the heated discussion among her coworkers as they gathered around the snack room table. As usual, the topic turned to President Rondell's recent requirement that all who resided within the United States must attend Sunday services, and that SIPS scanners be placed in all places of worship to monitor compliance with the rule. Now on Mondays, the first task of the day was to run printouts that listed names of those who did not comply. So much record-keeping and watch-dogging had clogged the system, making necessary additional staff and round-the-clock shifts to handle it. Of course, new staff had to be trained, and that brought its own set of problems. Almost overnight new workstations crowded the aisles, filling the work space to overflowing. There was a continual turnover of personnel, sadly because of Marloid's and AIDS. The office remained in a state of turmoil.

It was rumored that those who habitually did not comply with the law would be heavily fined or jailed. Holding her breath each Monday, Lucita scanned the list for familiar names.

"I feel sorta sorry for the Dissenters," Henley, a data processor, announced.

Aletha, who worked at the station next to Lucita's, jumped on him. "Sorry? After the trouble they're bringing on us? Don't you listen to the news, man?"

Henley tipped his cup and tapped it on his teeth to dislodge a piece of ice. "Don't get me wrong, doll. I don't agree with what they're doing, but it's against the Constitution to force how anyone worships. That's a matter of personal choice. Besides that, think of the number of Muslims there are in the U.S. They oughta have a right to their religion."

"Yeah, but all that personal choice is literally killing us," Aletha sneered.

Henley crunched his ice. "What makes you think forcing people to go to church on Sunday would change our environmental problems?"

Aletha threw up her hands. "Where have you *been?* Surely you've heard Taelon say that if people don't turn back to God, and *now,* it's curtains for us!"

"I'm no authority, y'know, but can't the president make his own laws in times of national emergency?" asked Diedre, a petite blond with the greenest eyes Lucita had ever seen. "Even if it's against the Constitution?"

The others agreed.

Aletha's hands trembled. "And we are in a state of emergency. Taelon says that God won't divert another asteroid like He did that last one." She turned on Henley. "Our world is in a terrible fix, and here you are taking sides with weird groups of people who claim to love God but refuse to serve Him and are causing all this trouble. Give me a break."

Henley tore the rim off the foam cup and slipped it over his wrist.

Aletha's eyes turned icy. "You know what I heard? They're going to clamp down on Dissenters. First of all a fine, I guess, but then they'll be in jail. They'll probably nab sympathizers too, and I wouldn't want to be one of them."

She turned to Lucita. "Hey, I see you sittin' around reading your Bible at lunchtime almost every day. You're pretty religious. What d'you know about all those bizarre groups that attend church on other days?"

Lucita squirmed. "Well, I really *don't* know very much, but I'm learning. There's too much to tell in a short time, but if anyone wants to join me—"

Aletha's harsh laugh cut off Lucita's words. "I say put these nut cases outta their misery and the sooner the better. They're not doing themselves any good, and for sure they're not helping the rest of us."

"God is love," Henley said softly. He stood up, dropped his foam bracelet into the trash, and left the group of women, silent, staring after him. And his words just hung there.

Later, in the lunchroom, Lucita took a bite of her sandwich and then opened her Bible.

"May we join you?"

Lucita looked up, surprised. "Oh, hi, Henley—Diedre." She moved over to make room for them.

"What's that thing got to say that keeps your nose in it all the time?" Henley asked, his eyes smiling.

Stunned, Lucita stared at her colleagues. *Blessed Lord, I can't explain everything I've learned—I hardly know it myself.* She looked at her Bible, and then back at her coworkers.

"Uh, what do you want to hear about?"

Diedre leaned forward, her voice a whisper. "My old babysitter always went to church on Saturdays. I haven't thought about her in years, but I remember her saying that God had set apart the seventh day of the week in a way that made it holy." She frowned, thinking. "Yeah, she said that God had *blessed* that day. I've never thought about it since then, but what does the Bible *really* say? D'you know how to find out?"

Their earnest faces moved her. What difference did it make if she didn't have *all* the answers? She'd share what she knew. If Henley and Diedre wanted to study with her, then so be it.

So opening Sadie Bannister's Bible, she flipped to the back page and found the Sabbath texts written there. "It starts in the book of Genesis when God first created the world. . . ."

~ ~ ~

The dreadful weight Lucita had carried for the past few weeks pressed down even harder. She'd begun meeting regularly at noontime with Pastor Bannister and Josie Perez, a young woman about her age who came along with him. Lately Henley and Diedre had joined them, as eager as she for answers to their many questions. And the more Lucita read and heard, the more certain she felt that the seventh day of the week was holy and to worship on any other day was a slap in the face of God.

Over the past few days she'd been consumed by a burden

to share her new beliefs with her parents. She just *had* to do it. She had to help them understand how important it was. Yet every time she worked up enough courage to do so, something prevented it. Another thing, Papa was inflexible about the family attending Mass, but her heart was no longer in it. She went through the motions to keep peace in the family and to allow herself a little more time to study, to be *sure*. She'd undergone quite a metamorphosis—for the better, she hoped. Now she realized that the images she'd so earnestly knelt before were nothing more than plaster and paint. God, the *real* God, was in heaven. He wanted her heart, her love, her devotion. Sadie's Bible said no one but God could forgive sin, that only He was to be asked for that forgiveness. Yet the priests decided at confession time whether one would be forgiven or not. They taught that those who died with unforgiven sins must wait in Purgatory while loved ones prayed and sacrificed them into heaven. Still, with Papa's watchful eye on her she dared not falter in her outward observance toward the things which used to draw her. Kneeling before her patron saint, taking Communion—these acts stabbed her conscience. They seemed a mockery now, for those who truly wanted to follow God must have no other god before Him.

It was obvious she would have to make a decision soon. Either be "one of them" or put the new ideas behind her and devote herself to the beliefs of her childhood church and hope and pray that Taelon spoke for God and all that the news media said was true.

~ ~ ~

As the days passed, Lucita tried to ignore the ongoing snackroom conversations and concentrate on her work. It was true that people who didn't belong to Sundaykeeping churches were being marked as adversaries of the law and, therefore, threats to society. President Rondell and the leader of the worldwide church had become close cohorts, surrounded by a militia of very vocal spiritual leaders who urged religious reform, and together they had drawn up new guidelines for Sunday activities.

Within the past couple months huge rallies had been held

in many of the larger U.S. cities. Panic because of vicious weather patterns that destroyed food crops, the Marloid's epidemic, and skyrocketing crime rates led government leaders to demand that everyone obey the religious rules Taelon had led them to put in place. To disobey, it was feared, jeopardized the entire nation. The scanning system in churches was perfected. Lists of Dissenters were published in the local newspapers. And it was true that Sabbathkeepers were particularly singled out as the hard-core lawbreakers to keep an eye on. It seemed that Taelon considered worshiping on Saturday almost a greater insult than not being in church on Sunday. All in all, the whole situation left Lucita with a queasy, jumpy feeling.

Forcing such things from her thoughts, she picked up the stack of forms in her "In" basket. One by one, she began to make corrections. Middle names of a pair of twins had been transposed. A juvenile's sentence had been appealed and dropped. Suddenly she stared at the next card, unable to believe what she saw. It held the name of Bill Ferandell, the head elder at Pastor Bannister's church. With numb fingers she moved the curser to the "Religion" field. *SDA*, it said. He was so nice. He'd seemed so devoted to the church that sat atop the long cement stairway. She'd sat in the church's fellowship room and eaten Saturday lunch with him and his family. He'd even given her a spare copy of a book called *Desire of Ages*. A band of ice tightened around her ankles as she watched the name of a Sundaykeeping denomination pop up on the screen. Bill Ferandell had changed his allegiance.

Later, when Lucita, Henley, and Diedre walked into the restaurant, Pastor Bannister and Josie had already ordered and were waiting at their usual table.

"I've got bad news, I'm afraid," the pastor said. "They're confiscating our church. Actually, they're taking over all the houses of worship that meet on any day but the first of the week. Going to use them for Lord's Day congregations instead." His shoulders sagged. "That means we can't use it anymore."

Diedre had been attending services. "Why can't we just go to church on Sunday, and then worship on Saturday, too?"

His sad smile reached out to them. "That's what some of our members are doing, but do you know, the Bible says that we should honor God's *Sabbath* day. It's a covenant, a sign between God and us. When we pretend to hallow Sunday I believe that we are acting a lie. We need to hold God's Sabbath in highest esteem before others."

Henley leaned forward. "But Pastor, what if they really do carry out these threats to arrest people who don't obey the Sunday law?"

The old man tugged on his lower lip. "Well, then that's how it will have to be. I must be true to my convictions."

"What about you? If you don't have your church work, what will you do?"

Pastor Bannister grew pensive. "I've got a couple of acres out in the countryside, but anyone could find me there. Anyhow, I'd worry about our parishioners and the others who are just learning, like you. Many of our families are leaving the city, but some won't be able to. I'd hate to leave them behind."

Lucita studied the big man, his face so kind, yet creased with care. "I don't get it. Why is everyone moving to the country? Where is 'the country' anyway?"

It was as though a great eraser brushed across his face, removing the worry that had been so evident a moment before. "Why child, I guess I shouldn't feel so sad. After all, this has been foretold in the Bible—it's a sign of the end. You see, Jesus is soon coming for those who are faithful to Him. Satan knows his time is short, and that makes him even more angry. He doesn't want anyone to be saved and will do anything to prevent it. He'll cause terrible things before Christ's coming. The Bible tells us that right before the end there'll be a strict law that all must worship on a substitute day or lose their freedom and suffer persecution. In order to survive, many will go to smaller places to distance themselves from prosecution by the law—to put it off for a while longer, that is."

"You said *'survive'?"*

"Ah, yes. It's too bad you're having to learn this in one short study, but time isn't cooperating very well now, I'm afraid. You see, Bible prophecy predicted what's happening right now. The tight surveillance possibilities SIPS has brought about, and this mandatory Sunday worship issue." He shook his head. "Mark my words—because the Bible predicts it—before this is over those who stay true to God will be sentenced to death. And to escape persecution and death, many will run and hide."

It sounded so outrageous Lucita couldn't hold back. "That can't be, Pastor, not in *America!*"

He looked at her, fatherly concern plain on his dark face. "Lucita, I don't know how many more times we'll manage to meet, but I'd like to feel sure that you really understand what's about to happen." He dug in his Bible case and pulled out some papers. "Sorry this is so rumpled, but it's still readable. All the Bible texts that explain what is about to happen are listed there. Read them in the order they are given. There are other texts that you can search out for yourself, of course, but these are the main ones.

"Here, too, are some papers that help explain the texts. Listen, I'm going to keep on studying with you—and these dear friends of yours—just as we've been doing. But if something should happen—" He glanced at Josie. "If something should happen, just know that I'll be praying for you. I know God is working in your hearts and He'll help you understand completely."

Josie slipped her arm around Lucita. "And I've come to say goodbye, my friend. Daddy's decided it's time for us to go, and tomorrow we're leaving, just like that. Keep studying—stay true. I'll miss you."

Everything was happening too fast! Lucita tried to swallow the lump that was caught in her throat. She had lived for being with these dear people and studying with them. They had been so patient with all her picky questions.

"B-but where are you going to go?"

Something flickered through Josie's eyes. "Daddy said not to tell anyone, but I know I can trust you." She pressed an envelope into Lucita's hand. "Read this later when you have time. If *you* ever need a place to go, well, there'll always be room for you."

The noon hour was nearly gone. Lucita tucked her Bible and the note from Josie into her purse, as Pastor Bannister began putting his things away, his sandwich untouched. "Just keep the faith, my friends." His voice sounded ready to break as he turned to Lucita. "I'll be in touch as I'm able, but I just want you to know that Sadie—"

A vicelike hand grasped Lucita's shoulder, and she looked

up to see Papa. His eyes bore into hers, then fastened on Pastor Bannister.

"Who are you?"

"I'm Washington Bannister." Pastor Bannister arose and offered his hand, but Papa ignored it.

Papa glanced at the open Bible. "So it is *you* who has given Lucita such strange ideas?"

He pulled Lucita to her feet. "Don't let this happen again, Bannister." His hand grew tighter as he guided Lucita away from the table. "And *you* will turn in your resignation at work this very afternoon. It's no longer safe to let you out of my sight!"

~ ~ ~

On the way back to her desk Lucita's thoughts whirled. She dared not defy Papa's command, so she must give notice today. What would they require, two weeks? And then under Papa's and Mama's constant surveillance. No more freedom to meet the pastor for study. *Help me, Father. I need to make sure I understand Your truth correctly. There's not much more time to learn, for I'll not be able to take my Bible home.*

Discouragement nearly overwhelmed her. She'd seen the last of Pastor Bannister, her lifeline to God. What if he was caught? What would they do to him? He was so old. Determination welled up in her. There was one thing she needed to do before she spoke to her supervisor and it had better be now, before they knew she was going.

A few minutes later Lucita ran a search for Bannister's file. When the record popped onto the monitor, she cursored down to "Property." With a quick touch to the delete key all record of Pastor Bannister's country place vanished. Whether this business about death penalties and all that stuff was true or not, at least if he went there, he'd be safe.

She glanced across the room and found Henley watching her. With a sympathetic shrug he resumed his work. *What will happen to him—to the others? I should have told them before.*

It was too much to think of right then. Instead, she cleared the screen, then went to find Melanie.

~ ~ ~

When she got home that evening, Papa was waiting for her. "You trouble this family, Lucita. You once brought us joy, but you've disobeyed again. You've let the heretics poison your mind."

"But they aren't heretics. Let me explain everything I've learned. You've often told me that things aren't always as they first seem. You taught me that I must be true to what I know is right so I'd be a credit to our family and God."

"Sí."

She swallowed hard. "I've tried to do that when young men have whispered things in my ear, and when others were doing things that would make the Holy Mother blush. Now I am asking *you* to listen to what I have to say without stopping me. And without making up your mind before you've heard it all. *Please,* Papa! Then I will do the same—hear everything you have to say."

Papa stood in the kitchen doorway for a long while, anger and uncertainty taking turns on his face. Finally he turned to Mama. "I have tried to keep heresy out of our home. And now I am to sit here and listen to it?"

Mama laid her hand on Papa's arm. "I am only a woman, *mi amo,* and no match for you. But perhaps Lucita is right. How can you know the lies she's been told unless you first hear them all?" Tears filled her eyes as she looked at Lucita, then turned back to Papa. "You could ask Father Matthew to come over. Together you can help her. That makes good sense, no?"

Papa threw up his hands. "All right, then. I will call Father Matthew. We will eat the good supper you have made, and then we will *all* sit down together and listen to her." He crossed himself. *"Madre mía,* in my very home this happens."

Later, as Lucita explained the things she had learned, she prayed they would understand as she did. Mama dabbed at her eyes while Papa sat, stiff as a rod, as though trying to shield off something evil. But there was something deep and formidable in Father Matthew's eyes that made her shudder. Still, she continued. Should she share the prophecies Pastor Bannister had explained that very day about the end and persecution? Perhaps not. She must study them more over the two precious weeks left to her. From work she could phone the pastor for help.

She longed for the comfort of Sadie's Bible as she tried to remember where all the important texts were, but instead was forced to use Papa's. She looked up the fourth commandment. "See, right here it says to worship God on the *seventh* day."

Lucita's sister, Teresa, came in from work just as she was explaining how useless it was to pray to saints when those people were no longer alive. Teresa crossed herself and let out a cry of dismay.

Papa raised both hands. "Enough! We'll hear no more. It's one thing to hear about right days and wrong days and turning backs on perfectly good food we have been eating for years. But you have mocked God by saying the saints He has set to watch over us are a trick of the devil himself! *Heresy!* You have been fooled. Why, those saints have carried my prayers to Our Good Lord for more years than you have breathed, and the Holy Mother has blessed us!" Furious, he sucked in his breath. "What do you say, Father?"

Father Matthew bristled. "The Dissenters have poisoned her mind. You must work quickly, my son, not to lose her."

Papa turned to Lucita. "Go to your room—now!" He fought for control of his voice. "I'll see you in the morning."

Shaken, yet glad for the few moments of privacy the family discussion would allow, Lucita dropped to her knees beside her bed. Papa's voice grew loud, then quieter. Why had she shut the door? This was all about her! She had a right to know what was being said. She arose and opened the door a crack.

Now Papa was talking on the phone. But it hadn't rung.

"Tomorrow about 10:00? She'll be ready."

The receiver clattered into its cradle. "It's arranged then." Papa's voice was barely audible. "The deprogrammer has worked with Dissenters before. With any luck Lucita should be herself again within a week." Papa's heavy footsteps thudded across the room. "You know, after they take her to the safe house we won't have contact with her until they finish."

She could hear Mama crying, and Teresa said something. Father Matthew answered. "There are women there, too. I know these people, and they will help her. When Lucita returns home she'll be as she was before, and I will talk with her—help her. I will bless and cleanse your house. Until then, though, I must do what I can to put a stop to this Mr. Bannister's work."

Papa's voice took over again after Father Matthew left. "Teresa, she's not to know what's planned. Mind you don't say a word. Now, let's work it all out."

Lucita's mind raced. Deprogrammers? She must get away, and quickly. But how? A moment later she slipped her nightgown on over her clothes and found her old book bag, into which she stuffed her hairbrush, wallet, and a change of underwear. Quickly stowing them beneath the bed, she turned off the light and slid between the covers, her heart knocking against her ribs.

Chapter 24

The first few Sundays after the church-attendance law had become effective had gone well for Nick and his family. After lunch they all—with the exception of Dusty—joined the Norawalts and went from one neighbor's home to another giving away special chapters of *The Desire of Ages,* a book on the life of Christ.

Each of them felt a burden for their neighbors. The closer they grew to God, the more unthinkable it became to keep His love to themselves. A sense of expectancy went with them. *Christ is coming! There is no better news than this for our aging, dying world.* "After all," Paul reasoned to the others, "we can't pinpoint the time when probation has closed.* It's possible that reading these beautiful stories of Christ's love will draw some of them to Him."

After careful deliberation they'd all agreed that it wouldn't be right for them to attend church on Sunday. Perhaps other Sabbathkeepers would see it differently and worship on both days for a while. But they didn't want to water down their witness as believers who kept God's true day of rest. Instead, they decided, they'd devote Sunday to soul-winning and doing things together as a family.

Tyler Norawalt, a serious but pleasant earliteen, had taken Gillie under his wing as they went door-to-door visiting their neighbors. And on this day the boys met the Porters, who seemed interested and friendly. They'd taken Nick and Marj back to see them.

Nick smiled to himself as he settled down to watch the

news that evening. Usually, when put on the spot for quick answers, his mind went blank and he ended up feeling like a fool. But God's commission was to *spread* the gospel, and then let the Holy Spirit do the work, and so he'd taken God at His word. He'd chosen to have faith that God would give him the right words at the right time. To his joy he'd found that in spite of his getting tongue-tied a few times, the Porter family were truly interested and had asked to begin studies the next evening. It had been a good day.

Nick clicked the remote, and Aaron Chandler appeared with his unique brand of news and commentary.

". . . churches reported problems with parking space for all the worshipers today. . . . Is this really a national turning of hearts to God, or just compliance with the new law? Does God accept a form of worship, or does He require 'the real thing'? Will swift retribution come to those who refused to worship today? Answers to these questions remain to be seen."

Chandler disappeared and a psychic replaced him. "Doom awaits those who did not pay homage to God today by attending the church of their choice . . ."

Nick switched the TV off, refusing to listen to the psychics. It was then he noticed a rumble which grew steadily louder. A moment later a force slammed against the front wall, rattling the windows and knocking down the heirloom picture he'd rescued from the yard sale. Overhead, greenish clouds sucked together. Debris from the street lifted and raced ahead of the wind. Nick watched the group mailboxes at the curb lean precariously, then collapse. A white finger reached from the clouds to the earth.

"Tornado!" he screamed. "Get in the bathroom!"

A moment later Marj and Elissa were sheltered beneath him as he prayed aloud for the Lord's protection.

Elissa struggled to free herself. "Gillie!"

Nick held her down. "He's at Norawalts!"

The rumble became a living thing. They were inside a drum, a thousand sticks pounding harder and faster. His eardrums felt like tissue paper, rattling, creaking. Wincing from the pain, he tried to cover his women.

The psychic said something would happen. And Dusty was out there.

Then everything went silent. Nick held his breath, waiting for the next onslaught. When it didn't come, he headed for the living room.

Corkscrew trees, roofless houses, and overturned cars littered their street. Already people scrambled frantically about, calling for missing loved ones. Nick glanced around the room. Only the one picture dislodged; no other damage. It seemed a miracle.

The tornado was over. Shaken, he returned to the bathroom, "I've gotta go help out there. You two go see if you can find Gillie."

~ ~ ~

By Monday night there were still residents of Kramerville listed as missing. But Nick and his family praised God that none of their church members had been injured. The tornado had cut a wide swath through several residential areas, including their old house, and a major part of the business district. Rescue crews still worked around the clock, pulling the injured and dead from the rubble.

Nick borrowed Gillie's Walkman so he could listen to news bulletins as he helped rescue injured people from a collapsed church. But nothing could distract his mind from Dusty. Where could his son be? Injured somewhere? Unable to get home? Heart heavy, he labored on, praying silently.

At last Nick paused to rest a few minutes and to listen to a special bulletin. It was beyond comprehension. Almost simultaneously with the tornado that raged through Kramerville, 71 other tornados had scourged the nation the evening before. Towns had been demolished as though knocked aside by the hand of a willful child. Even two commercial jetliners had been caught in the maze of swirling clouds and flung to the ground. When Hoover Dam collapsed, the source of power for a large section of the Southwest was eradicated, and record temperatures aggravated the situation. The nation was in distress, with tens of thousands of people unaccounted for.

The voice of the reporter continued. "Taelon appeared to Max Orcott shortly after the tornadoes ended to announce that the nationwide tragedy that struck yesterday was the result of God's anger toward those who refused to observe the Lord's day and worship Him. SIPS reports are not yet complete, but it is estimated that thousands of individuals ignored President Rondell's security measures for this country. It is past time to take this law seriously. The president has stressed that he will not allow a relative handful of people to jeopardize the safety of the nation.

"Taelon is quoted to have said that 'the carelessness and indifference of a few has brought God's displeasure upon the millions.'

"Riots have broken out in major cities, demonstrating against people groups who flaunt God's commandments."

~ ~ ~

On the Thursday after the tornado, Nick set aside the Bible story he'd been reading to Gillie and went to answer the doorbell. Two young men, wearing sheriff badges, faced him.

"Nicholas Wheatley?"

"Yes."

"We're serving notice, sir."

"What?"

"You were not in church last Sunday. You *do* know the law?"

Adrenaline shot through him. "Yes."

"Were you ill?"

"No. I keep Sab—Saturday. The day God set aside for us. The *Bible* Sabbath, you know."

The officer sighed. "The law does not prohibit worship on Saturday, but it *does* require church attendance on Sundays."

The shorter deputy spoke up. "Y'know, I can't understand you guys. Supposed to be such smart people, *healers* with all your doctors and hospitals. You say you serve God but then you slap Him in the face by breaking laws and thumbing your noses at His holy day."

"We—"

"Save it. We're taking you down to the station. You can tell them." He pulled a pair of handcuffs from his pocket. "I've gotta arrest you. You have the right to . . ."

Nick's stomach lurched. Marj and Elissa were shopping—Gillie had stayed behind. He glanced at the boy's panic-stricken face.

"You leave my dad alone!" Gillie shrieked, hurling himself across the room. Protective, he bear-hugged his father.

The deputies pried Gillie away. "Sorry, buddy." The man's tone was gentle. He seemed genuinely regretful. But then he turned toward Nick. "It's too bad that a dad's sins affect his kids, but that's how it goes. Now if he *really* cared what happened to you—"

Nick interrupted. "Could I have a word with my son before you take me?" He slipped his arm around the boy. "Remember what we talked about?"

As though supported by kind hands, Gillie squared his thin shoulders. Struggling with his tears, he stared at the officers who held his dad. Then his expression changed to one of new understanding.

"I remember." He brushed the tears from his cheeks and nodded. "I'll take care of stuff, Dad. Don't you worry."

The officers shoved Nick down the sidewalk and stuffed him into the squad car. When he glanced back, Gillie stood in the doorway with his hand lifted in a silent wave. Nick swallowed hard. His family had been through so much, and now he wouldn't be there to look after them. *God help us all.*

The squad car peeled away from the curb and opened its shrill throat, its siren screaming as though warning the bystanders that it held public enemy number one.

~ ~ ~

The pungent odor of vomit filled the city jail's holding tank, turning Nick's stomach. How long had he stood there, hands cuffed behind his back, waiting for Sergeant Clay to question him? Three hours—four? Nick eyed the others—a couple drunks, a punk kid with a filthy mouth, a shifty-eyed but well-dressed man who held himself aloof from them all. Yet, in spite of their differences, they had one thing in common—fear.

His thoughts trailed to Marj and their contingency plans

should the law actually prosecute any of them. There was Dad's old place in Minnesota, remote, humble, but with space for a garden and the spring for water. Their plan had sounded sensible. But they'd not counted on being separated when the time came. Since Dusty's arrest for possession of drugs, nothing had worked the way they'd planned. Funds depleted, and left with only the barest of necessities, they were not as mobile as before. But at least Dusty had returned; he didn't know where from. Perhaps he'd help the family.

Nick had the gut feeling that this was it, that he wouldn't get away from this one. Things were tightening down, and it was hard enough for those who didn't have Mayor Jordon for an enemy.

But Marj hadn't been in church either. Maybe they'd gone back to pick her up and left the children alone, or maybe forced them into a foster home. His heart lurched. He just couldn't let that happen.

Lord, be with my family.

Finally, a guard, fuzzy-faced and full of importance, ushered him into the questioning room. The place smelled of stale smoke and nervous sweat, yet Nick gratefully dropped onto the chair that the boy shoved toward him.

Sergeant Clay sat at his desk.

"So we meet again. Between you and your boy, the Wheatley name is getting rather common around here." He wiped his nose on the back of his hand. "If I had to pick between a drug runner and a Dissenter, I'd choose the runner any time," Clay smirked. "At least you can understand what they're doing."

The interrogation had been one-sided, leaving him little opportunity to explain his position. He'd clearly broken the law, and willfully, at that.

In the ID room they scanned and fingerprinted him, took his wallet and watch, and then keyed his arrest information into SIPS. Then, before being locked up, he was allowed to dial Marj.

"Call Paul, honey," he'd whispered. "And remember what we talked about before. It's time."

Crying, she started to ask a question, but he stopped her, afraid that the call might be monitored. "Marj, please don't say anything more. And don't come down here. I'm going to be locked up, and there's nothing anyone can do. They're going to take this all the way." He searched for words to guide her without giving their secret away.

"Remember what we discussed!" *Lord, help her understand that I mean for them to go to Minnesota!*

His time was up. He barely had time to stammer a last "I love you" before the guard snatched the receiver.

"C'mon, Wheatley, let's go."

~ ~ ~

The next afternoon, handcuffed and without opportunity to bathe or shave, he stood before Judge Rochetti and Mayor Jordon.

"You can save yourself a lot of trouble, Wheatley, if you just give up this Saturday nonsense," the judge said. "Look, we have to enforce the law, so you have no choice. And you've got a wife and kids to care for. Your shop's sitting there untouched, and business will be good again now since Beckett's was demolished."

"Just say the word," Mayor Jordon added condescendingly. "I can help you put things back together. We need a mechanic just now."

How good it would be to go home for Sabbath—to leave the wretched jail. Maybe his decision to dig in his heels about Sunday had been wrong, was bringing trouble to his family earlier than necessary. Maybe he should just go along with things for a little while, worship on *both* days, hold back the winds of strife that the Bible talked about. That would give them time to lay new plans.

Blessed are they which are persecuted for righteousness' sake: for theirs is the kingdom of heaven.†

Nick sucked in his breath, clenched his fists against his longing to go home. "I'd like that, your honor, but I can't ignore God's commandments."

Judge Rochetti laughed. "Let's make sure I have this right. You're putting your wife and family at jeopardy because you refuse to attend church on Sunday?"

It sounded awful. It sounded ridiculous. "I don't think—"

"Obviously. Don't you *care* what happens to them?"

Memories of Gillie standing alone haunted him. And he could still hear Marj's sobs. His SIPS record, tied to hers, would already have frozen their slim bank account, would warn of a problem. He tried to think how much money was in the drawer at home. How far could Marj and the kids get? Was Dusty with them?

Shannon's face returned—taunting, mocking, her *loser* routine loud in his ears.

Lord, I thank You for Your help.

He straightened his shoulders. "I must stand firm, sir, because I *do* care what happens to them."

The judge shrugged. "Not much left but to let things take their course, then." He beckoned the guard. "Put Wheatley away. Alone, and no visitors."

~ ~ ~

Nick looked at the little square window high in the moldy cement wall, thankful for the tiny patch of sky he could see. Relieved that the handcuffs had been removed, he lay back on his plywood cot, the one brown blanket folded beneath him for cushioning. No longer were jails places of even marginal comfort, for in recent years an outcry from the public about using tax dollars for prisoners had stripped the lockups of anything more than bare necessities for survival.

How many days had passed? When would his trial be? With crime escalating, and arrests at an all-time high, it might be months. Sergeant Clay had said that his would be a full-blown court trial because he was the first Dissenter to be apprehended in Indiana. Confined with muscles getting flaccid, he wondered what he could say to convince the jury that his spiritual reasoning was sound.

But that wasn't his worst worry. It was hard with no news of Marj and the kids. He felt disconnected, not knowing what had happened to them, or what went on in the outside world, for that matter. But when you were considered a felon . . .

He knew a few things, of course. It had rained constantly since he'd been arrested. He'd overheard a guard say that flooding was at an all-time record, that most crops in the Midwest had been drowned out. Naturally, that caused food shortages. Dissenters were being blamed, so SIPS had tightened its hold upon purchases to provide first for law-abiding citizens. Then there was something about another asteroid.

He whispered to the only company he had. "Dear Father, I know I shouldn't worry, that I can trust You to take care of everything. But I'm used to being able to *do* something. Please be with Marj and the kids, wherever they are. And help me to stay true to You, no matter how hard things might get. I don't know what to say in that courtroom. You know how I stumble all over my words when I'm up front. What if I make You look foolish?"

Shannon's face threatened. He pushed it away.

He thought back over the past months. He'd been so annoyed about how everything had gone—about selling his house and Dusty's obvious disdain of everything he knew was right. Had he been the Christian father example he should have been during that time? He'd been pretty angry sometimes, had to bite his tongue to hold back words he'd heard a lot but never used. Perhaps he hadn't given the unconditional love he should have. But then, what *was* love? Maybe he was only fooling himself that he was close to God, that he loved Him. Nick was smart enough to know that people told themselves all sorts of things to make themselves look good in their own eyes. Could it be that his motives for obeying the Sabbath commandment were only for what *he* could get out of it, not because of true devotion for his Saviour? It was so hard to know.

The nights and days got all mixed up, agony of soul his constant companion, terrible memories pelting him. *What if I'd been different? Did I remember to apologize to Gillie that time I snapped at him? What about all those lies I told Mom when I sneaked off with the boys? Those words rolled off my lips so easily! Did I ever confess to Mom?* He thought not. Shannon's face reappeared. *Did I do all I could for her? We said some ugly things a few times. Maybe she would have been different if I'd been different . . . I've been pretty proud of my business. Was it wrongful pride? And all those times I could have spent in worship and soul-winning but did other things instead. Have I made things right with my Saviour? Or have I hurt Him too much?* Nothing was worthwhile if he'd turned Jesus away.

Cold and abandoned, sorry tears poured down his cheeks.

Lord, can You save someone like me?

Something outside rumbled and his bed lurched then the young guard stood at the door. His frightened eyes peered through the bars. "We gotta earthquake!" His mouth formed a circle as he stood there. Nick couldn't help noticing the scabby yellow place in the corner where his lips joined.

~ ~ ~

A few days later the clatter of keys pulled Nick from his half sleep. A new guard poked his head in. "Come with me."

Nick drug his hand across his stubbly chin. "Where's the old guard?"

The new guard avoided his eyes. "Marloid's. Now come on."

Marj? He looked at his rumpled orange jumpsuit. Though he'd done his best to stay clean, it had been impossible. He sighed and rolled off the cot. Wordlessly the guard led him down the corridor between the crowded cells. Envious eyes that held no hope watched as he left the dank basement.

Pemberton Jones awaited him in a small room off the main area of the police station. He waved the guard away and motioned Nick to a chair. Jones's lips grimaced into a half smile. "So we meet again."

The myopic lawyer eyed him for a moment, cleared his throat, and adjusted his thick glasses. "You really must do something about your appearance, Mr. Wheatley. Didn't your wife bring some fresh clothes for your trial?"

"Trial?" Nick stared at the man.

Jones's mouth sagged. "You didn't know you're on today?"

Nick stiffened. "No. What day is this?"

"It's Monday, man. You've been here almost two weeks. Your trial's in an hour. Court just appointed me as defense."

There was nothing to say. Nick smoothed his pants, now even more aware of his musty odor and appearance.

Jones cursed as he reached for the phone. "You can't go in there looking like that. What's your phone number?"

Nick told him. Breathless, he pressed his hands against his knees to keep them from trembling. Would anyone answer the call?

A moment later Jones hung up. "Line's been disconnected." *So they got away!*

The attorney glanced at his watch. "Well, we better use this hour to talk. Your trial begins at 2:00." He hauled himself out of the chair and stepped to the door. "Sergeant? Someone's gotta get some other things for Wheatley to wear. And he'll need a shower. Fix us up, will you?"

He closed the door and settled into his chair again. Folding his hands together, he pressed his index fingers into his lips, deep in thought. Finally his eyes brightened. "You are here because you did not attend church on the Sunday in question."

"Yes."

"Can you come up with some reason you couldn't attend—kids sick, a fight with the wife? Car wouldn't start?"

"No."

"Man, surely you can think of something." He took his pen from his pocket and removed its top. "Why didn't you go?"

"I-I chose not to. I honor the Bible Sabbath."

"But *why?*"

Nick tilted his head, sorting through his thoughts, before he spoke. "Because God set aside the seventh day of the week as the one day in seven that He made holy. Exodus 20:8-11 tells us that God *sanctified* the seventh day." He cupped his hands as if holding a gift. "It's the day I meet with God, as He's asked me to do."

Jones's expression changed to one of pity. "But that's the *Jewish* Sabbath. Everyone knows that it was changed at the cross."

Suddenly Nick's mind went blank. *God, help me. I need to get out and help Marj with the kids. I can't stumble over my tongue now.*

"Uh, well we believe—" It was no use.

Pemberton Jones shook his head. "How can I give you any defense if you can't even explain what it is you believe?" He stuffed his pen into his pocket and stepped to the door. "Guard, take Wheatley to the showers. Trial's in a half hour."

He eyed Nick again. "Try to clean up, will you? I'm afraid it's the only hope you have."

---

*Revelation 22:11.

†Matthew 5:10.

Chapter 25

Lucita eyed the green numbers on her bedside clock. The little dots between them blinked back at her, counting off the seconds she had left. With each moment her tenseness doubled, the unknowns in her immediate future a frightening specter. What would happen to her family if she followed her plan? Would she ever see them again? Silent tears dribbled onto her pillow. Her family meant so much to her, but then, so did God and doing what He asked of her. Maybe if she went now, when Papa settled down a little she could come home again and explain the wonderful truth she had learned.

Heavyhearted, she glanced at Teresa, who had slipped in as quietly as a spirit and long since fallen asleep. They'd always been close, but since Lucita began working at SIPS there had been little opportunity to do things together. *Blessed Father, what will become of her?*

Pushing away her desire to confide in Teresa, Lucita prayed for her. Then she looked back at the clock, rehearsing in her mind each move she must make. At last the numbers blinked "2:00."

Holy Father, help me, please.

She slid from beneath the covers, then, heart pounding, removed her nightgown, pulled on her sweater, and reached beneath the bed for her bag. At the bedroom door she stopped to listen. If she made too much noise, there would be no second chance.

Papa's bedroom door was ajar as usual, and she could hear his gentle snore. She tiptoed down the hallway and through the darkened living room, her mind memorizing every detail she loved so well. Carefully, she undid the three safety locks that offered a measure of security against break-ins. Now she was trying to break out. Thankful that Papa had not yet installed an audible alarm, she eased the door open and stepped outside.

Somewhere in the cracks of the old foundation, a cricket scratched out its rhythmic melody, but so quietly did she move that it didn't falter. At the edge of the yard she stopped to check the street. Even at this hour people were out, going about their shadowy business.

Her chest tightened. It wasn't safe even for men to walk the streets alone at this time of night. Who would hear if a frightened girl should scream?

Her thoughts reached for confirmation. *Lord, is this what You want me to do?*

Fear of the deprogrammer spurred her on. With a last glance toward home, she inched up the street, her eyes sweeping the area ahead for possible danger. Two man-shaped lumps were propped against an old hotel on the block next to theirs. A woman in a thin, scanty dress stood beneath the street light on the corner and turned to watch as a car eased through the intersection. Five more blocks to the all-night grocery. Lucita hurried.

In the last year crime had mushroomed. No one was safe anymore. Home had offered the only security she'd known until she had begun to read Sadie Bannister's Bible. Tears pushed at her eyes. Sadie's Bible! Now she'd have to do without it, for she dare not return to SIPS to get the precious book. If she waited that long, Papa would find her.

For a moment she felt utterly alone. In a manner of speaking she'd turned her back on both her religion *and* her family. Mother, father, siblings—she was erasing their places in her immediate life. They would worry. Mama would be frantic, and Papa would be outraged. And the others?

Lord, is this right?

A warm feeling touched her deep inside.

Nothing is too much to give up for You, Lord. Now You will be my family.

She had just crossed Third Street when four men stepped out of a doorway in front of her.

"Guess Spike'll find out what's good for him," one laughed.

The others hooted.

Then someone spotted her.

"Hey lookie, guys." As though moved by one hand, they spread out, leaving about three feet between them. "An we was thinkin' we'd hafta go home all lonely tonight."

The memory of the last time she'd been in such a situation shot adrenaline into Lucita's veins. *Lord, help!* She sidestepped, then half turned, not sure whether to try to run home.

"Oh, we gonna play tag?"

"Nah! Cat an' wee mousie!"

They surrounded her in a heartbeat. Feet nailed to the roadway, Lucita remembered the text she'd found in Sadie's Bible. *Lord . . . shepherd . . . valley of the shadow . . . will fear no evil . . .*

Suddenly her fear vanished. She stood tall, and in the most firm way she knew she faced the talkative one. "You can't do this to me. My Father won't allow it. Now, step aside."

Mouths hanging open, they fell back as she hurried to the opposite corner. Her ears strained for the footsteps that surely would follow, but she forced herself onward. *Don't run!* Twenty steps. Thirty. Still nothing. Cautiously she glanced back. They stood where she'd left them, arms hanging loose, watching. She did not look back again.

She was leaving the safety of her home for a new kind of safety. *Lord, thank You for watching over me.*

Inside the market, she dug into her purse and found Josie's envelope. *"And if you ever need a place to go there'll always be room for you."*

She unfolded the paper. Josie's family was leaving tomorrow—no, today. *Let them still be there.* She dug change from her pocket, then dialed the number.

The phone rang four times before a man answered.

"May I speak to Josie, please?"

There was a long pause. "Josie's in bed."

Lucita glanced out the store window. Four men leered at her. There was no time to waste.

"I'm sorry to be calling so early, but I'm in trouble. I'm a friend of Josie's."

She could hear whispering in the background. "What's your name?"

"Lucita."

"Why, child, what's happening? Josie told me she saw you yesterday."

"Mr. Perez, Josie said you're leaving the area. My parents have contacted deprogrammers who are supposed to pick me up in the morning. So I left home. Now four men are standing outside the grocery store waiting to get me. Josie said if there was trouble—oh, I shouldn't have called."

"Of course you should. Now, where are you?"

"At Tucker's Market, just off Broad."

Mr. Perez sucked in his breath. "Well, you just stay put. I'll be there in 10 minutes. White car. Back seat's filled with boxes and stuff."

The phone clicked dead. Lucita looked out the window again. The pock-faced man said something over his shoulder, then ambled inside.

"Maria, please don't leave me. Come home. We can work things out, you'll see."

Lucita glanced around to see if she had missed someone else in the store, but there was only the lone clerk. Nervous, he eyed her.

"Better go, ma'am. We don't want no trouble here."

Pock grabbed her wrist. "C'mon, honey."

"No!" Her scream echoed against the ceiling as she tried to wrench free. "Let go of me! I don't even know you!"

Uncertain, the clerk reached for the phone. "Should I call the police?"

Pock clasped Lucita in a bear hug, his breath sour from liquor. "C'mon, baby. We'll be OK."

"Help me!" She yanked away.

The clerk's voice rose, sounding like an excited Barney Fife. "I said I'd call the police!" he warned. He picked up the phone, began to dial.

Battle went on in Pock's eyes. Then, with a jerk, he flung Lucita's arm away and turned on his heel.

Shaken, the clerk replaced the phone. "I can still call 'em, miss."

For a moment she wished he would. But police would ask questions. They'd want her address. Would call home.

"No thanks. Someone's coming to pick me up. I'll be OK."

CHAPTER 26

The jury sat in their box, suspiciously eyeing Nick as the guard guided him toward his seat. Nick scanned the courtroom for one congenial face. He saw his favorite bank teller, some previous customers, and the parts man from Beckett's, but no one from the church. A moment later he looked away, for the revulsion on so many faces was impossible to miss.

To his surprise, press equipment lined the outer aisles of the courtroom. Already the cameras were grinding away, following him as he moved in his too-small shirt and slacks across the room. He looked away, suddenly shy. Were they zooming in on his face, waiting to catch every fleeting emotion as he'd watched happen to other unfortunates in the past?

Unnerved, Nick sank into his chair and stared at his lap.

Pemberton Jones nudged him. "Hold your head up, man. You're looking guilty."

Nick forced his shoulders back and glanced across the aisle. A man, his briefcase open on the table before him, avoided eye contact.

"Who's that?"

Jones's eyebrows climbed his forehead. "Why, that's Randolph Grayson—from Chicago—your high-powered prosecuting attorney."

"They brought someone in?"

Jones nodded. "President Rondell appointed him chief prosecutor against religious criminals." Jones leaned closer. "You've made quite the splash in the news, you know. Actually, it wouldn't surprise me if your trial gets moved elsewhere. You're sort of a test case, I guess. Everyone'll want to hear what you have to say."

Nick went cold. "I'll have to *testify?"*

Jones gave him a look. "Of course. Weren't you listening when I told you that? I can't explain all your mumbo-jumbo. I can only guide you."

Nick's stomach turned to lead. *Lord, You know I can't do this.*

You don't have to. I am with you always . . .

Something warmed Nick deep inside. *I keep forgetting.*

He looked back at Randolph Grayson, trim in his gray suit and maroon tie. About age 50, Nick supposed, composed, efficient. Grayson whispered something to the woman who sat beside him, then faced Nick square on as if to size up his prey. Their eyes met and held. What he saw there was neither hostile nor compassionate. *The man's just doing his job. He's going to squash me.*

When the side door opened everything went quiet.

"Please rise for the honorable Judge Rochetti."

Stiff from inactivity, Nick stood.

"The Court will hear the case of the State of Indiana versus Nicholas Wheatley, Dissenter. Be seated."

Judge Rochetti stared long and hard at Nick before turning to the jury. "The defendant, Nicholas Wheatley, was arrested on the suspicion of breaking the National Worship Law. Your duty is to clear preconceived opinions from your thoughts as you listen to the coming testimony. Remember, one is considered innocent until proven guilty. With this caution, we will now proceed."

Cameramen vied for better positions as Nick sat down. Surely all eyes in the room were on him. His head spun with thoughts. Yes, he'd broken the law of the land but had remained true to his God. Why, then, did he feel like such a despicable piece of humanity?

He sighed, and faced his jury.

~ ~ ~

Nick leaned back against the rough cell wall of the city jail, relieved that he hadn't had to speak on his first day in court. But there was always tomorrow. Nauseated from the thought of facing the hostile observers again, he drew a deep breath and tried to clear his mind.

How he wished he had his Bible—he needed its comfort, wisdom, direction.

Father, I know I shouldn't be scared, but I am. I can't even line up my thoughts now, let alone my words. I don't think Jones cares one way or another what happens to me. He was appointed, and no matter what happens he'll get paid. But I want to get out. I want to go find Marj and the kids. You know they need me, Lord.

He looked at the patch of sky high on the wall. Darkening. Ahead, another lonely night on his hard, cold bed.

Father, can You help me think through what to say tomorrow? I can't even remember where to find the texts to prove that what I did was biblical.

He glanced down at his hands and spread his fingers. *I keep thinking that maybe someone in that audience is still open to the truth about You. If I could say the right things, show the right attitude, maybe they'd accept You. Please, Lord, help me. If there's someone—anyone—don't let me mess it up for them.*

The guard came to his cell and slid a tray through the slot at the bottom of the door. A bowl of thick soup, two slices of white bread, and an apple. The aroma of the hot soup rose up to meet him, heightening his intense hunger. He picked up his spoon and stirred through the conglomeration, then with a sigh put the spoon down and took his bread and apple.

Why should he be surprised? A thick pork-laden soup was exactly what he should have expected. Was it intentional because he didn't eat pork? Or simply the cook's choice? He smiled to himself, in spite of his disappointment. *Thank You, Lord. You said that our bread and water would be sure. Besides that, You've given me fruit!*

~ ~ ~

The next afternoon Nick relaxed for a moment, thankful to be in one of the court's anterooms while he awaited the afternoon's proceedings. There was a window to look out of, no press watching him, and lunch—this time one he could eat—and it had lifted his spirits. It was a good thing, for the morning had been a grueling one, what with Randolph Grayson making him look like public enemy number one. The man was so persuasive that before Grayson had finished his presentation Nick was nearly convinced that he truly *was* responsible for all the environmental disturbances, the latest terrorist bombings, and last week's midair collision of two airliners. Grayson, at last, had faced the jury as he finished his preliminary statements. "It is not so much what a man does that counts, as his *attitude* toward his fellowmen and their welfare. A person who flaunts the law in order to please himself doesn't care what becomes of those around him. Dissenters fall into this category. Written in their Bibles is the same rule that God gave in *my* Bible. 'Render unto Caesar that which is Caesar's,' which is a command to obey the laws of your land. This is the will and testament of God.

"One who disregards this most basic guideline will trample on other portions of the law as well. In our testimony you will clearly see that the defendant has closed his eyes to what is around him, and is not interested in the health or welfare of the people with whom he lives in this great country. This is an attitude that neither the State of Indiana nor the United States of America can afford to tolerate. Freedom for all is guaranteed. Personal rights are a part of that freedom, yet one's personal rights remain rights only insofar as they do not compromise the rights of others. It is my purpose to prove that Nicholas Wheatley, as a Dissenter, has done just that."

Nick nudged his lawyer. "This doesn't sound so good."

Jones faced him, looking resigned. "You're right," he agreed with a shrug, "and I hate to lose cases."

Sweat trickled down Nick's neck as he watched the men and women who'd come to witness his trial. For a grueling hour he'd been in the witness stand, trying his best to answer Randolph Grayson's carefully crafted questions. He glanced again toward the back corner of the room, beyond the news media setup, to where the golden-haired woman sat with the boy—their son. He stared for a moment at Dusty, whom he had not seen since the day of the tornado. *Thank You, Lord, for watching over him.* Then he tore his eyes away from them, willing himself to concentrate instead on the real issue—God's authority to declare a certain day sanctified by His presence. And his love for his God as well as his responsibility to honor Him by keeping that specific day holy.

Grayson shuffled through some papers on the table, then came back to face him in the stand.

"Mr. Wheatley, you said you have been a law-abiding citizen your entire life, until this recent incident. Is that correct?"

"It is."

Grayson glanced at the paper in his hand. "I have here a copy of an arrest warrant. The charge states that on the Sunday following Kramerville's adoption of a Sunday-closing bylaw you were in your garage with a customer on that day. Is this correct?"

"I was—"

"Just answer yes or no," directed Judge Rochetti.

Nick's heart knocked against his chest. "No."

Grayson smiled. "We heard Mr. Arnie Tate admit that he was in your garage on that day, that he had trouble with a tire he wanted you to fix. Do you recall that testimony, Mr. Wheatley?"

"Yes."

"Then how can you say you weren't with a customer at that time?"

Nick licked his lips. "Because I did not work on Tate's car, nor did I intend to."

"But the wheel was off. Mr. Tate was in your garage."

Lord, why isn't Jones objecting, doing something to get Grayson off my back?

"But—"

"And your diagnostic equipment was connected to a vehicle, isn't that correct?"

"It was—"

"Just answer the question."

"Yes."

"The apparatus was operational while Mr. Tate was present, is that not correct?"

Nick glanced toward the back of the room. Shannon wore a "they've-got-you-now" expression.

"Yes, sir."

Grayson rested his hand lightly on the railing between them. "Who attached the apparatus to the vehicle?"

"I did."

"And this was on a Sunday? The first Sunday mandating church attendance and forbidding optional employment?"

Nick glanced at Jones, who was picking at his fingernails. "Yes, sir."

Murmurs arose from the audience. Eyes from everywhere measured him.

But Grayson was not finished. He began now to talk about religion, man's responsibility to God, and to others.

Lord, send Your Holy Spirit to give me words. Open the hearts of these people listening to my testimony. Keep my attitude right. He glanced again toward the back of the room. *And Dusty, Lord. He looks confused sitting there by his mother. Clear his mind. Draw him back to You, please.*

There was something new in Grayson's manner as he approached Nick again. He opened his mouth, looked puzzled, then turned to Judge Rochetti.

"Your Honor, I ask the Court's permission to depart from usual procedure and allow the defendant to explain his strange confusion between Saturday and Sunday in relation to his duty to God and the State."

Judge Rochetti leaned forward. "To what purpose, Mr. Grayson?"

Grayson straightened. "I think if he is allowed to speak in his own way it will be much clearer to the court and the jury what kind of man we have here."

Judge Rochetti frowned. "I'm not convinced of your reasoning, but I will allow it."

Grayson leaned across the railing, toward Nick. "Now, Mr. Wheatley, suppose you explain why you think your honoring the Sunday law is not important."

Nick glanced toward the back of the room. He *had* to do this. It might be his only chance. *Help me, Lord.*

Dry-mouthed, he gripped the chair arms, then pinned his eyes on Grayson. "It's like this. I-I believe in the *entire* Bible. In the very beginning after God created the world He rested."

Lord, help!

"Because God wanted special companions that were in His image, He created a beautiful place for them to be—a place that had everything they'd ever need in it, a place filled with comfort and the potential for unending joy." He coughed. Swallowed hard. Continued. "It took Him six days to do this. When He had finished creating this special place, God created two people and set them over all the earth and everything in it. It was His desire to have these people for His friends, to cherish and enjoy, and He wanted time set aside just for that. And so, to make earth and everything in it complete, He created yet another day, the seventh. This seventh day was dedicated to communication with them and was always to be a covenant of eternal friendship between them and all human beings that would follow."

Nick scooted to the front of his chair. "In the earliest days, Sabbath—the seventh day—was always kept by those who were dedicated to staying close to the Lord. But sin had come into the world, and gradually most of its inhabitants turned to serving themselves and their desires rather than staying close to God. Many began worshiping the sun. This separated people from God, and grieved God.

"Because God loved us so much, and because sin must be paid for, He eventually sent His Son, Jesus, to live and die here on earth as the sin sacrifice for us. God had written His laws, the Ten Commandments, on stone, with His own finger, and given it to Moses and the Israelites. He said that if they loved Him, they would keep those laws, made for people's well-being. The seventh-day sabbath—this 24-hour period that God had made holy—was one of those laws.

"There is a verse in the Bible that states that God doesn't change. This is proven in the New Testament when Jesus Christ was on earth for the purpose of bringing the good news of salvation. He said, 'If you love Me, keep My commandments.' He spoke of the commandments given on Mount Sinai, the ones written both to show man's duty to God and responsibility to one's fellowman."

Nick looked over the silent room. *Lord, please help them understand.*

"During His lifetime here on earth, Christ went to the synagogue on the Sabbath—the seventh day—which is now called Saturday. After His resurrection the disciples still kept this day as they went about preaching. But later on in time, seeing that Christianity was beginning to wane again, certain religious leaders decided something must be done to keep their church large and financially stable. A plan was drawn up to incorporate pagan sun worshipers into the Christian church—a compromise, if you will, to bring them together. It was decided that since pagans worshiped the sun on Sunday, it would be a wise compromise to move Christian worship to Sunday, as well, thus making Christianity easier for the other group to accept. And since Sunday was the day that Christ *arose* after His great sacrifice, which the Christians could accept, Sunday would forthwith be set aside for worship. So the seventh day the Lord God had created for His communion with His created beings was discarded in favor of the first day, which they named 'The Lord's Day.'"

Nick, aware of Grayson's unblinking stare, met the attorney's eyes. Surprised at the interest he saw there, he continued.

"It was not God who designated Sunday to be a day of worship. God says that He does not change. There are no texts in the Bible in which He states that He changed the sanctity of the Sabbath to Sunday, the first day of the week. There is a church that boldly claims that it is the sole authority that made this change, and if you wish, I can tell you more about that. But what it all boils down to is that man has gone his own way, not *God's* way. And when man takes things into his own hands, you can see what happens."

Nick turned toward the judge, then to Grayson, then to his dear son, Dusty. "This is why I keep the Sabbath—Saturday—because God has asked me to, and because I love Him I want to honor Him. To hallow any other day would not honor Him. I pray, and do my best to serve Him on all days of the week, but in His great love He has set aside the seventh day for *communion* between us. This is our *special time,* and God has not given the right to anyone to change what He set up. He longs to spend that special time with each man and woman and child. I would urge *all* of you to give study—"

Judge Rochetti tapped his gavel. "That will be sufficient, Mr. Wheatley. I think we have heard enough to understand your method of reasoning."

Muffled conversation broke out all over the courtroom, but above that hum Nick heard a commotion at the rear of the room. Then he saw Dusty burst through the back door. Perplexed at the boy's hasty exit, he glanced at Shannon, who pinned him with her dark eyes.

Judge Rochetti banged his gavel. "Order!"

The room quieted as the judge peered across the bench. "It's late in the day. We will recess until tomorrow morning at 9:00, at which time Mr. Grayson can resume his questioning."

He addressed the jury. "You are not to discuss this case with anyone, even among yourselves. Draw no conclusions, for you have not yet heard all the facts. Court dismissed."

Nick sagged in his seat, exhausted. He had made a speech. God *had* given him words, and as he spoke, he had forgotten about himself. He glanced up to find Randolph Grayson's eyes still on him. His expression was not hooded or aloof. Was that a warmth he detected?

Then the guard was there—snapping on his handcuffs. It was back to the cell for the night. But this night would be one of joy, for the Lord had surely shown His hand.

Now, if He can only do something for Dusty . . .

~ ~ ~

Nick had finished his two pieces of white bread when the outer door to the cells opened. It had opened several other times during the evening to admit new prisoners. Angered, they often cursed and fought as they were stowed away. Nick turned over on his hard board bed. He wouldn't get a cell mate, for he was considered too dangerous.

Like a leper.

He heard the guard coming down the hallway, stopping at his door.

Nick turned over. It was too dark to see well, but as the guard slipped a key into the lock, he noticed a form behind him.

Dusty?

"I can get in trouble for this," the guard whispered. "Make it quick."

"It'll be worth your while."

The door snapped shut behind the visitor.

Nick stood up. "Who's that?"

"It's your prosecuting attorney, Grayson. I must talk to you."

Fire sliced through Nick's veins. "But you're not allowed."

"I know," Grayson chuckled, "and you weren't allowed to skip church that Sunday in question, but you did. May I sit down?"

"Sure." Uneasy, Nick stepped back.

Grayson sank onto the cot. "What you said today about Sunday worship being instigated by people, not God. I looked up the background to that in the library this evening. You were right, and everything has fallen into place all at once for me. There's always seemed to be a piece missing. I think perhaps you're right about the importance of Saturday worship, though I do need to study into it a little more. I'm wondering if you could list a few texts for me that might help me in my study."

Nick sucked in his breath. *What kind of sick trick was this man playing? Surely, this wasn't even legal!*

The lawyer touched his arm. "I've got to study this matter out, and immediately. You can understand that."

"Sure."

A hunch that Grayson was in earnest settled over Nick. He had asked the Holy Spirit to work on honest hearts, after all. But now *he* was in new trouble, for his mind was blank. He couldn't remember where the pertinent texts were found.

God, help me.

"Uh—the commandments are listed in Exodus 20. Other texts that follow through are Genesis 2:3 and Isaiah 58:13, 14, and Matthew 28:1 tells when Sabbath *is.*"

Grayson was scribbling fast.

"Then there's the unchangeableness of God in Ecclesiastes 3:14, and in Matthew 5:17 through 19 Christ said that He didn't come to destroy the law or prophets, but to fulfill them. And that not even a comma will pass from the law until everything's finished. Romans 3:31 mentions that too. If you can find a Bible with a concordance you can look up other references to the Sabbath. If I had mine I'd lend it to you."

Grayson squeezed Nick's shoulder. "That's all right. I always take mine with me on trips. I'll study this out tonight."

He scooted to the edge of the cot. "Now, I don't know how to ask this, but—well, could you not tell *anyone* I was here tonight? It really is quite irregular."

"No problem."

"Thanks," Grayson whispered, clasping Nick's hand. "Please pray for me . . . and God bless you."

Randolph Grayson had been gone only a few minutes when the guard came back. "Someone to see you upstairs."

Puzzled, Nick followed the young guard down the hallway. A moment later he faced Shannon through a glass window. It was the same old Shannon, eyes filled with fire, mouth with venom.

"You *scoundrel!* You *scum!* Even from the witness stand you had to reach out and manipulate my son! Haven't you done enough to mess up his mind?"

Nick tried to make sense of her words. "What happened?"

Anger tugged at her mouth. "Don't pretend you don't know," she spat. "What you said on the stand, that God 'longs' to spend time with people. Of all the notions. But it sunk Dusty."

"God wants you, too, Shannon."

Her eyes were slits of hate. "You weasled Dusty away from me when he was a kid, and you're doing it again. He said he couldn't ignore God anymore, couldn't *fight* Him, of all things. And then do you know what he said?"

Her voice rose to a screech, hatred burning in her eyes. "He said he was *going to find his mom* and put his life back to rights again, before it was too late! I'm so angry I could, could . . ."

Nick stared at the beautiful woman he'd once loved. As Dusty's words seeped into his weary mind, tears filled his eyes. Now it didn't matter what happened to him personally. No matter what happened in the courtroom, his job was to keep praying, and God would take care of the rest.

Chapter 27

For weeks the days and nights had blurred together, a terrible mixture of scorching heat and the night's high-desert cold. Brenna huddled with Jared and Keely in their "efficiency room" on the eastern edge of the camp that had ballooned to nearly 50,000 of The Chosen. Hastily built like 1930s clapboard motels, the dwellings sprawled across the desert floor, offering little more than protection from the blowing sand and direct sunlight.

In spite of help from the small swamp cooler Wally had purchased, the children's faces flushed from the noonday heat beating down upon the treeless encampment. Quiet now, except for the sound of an occasional vendor truck or someone on the way to the toilet block, the sprawling camp lay awaiting the sun's drop behind the bony mountains. Yet, in spite of the heat, Brenna willed the sun to stay high in the sky, to mimic its action of so long before when it had stood still for Joshua.

This was no less a battle—the battle between good and evil. And it seemed that the side of evil was winning, except when she looked into the eyes of her two children as they sang of Jesus and prayed to God.

Jared took a bite of his peanut butter sandwich, then spoke with a full mouth. "Mama, tell me again what to do tonight."

Each day during the few hours when they were alone she'd spent time trying to prepare the children for whatever might come, to teach them to trust the Lord for safety and direction. But today it was simply too hot to talk. To breathe. To *think*.

She forced herself. "Daddy says Taelon is coming tonight."

Taelon, the being she both dreaded and felt fascinated by each time he appeared.

The boy stretched out his bad hand and looked at it. "To heal my hand?"

"Yes."

He frowned. "Will he touch my hand?"

Brenna forced back the memory of "Mama" touching her foot, of the shaky feeling she'd experienced when that had happened. Taking a deep breath, Brenna knelt beside Jared. Once again she explained her plan, the only thing she could think of in their overwhelming circumstances.

It would not be long now. Outside, the Beckoning Music already throbbed its hypnotic beat. The frenzy had begun, worshipers making ready for the appearance. Brenna knelt on the plywood floor, holding her children close.

"I'll be praying the whole time, Jared, and you must do the same. No matter what happens."

In spite of the hours of instruction forced upon them by those who believed Taelon was sent as the forerunner of Christ, she had kept her mind clear, had pinned her thoughts on Jesus, and had sought His guidance. There had been no one to offer her comfort, to encourage her in her quest to "remember the Sabbath day," and to "have no other gods before me." Yet, in the wee hours of the morning as Wally slept beside her and the children slept on their thin mats, she had felt Jesus' presence, heard unspoken words encouraging her from deep within. For the first time she understood the meaning of praying without ceasing.

"Don't forget to sing," Keely said, hugging Jared. Softly now, the child began to breathe the words, to touch them lightly, to offer them as a gift to her brother. Jared gazed at her and began to mouth the words, too. *"Jesus loves me, this I know . . ."*

Voices outside. The door opened. It had grown dark and Wally was there, tense, sober. "C'mon. It's time."

Jared's eyes clung to Brenna's as he inched toward his father.

Wally caught Jared's good hand. "C'mon, Brenna."

"Keely and I will stay here."

"You and Keely will *not* stay here. You must be there to accept the gift about to be given our son. Now, come along."

But she didn't want Keely to see what happened, no matter what it was. What if Jared were actually healed? What if Satan was able to pull it off? How could she keep Keely from being fooled? Together, she and Jared had decided the little girl must not watch.

"We can't."

Keely's arms tightend around her mother's legs as Wally dropped Jared's hand and strode across the room. His strong fingers dug into Brenna's wrist as he propelled her through the doorway and into the night. The perfume of desert sage filled the air, but to Brenna it was the odor of death.

Light from the flickering fires set at intervals around Taelon's platform, the throb of Beckoning Music, and the dancers who undulated their prayer rituals through the smoky haze filled the night. Wally kept his iron grip on Brenna until she and the children were in the guarded area near the platform. Here the family would be safe from the hundreds who desired healing and might rush the platform in their eagerness. Brenna sighed. *Oh, Lord, help us.* There would be no escape tonight.

Static bristled through the still air, the sensation that always occurred just before Taelon appeared. The music heightened, the dancers spun faster, expectancy spreading through the crowd, drawing them like a magnet. And then everything went still. Sparks, like a million fireflies, shot over the platform. They were bright, shining hot, too vivid to watch without shading one's eyes, but almost impossible to turn away from. They flickered noiselessly, then gradually disappeared, exposing the most beautiful being she'd ever seen.

Sick folks crowded in. Unwillingly, she watched a young soloist who'd been left a paraplegic after a ski accident grow strong and abandon her wheelchair. Two men in the last throes of AIDS drooped before Taelon. He passed his hands above their heads. "Be healed, faithful ones." When she looked again they were laughing and kissing one another, as healthy-looking as children. Then a boy, blind from birth, was given the gift of sight.

Shaken, she looked away. What if she was wrong? What if

Taelon actually *was* God's messenger and she was too stubborn to see it? It would be so easy to believe his words. So easy.

Lord, what is truth? Help me!

A stillness surrounded her. *Whatsoever is clean, pure, beautiful, think on these things.*

She watched the healed, many of them baring their bodies and undulating to the Beckoning Music, giving themselves over to its rhythm, praising Taelon rather than God.

She brought herself up tight, drew the children closer. She had to get them away from this, but how? She wanted to stand up, to scream at Wally, to wake him up to what was really happening. But the guards clustered around her, watching her every move. There was nothing she could do but pray.

Softly, she began whisper-singing "Jesus Loves Me." The children pressed closer as they joined in, so quietly she could barely hear them.

"Jesus, be with us tonight," Brenna murmured into their ears. "Keep Jared safe. We know You love us, and we want to be true to You."

And then Wally pulled Jared away.

Brenna pressed Keely's face to her bosom. "Keep singing."

Wally hoisted Jared onto his shoulder and made his way through the crowd. A moment later her son, stiff and small, stood upon the platform.

"This is my son," Wally said, and knelt before Taelon. "Please heal my son."

Taelon's great arm moved out to take Jared's twisted one. Jared's eyes squeezed shut, his lips moved, mouthing the words Brenna sang to herself.

Suddenly Keely's childish voice broke through the stillness that had settled over the crowd. ". . . Little ones to Him belong, they are weak but—"

Jared spun around and looked at his sister. "Yes!" he sang out, "Jesus loves me."

Brenna sang louder, too.

Taelon seemed to shrink as his eyes caught Brenna's. Something about them was so familiar. So strange . . .

"Quiet!" Wally yelled, reaching out for Jared. "Kneel!" he commanded his son.

Jared dug his heels into the platform.

"Bow before Taelon!" Panic filled Wally's voice.

"Jesus loves me, He who died . . ."

Wally's hand shot out to silence the boy.

"I cannot heal this child because his mother is an unbeliever and has *poisoned* him against truth," Taelon pronounced.

"But your majesty—"

"She must first repent."

"But—"

"Enough! Remove this child and his mother or I shall go. I shall tell God that He is not honored here."

A cry of panic arose from those who had not yet been healed. They pressed toward Taelon, begging him not to leave. Some moved in on Brenna, anger twisting their faces, and they struck at her as they tried to snatch Keely.

Suddenly a new guard stepped up. "Stop!" he commanded. His voice was rough, sharp. His eyes narrowed. *"I'll* take care of her."

Then Wally was there, pushing Jared toward her. "Are you satisfied now? Wrecking everything? Go back to the room." He started back toward the platform as the crowd inched toward her again.

The guard shielded her. "Come follow me."

Others had commanded her before—had tried to compromise her. Only by the grace of God had she been able to avoid being defiled by those who cared little for His ways. She eyed the big guard, then took the children's hands and followed him.

He led her to their door. "You don't believe in Taelon?"

She shook her head.

"Please, why not?"

Was he trying to stall her, to gain entrance to their room? *Guide me, Lord.*

"God gave us the Ten Commandments. He told us not to bow before other creatures, to be good to each other, to honor the seventh day because it is holy. But Taelon promotes Sunday as the day of worship. Taelon blesses impure actions and takes honor to himself, though he does not claim to be Christ. But he can't be what he says—a messenger from God.

He can't forgive sins. Only God can do that. And the Bible says that God does not change. God has not changed His rules, the truth about Himself."

The guard stood quietly, his eyes troubled. "You know, I believe you're right. What's happening here isn't according to the Ten Commandments. I was a pastor once. I should have known better." He straightened, a relieved look on his face. "Tomorrow I'm going to leave and beg God's forgiveness for getting caught up in all this. You must get out of here, too, for it's rumored that something momentous is going to happen before Monday."

He turned to leave, then paused. "Anyhow, thanks for talking to me. If I don't see you again, I'll see you . . . *up there."*

As Brenna opened the door and helped the children up the high step, the guard cried out. She turned to see a mob surround him, heard heavy blows. Moments later when the men left, he lay upon the ground, broken and still.

"Yes. I'll see you up there," she whispered, forcing back the bitter nausea that climbed her throat.

~ ~ ~

Wally returned after they'd all gone to bed.

He snapped on the lamp and yanked her to a sitting position. "Look at me and hear me clearly." Eyes glazed as though he'd been drinking, he measured his words. "I begged Taelon to forgive your stubbornness and for training Jared to rebel." He slammed his fist into the mattress. "I want Jared to be a normal little boy. And I want you to be saved, too, but you're so hardheaded. You'll cause the loss of yourself and both children if you aren't careful."

He was losing control. "Taelon told me something that only Luke, Max, and myself know. I'll tell you only because it's important that you cooperate."

Lowering his voice, he glanced toward the door. "On Sunday Christ Himself will come with Taelon, and The Chosen will be allowed to make special offerings to prove their devotion to Him. If we both cooperate, Christ Himself might be coaxed to heal Jared."

Wally's fingers bit into her arms. When he spoke, he was almost begging. "Please, Brenna, *pretend* to believe if you have to, but *don't* wreck this opportunity. Taelon says they can't do anything against your will."

Frozen, Brenna couldn't respond. To face one who *appeared* to be Christ? It was too much.

"If you don't repent, I must make a sacrifice or even *I* will no longer be accepted as one of The Chosen." He shuddered. "You understand that you *must* make the change, for I couldn't *bear* to sacrifice what 'Christ' would require." His voice broke. Tears poured down his cheeks. "Oh, Brenna, try. Try!"

"Sacrifice?" Brenna pushed thc word out.

"He cannot accept something spoiled, old, or worn."

"What would you give?"

Torture filled his eyes, and his breath came in ragged gasps as he slowly formed the words. "Taelon says that husbands are responsible for decisions their wives make." His nails clawed deeper. *"The Sacrifice of Abraham,* he called it. If we don't both cooperate, he will ask our *whole* child as penance for my failure to properly guide you, and proof of my personal dedication to him. As a covenant between us."

The words filled up her heart, her mind, her mouth. The awfulness sucked her in, as real as quicksand.

"Keely?"

She flung his hands away and leapt toward her sleeping child. "No. You can't do that."

He followed, his voice a whisper. "But I can."

"You—"

His eyes glinted. "Only *you* can keep the sacrifice from being necessary."

The sound of a thousand winds shrieked through her head.

"Repent!" Wally's voice chased her, grabbed her, dropped her to her knees.

~ ~ ~

Later that night as she lay awake beside Wally, Brenna reached for God.

Father, it's my duty to protect my child, both my children. I have to keep them safe. But how can I turn my back on You? Still, if I don't give in the kids will be damaged beyond repair. And if I do . . . The thought was too ghastly to pursue.

Cautiously, she slid from the bed and knelt on the rough plywood floor. *Oh God, help me to be faithful. Show me the way. I can't give up Keely, or Jared, and I can't turn away from You, either. Father, I'm so scared. I can't handle this alone. I'm not sure I can even handle it with Your help.*

The silence was deafening. She didn't feel God's arms around her or His impressions filling her mind.

Father, where are You?

She waited, but there was nothing. Had she offended Him so that He no longer heard her cries?

God?

Maybe she had it all wrong—hadn't acted wisely. Perhaps she should pretend to go along with Wally—fake a change—then watch for a chance to slip away with the children. Surely God wouldn't hold her guilty for trying to save Keely's life.

Ever since they'd arrived she'd plotted escape. But she was watched so carefully. Wally's friends had talked, reasoned, even become angry with her. They said that she was preventing Taelon's full blessings to the camp. The wives of the other Chosen understood and worshiped as they were taught. Why couldn't she?

Twice she'd been allowed to walk out onto the desert with the children. They might have slipped away then, except for the watchful eyes. No, there was simply no getting away. She and the children would have to go through this trial. She must make a choice. Either she must recant and let Jared be healed, or she must stay firm and let Keely be . . .

Terror clutched her. To die would be much easier than this—making an unthinkable decision either way. She peered across the dark room to the corner where Keely slept. *My precious child, how can I let you go?*

Ugly visions lurked in her thoughts, leaving blinding pain in their wake. Her heart raced, her hands turned clammy.

Oh God, please be merciful. Show me what to do. I can't *choose to go against You. You've led me from the day I was a child, You brought me into Your church, taught me to love You better than my own life. But You* can't *ask me to turn my back on Keely and let her be sacrificed to die in torture. You can't want that, can You? Please don't leave me now!*

A sinister question kept returning. *What makes you think God has time for a sinner like you?*

She shoved it away and climbed back into bed.

The lonely silence of the sleeping camp surrounded Brenna. How she longed for someone to talk to, to pray with. She tried to reach beyond the agony devouring her. *God, what do You want of me?*

She waited.

God?

Why wouldn't He answer?

He who loves son or daughter more than Me is not worthy of Me.

Brenna took a ragged breath, the wound in her heart greater than ever before.

I do *love You, Lord. And I love the children You've given me. I just don't know how—*

Trust. I will make a way. Just trust.

Brenna curled into a little ball and hugged herself. With all her strength she concentrated on that last thought. God *was* there for her. He *would* make a way. He had promised. She must trust in that promise.

~ ~ ~

Sunday dawned hotter than usual. Wally had left them early to prepare for "Christ's" appearance. Word that something special would happen sometime that day had leaked out, and the news media poured in with their equipment, eager to beam whatever would occur to the entire nation.

Brenna had just finished feeding the children when a guard forced the door open. "They want you in the big tent. Now." His eyes caressed her. "Bring the children, too."

Brenna thought fast. "We need 15 minutes to get cleaned up. Then we'll come."

The guard left.

Brenna spun around. How could she prepare the kids for what was to come? She had so little time.

She reached for their clothes. "Now, listen carefully to what I tell you. A *pretend* Jesus will be here today. He will look real, but we must not believe him. They want Mommy to disobey the *real* Jesus—to say Sabbath isn't His special day anymore."

Jared's forehead puckered. "But Mommy, Jesus won't *like* that. Sabbath's His special sign."

"I know, and I won't change. But things might get pretty hard for all of us for a little while. Daddy wants the pretend Jesus to heal you."

"But you don't want me healed, do you, Mommy?"

Tears sprang to Brenna's eyes. "Oh Jared, you know I do. But not by Satan or his followers."

He nodded wisely. "We don't want him to touch me."

Keely's somber eyes sought Brenna's. "I sang 'Jesus Loves Me,' didn't I, Mama?"

"Yes, and we'll need to sing it again." She took the child in her arms. "Honey—if I don't do what they ask they may take you away from me."

Keely stiffened. "Where to?"

Brenna couldn't tell her. Besides, God was going to—

Jared took Keely's hands. "Don't worry, God will take care of us. Mama's told us all about this end of the world stuff, and when it's over we get to go to heaven and play with Jesus and see those lions and tigers, remember?"

Keely brightened. "And I can ride on Jesus' shoulders!"

"So don't be scared. Just remember to sing. If they take us away from Mama it will be for only a little while. We can be brave, just like Daniel was, OK?"

Brenna clutched his words to her heart. How she wished for the faith her small son expressed.

Fifteen minutes later Wally sent the children off to play with other youngsters. And now eight men and four women surrounded her, frustrated, angry.

"How can you turn your back on God like this?" Max asked. "You've seen his messenger. Wally's explained what it's all about."

"Taelon is not God's messenger. And God doesn't change."

"So you're schooled in religion? You hold a doctorate of

divinity? You're fluent in Greek and Hebrew and can decipher these things?"

"No."

"Now wait a minute," Luke Whalen interrupted, motioning Max to stop. "She's not on trial here."

He moved closer to her, his eyes kind. "Brenna, I know it's a big step to take, but just think. What difference does it really make what day we keep, as long as we worship Him? God is loving and kind, isn't He? He knows what's in our hearts. How can doing as Taelon asks change God's love for you? Why not just go along with us? It's for the best of everyone else involved." His eyes clouded. "I don't know what might happen if you further anger Taelon."

Brenna couldn't keep quiet. "Remember the Sabbath day to keep it holy. Six days—"

"The price of disobedience will be terrible, Brenna," put in Luke's wife. Tears sprang to her sky-colored eyes. "I couldn't give up my kids, if I had any."

"Thou shalt have no other gods before me."

Wally fell to his knees beside her. "C'mon, Bren. Just *do* it. You're not turning your back on God. You'll be saving the kids."

Lord, help me!

Silently she looked at each of them. Then she dropped her head, thinking, praying. From somewhere outside she heard singing. But it wasn't Beckoning Music. Instead it was children's voices—*many* children's voices singing the sweetest song in the world. *Jesus loves me, this I know . . .*

~ ~ ~

That afternoon Taelon hovered on his platform, his fiery eyes boring into hers. "Repent!" he demanded, his voice shaking her mind and the earth beneath her feet. "Repent, or you shall suffer as you never have before."

The children clung to her, their faces blanched with fear.

"Turn away from your wickedness and save your children," he thundered. "Bow before me."

"I can't!"

He seemed to hover over her, both hideous and beautiful. "Then, perhaps you can bow before *him!*"

Fifty thousand breaths sucked in at once. An ocean of worshipers fell to their knees. Brenna looked up, and there beside Taelon was the most beautiful person she'd ever seen. His face radiated such kindness and goodness that Brenna could never mistake who he was. The warmth of total belonging encompassed her as "Jesus" raised his hands, setting the sleeves of his long white robe moving gently in the cool breeze that flowed around him. He would set them straight. He would explain Taelon's lie.

He gazed at her for a long moment, deep love and acceptance in his eyes. After an eternity he turned to the crowd. "Peace be with you, my children. I have longed to come to you."

His firm but gentle voice filled Brenna with hope. God had promised that He would help, and He had sent Jesus to do just that. Love welled up in her heart, blurring her eyes.

He spoke on, encouraging them, and declaring his love for every person alive.

"I have protected the earth, waiting for all to accept my holy day. But some have closed their eyes to new truth. I cannot cover their sins much longer. You have seen the earth suffer from plagues and tempests. You have watched Marloid's disease devour previously healthy men, women, and children. These catastrophes result from humans' unwillingness to follow God exactly as He asks. Instead they honor the ruler of darkness. If I can again protect the earth and those who live on it, all must turn to me."

He turned to Brenna. "My precious child, you have tried to be my servant, to teach your children of me, and I love you for that. But you have been wrong. The holy men of the Bible tried to honor me, too, but they did not always understand what I told them. As weak humans sometimes do, they wrote error into the Bible. Trust me now and join with your husband in worship of my Father and His representative, Taelon. Stand and be a leader in righting the wrongs in this world. Save your children and yourself. Think of others. And keep my holy day in remembrance of my resurrection." His voice grew even more tender. "Please . . . I love you."

His eyes were drawing her, sucking her in. His sweet voice, one she'd long awaited. Everything she saw showed that the magnificent one who stood before her truly *was* Jesus Christ of Nazareth. She wanted to run to him, to wrap her arms around him and ask him never to go away. But there was something . . . She fought to remember.

Every eye shall see him . . . coming in clouds of the sky . . . go not to the desert . . .

The realization crept over her, slowly, convincingly. Horrified at what she'd almost accepted, she found her voice.

"I will *not* bow before you, nor will my children!"

Wally scrambled up, grabbed her, clamped his hand over her mouth. He struggled to yank her to her knees, but she would not bend. Finally he let her go, an ugliness she'd never seen before upon his face.

"You're *evil!* I'll see you burn in hell!" he hissed, then turned back to the being.

The being spoke again. "Very soon those who have not submitted to me will suffer grave consequences. My sheep obey my voice, but they will not remain as sheep. In an effort to rid the world of the stench of sin, they will soon wreak vengeance upon those who reject me. The Dissenters will be unable to buy or sell. Their children will starve in the gutters and rot on the hillsides. God-fearing men and women, sent by him, will mow them down and put this earth to rights again. There is but little time left. Now is the time to repent. Now!"

"And you." He motioned to Wally and two others who bowed before him. "You have not been faithful servants. You have not subdued your families and brought them to me. Of you I require proof of allegiance!"

"I am ready to make any sacrifice," Wally cried, lifting his arms in supplication.

"Even a blood offering?"

"Even my daughter," Wally sobbed.

"No!" Brenna shrieked.

A heavy hand knocked her to the ground.

The being's words found her, twisted her in agony. "Will you repent?"

She looked up, first into her son's eyes, then at Keely, now suspended high over Wally's head. Then she met the being's gaze.

God, help me to do the right thing!

She got to her feet, stood tall, then began to sing. "Jesus loves me, this I know . . ."

Jared joined in, and then, high-pitched and off-tune, Keely's voice joined theirs.

"Very well." The being zeroed in on Wally. "Your wife is beyond salvation. To rid yourself of blame, I will accept your child in her place—a sacrifice that will prove your allegiance to me. Bathe the child. Dress her in her best, and bring her when you have finished. When the sacrifice is complete, I will heal your son."

The thousands scrambled about, running one way and another. Men hurried to the edge of the encampment and carried back stones. Quickly an altar was built.

Brenna sucked in her breath. Would they *burn* Keely alive?

Go now. Go and take Jared. I'll show you the way.

She'd been scrambling after Wally on his way to the cabin, Keely's frightened face bobbing over his shoulder. But now she stopped in her tracks. All around her people were jostling for a good place to watch what would happen when the being reappeared. She looked at them, plastic people who moved and talked and breathed as one. People subject to an awful pseudo-god.

Go now, and take Jared into the desert . . . I will shield you.

"But *Keely,* Lord."

I will take care of Keely. You go.

"How do I know this is You speaking?"

My sheep know My voice.

"What about the guards?"

Go.

So they walked away from camp with no food, no money, no canteen in which to carry life-giving water; only Jared's little Swiss knife that he always kept in his pocket. Ahead lay parched desert. Nothing more.

Brenna's heart remained at the camp. There her girl child would—she dared not think of what might happen. But God had promised. God would help.

She paused by a scrubby tree and looked down at Jared who stared toward camp. She, too, located the platform, plainly visible in the distance. She heard the Beckoning Music begin, its thrumming reaching out to them.

A cry went up as the being again appeared.

"Don't look, Jared," Brenna said, turning him around and pressing him to her.

She could see Wally making his way forward, carrying Keely in her white church dress high over his head.

For a moment Brenna froze. If she hurried back perhaps she could make it all stop. Wouldn't it be better for her to lose eternal life than to let her child suffer so? Her heart slammed against her chest. But deny her God?

She drew in a long breath and forced her feet to turn away. Heart heavy, she began walking. Every step, every breath was a prayer. There was nothing more she could do. The nightmare that had begun on the evening of their anniversary was drawing to its conclusion. She'd fought long and passionately, but she had no more strength. It was all up to the Lord.

Chapter 28

Other reporters and cameramen were already recording the sparkling above the platform when Aaron and Buzz pushed through the crowd to their spot in the media tent.

"Hurry," Aaron growled, opening the tripod.

Buzz fumbled the camera, almost dropped it, but finally got it secured.

The competition's cameras whirred as the sparks sucked together, then faded at Taelon's greater light. Aaron yanked the lens cap off. "Pan the guys by the platform, those guys in red scarves. Get that pile of stones, then fasten on Taelon."

A vague restlessness stirred Aaron as he watched what was happening. There, at the front of the crowd, three men wearing red scarves dropped facedown upon the sand. A hush fell over the crowd as the Beckoning Music ended and the dancers stopped their sensuous twisting and turning. At the end of a great hush, Taelon made some preliminary remarks, then continued.

"The God of heaven knows of your trials, and how mother earth is suffering from the wickedness of men and women. He sees the illness. He hears your hearts crying out to Him. He knows that most of The Chosen are true to Him and would give all for Him." A darkness crossed his brow. "But there are those with divided allegiance who cling to worldly mates. These so-called Chosen, and the Dissenters that have mesmerized them, are a thorn in God's side. They sow seeds of distrust and challenge God's authority. And retribution will be had."

Taelon raised his arms.

"Three such repentants now seek pardon for not fulfilling God's commission to bring their families with them to the feet of God. One is the husband of a Dissenter. Two have committed crimes against the Knights of Truth and seek forgiveness. By making their offerings they show their complete submission to the Lord.

"I ask you now to prepare yourselves to worship before the lord of Earth, to bow on your knees before him."

A long and pregnant silence blanketed the camp as the evening sky darkened. Buzz had his camera trained on Taelon, but then, in a flash brighter than lightning, a new being stood on the humble platform.

"Jesus!" The shout arose from the crowd. The God-man, the one Aaron had convinced himself was just another character from a fairy tale. Aaron squinted. "Jesus" was taller and more magnificent than Taelon, and strangely, he looked just like the pictures Grandie had shown him so many years before.

He lifted his hands. Aaron saw the scars ridged and red in his palms. "Bless you, my beloved. I have longed to be with you," he intoned. "Soon I shall take you to heaven and eternal happiness, but there is yet a little work to be done.

"Some here tonight wish to make a covenant offering to my Father, to prove their allegiance to Him. He is displeased with the disobedience of some, but He will gladly receive the incense of your earnestness as you bow before Him."

Aaron watched as Max Orcott approached the platform. He motioned to two of the men who lay prostrate upon the ground. They arose, something in their arms.

"Sheep, like in Bible times," Buzz muttered. "All we need now is Mount Sinai."

"Get all of this," Aaron directed, not taking his eyes from the scene.

"Christ" stepped closer to the edge of the platform, directly behind the altar. Crouching reverently as they walked, the men placed their animals upon the stones. Their legs were tied together, and they bleated with fear. Then stepping back, the men lifted their hands toward "Christ."

His hands outstretched as though in blessing, "Christ"

looked heavenward. Suddenly fire flashed from his hands and engulfed the altar.

"My Father has accepted this token of your devotion," "Christ" said, with tears in his voice. "Go in peace. Your sins are forgiven. Your salvation is sure."

Music broke out, and the dancers began whirling once more, their voices raised in praise and adoration. But again "Christ" lifted his hands.

"There is yet another gift to be offered to my Father."

A hush fell over the crowd as the third man arose. Aaron squinted. Wasn't it Kenrick, the young professor he'd interviewed?

"Have you brought your lamb?" "Christ" asked, his voice permeating the dusky evening.

"I have. My most prized lamb. I offer it to you with open hands."

Making his way to the platform, Kenrick raised his offering high. Aaron gasped. This was no lamb. It was a child, dressed in white.

"My daughter!" Kenrick cried out. "My daughter, for life or for death. Whichever pleases my lord."

Onlookers sucked in their breaths and flung themselves to the ground.

"Jesus" looked down, a smile widening his lips. "This is a great sacrifice for you to make, yet I am the creator. I give life, and I can take it. I will test you to see that your heart is pure, that you have truly submitted all for me."

The child, still raised above her father's head, squirmed, then quieted. Then over the clear air came a thin sound, a clear, high voice. Was that singing? Yes! And the tune. It pulled Aaron back to Grandie's lap.

"Jesus loves me, this I know . . ."

"Silence!" "Christ" roared.

". . . Bible tells me so."

Buzz caught a priceless frame of the child's face as Kenrick lowered her and whispered into her ear. She shook her head defiantly, then began to sing again. Once again Kenrick lifted her above his head and approached the altar. Then just before the child's father placed her on the stones, Aaron saw her body go limp.

Kenrick gently placed her across the altar amidst the ashes of the burnt lambs. Then he bent down and patted her cheeks; shook her as though to waken her. And then with a howl as though his very soul was being torn from his body, he fell to the ground, weeping.

"No!" he wailed. "No! No! NO!"

"Christ" drew himself up. His lips curled. "My Father does not accept inferior offerings. The child is dead. Take her away."

Pandemonium broke out, telephoto lenses sucked the child's face in, playing upon her lips relaxed into a gentle smile. Kenrick stood over her, weeping, pulling at the red band around his neck, his eyes wild, his mouth contorted.

Nauseous, Aaron nudged Buzz. "Try to locate the girl's mother. Get her face."

~ ~ ~

The late-night lights glared in Aaron's eyes as he continued his on-the-scene report. "Authorities are even now combing the surrounding area to find Brenna Kenrick, mother of the child who was to be sacrificed upon an altar in the manner of lamb offerings of Old Testament times. Though it is rumored that she and her young son vanished into the desert, officials speculate that the pair found a ride with an unidentified truck driver who left the encampment during the sacrifice. All roads have been blocked as searchers comb the area."

Aaron paused while Buzz moved to another angle, one that played on the frenzied worshipers in the background.

"In the event that the pair escaped into the desert, the latest infrared technology will come into play. Tomorrow morning an intense search will take place. With these measures Kenrick and her small son will surely be in custody before tomorrow night. Stay tuned for live coverage."

Chapter 29

Darkness surrounded them, the moonless night hiding dangers Brenna didn't want to consider. Far behind she could see the fires flickering around Taelon's platform where Keely had been offered as a sacrifice. Heavy hearted, she urged Jared onward, stumbling toward the sand-streaked mountain. Some of the people had talked about that mountain, those who interrupted their religious frenzy long enough to hunt for rabbits or coyotes. They claimed it held a sweet-water spring in a mountain cove, a place where the desert birds and animals came to drink when the shadows deepened.

Now, with thirst thickening her tongue, it seemed the best place to go, though she knew they couldn't stay, for that would be the first place to be searched. But if they were there by morning, they could drink and then find a place to hide until dark. As they rested, she would pray. God had said He'd care for Keely. Surely He would care for Jared and herself, too.

She took Jared's hand again. "How are you doing, sport?"

"I'm cold, Mama."

"I know. If we keep walking we'll stay warmer."

Jared stumbled, then cried out. At every turn, sagebrush snatched at them, twisting itself between their clumsy feet, gouging their legs. Her heart went out to Jared, for she had nothing but kisses to put on his little-boy hurts.

It must have been well past midnight when they finally stopped for a rest. *Lord, do we dare sit down on the ground? What about snakes? Scorpions?*

She settled onto the rocky sand and pulled Jared close,

wrapping her arms around him, trying to provide some warmth. The sky was alight with stars and planets—ones she'd learned about in Girl Scouts. God's handicraft brought strange comfort. If He could take care of billions of stars, surely He could care for one small boy and his broken-hearted mother huddled on the desert floor.

Too keyed up to sleep, Brenna studied the sky. Even the usually dim Seven Sisters shone brightly. Low, climbing from the eastern horizon, Orion began his sideways crawl across the early-morning sky. She noted the sword hanging from his belt and pondered that it harbored the great nebula through which the Holy City would someday pass. Oh, if only Jesus had come yesterday.

Pain exploded in her heart, making her literally sick. Jared was at her side, but where was Keely, who should also be in her protection? If God truly was love, why hadn't He delivered her? Why had He left an innocent child to suffer at the hands of His enemies?

Brenna yanked herself up short. *Lord, keep me from this kind of thinking! I know You love Keely more than I possibly can, and will make things come out right, though I can't see how. Don't let Satan make me doubt. Help me trust.*

Jared whimpered, and she drew him closer.

Help me to be the right example for Jared. We must lean on You, because we have nothing in our hands—no place to go, not a crumb to eat.

Her stomach growled. *How can I explain to Jared that he can't have breakfast? And how can I tell him what happened to Keely, Lord—oh, how can I bear this?*

Tears flowed down her face, dripped from her chin. In her mind's eye the scene played over and over, each time going further. She could see Wally holding Keely high, then placing her on the rocky altar. Had he tied her like an Old Testament lamb? Did death come quickly, or did the flames linger—taunting, tasting?

Brenna shuddered. What could happen in the heart of a man to enable him to give his daughter as a gift to placate the devil?

And how could you just walk away? The accusing thought slammed into her mind.

Surely there's something I could have done! Maybe if I'd tried harder . . . oh God, please help me. I'm going to lose my mind, and then where will Jared and I be?

Suddenly a warmth surrounded her, though from where it came she could not tell. Still, something had changed.

I told you not to worry, My child. I said I'd care for Keely. I'll take care of you and Jared, too. Your part is to stay faithful and to trust Me.

"But where shall we go?"

You've already begun. Go to the mountain.

"And what will I feed Jared? He's just a little boy."

No answer came, yet the sense of a Holy Presence remained.

She relaxed then. God would provide—she *had* to remember that. She was only human. She couldn't see ahead, but He could.

Orion had climbed higher when she jerked awake, heart racing, a faraway hum grabbing her attention. She eased away from Jared and stood. The camp was only a distant speck, but between it and herself she could see three small lights bouncing through the darkness like busy ants carrying flashlights across the desert floor. As they drew closer, the single dots became twins. Headlights.

Her knees weakened. Were those the camp Jeeps, bringing Wally to look for them? She scanned their dark surroundings. Was there any place to hide?

Go to the mountain.

Brenna paused for only a second, then awakened Jared. "Let's go, honey."

The child scrambled to his feet.

"Mommy, I'm cold."

"Me, too. Walking will keep us warmer."

She glanced back at the headlights. "Let's see how fast we can get to the mountain."

Their breaths came hard as they topped a sharp rise. Then Jared caught the sound. "Somebody's coming. Maybe they'll give us a ride."

Brenna hurried him. "Remember, we don't ride with strangers."

They stumbled down an embankment, feeling their

way. Then up the next rise. Now the engines were louder, easy to hear.

"Mommy, why are those cars driving around like that?"

"Maybe they're looking for something."

"Us?"

"Maybe. Look, we need to find a place to hide."

Two headlights topped the rise they had just left. Instinctively, Brenna pulled Jared to the ground beneath an outcropping of sagebrush. She sucked in her breath as sharp rocks tore at her elbows.

"Hold still, honey. Don't make a sound."

A door slammed and feet shuffled. Another vehicle arrived.

"They couldn't have gotten this far," someone said. "Probably went to the highway and hitched."

"It would be suicide for them to come out here anyhow." It was Max. "The spring in the cove's gone dry. Don't worry, when they get thirsty enough they'll head back."

When the third vehicle drew up Brenna knew it was over.

"Jared. Jaaa-red!" Wally's voice broke through the night.

Jared tried to answer. Covering his mouth, Brenna held him tightly, but he squirmed free.

"It's Daddy!"

She covered his mouth again. "Shhh!"

The child finally relaxed in her arms. He would obey.

"I must find them before Taelon changes his mind," came Wally's voice. "I can't lose both my kids in the same night. Let's drive just a little farther."

"I say we head back now," Max stated. "We'll ask around town. Someone surely saw them—a woman and a little kid out walking alone." He laughed harshly. "Brenna's too foolish to believe what she sees with her own eyes, but she's not stupid enough to go into the desert. That's suicide. If they don't turn up in town we'll track out this way again come daylight."

One by one the motors started and the Jeeps pulled away. Still Brenna waited quietly, just in case. At last she sat and looked onto the rise. It was empty once more.

~ ~ ~

Five days had passed since they'd fled the camp. How

they'd survived daytime's blistering heat and the frigid nights she couldn't say. Only impressions told her what to do.

They were now far beyond that first mountain with its thread-trickle of water, and ahead lay barren wasteland. And yet, here was the skeleton of an old car. Amazed, she looked at the only sign of civilization they'd seen since a plane had crisscrossed the sky on their second day out.

Now the sun had broken over the eastern hills, and would soon glare upon the land again, sucking up every bit of moisture it could find. Away from cover, they were vulnerable, especially with Jared's red shirt. Exhausted, she reached for his hand.

"Lookit, Mama. An old hubcap," Jared said, pulling it from the sand.

"Umm."

"Maybe we could use it for a dish."

For what? There was no food. Even now her belly cramped. They had found a few pinion nuts, and by the old spring some dried-up berries, hardly enough to sustain life for more than an hour or two. Yet they were still alive.

"It would hold water."

Brenna looked at Jared with new eyes. She saw a dented hubcap, but he saw possibilities.

"You're absolutely right. When God leads us to water we *could* save some in that." She eyed the car. "Maybe there's something else we could use. I'm sure no one wants this old car."

They left with the hubcap, an old bucket, a rusty tire iron Jared insisted they'd need, and two old slip-on seat covers, now thin and bleached to a see-through beige, yet better than no protection at all. The rearview mirror and a windshield wiper completed their collection.

By the time the sun was half-high they were climbing hard onto some open rocks. There on the hillside, more apt to be spotted from afar, Brenna had insisted that Jared drape one of the seat covers over his shoulders.

"Mama, it's too hot to wear this."

She sighed. "I know. But it covers your red shirt. Red is too easy to see."

"Where are we going?"

There was a drop-off. Across a dry wash stood an embankment. Halfway up she spied an overhang large enough to create good shade until late afternoon.

I will lift mine eyes unto the hills.

She pointed. "Let's go over there and rest."

After they'd climbed the embankment Brenna put the bucket down and stepped into the welcome shade. A cool breeze greeted her. Surprised, she peered into the darkness, only to discover a cave. She cautiously tapped the ground to warn away snakes as she inched inside. The cave was about 15 feet deep with a ceiling that sloped to the floor in the back. Disturbed, a spider skittered across the sandy floor. Was it poisonous?

She shuddered. "Jared, may I use your knife?"

Outside, she cut a branch of sagebrush, then swept the ceiling and the floor. Only then did she spread out the seat covers so they could lie down.

Though Jared slept immediately, Brenna sat at the mouth of the cave and looked down into her "front yard," studying landmarks and possible ways of entry. Their biggest problem—a place to hide—had been solved. The next was water. They *must* have it, had already been without it far too long.

She eyed the rough terrain below. Toward the north, behind a cluster of rocks, was a green smudge. Brenna's heart quickened. Where there was green there was water. She jumped up and grabbed the bucket. Then she sat back down.

The sun was getting high. If she left, Jared might awaken and hunt for her. Or someone might stumble upon her, away from cover. Better to wait until evening and go together. With that thought she tried to ignore her swollen tongue, and curled up beside her son to sleep.

The sun was low by the time they'd gathered their cattails, dandelion greens, and water and started back to the cave for their first night in a shelter. They'd just inched down to the lowest point of their journey, an exposed area with no cover, when Brenna heard the throb of a helicopter.

Startled, she searched for a place to hide before it came into view.

"Lie down!" she screamed.

Brenna flung the food from the seat cover pouch and covered Jared's shirt. Unable to get under it herself, she curled into as tight a ball as she could and prayed.

The helicopter burst into sight, following their rocky gully. Then it disappeared around the mountain. Just as Brenna decided it was safe to get up, it returned.

Dear God, please help us!

This time it barely inched along, rose, and paused beside the cliff, then continued on, just below the level of their cave.

As it neared them, Brenna prayed again. How foolish she had been to venture away from the shelter of their rocky hide-away before it was wholly dark. Surely they had been seen, for how could the pilot miss them, sprawled as they were on a naked desert floor? She listened as it paused overhead, waiting for it to land.

Thy will be done, O Lord. Thy will be done.

CHAPTER 30

September Again

Lucita awakened with a start, sensing someone outside the window of the small bedroom she and Josie shared. Skin prickling, she waited to be sure her imagination wasn't tricking her. And then shadow hands raised the window.

She screamed and sprang from her bed. Antonio came on the run.

"You're sure it wasn't just a dream?" he asked after hearing the story.

Josie clutched his arm. "I saw him too, Dad. It's no dream."

The scream had awakened the rest of the household, as well. Pastor Bannister, his face puffy from sleep, sat in the lamplit kitchen with the girls while Antonio checked around outside.

Satisfied that the intruder was gone, he soon returned.

Lucita shuddered. "Maybe it was the deprogrammer."

"I don't think so," Antonio encouraged. "How could he know you're here?"

"Well, let's have some hot tea before we go back to bed," Pastor Bannister suggested. "We'll read a few Bible promises while we wait for the water to heat."

Lucita glanced at those who now surrounded the table. She, Josie, and Antonio had been at Pastor Bannister's cabin for a few days, but the pastor and Carby Peters with his three preschoolers had arrived only last night.

Carby, a redheaded lab technician from Seattle, seemed a joyful sort, even though his wife had recently died of pneumonia. He was obviously devoted to Zach, Zeb, and baby Zina.

"Let's catch the news," he said, reaching for the radio after Pastor Bannister had set the Bible aside.

". . . earthquake measuring eight points on the Richter scale has leveled two thirds of the city of Paris. A Red Cross airlift will leave Germany, where they were providing aid following the tornadoes and massive flooding. Medical supplies are nearly depleted from providing for these disasters and treating Marloid's victims. Requests for supplies from the United States and other nations—uh, breaking news just coming in, ladies and gentlemen. Eyewitness report seeing what they describe as a giant white-hot fireball shooting from the clouds above New York City. Several city blocks near the Empire State Building appear to be ablaze. Stay tuned for . . ."

Static drowned out the words.

Antonio shook his head and sighed. "Things are getting pretty bad out there." He took the radio and found a new station.

". . . Christ is our only rock. We must rid this world of Satan's followers, spiritists, the agnostics, but worst of all, the Dissenters who mock God at every turn. They ignore His sacrifice on the cross and have brought untold suffering upon the world in the name of the *old* Sabbath—Saturday—the day hallowed by ancient Jews. It is clear that the Dissenters, with their poisonous message, are a national danger. They trick others into turning their backs on truth."

Music swelled behind his voice as the radio preacher continued. "We embark upon a holy war, my friends. It is time to stand up and call sin by its right name, to boldly demand that the Lord's day be honored as He requests, by *all* mankind. Both Christ and Taelon have plainly stated that God is angered and will withdraw all protection from this planet if order is not restored.

"In response to this, President Rondell has announced that Dissenters will be given until a week from tomorrow to repent from their ungodly ways." The music swelled. "If you know Dissenters, *plead* with them to turn their hearts to the Lord and reverence His holy day. *Pray* for them. Do what you can to save them. But if they won't listen, *report* them to the nearest authorities. Their time is short. If they are not summarily taken care of as the public enemies they are, then, brothers and sisters, our very lives are in jeopardy."

Music surged through the room, a beautiful song Lucita had heard before, but it brought no peace to her heart.

"Things are closing down quickly," Pastor Bannister said with a sigh. "It's no longer safe to walk the streets, even in the daytime. You know, the government warns of the death penalty, but gangs who've fought each other for decades have joined forces and are already killing anyone they think looks like a Dissenter. Hundreds in Seattle alone have been jailed. You know that old warehouse by the docks? They've turned it into a holding tank. Things are pretty rough in there, I guess."

"But we didn't have that many church members left in the city," Carby said.

Pastor Bannister smiled. "That's the amazing thing about this whole situation. Just like we've been taught, many devout people, like Lucita here, have accepted the Sabbath truth and been baptized. Remember that mechanic on trial in Indiana? The pastor of a small congregation followed that case closely, studied into the situation, and as a result his whole group accepted the Sabbath. That angered an evangelist in his city. When he studied into how a whole congregation could be 'duped,' he became convinced of the truth they believed. So he preached it publicly—over the airways and even the Internet—and now has brought a great number of people with him. Of course, they're trying to keep that one under wraps, but word is getting around. Unfortunately, many of the new followers are now in that warehouse, awaiting their fate next Monday." His shoulders sagged. "I was kind of hoping to be put in there myself to have a chance to encourage the new believers."

Lucita stared at the preacher's trembling hands. He was old, and weak, but his God—*her* God—was mighty, and who could tell how He would work?

She thought for a long moment before speaking. "Pastor, you know I haven't been baptized."

He laid a fatherly hand on her shoulder. "I'm sure God understands it hasn't been possible."

Yes, God would understand, but a longing to take the visual step filled her. "I really wish I could be baptized, anyway."

Pastor Bannister stared at Sadie's picture on the wall. "Well, it just might be possible. There's a hot spring along the trail a mile or so from here. Sadie and I used to hike over there on Sabbath afternoons. The water would be warm—even if the weather isn't."

A sweet peace fell over her. "Oh, please, can we do it?"

The old man patted her arm. "Tomorrow, lass. I will baptize you outside, like John baptized Jesus. Maybe that's why God brought me here instead of letting me get jailed."

Josie got up. "Not to change the subject, Pastor, but are you sure you weren't followed here?"

"I don't think so."

"Did you buy gas on the way—get scanned? SIPS knows everything, you know. Bank accounts, relatives, *properties.*"

Pastor Bannister rubbed his eyes. "That's right. Could be that tonight's snooper was—maybe we oughta press on into high country. They can find this place."

Lucita swallowed hard. "Uh—I took care of that."

"What do you mean?" Carby prodded.

"The last thing I did before I left SIPS was to—well, I deleted part of your record, Pastor. About this place."

The old preacher's eyes widened. "You didn't."

She nodded. "Oh, but I did."

~ ~ ~

The next afternoon as they celebrated Lucita's baptism, Pastor Bannister answered a knock on the door. A heavy-set officer pushed his way in. "I'm Sergeant Clark. Just makin' a friendly call to let you folk know we'll be running three church services at the Community Center next Sunday. You folks should come to the 2:00 meeting."

He stared at Lucita. "What's your name, miss?"

"Lucita."

"Lucita. Pretty name. Is your husband here?"

"I'm not married."

He winked at her. "Well, I'll be on my way, but I'll see you soon."

When he had gone, Pastor Bannister sighed. "Our presence is no longer a secret. We probably should move on."

~ ~ ~

The sky was just beginning to lighten the next Sunday as the group followed Pastor Bannister onto the trail that climbed from the cabin into the back country. Outfitted in the assortment of jackets and sweat pants that Sadie Bannister had kept at the cabin for visitors' use, they looked like a casually-prepared group of hikers who'd escaped the city for a short Sunday outing.

The pine cover, along with predawn dimness, made the rocky trail difficult to see. Stumbling over snarled tree roots, Lucita followed Josie. And so did 4-year-old Zack, who insisted he could walk instead of being carried.

Concerned about his slowness, Lucita squatted down and captured his wrist. "Hey, buddy, ready for a camelback ride?"

He giggled as Lucita swayed up the trail.

~ ~ ~

Monday dawned quietly as the little group huddled deep in the forest, away from their beds and the comforts of civilization. As Lucita lay on the ground she tried to imagine what she'd do if someone pointed a gun at her—if she was forced back down the mountain—if that deputy came and *looked* at her again. With a shiver she turned over and snuggled against Josie, who still slept.

But as she lay there a dark fear pushed into her mind. Where would they go? From whom exactly were they running? They'd brought only a little food—flatbread they'd made of flour, oil, and water, then dried in the oven so that it wouldn't spoil, some dried fruit that Sadie had left in the cupboard—things that didn't need cooking and that could be stuffed into their pockets. Pastor Bannister said God would supply their needs. He'd preached it for years. Now it was time to prove God's promises, he declared.

Blessed Lord, do You see us here on this mountainside? I'm cold and scared, and yet Pastor Bannister doesn't seem afraid. I don't know You as well as he does, but I'm trying to follow You. Help me to trust You, whatever happens. I love You and the Sabbath, and these people

You've put me with. Help me not to disappoint them. And Lord? Be close to my family. Help them to understand why I left and to learn the truth about You. Please.

~ ~ ~

On Friday, with the sun sliding toward the horizon, they worked their way around the face of a mountain, seeking a sheltered place to spend the Sabbath. The night before, they'd listened to the radio Antonio had brought along. World news had grown only worse. A new strain of Marloid's had been isolated. It progressed in the same manner, yet its victims did not die as quickly—just suffered on. Torrential rain hampered rescues from the New York fireball tragedy, and the famine raged on in Western Europe, now complicated by hoards of grasshoppers that ate what little vegetation farmers had been able to grow. Megatwisters rampaged throughout the southern states, and seismographic measurements indicated increasing tension beneath the Pacific Rim. Tidal waves were predicted from earthquakes at sea.

Seattle news reported that Dissenters jailed in the warehouse had escaped, and an all-points bulletin had been issued for their arrests. Reconnaissance planes using infrared radar had spotted many pockets either of humans or animals, deep in the forests of the Cascade Range. Trackers were on their way into the back country to check out the surveillance reports. Taelon had made it clear that until every Dissenter repented or paid the ultimate penalty, God would do no more to protect Planet Earth. Furthermore, persons found aiding Dissenters would be treated as enemies of the State.

Lucita sighed. Her little group was in trouble too. Their food was gone, and they'd had no water today. But they had found a U-shaped ledge on the mountainside that would provide some shelter from the northern winds. It was fairly large, with room enough to walk around comfortably. As they sat on the boulders discussing what they should do, Lucita noticed a thrumming sound.

She pointed toward the horizon. "Look over there."

A helicopter grew larger as it inched toward their hiding place.

"Lie down!" Carby hollered.

"The trail!" Josie shouted, pointing to the pathway they'd just followed. "Someone's coming."

Lucita pulled Zack close as they watched the hikers and the helicopter. A dog scampered ahead of the hikers, his nose to the ground. They'd be easy to find now, exposed on the barren ledge as they were.

"Shouldn't we move on?" Josie called over her shoulder.

The edges of fear fought with Pastor Bannister's usually placid expression. But then he smiled. "It's testing time, folks. Remember the words we've quoted so often. 'I am with thee, and will keep thee in all places.' * We'll just settle here until the 'copter moves on, trusting that God will provide whatever we need."

The 'copter worked its way along the ridge, lost altitude, then made another pass so close that Lucita could see the pilot's face. He hovered, sizing them up. Sharp granite pressed into Lucita's chest, bit into her hands as she lay motionless. Finally the helicopter turned and sped off.

"Our only hope is to move as far away from here as we can before they can send someone up," Antonio said. So they hurried onward, holding the children's hands and praying for good footing. Carefully, they crossed a natural bridge, only to find themselves on a narrow, dead-end cliff with steep walls towering over them. They were trapped. The only way of escape was the way they'd just come.

It was over, for the hikers—the law—were not far behind.

Pastor Bannister sank onto a rock and pulled Zeb close. Still panting, he began singing, his velvety voice offering up words of comfort.

"Under His wings I am safely abiding;
Though the night deepens and tempests are wild,
Still I can trust Him; I know He will keep me;
He has redeemed me, and I am His child."

As he sang Lucita hummed along, her trust growing.

". . . Sheltered, protected, no evil can harm me;
Resting in Jesus I'm safe evermore."

Blessed Father, please take care of us. Help me to be true to You, and to encourage the others. Help me to be brave . . . no matter what.

She glanced at the little group, so tired, so hungry, and with no safe place to go.

We need water, Lord. And food. But mostly protection. Thanks so much for giving us these things.

"Over there. I see them," came a shout. "Sic 'em, Gray. Hold."

Lucita heard the dog's claws seeking footing on the rocks. Even at a distance she could see his eager eyes, his tongue lolled from his mouth.

Zack whimpered.

"It's OK," Lucita murmured, holding him close, but her heart flailed beneath her shirt.

Then three men appeared on the rocks they'd just crossed, Sergeant Clark in the lead. He raised his gun and held it steady.

"You folks lost or something?" he called to them.

Carby tucked Zeb behind him. "No, sir."

"Don't you know they're combing these mountains for Dissenters, shootin' 'em on sight? Don't wanna be mistaken for them, would you?"

The second officer interrupted. "Where you from?"

"The valley."

"Well, it's obvious by lookin' at you that you ain't all one family," he laughed. "Now, what's your names?"

If they told their names—

The guns zeroed in on them. "Your names!"

Pastor Bannister struggled to his feet. "I'm Washington Bannister."

Sergeant Clark typed the name into his InfoTel, waited, then grinned. "Well, do tell. We got a warrant for your arrest, boy. Preacher, huh?" He jerked the muzzle toward the others. "Who are they?"

"I'm Antonio Perez."

"Carby Peters."

Sergeant Clark eyed his quarry. Then his gaze fell on Lucita. "And you're Lucita. Last name?"

"Fernandez."

Sergeant Clark checked the InfoTel. "So you're the kidnap case. Dissenters got you, huh?" The three officers trained their guns on little group.

Lucita jumped to her feet. "No. I—"

"C'mon over here, sweetie. We'll getcha back home."

The pursuers advanced, guns at the ready.

Fear gripped Lucita. If she stood her ground, she might be shot. It was not too late for her to save herself. She could go back with the men—back to Papa and Mama. Maybe—just *maybe*—she could help them understand that God's way was not the way they'd chosen to follow.

Confused, she glanced over her shoulder. Pastor Bannister's head was bowed; his lips moving.

She closed her eyes. *Blessed Jesus, help me make the right decision.*

Her mind cleared. Leaving now would be denying God. She straightened her shoulders and looked the man in the eye. "I'm staying," she told him.

Sergeant Clark's gun zeroed in on Pastor Bannister. His eyes were cold. "Waste the leader first," he barked. The shot ricocheted off a rock. The lawman swore. He gripped his gun with both hands and fired once more. He wouldn't miss again.

Terrified, Lucita spun around. Pastor Bannister still stood, his head bowed.

"Sic 'em." Another shot. A vile curse. Feet scrambling toward them. The dog loping ahead of the men.

And then all nature went crazy. An ominous growl belched from beneath their feet and the rocks that had seemed so sturdy wobbled like gelatin. Pastor Bannister toppled to the ground while Lucita clutched at Zack to keep him away from the drop-off.

Then the ledge tipped and a boulder tumbled into the precipice. Lucita winced as her elbows ground into the rocky surface.

The children screamed as their pursuers scrambled toward them on all fours. "God's doing it again!" Sergeant Clark bellowed. "And you nut cases are the reason." He flopped onto his belly and carefully aimed his pistol at the pastor.

Just then an earsplitting crack reverberated between the rocks, then out and across the valley. Panicked, Lucita tried to see what had caused the noise. She gasped as she saw the natural bridge buckle, then crumble and fall with a deafening roar.

The officers' guns clattered over the edge as they scurried back the way they'd come, clinging to the rocks. The dog cowered, tail between his legs.

A lifetime later it was over. The echoes of the collapsing bridge faded, leaving only the sounds of unsteady breathing and the breeze brushing through treetops that now lay directly below them.

Pale, Sergeant Clark scrambled to his feet. "God's trapped you now!" he shouted. "Wait'll that wall crushes your heads. You won't get away."

Their pursuers, so recently terrified, grew bold again. "We'll be back!" they yelled over their shoulders as they hurried back down the pathway.

Lucita slowly got to her feet. She felt disoriented, but she lifted Zack and kissed his skinned elbow. And then Lucita felt Josie's arms around her. "Did you see God rescue us from those men?" Josie asked, crying and laughing at the same time. "I was so scared, but He'd promised, and He did it!"

Pastor Bannister tipped his head back and raised his arms, stretching them toward heaven. "Mighty God, thank You for Your protection. You have shown Your hand to us as surely as You showed it to the children of Israel so long ago." He sank to his knees, bowed his head, and covered his face with his big hands.

His voice grew soft. "I know that Your coming is soon, and we'll see Your dear face at last. Oh, Lord, please hurry! Keep us faithful to You. Calm the human fears that threaten us, and lead us in the way we should go. We *praise* You, Lord."

They knelt there for a long time, silently communing with their Father. Only gradually did Lucita become aware of a splashing sound. She finally opened her eyes.

Where the cliff above had separated, a large crack had formed. From it flowed a ribbon of bright, clear water. She watched it tumble onto the stones just a few feet away, work its way along a low place on their ledge, then drop to the valley below.

Water. Coming from the rock. Pure water, clean and cold.

Thy water shall be sure.

Together they headed for it, their trembling hands lifting the crystal liquid to their mouths. And then something brushed Lucita's cheek. She glanced up. Giant flakes wafted down upon them, dropping lightly on the stone and brush floor. *Snow? Falling from a sunny sky?*

She caught a piece. It wasn't cold, though it was white and soft.

Pastor Bannister tasted a flake. "Praise the Lord, it's Moses' food!"

"Manna?"

Zack grinned up at her. "Hey, we can play children of Israel."

With the prospect of food, they were suddenly ravenous, their bodies crying out for nourishment. They fell to their knees and began to stuff the lightly sweet "bread" into their mouths. But then a hush fell over them as they realized what had just happened. As the food from heaven continued to drift around them, Lucita forgot about eating. She lifted her eyes to the sky above the towering rock walls. "Father, thank You for the water and food You have provided," she called. "I praise You for taking care of us. I know now that I can trust You for everything."

They ate their fill for the first time in many days. Perhaps others would come looking for them. They might be cold. Maybe they would hunger and thirst again, but it didn't matter. They were children of the King, and as Psalm 46 told them, God was their refuge and strength, and a faithful help in trouble.

And *that* was all that mattered.

---

*Genesis 28:15.

CHAPTER 31

As the cell door slammed shut Nick collapsed on the cement floor, too weak to stay upright. His mind raced, wondering if Freed had followed him into this new cell, and he fought the dry heaves that threatened to drag his stomach into his throat. He'd been warned not to talk about the Sabbath to other prisoners, but what else could he do when they asked questions? Time was so short . . . But his disobedience had bought him another beating and this cold, narrow cell.

Determined not to antagonize the explosive guard further, Nick forced himself to lie just as he'd fallen, and awaited the next kick.

How long was it now since they'd brought him to the work camp after Randolph Grayson had resigned as his prosecuting attorney? Two weeks? Three? He'd lost count of the days, and the number of beatings at Freed's heavy hand. Waiting for trial, he'd been moved from cell to cell so he wouldn't "contaminate other prisoners" at the minimum-security work farm.

Hearing footsteps, he braced himself for the next blow. Instead, a gentle hand touched his shoulder.

"Nick? You're OK. We're friends."

It was a trick.

"Ken Walsh, the doctor from Hayworth, is here," said a familiar voice.

Nick tried to open his eyes but couldn't. He tried to push words between his swollen lips. "Who's talking?"

"It's me, Tong. Remember, you taught me about God."

A warmth stole over Nick. "Tong?"

Other voices joined in. Someone pressed a damp cloth to his eyes, held it there. And then everything went black.

The next morning only one eye could open. As Tong spooned watery oatmeal into his mouth Nick studied the others—Brother Ramsey, who always sat on the front row at church, Dr. Walsh, and a boy who couldn't be more than 12.

Gillie? He tried to focus. Hair wrong color, stance different, but a boy, just the same.

Nick was curious. "What's your name, lad?"

"Roddy."

"Why're you here?"

The boy fought tears. "Same reason you are, Mr. Nick." His voice cracked. "Mom and me were going to Gramma's near the Smoky Mountains. She's got a little farm . . ." His voice trailed off.

"What happened?"

"We had to get gas and they scanned Mom. Dad—" His voice broke. "When Dad died a couple years ago I promised to take care of Mom—but they just yanked her outta the car—there wasn't n-nothin' I could do." Roddy buried his face in his arms.

"She's probably in the women's section," Brother Ramsey said. "It's been real hard for Roddy."

If this were Gillie . . .

Nick reached out. "C'mere, boy."

A moment later a youthful hand slipped into his, slender but calloused.

"I don't know where my Gillie is, either, and I kinda need someone right now. So suppose we stick together while things sort themselves out."

Sheepish, Roddy brushed away his tears.

"You don't need to be ashamed of your feelings, son. It's hard to stand by and not have any control over what's happening. But say, you know God will take care of your mom, don't you?"

Roddy's hand stiffened in Nick's. "Yes, but—but she's not very strong and—"

"Remember His promise, 'I am with thee—' "

" '—and will keep thee in all places'?"

Nick ran his tongue over his cracked lips. "God has *promised* He won't let anything come to us that we can't bear. It's tough, but He always keeps His word."

"And He'll be with Mom." It was a statement now.

The boy scooted closer, and Nick somehow got his arm around the thin shoulders. "Now, how 'bout just sitting by me for awhile. I think we both need to rest and to pray for strength not to let these temporary circumstances get us down. What do you say?"

~ ~ ~

For the first morning in several days they awoke to silence, for the rain and hail that had pelted the window ended. The sodden walls oozed. It had turned cold, and with the dampness life was miserable. Beneath their thin blankets, the men huddled on shared cots.

"Hope we get oatmeal today," Roddy chattered from his spot beside Nick.

Nick pulled the boy closer, trying not to notice the ribs that jutted from his sides. It was hard enough to suffer hunger as a man, but for a growing boy . . . The rattle of the food cart down the hallway triggered Nick's saliva.

At last Freed appeared.

"It don't make sense," he grumbled, rattling the dishes. "Food's gettin' short. Law-abiding guys can hardly buy any, but they feed the likes of you. God's really mad if you ask me. He's sending these storms to shake sense into folks. That drought in the prairie states? And Florida being pounded again? You ask me, it's *your* fault. And they might not be able to explode the newest asteroid, either. If they don't, that's all she wrote."

He poked his nose through the bars. "Didn't know that, did you? Protected like you are in here, you don't get no news—don't know what the common man hasta go through. You just sit and sap off tax-payin' men. Well, they shoulda listened to Taelon sooner, if you ask me. He predicted all this stuff, told 'em what they'd hafta do."

Freed slid a tray of half-filled bowls across the floor. "Yep, you Dissenters are gonna be an endangered species before long."

He glared at Nick. "By the way, *gents,* you'd best get ready. You're goin' on flood cleanup today. 'Bout time you do somethin' to earn your keep."

~ ~ ~

Later, Nick dropped another beer can into his sack. The clouds had peeled back and the late September sun beat down upon him, too hot for comfort, but comforting just the same. After the cell's dampness, exercising his stiff muscles seemed a blessing indeed.

Give thanks in all things. Yes, thanks that they were alive, could work, could *hope.*

He stepped into the roadside gully. Knee-deep from the latest wash-off, the culvert held a tangle of debris. Nick pulled out an old tire and slung it to the edge of the road. Next came a broken fishing rod.

"Nick!"

Rook, a cellmate on his first day at the county jail, approached. The jagged scar that stretched between Rook's mouth and ear puckered—causing a lopsided grin. "Look busy, man, we gotta talk."

Nick resumed his task.

The petty thief had bragged about the times he'd been jailed but freed on technicalities. Now he lowered his voice. "I don't think I'm going to shake this rap, man, but I don't intend to stay here long. You said you was a mechanic?"

"Yes."

"Know how to hot-wire?"

Nick stood up. "Sure."

Rook pretended to put something in his orange sack. "Keep workin', man, so they don't know we're talkin'." He lowered his voice. "I got me some friends that'll help if I can just get to 'em. Cops'll never find me where they are. Just thought you might wanna go along, mebbe help me getta car."

"Running won't work, not with SIPS in full swing. Did you think any more about what I told you?"

"Nah. Religion's not for me, man." He traded his empty bag for Nick's filled one. "Be nice if God was like you said, all kind and stuff, but it just ain't so. Too much has happened that prove that's just woman-talk."

"You're wrong, Rook. And think about the escape."

Rook brightened. "Escape?"

"Yeah. Leave this whole mess behind."

"Go to heaven, you mean. That flyin'-around-in-the-sky stuff. Rescued by a big cloud. You been watchin' too much TV."

Nick unearthed an oversized canning jar like the ones his mother had filled each summer. About to drop it into the bag, he stopped cold. His stomach lurched.

Rook noticed too, caught his breath, and swore.

Nick set the jar down and called to Freed. The guard ambled toward them, his hand resting lightly on his pistol. "Wha'cha want?"

"Look at this."

Freed reached for a cigarette. "Well, I ain't comin' down there."

Nick climbed the bank and handed the jar to him.

The guard blanched. "It's—a baby, ain't it?"

Perhaps six fetal months old, it had only just begun to decay and bore the signs of brutal removal from the womb that had once nourished it. *Somewhere there's a woman who's hurting right now, probably wounded by her do-it-yourself abortion, and her wounds aren't all physical, either.*

Freed thrust the jar at Nick. "Put it in the sack."

"But—"

"Nothin' we can do for it now."

Nick eyed Freed. "What about the police? Shouldn't it be reported?"

Freed laughed bitterly. "Nah. No way to trace whose it is anyhow. Somebody just got tired of it, that's all. Too many brats in the world anyways. Just starve to death if they live, way thing's goin'."

"But abortion at the age of *this* baby's against the law."

"Yeah?" Freed smirked. "Well so's Sunday-breakin', and that didn't stop *you* none."

The day's beauty had vanished. Nick's stomach churned as he returned to the gully and away from the hatred in Freed's eyes. Ever so gently, with a prayer for its mother, he lowered the babe into the bag.

Rook paled. "Don't know how anybody could do that—dig a baby out, y'know? But they do it all the time. You gonna break with me or not?"

There was nothing he'd like better than to go find Marj and the kids, but if that was to happen, it would have to be a break of God's making, not his own.

"Nah, but thanks for thinking of me."

Rook's shoulders drooped. "Well, see ya, man." He hoisted Nick's filled bag, then headed toward another prisoner a few yards away.

As Nick continued to unclog the gully, he remembered the day after Randolph Grayson had visited his cell. Twenty minutes after time for his trial to resume, he and Pemberton Jones had sat in the courtroom. The judge had not arrived, nor had the prosecuting attorney.

Jones had fidgeted. "Wonder what's keeping them? I hoped to be done here by noon—got other things to do."

Finally Judge Rochetti took his place. His eyes bored through Nick then swept across the spectators. "Our prosecuting attorney has resigned for personal reasons. To demonstrate to you how deadly dangerous the Dissenters are, I am going to read his letter of resignation to the court."

The cameramen scurried; whispers circled the room.

Judge Rochetti adjusted his glasses. "'Upon hearing Nicholas Wheatley's testimony regarding his reasons for Saturday observance I have decided that I must step down as prosecuting attorney. It is my belief that Wheatley is acting in accordance with his religious beliefs, which, upon scrutiny, I discovered are based upon sound biblical injunctions. After a thorough search of the Bible and historical records that support the information he offered regarding the background of Sunday worship, I found no biblical support for worship on the first day of the week. Though I know and understand the Sunday law as written, I too feel that it goes against God's direct commands, and has no biblical right for enforcement. Therefore, with due respect to the powers that be, I tend my resignation as prosecuting attorney in this case. Sincerely, Randolph Grayson.'"

Stunned silence blanketed the courtroom. An instant later newsmen fled the room and observers sprang from their seats. A camera zeroed in on Nick's face and stayed there. Flabbergasted over the turn of events, he'd tried not to smile. His words had actually meant something. What would happen next he couldn't even guess, but a warm feeling had surged over him. Perhaps there was still time to share the good news of God's great sacrifice. He'd best keep his mind on that fact.

Soon Judge Rochetti had banged his gavel. "I read you Grayson's letter because you must realize how quickly religious poison can be spread by word of mouth to intelligent but gullible people. The outcome of Grayson's resignation is that we must scrap this case and reschedule it. It's a waste of the state's money, but that's the law." He motioned to the guard. "Take the defendant away."

The next day Nick had been moved to the work farm. There was still no word on a new hearing date, and no one seemed willing to talk about the event. Not knowing what had happened to Grayson, or if his case was even on the docket, was discouraging. Deep depression dogged him. He reached for God, pleading for help, but only his failures came to mind, haunting him, pulling him down. When would it end?

That night, after his long day of work in the ditches, Nick was allowed a shower—five minutes of delicious warmth trickling down his back, over his still-swollen face. He spent his moments, not only in scrubbing every square inch of his body, but in praying for strength, for forgiveness for wrong tendencies, for Grayson, and for his family wherever they were.

~ ~ ~

Five more men had been crowded into Nick's small cell by the time the next Sabbath came. Not knowing how long they'd be together or what events the day would bring, they prayed, recited Bible passages, and shared experiences of God's care and protection. And they waited in dread for the guard to return.

It seemed as though Freed was determined to antagonize them, to cause them to fight back so he could unleash his full fury upon them. Taunting that morning, he had prodded

Brother Ramsey, then announced that the old man, along with the others, was scheduled for a road crew that day. It had riled Nick to see the old man singled out as the morning's target, and he didn't know what he might have done if Freed had taken a swing at him. But he had prayed, as he knew the others were doing, and Freed backed off, leaving with a sneer and the promise of a hasty return.

Bud, who'd arrived only that morning, sighed and leaned back against his narrow spot on the wall. "They ever feed ya' in here?"

Roddy perked up. "Twice a day, usually. They're late this morning."

Bud's hand rasped across his stubble. "You guys hear 'bout the newest law—can't buy food if you're a Dissenter?"

Nick went cold. *Marj. The kids.*

"Regulation came into effect last Tuesday, it was. They're using them scanners. Won't sell ya nothin' 'ceptin SIPS says yer a Sundaykeeper." He gave a mirthless laugh. "Surprised they don't scan you here, it's gettin' so tight."

As though on cue, the food cart rattled down the hallway. When Freed opened their door, he stood, his legs widely braced, hands on his hips. "Looks like a banquet for you today. Scrambled eggs, hash browns, toast done just right and smothered in strawberry preserves. Any of you want bananas? Grapefruit?"

Roddy's hand shot up.

Freed darkened. "Then you'd better leave off being a Dissenter. Likes of you gets only *slop*. He picked up a tray and slid it across the floor. Most of the thin oatmeal sloshed onto the tray.

"You men have 10 minutes to eat. Then you're gonna work."

Dr. Ken cleaned his hands as well as possible, then went to the tray in the middle of the floor. "You guys come and get your bowls. I'll pour the spilled stuff back into them."

Bud eyed his bowl, then shook his head. "Thanks, but I ate real good last night. Give my share to the boy—he needs it more."

It didn't take them long to eat. When they finished,

Tong set his bowl aside. "What are we going to do about working today?"

They just looked at each other. Nick knew what was going to happen. And it wouldn't be pleasant.

"Not much we *can* do, is there?"

Brother Ramsey smiled. "We stand together, then. For Sabbath—for our God."

"Just remember to pray," added Roddy, running his finger around the inside of his bowl. Freed and another guard had come for them, and when they refused to work on the Sabbath, called them lazy, hailed them with words that Nick had never heard, and then, surprisingly enough, left. But they did not return with the usual weak soup for supper, nor with oatmeal the next morning.

"Good thing we've got our own water," Ken said, going to the faucet for the dozenth time on Sunday. "Just keep drinking. They'll bring something pretty soon."

~ ~ ~

By Tuesday, hunger-nausea was heavily upon them. Nick eyed his cellmates, then young Roddy, tucked so quietly under his arm. By unspoken agreement, they'd not mentioned food since Sunday when no supper was provided. It would do no good to talk of their hunger, to visualize what was not to come. They'd fallen silent, each taken up with his own thoughts, individual fear, and pain.

As they waited, Nick spent hours thinking about God and heaven, and about his life. Fear gnawed at him as he realized how little time he'd devoted to Bible study and developing a solid relationship with Christ. What of his past behavior? Had he done things that would hurt the church? What if he'd fooled himself into feeling safe when actually he was not saved? The mental torture was constant. If there was no chance to be with Christ, his life would have been for nothing.

Ken broke the silence. "Wonder when our court date will be?"

There was no answer, for there was nothing to say.

~ ~ ~

The next Sabbath morning Freed opened the cell door earlier than usual. "Y'all have company," he drawled almost pleasantly. The light flicked on to reveal Blake Munsey, their pastor.

So he'd been caught too. *Maybe he knew about Marj.*

Freed shut the door. "Just call out when you're ready."

Brother Ramsey struggled to a sitting position. "They putting you in, too?"

Blake's face widened in a smile. "No, and it's a good thing. You don't have room to turn around in here," he joked. He shook hands around the circle, then stopped in front of Roddy. "And who are you, young man?"

"Roddy Cole, sir. Are you the preacher?"

"That's what they call me."

"Then do you know where my mom is?"

Blake patted Roddy's shoulder. "Maybe I can find out. Suppose we talk a little bit, and then we'll see what we can learn. How'll that be?"

The preacher sat beside Brother Ramsey. "I can't stay long because I must try to contact our remaining church members. Quite a few didn't get away." He seemed to be searching for words. "I'm doing what I can to ease the situation."

Nick interrupted. "Do you know where Marj is?"

Blake sobered. "Sorry, she disappeared about the time you were arrested. But I'll try to find out. We can contact SIPS to determine her last contact."

Nick went cold. "Please don't."

Pastor Munsey leaned forward. "Now, the reason I'm here. It looks like you all might be getting out."

Nick held his breath.

"All my life I've tried to lead in the right way. In the past when I've discovered I was wrong, I wasn't silent about it, and I changed. Still, it hurts to know that however innocently, I've misled my congregation."

Brother Ramsey's eyebrows shot up. "You've *misled* us?"

"When Taelon made his predictions and said things that I felt were contrary to Bible teachings, I studied into his claims so I could explain the error to my congregation. It goes without saying that the church has been deluged with error in the last few years. Anyway, I began to find quite a few discrepancies in our teachings—nothing wrong with the Bible, mind you, but with the way *we've* interpreted it."

Tong tensed. "So what wrong did you find, Pastor?"

"Two major things, I'm afraid." He glanced at Nick. "One is what happens after death. Our church puts a twist on those verses about the dead knowing nothing, but when you read them correctly, you realize that they are referring to 'knowing' in the sense of knowing the need for food, for rest, for warmth. I've learned they retain their thoughts, and can communicate, given the chance."

Something cold slithered down Nick's back. "That's not true."

"I can prove it. However, they've allowed me only a few minutes with you, and I need to tell you the rest." He glanced at the others. "Taelon made an announcement—you probably didn't hear it. It seems a very important section of gospel scripture was withheld by Sabbathkeepers when translating the Bible. This manuscript, just found near the Dead Sea, records Christ's words as He rose from the earth to go back to heaven. Here, I'll play it for you." He pulled a tape recorder from his pocket.

"Our Lord sends this message to you. 'Ye have reverenced my Sabbaths,'" said the beautiful voice of Taelon. "'But old things are passed away; and a new work I do. Bring your tithes and reverence me on the first day as a remembrance of my resurrection, and my gift of eternal life to you.'" Munsey switched off the tape.

"Now, that's clear enough, isn't it?"

Ken jumped up. "Clear blasphemy!"

"Now wait," Blake soothed. "Our church historians have been discussing this on Internet. Everything checks out. This thing is valid."

Lord, guide our thoughts. Make us wiser than we are. Keep us strong.

Distrust nagged Nick. "And so you've discarded the idea of Sabbath sanctity?"

Blake laughed lightly. "Of course not—not *pre*crucifixion, that is. The Sabbath *was* the Creation sign between God and humanity. Now *Sunday* is the sign of humanity's *accepting* the sacrifice God made on our behalf."

Munsey eyed the prisoners. "I don't ask you to take my

word on it. Five minutes certainly isn't enough time for you to study it out—it wasn't for me, at least. But what you *can* do is agree to look at it—to give it a shot, and then you'd stand the chance of getting out of here. Your jailers aren't trying to be unreasonable. Look, they're just enforcing the law. They're just cooperating with those who are trying to bring balance through undivided allegiance to God. Now, you're separated from others because you spread falsehood, however innocent you are in doing it. However, I've convinced them that you knew nothing of the latest findings because you've been behind bars with no access to news. That's like trying to drive on an empty tank."

Wordless, the men stared at Munsey.

"And are you going to tell the women the same thing?" Roddy asked.

Munsey nodded. "You're pretty young to be in jail, aren't you, son?"

"I guess so."

"Maybe they'll let you come help me explain the truth to your mom. Would you like that?"

Roddy was quiet for several seconds. *Lord, help him—help* us *to know the truth.*

The boy fiddled with his shoelaces. "I'd like to go, Pastor Munsey, just to see if she's OK." His forehead wrinkled up. "But I can't." Tears brightened his eyes. "I-I'm young, I know, but I'm not too young to know that what you're telling us isn't true."

Atta boy, Roddy!

"You see, I just got baptized. One of the things my Bible says is that God never changes His rules, and I can find that text. He doesn't tell us to do one thing now and something else later. I think Taelon's the devil, and you shouldn't believe what he says. Anyway, if there *is* a manuscript out there, then I'll bet it's a fake. God would'a let us know earlier if it wasn't."

"I can see you're 'a thinking man,'" Munsey complimented. "And I like men that think. That's all the more reason you should come with me and let me explain it all."

Roddy wavered, then straightened his shoulders. "I can't. Mom's counting on me to do the right thing." Tears sprang to his eyes.

A little child shall lead them.

Munsey turned to Nick. "Your trial's coming right up," he told him.

"When?" Nick's stomach soured.

"Think about what I said. It still may not be too late."

After Pastor Munsey left the men fell silent. Roddy leaned into Nick, shaking with silent sobs. Nick felt like crying, too.

It was hard for the boy, hard for them all. Tomorrow would be difficult, and the next day and the next. Nick's thoughts closed in on him. What about that manuscript? Did he really know what he believed? Or had he gone on tradition and old memories for too long? Was he sticking with what he knew just because that's what he'd always done? Did he worship God only for what he could get out of Him?

Lord, please keep my motives pure. If I do Your will for selfish reasons, it's as though I haven't done it at all. Be with us—sustain us. And please watch over our loved ones . . .

The cell door burst open, interrupting Nick's silent prayer.

"Wheatley, the judge needs to see you. Get on out here. And bring your stuff."

CHAPTER 32

October Again

The putrid breeze wrapped around Aaron like devil's breath as he stood with his back to the great Mississippi River. Even the gas mask, which he'd worn since leaving the 'copter, had not quelled the penetrating odor of rotting fish.

Every ripple of the reddened water behind him brought more fish to shore—bloated things, bellies up, their glazed eyes protruding from their heads. It was foolish to be here, even for the sake of sensational news. Even the carrion-eating birds had more sense than he. They'd long since winged away from the stench.

The seers, guided by Taelon, had been right again. They'd predicted that God's finger would next point to fresh waters, though Aaron wasn't sure God had much to do with this mess. It had been news when the Black Sea had reddened and killed everything that lived in it. The strange malady had then overtaken the Mediterranean, sending famine and death to its shores. But when it came to America!

Masked fishermen and cleanup crews poked halfheartedly among the piles of dead fish behind him, trying to burn them, bury them, anything they could do. Only the destitute who could not leave would stay around much longer.

Aaron was just ready to start his report when Buzz motioned to him to wait, laid his camera on the ground, and stumbled into the parking lot. Jerking his mask off, he bent over and lost his $18 lobster dinner. Then he returned, grinning sheepishly. "Just couldn't hold onto that one. Now, let's try again."

He refocused. "OK. Do it, and let's get out of here."

Aaron adjusted his mask, then began.

"Some say it's because the planets are in alignment that trouble has come to the great Mississippi. Some say this fall's intense heat has caused chemical reactions in plant life, which in turn have poisoned the water. But the Knights of Truth and their messenger, Taelon, say that the hand of an angry God has brought trouble to these shores, killing fish by the hundreds of thousands. Whatever it is, life is hard here along the Mississippi."

Though it was impossible to find the right words to describe the scene or stench around him, Aaron continued as Buzz panned the dock and the water's edge. Twice he stumbled over his words as he concentrated on keeping his dinner down. By sheer willpower he determined to get through this, get in the whirlybird, and leave the place.

"Fish and game authorities are working around the clock with a team of aquatic scientists to determine what has caused the pungent turn of events. Though President Rondell has not come to the area, he has declared a state of emergency. It is yet to be decided how cleanup will proceed.

"The hope of those whose homes line the river edges is that a solution can be worked out, and soon."

Buzz zeroed in on the mass of rotting flesh at Aaron's feet, then panned to his face. With his usual flair for dramatic endings, Aaron slowly pulled off his mask, then held his nose. "This is Aaron Chandler, reporting to you from Greenville, Mississippi."

Fifteen minutes later they were aloft, heading for the airport. But the stench clung to them like sewage. "We'll probably have to throw our clothes away, or go to our next assignment reeking of dead fish," Buzz grumbled.

Head throbbing, Aaron leaned back in the seat and tried to ignore the nauseating odor. The evening's assignment, a religious rally in Houston, would be tension-filled, of that he was certain. Word was that a new plan regarding Dissenter control would be revealed. But he was tired of running all over the country just to come up with shocking reports to keep the public glued to the screen. And getting tired is what had happened to other good reporters before they went down the tubes and their ratings went flat. Maybe it was time to quit—while he was still on top. He'd set aside enough for a good retirement. No problem about that. And he was different from many of his cohorts. His major aim hadn't been big bucks. He'd worked for the sheer love of creating crisp reports that kept people begging for more, for the joy of a well-turned sentence, the ability to create concise word-pictures. He hadn't bought a fine house, but still lived in the same dingy apartment he'd rented for the last 15 years. He didn't drive a sporty car. He didn't even spend money on doctors who might do something about the fire in his belly.

He rummaged in the cooler behind the seat. Other reporters chased their problems over a beer—or liquor, or worse. He chased his with milk.

He took a couple swigs, then shuddered. Even the white stuff smelled like rotting fish.

~ ~ ~

That night the stadium overflowed with world dignitaries and religious leaders, drawn together to solve civilization's worsening problems. Buzz worked fast to scan the crowd for church and civil liberties groups that pressed in, banners held high. The loudspeakers thrummed out religious rock as Aaron took inventory of Renton Pierce and other famous Protestant evangelists who sat on the platform. They looked sober, bent, and overwhelmed with their burden of trying to lead wayward sheep home. Grandie had said that serving the living God was a joy. Well, he saw no joy on their faces.

"Scan the platform—face shots," Aaron directed, jotting notes as he spoke. Buzz complied, getting good closeups of Pope Corrado who sat on his raised throne, the lesser religious leaders surrounding him, and of White House personnel. Then after a spectacular welcome, as the vast audience knelt in supplication to the God of all, a cry went up at the back of the stadium.

"Just demonstrators," Aaron said. "Stay with the platform."

But the commotion grew, a great scrambling, with people rising and waving their arms, pouring over the walls and onto the field. Aaron lifted his field glasses.

"Get it!" he snapped.

As he watched people fling themselves to the ground in worship, a great sound arose as others cried out. And then he noticed a tall man in a white robe gliding slowly forward, golden hair falling to his shoulders, his hands lifted in blessing. The man began to work his way across the field, touching one, then another. Those he touched leapt up, running about, laughing, singing. Aaron's heart lurched as he watched "Christ" for the second time in his life.

"Christ" passed in front of him before he glided up the platform stairs and stepped to the pontiff's side. An electric hush settled over the stadium as the two spiritual leaders—heaven's and earth's—stood together, their hands joined high so all could see. Then "Christ" held out his other hand to clasp Renton Pierce's hand.

Finally Pope Corrado stepped to the mike. "Your eyes do not deceive you. 'Christ' has come to explain the Father's wishes. We who do the work here on this earth should listen and pay heed."

The crowd pressed closer as "Christ" raised his hands, evoking silence. Then without using the mike, his beautiful voice rang out. "I long to bless you. My Father longs to bring peace and safety to this world once again. But you have not followed His will in bringing Dissenters back into the fold. Some of you have thought yourselves merciful, harboring Dissenters, sparing some for special skills they possess or because of blind allegiance. This can be no more. . . ."

~ ~ ~

In the wee hours of the morning Aaron lay awake in his hotel room. Milk hadn't helped, nor had the antacids he ate like candy. His only companion was the pain that had become so familiar it was almost like a grumpy old friend.

He'd spent a lifetime reporting what he saw. Nothing had been too complex for him to present in his clear-cut, no-nonsense manner. He'd prided himself in that. But now with the pain and darkness he realized his thinking hadn't been so clear-cut after all. An uncomfortable thought kept pushing into his mind, though he had tried to keep it out. Now he let it come, too weary to resist any longer.

Grandie. If she were alive, the law would be after her. They'd call her a Dissenter. They'd drag that poor old woman onto the streets and finish her.

He shuddered. *Precious Grandie.* Remembering all that had happened during the long day, bitter laughter caught in his throat. This was what Grandie had tried to warn him about—the coming of the day of the Lord. And here it was—she'd been right after all. Why hadn't he listened to her? Once he'd been convinced—felt what she said was truth—and he had sensed the Lord calling him. But to worship a God that demanded such a stringent lifestyle? One couldn't live that way and still get to the top.

The memory of sitting with other leg-swinging children in tent meetings assailed him. There was that funny woman who put colorful felts on a board as she told stories. Then the summer he was 12 when the story of Jesus' sacrifice tried to pull him down the aisle of Grandie's old church. How he'd struggled not to be swallowed by the desire to change his life plans and walk to the front with the others. He'd practically had to clutch the seat of his chair with his hands. From then on it had been mind over feelings for him. He'd learned to manage his desires, to do what he decided, not what he felt. And he didn't really regret his choice.

Over the years he'd brushed away the responses he'd occasionally wanted to make to God; at least "until later" after he'd realized his goals. Assuring her that he'd be OK, he'd busied himself with climbing the ladder to grasp success. And now he had it.

Had what? A tired, sagging body, one riddled with constant pain. Thoughts that seethed like wasps around a nest, but could never settle. And no one. Not one person to share his pain or the emptiness that was the framework beneath what the TV viewers saw.

Yes, Grandie had been right. And those Dissenters, they were right, too. If he had any guts he'd line up with them, if only for Grandie's sake. He felt the familiar stirring—the pull. He lived into it for a moment, then forever shut the door. It was too late to change—to follow God. Besides, he wasn't sure he wanted to live with all that glory stuff anyhow.

He clasped his fists over his stomach. Pressed inward to stop the burning that threatened to eat through the walls of his body. Grabbing the bottle of Mylanta from the night table, he took a swig. Then another. And with a reluctant sigh he shooed Grandie back into the place she belonged, to the one pleasant corner of memories he reserved for her.

Chapter 33

November Again

Longing for warmth, Nick curled into a tighter ball on the cell floor. How many days he'd been separated from his friends and shut in this dismal place, lying in his own filth, he couldn't guess. He passed his hand across his ragged stubble then pressed against his belly. The nausea was back. Once he'd read about a mountain climber who nearly starved to death, and of the terrible sickness he'd experienced as his body literally began to consume itself.

He forced himself to a sit-up. A skittering in the far corner of his windowless, unlit cell proved that he really wasn't alone, that the vermin which inhabited such places were just waiting. Dizzy, he sucked in a ragged breath. If only there were someone to talk to. But even the guard would not speak when he brought the watery soup once a day. It was as though Nick were already a dead man, unseen, unheard.

Where were Ken, Tong Wu, Brother Ramsey? And young Roddy? Had they been freed after he was taken away that fateful Sabbath morning?

The memory was a sour taste in his mouth. Handcuffed and hustled to Judge Rochetti's courtroom, his sentencing had taken only 10 minutes—life in prison with no chance of parole. A baffling sentence for a nonviolent crime. Was Mayor Jordon *that* powerful? Or was it something more, something bigger than a self-important mayor's vendetta against a poor grease monkey? He'd puzzled it through his mind until he thought he'd go insane. *Life without parole?* Because he was faithful to the One who gave life. Scathing rebukes had beaten his ears as guards rushed him to a new cell at the work camp, then hustled him right back out to service the prison vans. But it had been Saturday.

"I'll be glad to work after my Sabbath," he'd told them. Nervousness had made his voice quiver.

Freed's deep-set eyes glistened as he backhanded Nick. "You'll do it now!"

Something warm had dribbled from Nick's chin.

The Bible recorded Jesus as saying "Blessed are ye, when men shall . . . persecute you . . . for my sake. Rejoice, and be exceeding glad." * But it was hard to be truly glad when you were told that your rations for the next week would be cut in half because of the "No work, no eat" rule. There in his lonely cell he'd prayed for strength to stand firm, and God had provided it. It was only on Sabbaths that Nick was taken to the motorpool. He eyed the cars, longing to feel the cool metal beneath his palms, to grasp a wrench and take control of *something* in his life. But each Sabbath he'd refused, humbly quoting Scripture in explanation of his choice. Week after week Freed's grin seemed more maniacal, and he always grinned before beating him—cuffing his head, loosening teeth, socking him in the gut. Jerking Nick off the floor so he could knock him down again before hauling him back to solitary and laughing because his rations would be cut yet again.

Alone in the cold darkness, Nick pondered the essence of good and evil. Freed's hatred was beyond reason and comprehension. How could the guard hate a man he didn't even know? What about Nick drove him to such violence? Or was this thin, filthy man a symbol of something or Someone he hated more? With a moan Nick slumped against the wall. "Lord, God in heaven. Forgive me for not being able to love him as You have commanded that we love our enemies. Send Your Holy Spirit to me. I'm afraid. So afraid."

It was getting harder and harder to tell which day was Sabbath. Night and day were the same, for his cell was dark and he had no way to mark time. Then after one Sabbathday's beating he discovered that part of the wall was crumbling, and had scratched seven small pebbles from its surface. He put them into a small pile in the left corner of the cell.

Each day when his water-broth was shoved through the slot at the bottom of the door, he moved one pebble to the right corner. When they were all on the right side, it was Sabbath. *Unless they'd skipped a day feeding him.*

Not that it would matter, anyway. Every day was a worship day for him now, with nothing to distract him. He prayed for hours, praying that he might remember any past unconfessed sins, praying for his family, his old cellmates and the church members, and that his witness would be flawless. Only God knew if the time was past when words of kindness or the presence of the Holy Spirit could lead a hungry heart to truth.

From time to time Nick struggled to his feet, hobbled the three steps to the longer wall, made a left turn, then five steps to the short wall. Today the exertion heightened his nausea. Sinking to his knees he pressed his hands onto the cold floor—and into something cold and slimy. He retched, but there was nothing to heave. Finally, he leaned against the wall as cold perspiration trickled down his face. He was so tired. Every bone in his body felt as if it were breaking. More than anything, he needed rest. No, not rest. *I just need to die,* he thought suddenly. Suddenly oblivion seemed sweet.

A rattle at his cell door awakened him from spotty slumber.

"Thank goodness, I won't have to bring this slop much longer," Freed spat at him. "Soon they'll let me throttle you."

Silhouetted in the dim light cast when the trap flap was opened, Nick watched the tray slide under the door. There was the familiar crockery bowl. His heart leaped.

"Thanks! God bless you."

And thank You, Lord. I'm so hungry.

He lifted the bowl to his cracked lips, tipped it. The bowl was empty.

He sat holding it for a long time, remembering the times when it held warm liquid. Tears rose unbidden to his eyes. Then, with a sigh, he crawled across the cell and put another pebble in the opposite corner.

Nick didn't know if it was day or night when he sensed The Presence. Too weak to open his eyes, he simply listened. If it were rats scratching around, let them have him. If it wasn't, he'd know soon enough.

Hearing a brushing sound, then the slosh of water, Nick forced his eyes open. The door was ajar, letting in a thin wedge of light, enough that he could just make out someone scrubbing his floor. What an odd dream.

Then something splattered onto his hand. Nick touched it. Water? He bent down to taste it. Water! Puzzled, he watched as the scrubbing continued. Finally, his weary mind found the words to speak aloud.

"Who are you?"

There was no answer. Instead, the stranger set a basin beside Nick and pressed a cloth into his hand. Nick understood, somehow, that he was to wash himself.

The hot water felt heavenly. He bathed the crust from his eyes, his beard. In spite of the cold, he removed his shirt and began to wash his body. From time to time the stranger gave him clean hot water as Nick concentrated on his pleasant task. The whole situation had a dreamlike quality, and he didn't even wonder where the water came from.

Finally, he finished. His body felt clean and warmed. "That was wonderful. God bless you." Lifting his hand in a silent salute, the stranger set his equipment in the hallway, then handed something soft and heavy to Nick. His fingers explored it. A sweatshirt.

Then the visitor set a tin on his lap. "Have faith," he breathed as he left the cell.

After the door clicked shut, Nick sat motionless, pondering the precious contact. Had he imagined the vaguely familiar visitor? Impossible, for the sweatshirt already warmed him. Puzzled, he opened the tin. An aroma, sweet, yet substantial, filled the cell. He lifted a morsel to his mouth—tasted it. It was breadlike, only better. Sweeter. No, more filling. No, more satisfying. He wanted more.

Within minutes he'd devoured the entire lot, leaving not a crumb, and with thanks bursting from his heart he gulped the water that was piped into his now-clean cell. As new strength surged through him his mind cleared. Then he struggled to his knees. *Thank You, Lord, for food, for the stranger who cleaned my cell. Bless him, for I know he took an awful chance coming in here like that. No wonder he wouldn't talk.*

Nick crawled back across the cell, found the lid, and then the tin. He must shove them into the corner so Freed wouldn't notice them. As he tried to close the tin, his hand slipped inside. It wasn't empty! Unbelieving, Nick touched the food beneath his fingers again. Again he tasted. Had the stranger left two containers? He covered the one, set it aside, groped across the dark floor, but found nothing else. Awed, he tried to gather up his impressions, to make sense of it all. And then he understood.

Manna. Food from heaven.

Bowing his head, he reached out to the One who loved him so much He'd sent the comfort of hot water, a clean, warm shirt, and something to eat. The One Who so often during the past few weeks had spoken to his heart, though his ears heard no words. The One Who had suffered so much more than any human ever could.

"Thank You, Lord. I'm humbly grateful." Tears dribbled down his cheeks as he basked in the warmth of God's care. Tears of joy in a cell of darkness.

---

*Matthew 5:11, 12.

Chapter 34

Glancing toward the mouth of the cave, Brenna pulled the seat covers around Jared's thin body and herself. It had been snowing for two days and still the flakes flew, filling the mouth of their hiding space. She needed to go outside to relieve herself, but she was hesitant to knock down any of their snow wall, for it helped to block the wind.

Jared squirmed into a more comfortable position. "You think there'll be snow in heaven?"

She watched a flake sift down. "I don't know. God has lots of nice things planned for us. There could be snow."

"Do you think He'll have soup for us?"

"Mmm. I'm pretty sure He will."

"Alphabet soup?"

Brenna laughed. "Probably. With crackers and—"

"And manna!"

They giggled, then fell silent. They were safe here, she knew that now. The helicopter that had hovered over their heads had never returned. Several times they'd heard dogs baying, and once saw two men with bloodhounds walking through the ravine toward the pond, but that was all.

Everything was fine, except for the bone-chilling cold—and her loneliness. God had provided food for them, not bounteous, but enough. And now they could fill their bucket with snow each morning so she didn't have to chance leaving tracks as she walked to the spring for water. Brenna spent hours telling Bible stories or discussing heaven with Jared. But they could talk only so long before drifting into silence to think their own thoughts. They'd huddle together, trying to keep warm, and memories of Wally and Keely were sometimes so strong that it almost seemed they were there.

Her struggle with the guilt of leaving Keely defenseless often pierced her heart. Long ago she'd given God the pain of that abandonment, but the scene frequently replayed itself. Wally taking Keely back to the room and she running to the desert with Jared. Watching from the faraway hill as the dreadful light from the altar fire flared in the dark sky.

Oh Wally, why did you leave God?

She longed to feel the comfort of his arms around her. She needed his smile and the joy they'd shared. How was it that someone could wound your very soul, and yet you'd forgive and want him to return? Oh, not the way he'd become. But the man that he'd once been. Sometimes she fantasized about Wally bending over her and gently waking her from a bad dream. She remembered the companionship they'd shared, sitting together after the children slept, his big hands turning the pages of his Bible, reading to her, explaining, discussing. She had to turn off the memory or it would crush her. But it always nibbled at the edges of her mind.

When had it fallen apart—Wally's life with the Lord? She didn't know, couldn't think, but if she'd been more perceptive, maybe she could have done something about it.

Was it those Sabbaths when he'd chosen to sleep late instead of going to church? Or his decision to read widely of secular religious opinions, and finally choosing devotional books over the Bible because they were like spiritual fast food—quick and easy to read?

Or maybe it was his growing fascination with New Age materials as he'd tried to explain their dangers to some of his students. As a result he'd met Luke Whalen and Max Orcott, and had been sucked into the philosophy. And she hadn't protested enough. Surely, if she'd been more articulate Wally would have seen that his interest was drawing him into the occult. Yes, she was to blame, too.

As always, regret hemmed her in, and in her anguish she cried again to the Lord—not aloud, but from deep within her heart, a place so filled with hurt there was no room for tears.

Jared was asleep, and the sun at its highest when a shadow

darkened the cave entrance. She swallowed a scream as someone kicked in the snow wall. A great form bundled in a heavy ski jacket and wearing hiking boots filled the opening. Terrified, she willed Jared not to stir.

The stranger took a wary step into their home. Then another. Then he bumped the crowbar.

Brenna tried to smother Jared's cry, but it was too late.

"Jared? Is that you, boy?"

The child struggled free, then hurled himself at Wally. "Oh Daddy, did you come to wait for Jesus too?"

Wally laughed and scooped Jared up, holding him close. "We don't need to wait. He's already here. But where's your mom?"

There was no use trying to hide. Leaden, Brenna struggled to her feet.

Wally grabbed her arm. "Where's Jared's jacket?"

"We're using those seat covers."

He went further into the cave, deliberately tipped over their water bucket, eyed their makeshift bed, then turned back to her. "Where's your food?"

"Jesus sends manna, Daddy."

Wally bristled. His eyes had adjusted to the dim light and he could see her now. "This amounts to child abuse, you know. Let your kid freeze, starve him, all because of your stubborn notions and your refusal to do what's right. Good thing Taelon told me where you were hiding. The boy could have died."

"Wally—"

"I should kill you on the spot. It's legal, you know."

So the death penalty had actually gone through. Her knees wobbled. He shook his head as though to clear it. "I'll let the others take care of the deed after we're back at camp."

"We're not going back."

Wally just laughed. "*You* may not be going back, but the boy will."

Brenna clutched at the floor of the cave. After all they'd been through, they'd been found! She couldn't let Wally take them back, not to that place so steeped in evil. But she was helpless, and already Wally had started down the trail with Jared—now struggling and crying—in his arms.

Lord! Do You see what's happening? Help us! She followed for a moment. Stopped. Followed again. *What can I do? What can I do!*

Wally was walking fast now, too fast. Brenna was afraid he'd stumble, fall with her son over the edge.

"Wait! I'm coming."

Wally tossed her an angry look. "Well, hurry. This kid needs food. Medical attention."

She followed as quickly as her numb feet allowed. Then she sighted the Jeep, and the man waiting beside it. As they neared he fingered his gun. "You want me to take care of her, boss?"

Wally deposited Jared in the back seat, then tucked a thick blanket around him. He paused to consider the suggestion.

"Nah. Bring her along. Let 'em see what a scarecrow she's become. Manna? Ha."

He shoved Brenna into the front seat, but there was no blanket for her.

As the Jeep jounced over the desert floor Jared sobbed quietly. The driver's lip curled each time he looked at Brenna, and he edged away as though she had Marloid's. Brenna's thoughts churned. If they separated them back at camp, what would become of Jared? He was a good boy and loved Jesus, but it had been hard even for her to tell the difference between truth and falsehood when she saw the majestic beings that appeared there. Would a second child be sacrificed to Satan's cause?

Thy will be done, Lord.

She glanced heavenward. According to the Bible the Lord would come when there was no longer a way out. But the sky stretched blue and cloudless overhead. *Oh, please, Lord. Please. Keep him safe. Make me strong.*

The cold in the unheated Jeep seeped into her bones, stealing her sense of touch, but soon the tingling in her feet and arms lessened. They seemed like heavy rocks, somehow fastened to her body to hold her down. At last she dozed, stirring only to call out to the only help she knew.

"Jesus!"

She heard Wally laugh. "He can't hear you. He's back at the camp."

Heart-stricken at his faithless words, she closed her eyes again. *Lord, I love You so much, and I know You'll take care of us somehow, but please . . . can't You hurry? It's so cold. They'll take*

Jared. It's OK if I die, Lord, but Jared needs me. We both need You.

She was barely conscious when the Jeep pulled into the camp. From far away came shouts, angry voices, thrumming Beckoning Music. Careless hands lifted her from the Jeep and deposited her in a warm, dark place.

She struggled to remain conscious. "J-jared."

But there was no answer.

~ ~ ~

Night had fallen when Brenna wakened. Someone stood by her bed—her *bed?* She was in their little room at the camp.

She stretched her hands, wiggled her toes. Fire shot through her feet, but she raised onto her elbow. "Jared?"

A light switched on, revealing a middle-aged woman in a white robe.

Brenna sucked in a ragged breath. "Where's my son?"

"Hospital unit. Doctor says he's fine, though I don't know why. You don't look so good."

"Could I have some water?"

The woman shrugged. "It's over there."

As Brenna struggled onto her thawing feet, flames shot through her feet and legs. Slowly, cautiously she inched across the room for her drink. Then she took her sweater from its hook and hobbled toward the door. "I'm going to see Jared."

The woman's stone face did not change, but she blocked the door. "Can't."

"But he—"

"You've seen the last of him, Missy," the woman smirked.

Brenna froze. "Are they taking him away?"

It seemed hours before the answer came. "No. They'll be sending *you* away, if you get my drift. You and the other Dissenters they've culled from the desert."

Chapter 35

Lucita lay on the rock-strewn ledge and gazed into the valley. It seemed like weeks they'd been trapped on the mountain shelf with no way to get off and nothing to do but wait for their pursuers to return. Here and there brush provided minimal shade or cover. Time weighed heavily on their hands. They had no shelter from the elements or from prying eyes, and were keenly aware that should the helicopter return, there'd be no place to hide. Even the radio was gone—their last connection with a lunatic world. Zack had accidentally knocked it over the edge.

Sometimes they sang, and Pastor Bannister often led out in times of worship throughout the day. But mostly they sat quietly, busy with their own thoughts, waiting. When she pondered it, Lucita could trace how God had led in her life. Still, she wished she'd been quicker to cooperate with Him. Perhaps, then, things would have gone differently with Papa and Mama.

Squirming to get comfortable on the hard rock floor, she remembered how she'd sometimes disobeyed Papa's rules or God's, planning to make confession and to pay a few of her saved-up dollars and do some penance. But she'd learned that penance and confession to someone sitting behind a curtain could not forgive her sins. But God, in His mercy, had whispered words of encouragement to her and somehow changed her heart.

Her stomach lurched. What if her heart still held some sin she'd been too proud to confess, something she'd skillfully shoved to the back of her mind so she didn't have to face it?

What then? Would it so separate her from God that she could not be saved?

It was during these times that her eyes filled with tears and she turned her back to the group. They were sensitive to her moods. Each of them, at one time or another, withdrew into their own thoughts and fears.

When the daytime vanished she listened to night sounds—animals foraging under the protection of darkness. And she'd sleep, lying on her side, knees drawn up and her hands beneath her cheek. Each night seemed an eternity of cold dark hours, but finally the sky behind their mountain would lighten and they'd see manna blanketing the ground again.

Now, restless in the early afternoon of this bright, clear day, she fidgeted on a wide, flat rock, making room for little Zack, who had glued himself to her. She smiled down at his dirty little face, the grubby fingers now relaxed in sleep. Oh for a child's ability to fall asleep in any circumstance. The quiet of a pure conscience . . .

A muffled *pop-pop* disturbed the mountain stillness.

Josie sat up slowly. "I think they're coming again."

It was only a moment before the helicopter burst over the mountaintop, then hovered above them, spraying dust and gravel across their ledge. Lucita squinted at Pastor Bannister. His eyes were closed, but his head was tipped toward heaven, his lips moving, his hands lifted in supplication to God. Though his words were drowned in the clatter, she was comforted. *No matter what happens . . .*

The 'copter banked abruptly and sped off, then turned and started back. The little group crowded together, watching, and then Josie began to sing.

> "There's a sweet, sweet spirit in this place,
> And I know . . ."

The clatter of the motor masked the words.

Lucita clasped Josie's hand, then glanced at Carby and the children and at Pastor Bannister. His face was aglow—a curious way for a man to look when his pursuers had returned. He smiled at her and kept singing the words of the song.

Had she ever told him how much his kindness had meant

to her? He was an old man and had suffered many losses, yet he obviously thought only of others.

"Thanks, pastor, for what you've done for me," she mouthed.

He lifted his hand, grinned, and then glanced again toward the bright blue sky.

It was only a moment before the helicopter hovered beside their embankment. Inside, three grim faces turned toward them. Then the side door slid open and a machine gun barrel took aim. She could see its scope and the man behind it. The pilot steadied the craft.

Shots rang out above the thrumming engine. Lucita closed her eyes and kept singing the song of Jesus' presence. It no longer mattered what happened here on the mountainside, for it was only temporary. Perhaps their accusers could blast away their lives, but they could not take Jesus' presence with them. Protection for their bodies was one thing. Protection of their spiritual selves was so much more.

As the gravel and bullets flew, Lucita focused on the Gift—Christ's offering His own body for her sins—and for the sins of all who would accept Him. He had paid the price for more than their temporary drawing of breath here on this mountainside. There was a much greater thing at stake when this whole thing was over—their hearts, and eternity at Jesus' side.

Lucita pulled Zack closer. This wasn't their problem anymore, but the Lord's.

Suddenly something hit her foot and she drew in her breath at the sight of a hand grenade. A thread of smoke drifted up from it, then died. Another grenade was sped toward them, but it fizzled, too.

The helicopter inched closer. The gunner locked eyes with her, pointing his weapon at her head. He would not miss, not unless— In that instant a deafening roar filled the air. The ground beneath them flailed, tipped, seemed to spin under their feet.

Lucita, thrown down, clutched the rocky floor. The helicopter was jolted up 20 feet, dropped far below them, then spiraled away like a drunken fly. Lightning clawed at the 'copter, caught it, and flung it earthward. Lightning streaked across the sky, for an instant hanging like a giant spiderweb above them. In the same moment a terrifying trembling nearly tossed her off the ledge. She clutched Zack to her chest as the great wall at the back of their shelf slowly sank, leaving them on a flat mesa at the top of the mountain.

Now they stood alone, the sky a huge dome overhead. Lucita followed Pastor Bannister's gaze. There, far away, she spotted a cloud, distinctively compact, moving toward them through the clear, cold atmosphere. It swelled rapidly, became a dark seething mass that cut off the sunlight. Awed at its quick approach, she was distracted by the clatter of another helicopter. She saw the rapid fire of submachine guns, but the bullets didn't reach them. More grenades were thrown. All duds.

The wind picked up, howled, and shrieked as the 'copter landed nearby. Three men jumped out, guns in hands, running in a crouch beneath the blades. *They're relentless. Why? What danger does our pitiful little band hold for them, for the world?* Zack buried his face in Lucita's neck as she glanced back and forth between the boiling clouds and their stalkers. There was nowhere to go, nowhere to hide.

And then came a voice, musical, distinct, borne on the peals of thunder. *Do not fear, My friends, for I am with you.* She turned to Josie, whose smile of joyful surprise spread all the way to her ears. Pursuers forgotten, they watched in awe as layer after layer of dense gray clouds peeled away, leaving only a thin haze. Lucita sucked in her breath. *Yes, my Father. Yes.*

Behind them the men cried out, faces twisted in terror. They begged for shelter, tumbled back toward the 'copter, tried to get it started. But as the cloud neared, Lucita forgot about them. It was still far away, but in the clear atmosphere it seemed so close that she could touch it. And the cloud swarmed with angels—smiling, singing, winging toward them, so beautiful that she wept. The angels reached out as though to pick them up, just like the Bible had said they would.

Then the glorious cloud parted like a living curtain and she caught her first glimpse of the One who had risked all heaven to save her.

Oh, Jesus, I've waited so long for You to come.

His eyes looked deep into her own. *I've waited for you, too.*

Powerful and majestic, the righteous Judge sat on a dazzling throne. Lucita turned away, for her eyes could not hold the glory of it all. But she was drawn back, and saw Him coming nearer and nearer. His face shone as the sun; the kindness in His eyes made her weep. In His eagerness to bring His children home, He stood and with a glorious shout stepped forward and stretched out His arms.

"Come, you blessed of My Father!"

What was that she saw glistening upon His bright cheeks? Tears? Jesus crying? He smiled, brushed the tears away, and then reached toward them again.

"Come! I've waited too long already."

Suddenly He seemed to be looking only at her—her, Lucita! Her heart leaped into her throat, and she stood on tiptoe and reached for Him—her Life, her Meaning, the One who had come to save her. And then she realized that her feet no longer touched the ground. She was rising—rising! As she watched His gentle face a new strength surged through her body—she felt strong, and filled. She was no longer hungry or tired or lonely. She was going home!

As she neared Him she could bear His beauty and the kindness in His eyes no longer. With a sob of praise she sank down before Him and spoke to Him in her mind as she had always done before. And then, realizing that now she could tell Him face-to-face, she uttered her words aloud.

"Thank You, Jesus. I *love* You."

Now others bowed with her, each one intent on personally thanking Christ for coming to save them. After a long while Lucita looked around. Angels hurried about, reuniting loved ones, now smiling and happy. There were hundreds of people, no, tens of thousands and thousands and thousands. An ocean of angels and people. An ocean of joy and worship. They bowed before Him, and His great gentle voice kept reaching out to them all, drawing each nearer, soothing them, bringing joy beyond comprehension.

They were high now, high above the earth, and the cloud had tucked beneath them when Lucita heard someone call her name. She turned to see who'd spoken and saw nearby a young Black man hugging a pretty girl about her own age. The girl smiled up into his eyes, then glanced at

Lucita. A moment later she grasped Lucita's hands.

Her voice rang like music. "I see you read my Bible."

"What?"

The girl smiled. And Lucita gasped. "Sadie?"

They were all hugging now. Then in the next moment she was caught up and enfolded in Mama's arms. Aunt Rosa bent to add her hug. And there—there was Myrtle Flemming. Why, she'd recognize those eyes anywhere, though the woman now stood tall and straight, flaxen curls falling upon slender shoulders.

How had this happened? She didn't know, but she had all of eternity to find out. Right now she had to look up again—into the face of her Saviour.

Her heart filled with the peace of the Greatest Love ever known and the promise of eternity spent with Him.

Chapter 36

"Move it!" the guard growled, prodding Brenna through the early-afternoon sunlight toward the rocky rise just outside the camp. Handcuffed and scantily clad, she fought to catch her breath. Only 24 hours before Wally had found them. Now he and Max stood ahead of her beside a ragged group of people at the crest of a sandy hill.

All Dissenters? They must be, for guards, fingering their guns, watched them too.

Where was Jared? Had they put him with the fugitives, up there surrounded by piles of greasewood branches? She strained to see him, but could not.

Lord, protect him!

The place teamed with onlookers, eager to witness the slaughter of those responsible for the world's troubles. Scarcely controlling their frenzy, they spat and slapped at Brenna as she passed. At last she reached the others—thin and hungry-looking, dirty and cold. Yet they looked like children of the King because of the peace in their eyes.

A disheveled woman reached for her hand.

A kind human touch!

"Have you seen my little son?" Brenna asked her.

The woman slipped her arm around Brenna. "No, dear, but keep your faith. God will protect him."

Something caught in Brenna's throat as she glanced over the throng encircling the knoll. *Please don't make him watch, Lord.*

"They've tried to kill us before, you know," the woman continued. "Everything's failed."

Brenna relaxed. "He kept *us* alive, too, in a cave with no jackets—fed us manna. It would be hard to believe if I hadn't lived through it."

The woman's arm tightened around her shoulders. "It can't be long now."

Brenna nodded. No matter how bleak things looked, God would be victorious. He had promised, and His promises were sure.

Wally, avoiding eye contact with his wife, took the microphone and turned toward the crowd. "The world is dying because a small group refuses to worship God. You've seen the results of God's anger—tornadoes, air crashes, Marloid's. And these people—and others like them—are responsible for that anger. Taelon has repeatedly commanded us to eradicate *all* persons who will not honor God by keeping Sunday holy." He glared at Brenna. "God has rebuked us because it hasn't been accomplished."

Wally, don't do this!

Max grabbed the mike. "A few days ago we attempted to follow God's directions through Taelon to cleanse our world of these—these *misfits*—but due to satanic interference, we were unsuccessful." He pointed at Brenna. "Yesterday Taelon sent us to pick up another one, and has assured us that execution will be accomplished this time."

She couldn't be hearing right. What kind of God do these people serve? The loving God who cared for me so gently from day one and has been guiding me through all this nightmare? My God would never demand this.

Hatred twisted Wally's face. He took the microphone back, then stepped back to Brenna, grabbing her arm and jerking her forward. His eyes, deep in their sockets, took on a frenzied look. "It was our child who died just before I put her on the altar, and you know God didn't accept that sacrifice—it *angered* Him. The spell that has consumed this woman could fall upon any of us."

Brenna caught her breath. *Then Keely wasn't burned alive?*

Wally flung Brenna aside, then pointed to those atop the knoll. "And these people. They've cast their own spell, mocking us with their silence and their pseudoprayers, their 'praise-the-Lords.' "

He faced the Dissenters. "All over the world The Chosen have been trying to eradicate vermin like you. You've refused to die, protected by evil angels who foiled those who would do the cleansing. But Taelon has promised that tonight the task will be completed. And when we've finished, your children will be schooled to understand what God *really* wants."

"No!" Brenna shouted.

Wally grabbed her arm, twisting it in his rage. "Ha! Jared's finally safe. He'll soon forget the garbage you taught him."

Brenna choked back a sob. "Wally, you *know* this isn't true, and it isn't right!"

He leaned over and brushed a kiss across her thin cheek. "Oh, my darling, but you're wrong." With a long, scornful look, he returned to Max.

Was she merely to stand here and let it happen, let them put evil thoughts in Jared's head? God had promised to protect through each situation. He'd done so every moment of their long weeks in the desert. If He could do that, couldn't He also care for the thoughts and understandings of one small boy?

She glanced at the branches piled high around them. She had a horror of being burned alive. Who wouldn't! But if her heart was right, if her trust was based on the truth that the precious Lord Jesus had uttered when He walked this earth, then it really didn't matter. They could destroy her body. Her heart was God's—and so was Jared's.

The Beckoning Music began. A crowd of curious seethed around the knoll, laughing, heckling. But where on their faces, Brenna wondered, was the God-given peace that shows the heart is right? An overwhelming sadness engulfed her. She glanced at Wally, who caressed the amulet of his chosen god.

Father, please keep Jared and me true and steady right now. And Wally, Lord . . . if You will, do something.

The music grew wilder. And then, nearby, the fireflies began to gather. She turned her face away for she could not bear to see Taelon again. But at the crowd's gasp she looked back.

Instead, the being, the great counterfeit of the One she loved and waited for, materialized in his flowing robe of white. And he looked right at her—through her—his deep and glowing eyes boring to her very depths. He seemed filled with the anger of the ages.

How dare you escape me? Though his lips did not move, his words thundered in her mind. *How dare you put Jesus first—He who thinks He can have this world and all my domain. I am king. I will have my way. I may have lost your girl child. I may lose you, but I will not lose your son.*

Brenna tore her gaze from the deceiver. "Lord, help us!" she cried aloud.

"Prove your loyalty," the being shouted to the crowd.

In response, several men sloshed gasoline onto the piled-up branches, and the crowd grew silent. Then Max held a lighter to the wood. Brenna could see the small flame flicker and sputter. But nothing happened. Again and again he tried, with the same result.

Anger, like a fever, gripped the angry mob. Led by Wally and Max—their hands reaching out like claws to snare the Dissenters—they surged up the hill.

"Kill them!"

The being urged them on, his face twisted and ugly.

Suddenly a blinding light flashed from horizion to horizion. People screamed and froze where they were. Immediately clouds covered the sky, snuffing out all sunlight. They boiled just above the mob, angry-looking, heavy. An ominous feeling—the electric, hair-standing-on-end sensation that occurs just before lightning hits—toyed with them. Then Brenna watched the clouds part for a split second and a beam of clear, beautiful light fall to the ground. It lasted a heartbeat, then thunder rolled from one side of the encampment to the other.

"Be not afraid," it seemed to be saying. *"I'm coming."*

"Kill them!" the being shrieked, urging the crowd toward them.

And then came the wind—a tornado? She could see it gyrating across the sand, peeling the screaming throng away from their small, huddled group. It took Max with it—then Wally and the being as well. It drew a line between them—a line their pursuers could not cross. And then, as quickly as it had come, it stopped.

Dazed, The Chosen lay in heaps where the wind had

dropped them. Gradually they began to get up, but now they kept their distance. And then the dark clouds drifted apart and glorious light filtered through—grew strong.

She watched, mesmerized, as the darkness evaporated. Light pushed through her eyes, into her brain, filling her with new strength.

"Mommy!"

She turned to see Jared hurrying toward her from the camp, legs pumping hard.

She wrapped him in her arms. "Honey, you all right?" She checked him over, took his hands. *His hands?* Sucking in her breath, she looked at them.

"Jared—look at your hand!" She held it up.

He giggled. "I know, Mommy. That's what I was coming to show you. It tingled right when that really loud thunder went, and then it just popped out!" He wiggled his fingers. "See?"

In that moment the ground heaved like waves of the sea. Brenna dropped to her knees, hugging Jared close. Her eyes scanned the heavens. She must find His face—somehow. The mist cleared. Yes, she could make Him out now, though He was far away. Jesus was that brightest spot, surrounded by a million, million angels. And amazingly, in spite of the distance, she saw His hands reaching out toward them. Music filled the air, her heart. Not Beckoning Music, but magestic, triumphal music flowing down from the clouds. It filled her very soul, bubbling through her body and into her fingertips—more beautiful than she'd ever imagined music could be.

She couldn't take her eyes from Jesus. She watched Him draw closer, closer, and her heart reached out and embraced the Coming One. In that moment she felt two little arms slip around her neck.

"Mommy! Where you been?"

It took great force to tear her eyes from the heavens, but she knew that lilting voice. Turning, she saw Keely in her little white dress, a puzzled look on her face.

"Where *were* you, Mommy?"

Brenna laughed and held her close. "I'll tell you all about it soon, honey. But look!" She pointed to the clouds. "Do you see Who's up there?"

"That's Jesus, Mommy."

"What a happy surprise to see Him."

The child sobered. "But Mommy, it's no surprise. You told me a long time ago that He was going to come."

Chapter 37

For days Nick filled his stomach with manna from the tin box, no longer missing the tasteless, watery soup. He had slept, eaten, then slept again—and grown stronger. And he'd prayed in his dark cell, content in the knowledge of God's love.

But now something was happening. Beyond his door cells were being opened, and he could hear Freed barking out commands. Shuffling feet, sounds of confusion. His door burst open and the light came on—excruciating after days in total darkness.

Nick shielded his eyes.

"Hurry up, we're going. Hey—what's this?"

He heard the tin skitter across the floor and clatter against the opposite wall. "Who gave you this?" the guard barked.

Nick pushed his stiff body into a sitting position.

"I'm not sure."

The back of Freed's hand slammed into his mouth. "Well, it don't matter. Today you're finished anyway." He jerked Nick from his cot and shoved him down the hallway. "Say goodbye to your home sweet home."

Doors ajar, the row of cells stood empty. Under heavy guard, he and the others were herded onto the tennis courts in the little square across the street. No talking was allowed, but Nick nodded at Tong Wu and Ken, glad to see them still alive. Dark clouds tumbled overhead—there was going to be a storm. Soak them all good.

Then a gunshot sounded, forcing all eyes to the far corner of the courts.

Mayor Jordon climbed four steps onto a platform, then stood there a moment, nervous eyes scanning the prisoners. "You've all been given a chance to obey the law of God and of the country," he bawled into a microphone. "Because of our longsuffering, your lives have been protected. But you've defied every opportunity to repent and be saved. Our patience and God's mercy have now ended. Bottom line is either you die or the entire world dies. The choice is obvious."

The guards lifted their weapons.

"A national order has sentenced Dissenters to death," he continued, "and it's my responsibility to carry out that order." He licked his lips and squared his shoulders. "You will line up along that fence."

Nick's heart rattled beneath his ribs as something hard jabbed into his back. Soon they stood, elbow to elbow, waiting.

An ominous rumble grew louder until it seemed a thousand freight trains roared through the little park. Lightning flashed through the clouds, and something slammed against the jailhouse across the street. Nick watched the wall peel away and the building settle down upon itself.

As those who'd come to watch the execution cried out in terror, the ground began to gyrate. This was not like other quakes—a momentary shrugging of the earth. This one twisted and pulsated—grew in intensity.

Onlookers were thrown to the ground as Nick and the other prisoners clutched the fence behind them. Soon it collapsed, throwing them to the ground, as well.

Then Nick felt a small hand grasp his. "Mr. Nick, what's happening?"

It was Roddy, his eyes dark circles in a scarecrow face. Nick pulled the boy close as hope and held-back joy swelled his heart. "I'm not quite sure, but watch the clouds."

The earth wrenched again. A splitting sound and music from somewhere. Music? Commotion. Shrieks. Screams of terror. As the darkness began to fade, Nick glanced around. Everyone's attention had shifted from the prisoners to what was taking place beyond the courts, for the last quake had opened the earth. The ground widened and a man crawled out of the crack. Puzzled, he brushed off his overalls and looked about. Then almost faster than it could be seen or comprehended, others came up from the ground, too.

"Roddy, it's—"

The boy's grip tightened. "The *resurrection?*"

Now winged beings stood beside graves which bore no markers, but which God had not forgotten. These creatures helped even more people scramble from their dusty beds. As their accusers' cries rang out, Nick fastened his eyes on the clouds, the beautiful, brilliant clouds. The clouds—and brilliant rainbow colors—flowed together, then separated to reveal shafts of crystal light falling toward the earth. And angels! The clouds were full of angels. Then as the mists thinned into wispy fragments, joy beyond experience flooded Nick's heart. For there, surrounded by dazzling angels, was—was *Jesus* on His throne. The Jesus he'd waited so long to see.

At the sight of Him the guards went wild, anger and fear prodding them toward a last-ditch effort to kill the Dissenters and to save themselves.

"You!" someone screamed, turning on Mayor Jordon. "You misled us!" A crowd engulfed the man as others scrambled to hide behind the rubble around them.

Someone jabbed Nick in the ribs, but it didn't matter. He had seen what he had waited his whole life to see—the dear face of his Lord. If heaven should be no more than this, it was worth it all.

How long he gazed upon Christ's glorious face he didn't know. Other graves must have opened for he saw a throng of men, women, and children being lifted toward his Saviour. And then someone called his name.

He turned to face an angel whose hand rested lightly on his shoulder. Nick sucked in his breath, looked hard at him, then grinned from ear to ear. Those eyes—he'd recognize them anywhere. This was his guardian angel, his angel with the eyes of the elderly man he'd helped in his garage and the voice of the kind, mysterious visitor who'd cleaned his cell.

In the next moment Roddy called out and hurried to a woman's side, and Marj, younger and more beautiful than he'd ever known, flew into his arms. "Oh, Nick, I was afraid I'd never make it," she sobbed. "They took me away, you know. It was awful. I don't know what's become of the children. The last thing I remember is the gunshot—"

She stopped at the sound of familiar laughter behind them. They turned, and there came the children, hand in hand, Dusty in the middle, accompanied by three triumphant angels.

Tears of joy filled Nick's eyes and he swallowed the lump in his throat. His arms weren't long enough to hold them all, but he'd try.

But wait. They were missing the greatest event of all history!

"Look!" He pointed to the cloud. "Jesus has come just like He said He would." He sank to his knees as he gazed into his Saviour's face. Relief washed over him, making his knees weak and sobs and shouts of joy flow from his heart. There would be eternity to talk to the others, to look for his parents, for Randolph Grayson, and all those who'd touched his life. There would be time to hear the stories of those who'd gone before him. He'd talk to biblical prophets face-to-face, ask Paul those questions he'd saved up, and hear the story of redemption, First Person. But for now his eyes held on to Jesus, and he savored the joy of knowing he'd soon be held in Christ's redeeming arms.

They were beginning to rise now, slowly, smoothly.

Thank You, Lord. He kept his eyes on Jesus—longing for his turn with Him. *Thank You for forgiving me, for dying for me, for guarding all of us. Thank You for keeping Your promise.*

And then Nick stood before Him. As Jesus reached out toward him, Nick sank to his knees, a sob caught in his throat. He was unworthy, a sinner. Gradually, he raised his eyes, dared a look at his Saviour. Pure love and warm acceptance shone from Jesus' face.

Filled with unspeakable joy, Nick lifted his hand and touched the scar in Jesus' palm. And when he did, a new strength surged through his veins. Young and alive, he'd finally come home!

And in a moment so pure and gratifying, his new eternity began.

CHAPTER 38

Eternity

With his arm encircling Marj, Nick drew a deep breath and smiled at his new friends as they waited together beneath the great tree that spread its translucent canopy above their heads. In the distance the crystal city rose high above the undulating fields, the shining river wending its way between the hillocks, and finally flowing beside them.

One by one they had shared their stories with each other, stories of fear and danger, faith and trust, and of Christ's final victory in them.

"Even in my most creative dreams as I lay in that dark old cell I never imagined how wonderful it would be here," Nick told them. "It's everything He promised, and so much more."

The young woman—Brenna had been her Earth name—smiled a smile that included them all. "I know what you mean. We've been here a dozen Sabbaths already, and still I need to pinch myself to make sure this isn't only a beautiful dream." She reached out and touched her angel, then looked down with pleasure at her son and daughter playing at the water's edge. "There just aren't words for it."

And then the soft notes of the new song began, and Nick watched the joy on the young Black man's face as the glorious melody rose in his throat. Nick, now able to carry a tune, joined in with his children, and with Tong Wu, Lucita, Josie, and his other new friends. The Song to the Lamb, they called it. Only those redeemed from the sad, shadowed planet could sing it.

They'd gathered here to await His appearance again, for it

was the Sabbath when everyone came together to worship the Father, Son, and Holy Spirit. Young Bannister's song spread to other groups of people until the air was alive with singing. Strangely enough, Nick thought, it wasn't just the words or melody that made the song so beautiful. It had something to do with his own experience, too. His heart reached again for the One who had done so much for him.

And then He was standing there before them, the true Meaning of heaven. Again the accepting arms reached out, the smile on His lips widened, those eyes so deep and full of love twinkled with joy.

What wonderful things were in their future, Nick could only guess. Thanksgiving and love overflowed his heart again. Yes, they would continue to share their stories, to live and explore and learn. But their focus—the focus of all heaven—would be their wonderful Saviour, and His Father, and the Holy Spirit who had ministered so faithfully to each of them.

With a satisfying sigh, Nick reached out and clasped the hand of the One who had done it all for him.

"But as it is written, Eye hath not seen, nor ear heard,
neither have entered into the heart of man,
the things which God hath prepared for them that love him."
—1 Corinthians 2:9